Trouble Ahead

I tensed, pulling my hand out of Logan's and dropping it down onto Vic's hilt, ready to grab the sword in case Vivian, Agrona, or any other Reapers decided to storm out of the vehicles and attack us.

But it wasn't a Reaper who opened the driver's door of the lead SUV—it was a tall, thin man with blond hair and blue eyes. His winter clothes were covered by a gray robe, embroidered with the logo of a hand holding a set of balanced scales. I recognized him at once.

Linus Quinn. Logan's dad. And, more important, the head of the Protectorate, the police force for the mythological world.

That dread I'd been feeling all day intensified, my stomach clenching tight once more. Because I doubted that Linus was here simply to visit his son. No, something was up, and I had a feeling that the quiet of the last two weeks had just come to an end.

Still, I couldn't help looking at Daphne in morbid satisfaction. "What did I tell you? Our first double date? Officially *ruined*."

KILLER FROST

JENNIFER ESTEP

KENSINGTON PUBLISHING CORP.

www.kensingtonbooks.com

KTEEN BOOKS are published by

Kensington Publishing Corp.
119 West 40th Street
New York, NY 10018

All Kensington titles, imprints, and distributed lines are available at special quantity discounts for bulk purchases for sales promotions, premiums, fund-raising, educational, or institutional use.

Special book excerpts or customized printings can also be created to fit specific needs. For details, write or phone the office of the Kensington special sales manager: Kensington Publishing Corp., 119 West 40th Street, New York, NY 10018, attn: Special Sales Department; phone 1-800-221-2647.

KENSINGTON and the KTeen logo are Reg. U.S. Pat. & TM Off.

ISBN-13: 978-0-7582-8152-4
ISBN-10: 0-7582-8152-8

First KTeen Trade Paperback Printing: March 2014

10 9 8 7 6 5 4 3 2

Printed in the United States of America

First Electronic Edition: March 2014

ISBN-13: 978-0-7582-8154-8
ISBN-10: 0-7582-8154-4

As always, to my mom, my grandma, and Andre,
for all their love, help, support, and patience
with my books and everything else in life

AND

To all the fans of the Mythos Academy series,
this one is for you

ACKNOWLEDGMENTS

Any author will tell you that her book would not be possible without the hard work of many, many people. Here are some of the folks who helped bring Gwen Frost and the world of Mythos Academy to life:

Thanks to my agent, Annelise Robey, for all her helpful advice.

Thanks to my editor, Alicia Condon, for her sharp editorial eye and thoughtful suggestions. They always make the book so much better.

Thanks to everyone at Kensington who worked on the project, and thanks to Alexandra Nicolajsen and Vida Engstrand for all their promotional efforts. Thanks to Justine Willis as well.

And, finally, thanks to all the readers out there. Entertaining you is why I write books, and it's always an honor and a privilege. I hope you have as much fun reading about Gwen's adventures as I do writing them.

Happy reading!

Library of Antiquities

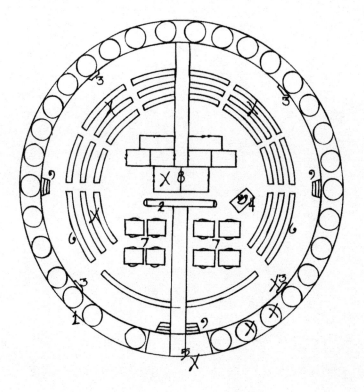

Chapter 1

"This is pointless."

Daphne Cruz, my best friend, leaned forward, stared into the bathroom mirror, and put another coat of gloss onto her lips. Sparks of magic the same princess-pink color as her gloss streamed out of the Valkyrie's fingertips and winked out as they hit the porcelain sink below the mirror.

"Pointless," I repeated. "*Point. Less.*"

"Mmm-hmm."

Daphne gave a noncommittal reply, capped her gloss, and dropped the tube into the enormous purse hanging off her arm. She reached into the depths of the designer bag and pulled out a hairbrush, ignoring me as she started smoothing out her golden locks. Which, of course, were already perfectly smooth. Daphne never went anywhere without looking her best.

"C'mon," I said, not ready to give up on my rant yet. "You know I'm right about this. The day is *sure* to end in disaster."

Daphne finished with her brush, put it away, and plucked a silver compact out of her purse. She smoothed a bit of powder onto her already flawless amber skin and gave herself a critical once-over in the mirror, picking a tiny piece of lint off her pale pink cashmere sweater.

I drew in another breath to continue with my tirade, but Daphne snapped her compact shut, interrupting me before I could get started again.

Daphne looked at me in the mirror, her black eyes finally meeting my violet ones. "C'mon, Gwen. Relax. We're out on a double date. We're supposed to be, you know, having *fun*. Not worrying about Reapers coming to ruin everything."

I glowered at her. *She* might be able to relax, but worrying about Reapers was something I did pretty much twenty-four-seven these days.

My left hand slid over to my right wrist, and my fingers wrapped around the bracelet that hung off my arm there. The bracelet itself was unique—several laurel leaves dangling off strands of mistletoe that had been woven together to form a thin chain, all of them made out of silver. I tightened my grip on one of the leaves and waited a few seconds for my psychometry to kick in. But the only sensation I got off the bracelet was the same cool, calm vibe I always felt whenever I focused on it.

To look at the bracelet, you'd think that it was nothing more than a bit of interesting jewelry. But it was one of the keys to finally defeating Loki and his Reapers of Chaos. At least, that's what Nike, the Greek goddess of victory, claimed. I served as Nike's Champion, the girl who carried out the goddess's wishes here in the mortal realm—and the goddess wanted Loki dead. Something the bracelet was supposed to help me accomplish, even if I hadn't figured out exactly what to do with it yet.

"Gwen?" Daphne asked, a bit of exasperation creeping into her voice. "*Now* what are you brooding about?"

I fiddled with the leaves on the bracelet for a few more seconds before tucking the whole thing back under the sleeve of my purple hoodie.

"I'm wondering how you can be so blasé about Reapers," I said. "Um, hello? In case you haven't noticed, Reapers have ruined pretty much everything at Mythos Academy the last few months. Homecoming dance? I end up fighting a Reaper in the library. Winter Carnival weekend? Another fight with a Reaper at the ski resort. Last day of winter break? Fighting Reapers at the Crius Coliseum. Winter band concert? More Reapers at the Aoide Auditorium. And don't even get me *started* on what happened when we went to the Eir Ruins."

One by one, I ticked the examples off on my fingers. When I finished, I gave her a knowing look. "So why should today be any different?"

Daphne rolled her eyes. She slapped her hands on her hips, causing even more princess-pink sparks of magic to erupt out of her fingertips.

"Because today is supposed to be about *us*—you, me, Carson, and Logan—not about Reapers," she said. "The rest of us have been having a great afternoon so far, even if all you've done is try to ruin things by looking for Reapers around every corner."

"The Valkyrie's right," a voice with a cool English accent chimed in. "You have been a little on edge today, Gwen."

I reached down, pulled a sword out of the black leather scabbard belted around my waist, and held it up to eye level. Instead of being plain, half of a man's face was inlaid into the silver hilt, complete with a hooked nose, a mouth, an ear, and a bright purplish eye that was fixed on me. Vic, my talking sword, the weapon given to me by Nike herself.

"I thought you'd be eager to run into some Reapers today," I said. "Considering that all you ever do is talk about wanting to kill them."

Vic didn't have a shoulder to shrug, so he rolled his one eye instead. "Even I need some downtime every once in a while, Gypsy. The Valkyrie's right. You should enjoy the quiet while it lasts. I, for one, am going back to my nap. You know the drill."

"Yeah, yeah," I muttered. "Only wake you if there are Reapers to kill."

"Precisely."

Vic snapped his eye shut. I gave the sword a sour look, even though he wasn't paying the slightest bit of attention to me anymore. I sighed, then slid him back into his scabbard.

"See?" Daphne said in a smug tone. "Even Vic agrees with me."

I glared at her again, though she and Vic were both right. I was being a total spoilsport today. But it had been almost two weeks since we'd heard so much as a peep from Agrona Quinn, the head of the Reapers, or Vivian Holler, the girl who was Loki's Champion and my nemesis. Two long weeks that had no doubt given the Reapers time to regroup—and come up with some new horrible plan to mess with me and the people I cared about.

Just thinking about what the Reapers might be up to made my stomach clench with dread. I'd already lost so much to Agrona, Vivian, and the other warriors, and I knew that it was only a matter of time before they struck again. But Daphne and Vic were right. There was nothing I could do about the Reapers today, and I should enjoy this time with my friends and boyfriend.

Because I might not have much longer with them, if Loki had his way.

"Okay, okay," I muttered. "I'll put on a happy face for the rest of the day."

Daphne gave me a sharp look. "Promise?"

I made an off-center X over my heart, tracing over two scars that marred my skin there underneath the purple hoodie and thick gray sweater I wore. "Promise."

"Good. Then let's go," Daphne said, clamping her hand on my arm and using her great Valkyrie strength to pull me toward the door. "Our order should be ready by now, and I'm in desperate need of a sugar buzz."

I sighed again, but I let her lead me out of the bathroom.

Daphne and I stepped out into the main part of Kaldi Coffee.

In many ways, Kaldi's was your typical coffeehouse. A long counter running along the back wall. A glass case full of sinfully sweet cheesecakes, cupcakes, and every other kind of dessert that you could think of. Lots of overstuffed chairs and couches. Wrought-iron tables. Espresso machines burping and bubbling away, flavoring the air with the rich, dark aroma of the coffee they were brewing up.

What wasn't so typical were the folks inside the coffeehouse.

Valkyries, Amazons, Vikings, Romans, Spartans. All kids around my own age, all descendants of ancient mythological warriors, and all armed with weapons. Swords, daggers, staffs, spears. Practically every person in the shop had a mug of coffee in one hand and something sharp and pointy within easy reach of the other. Morgan McDougall, one of my Valkyrie friends, had a crossbow propped up on the table next to her, the bolt in it aimed toward the door. Morgan had told me once that always having a weapon around made her feel better. Yeah. Me too.

I barely had time to wave at Morgan before Daphne strong-armed me over to two couches in front of the fireplace. As we moved through the shop, whispers sprang up in our wake. Or my wake, rather.

"Hey, look, Gwen Frost is here . . ."

"She must be taking a break from fighting Reapers . . ."

"I wonder when she's finally going to battle Loki . . ."

I grimaced and tried to pretend I didn't hear the other kids talking about me. Everyone at Mythos Academy knew that I was Nike's Champion and that I was supposed to find some way to save us all from Loki and the Reapers. Nothing like a little added pressure to make a girl worry and obsess that much more.

I sighed. Daphne was right. I was being totally paranoid today, and I couldn't figure out how to turn it off.

She let go of my arm and plopped down on one of the couches next to a guy with black glasses and hair, eyes, and skin that were all a dusky brown. Carson Callahan, her band geek boyfriend, and a truly nice guy.

Daphne leaned over and gave Carson a loud, smacking kiss, not caring who saw her do it or the fact that she'd just transferred all the pink gloss from her lips onto his. Carson gave her an adoring look in return and wrapped his arm around her shoulders, drawing her close. She hugged him back, her strength making him wince before she let him go.

"Is that my hot chocolate?" Daphne asked, her gaze zooming over to a tray full of mugs and plates of desserts on the table between the two couches. "Finally."

Practically every seat in the coffeehouse was taken, so we'd left the guys to brave the long line at the counter while Daphne freshened up in the bathroom.

Carson shot her another adoring glance. "I got you a piece of chocolate cheesecake too. I know how much you like it."

"Thanks, babe." Daphne kissed him again before leaning forward and picking up her oversize mug of hot chocolate.

I shrugged out of my hoodie, then sat down on the other couch next to a guy with ink-black hair and the most amazing ice-blue eyes I'd ever seen. He smiled at me, making a warm, fizzy feeling explode in my heart.

Logan freaking Quinn. My boyfriend. The guy I loved.

"It's about time you came back," Logan said, his voice taking on a light, teasing note. "I was starting to wonder if you'd snuck out the back and were ditching me for some other guy."

"Never," I replied. "It's not my fault that Daphne spent forever touching up her hair and makeup."

"Hmph," Daphne sniffed, but she was too busy canoodling with Carson and eating her cheesecake to really let me have it the way she usually did.

Seeing my friends so lovey-dovey made me turn toward Logan. I smiled at him and leaned forward, ready to kiss him, but he grimaced. It was just a twinge, just a small twitch of his mouth, really, but it was enough to make me stop. Instead, I changed direction, moved past him, and grabbed my own mug of hot chocolate, as if that was what I had meant to do all along. As if I hadn't noticed his wary expression—or the hurt that it sent shooting through my heart.

I leaned back against the couch cushions, still holding my hot chocolate. Logan hesitated, then reached out and put his arm around me. But he didn't draw me close like Carson had Daphne. Instead, we sat there, touching, but still with this distance between us—distance that I didn't know how to get rid of.

Not too long ago, Logan had attacked and almost killed me. Of course, he'd been connected to Loki at the time, and the evil Norse god had forced Logan to hurt me against his will. I'd managed to break Loki's hold on Logan, but the Spartan had left the academy as a result. I'd eventually convinced him to come back, but Logan still thought he might hurt me again, even though I knew he would never do anything like that. Not of his own free will.

Some days, Logan was just as fun, carefree, and charming as ever. But there were other times when I saw him looking at me, and I knew he was wondering if he'd really done the right thing by returning to the academy. I had thought we were past all of his self-doubt and worry, but the Reapers had left their scars on Logan just like they had on me. Just like they had on all of us—inside and out.

All of our friends told me that he needed more time. I knew they were right, but that didn't make things any better, especially when I saw how much Daphne and Carson trusted and loved each other. How *easy* it was for them to be together.

"Are you two ever going to come up for air?" I asked.

Yeah, I knew it was wrong, sniping at them, but heartache or not, there was only so long that I could watch the two of them suck face.

"Sorry, Gwen," Carson said, breaking their intense liplock, his glasses slightly crooked from how hard the two of them had been kissing.

"Just ignore her," Daphne said, planting one more kiss on his cheek before she finally moved away from him. "She's just grumpy because she hasn't had enough sugar today."

"I could feed you some cake if you want," Logan suggested, giving me a sly wink.

I huffed. "Please. I am perfectly capable of feeding myself. Besides, that way, I don't have to share."

I grabbed the plate containing the giant s'more that I'd asked Logan to get for me, picked it up, and sank my teeth into the sugary treat. Buttery graham crackers; grilled marshmallows; two thick bars of oozing, melting dark chocolate; toasted, slivered almonds for a little extra crunch. It was a perfect combination of sweet and salty flavors, and I savored every single bite. Yum. So good.

Logan chowed down on the vanilla cheesecake he'd gotten for himself, while Carson nibbled on a blackberry scone.

A few minutes later, a Viking who played the tuba in the marching band came over to talk to Carson and Daphne, and the three of them started chatting, leaving me and Logan to face each other again.

"I'm glad we did this today," Logan said in a quiet voice. "It's been nice to get away from the academy for a while."

Since it was Saturday, we'd spent the afternoon browsing through the shops in Cypress Mountain, the suburb where the academy was located. Well, really, Daphne dragged us all from one store to the next, but Logan was right. It had been a relief to leave campus and all the problems there behind for a few hours. Even if I had been secretly expecting Vivian, Agrona, and a group of Reapers to show up and attack us somewhere between the bookstore at one end of the main drag and the jewelry shop at the other.

"Yeah," I said. "Me too."

I closed my eyes so I wouldn't see him grimace again, and leaned my head on his shoulder. The motion made bits of metal press against my throat, part of the six silver strands that wrapped around my neck and formed the diamond-tipped snowflake necklace that I always wore, the one Logan had given me.

Thinking about the necklace reminded me of everything we'd been through, and I scooted even closer to him, feeling the warmth of his body soak into my own. He let out a soft sigh, although I couldn't tell what sort of emotion went along with it. Maybe happiness, or perhaps wariness again. But this time, Logan wrapped both of his arms around me and held me tight.

Even though I didn't think it was possible, I actually found myself relaxing and enjoying the time with Logan and my friends. We quickly scarfed down our desserts, coffee, and hot chocolate and spent the next two hours laughing and talking. Finally, though, we decided to head back to the academy. Everyone put their dirty mugs and plates on an oversize tray, which I grabbed and took over to one of the trash cans. I'd just tossed the last used napkin away when I realized that people were whispering about me again—three Romans that I recognized from my afternoon gym class.

"... you think the Gypsy girl will really keep something from happening?"

"Nah ... the Reapers will strike no matter what she does ..."

"I hope so, considering how much money I put down ..."

Money? Money for what? I frowned and looked over my shoulder at the three guys, but they were all absorbed in their laptops again. They didn't even look up as I walked past them. I peered at their computer screens, but they were all surfing the Internet and playing games. It didn't look like they were up to anything suspicious. Still, I knew from past experience that anyone could be a Reaper—no matter how nice and harmless he might seem.

"What's wrong?" Logan asked when I sat down beside him again. "You look upset."

I jerked my head in the direction of the three guys. "Them. For some reason, they were talking about me and Reapers and money. It was weird."

Logan exchanged a knowing, guilty look with Daphne and Carson.

"What?" I asked, my stomach clenching with dread again. "What's wrong? What are those guys up to?"

"There's a pool that the Reapers will do something at the Valentine's Day dance," Logan said. "Kids are betting on what they'll do and how bad the damage will be this time around."

The Valentine's Day dance was Friday night. According to Daphne, it was one of the biggest social events of the year at the academy, as big as prom at other schools.

So big, in fact, that she'd made me go shopping in Ashland last weekend too, so she could find the perfect dress to wear, and she'd made me buy something new as well. Logan had already asked me to the dance, but I hadn't thought too much about it. The way things had been going lately, I was just trying to get through one day at a time without being attacked by another Reaper.

"They're betting about Reapers ruining the dance? You've got to be kidding me," I said. "Why would they want to bet on something like that?"

Logan shrugged.

My good mood vanished. Because the three guys were right. The Reapers probably would crash and ruin the dance like they did everything else at the academy. Maybe the dance was *exactly* what they were waiting for, and that's why we hadn't heard anything about Vivian and Agrona since the battle at the Eir Ruins out in Colorado.

I stood up. "C'mon," I snapped. "Let's get out of here."

Logan got to his feet and threaded his fingers through mine. I squeezed his hand back, trying to calm my sudden anger—and worry.

We left Kaldi Coffee, with Daphne and Carson trailing along behind us. The four of us didn't talk much as we walked back toward campus. For once, it wasn't snowing, and the sun was shining brightly overhead, although it was still bitterly cold, even for February. Or maybe that was the fear seeping through my body at the thought of what the Reapers might do at the Valentine's Day dance—and how many people they might kill this time.

I was so busy brooding that I didn't notice Logan's steps slow and then stop. I looked up, thinking he was waiting at the crosswalk. Then I realized that three black SUVs were parked outside the main gate to Mythos Academy.

I tensed, pulling my hand out of Logan's and dropping it down onto Vic's hilt, ready to grab the sword in case Vivian, Agrona, or any other Reapers decided to storm out of the vehicles and attack us.

But it wasn't a Reaper who opened the driver's door of the lead SUV—it was a tall, thin man with blond hair and blue eyes. His winter clothes were covered by a gray robe, embroidered with the logo of a hand holding a set of balanced scales. I recognized him at once.

Linus Quinn. Logan's dad. And, more important, the head of the Protectorate, the police force for the mythological world.

That dread I'd been feeling all day intensified, my stomach clenching tight once more. Because I doubted that Linus was here simply to visit his son. No, something was up, and I had a feeling that the quiet of the last two weeks had come to an end.

Still, I couldn't help looking at Daphne in morbid satisfaction. "What did I tell you? Our first double date? Officially *ruined*."

Chapter 2

Linus wasn't the only one who got out of the first SUV. The doors opened, and two more men appeared, both wearing gray robes.

One of the men was short and stocky, with brown hair, hazel eyes, tan skin, and a face that always seemed to be smiling, while the other man was tall and slender, with black hair, dark eyes, and a far more serious expression. Sergei Sokolov and Inari Sato, Linus's friends and two more important members of the Protectorate. My unease increased. If all three of them were here, that meant something major was going down.

Had there been another Reaper attack? Maybe at another academy? I thought about pulling out my phone and texting my cousin, Rory Forseti, who went to the Colorado branch of Mythos Academy, but I decided not to. Not yet, anyway.

Linus shut the driver's side door and stood by the SUV, waiting, so the four of us crossed the street to meet him, Sergei, and Inari. Other Protectorate members, also wearing gray robes, waited in the other two vehicles, but they stayed inside their cars.

"Dad!" Logan called out, breaking into a jog and pulling away from me, Daphne, and Carson.

Linus smiled and held out his arms, and Logan stepped into his embrace and hugged his dad tight. After a moment, the two of them broke apart, dropped their eyes, and shifted on their feet, as if they were embarrassed by their PDA. Logan and his dad hadn't had the best relationship over the years, since Logan's mom and sister had been murdered by Reapers when he was five, but the two of them were slowly working things out. I was glad that they were growing closer, especially since Agrona, Linus's former wife and Logan's stepmom, had hurt them both so much by secretly heading up the Reapers the whole time she'd been in their lives.

Logan stepped aside, and Linus approached me.

"Miss Frost," Linus said, holding out his hand. "It's good to see you again."

A month ago, he would have been lying through his teeth. For a while, Linus had thought that I was a Reaper, that I was Loki's Champion, that I was responsible for all the horrible things Vivian Holler had done. Needless to say, he hadn't wanted me to have anything to do with his son back then, and he'd even gone so far as to put me on trial for my life. But the truth about Vivian and Agrona had come out, and Linus had apologized for his behavior toward me. He'd never be my favorite person in the world, but I would be nice to him—for Logan's sake.

"Mr. Quinn," I said.

I hesitated, staring at his outstretched hand. Linus knew all about my touch magic, but he still held his hand out to me. I wondered if it was some sort of test, although I had no idea why he would do such a thing. But I stepped up and took his hand in mine.

His memories and emotions hit me a second later. I got quick flickers and flashes of Linus over the years, fighting Reapers, talking with Sergei and Inari, and leading the other members of the Protectorate into battle. But mostly, what I saw was him sitting in a large kitchen, hunched over a table that was covered with photos and fat files of information, poring over every single document, and trying to figure out what the Reapers were up to and where they would strike next.

His memories of Logan growing up also crowded into my mind, along with all of Linus's deep, quiet love for his son and his unending pride in the fierce Spartan Logan had become.

And over all of that was sharp, agonizing worry—worry that Linus wasn't going to be able to stop the Reapers from murdering even more members of the Pantheon, including Logan. It was the same sort of constant, nagging worry that I experienced on a daily basis—that I wasn't going to be able to find a way to kill Loki. That the evil god of chaos would win in the end. That he would hurt, torture, and enslave everyone that I loved just to inflict as much pain on me as he possibly could before he finally killed me . . .

Linus dropped his hand from mine, breaking our connection. I blinked a few times, trying to clear the last of his memories and feelings from my mind.

"Are you okay, Miss Frost?" Linus asked.

"Fine," I said, forcing myself to smile at him. "Just fine."

"Logan, my boy!" Sergei said in a loud, booming

voice, finally jumping into the conversation. "So good to see you and your friends again!"

The boisterous Bogatyr warrior clapped Logan on the shoulder, making him stagger back a few steps.

"You too, Sergei." Logan grinned at the older man, then nodded his head. "And you as well, Inari."

The Ninja tipped his head, acknowledging the greeting, although he didn't say anything in return.

Logan looked at me, then turned back to his dad. "So what's going on? Why are you guys here?"

Linus smiled. "Can't a father come see his son?"

Logan kept staring at his dad, and the smile slowly slipped from Linus's face.

He cleared his throat. "Well, I do have something to talk about with Metis, Nickamedes, and Ajax. But I saw you and your friends walking toward the academy, and I thought I would stop and say hello."

Logan nodded. "Okay. I get it. So what's going on?"

Linus hesitated. "Perhaps it would be better if you and your friends met me in the library in a few minutes. Metis is already on her way over there. So is Alexei, Miss Frost."

This time, I nodded. Alexei Sokolov, Sergei's son, was the Bogatyr warrior who served as my guard. Normally, Alexei went almost everywhere with me. Today, he'd taken the afternoon off to spend some time with his boyfriend, Oliver Hector, since I was having my double date with Logan, Carson, and Daphne.

"Okay," Logan said. "We'll see you there."

Linus put his arm around his son's shoulder and hugged him close again. Then, he cleared his throat, nodded at Logan, and got back into the SUV. Sergei and

Inari took their seats again, and Linus cranked the engine and steered the vehicle away from the curb, heading to the secondary entrance and the parking lot behind the gym. The other two SUVs followed the first vehicle.

"Well, that was totally cryptic," Daphne sniped when the cars had disappeared from sight.

Carson nodded his agreement.

Logan shrugged. "That's my dad for you."

I looked past my friends and over at the stone wall that ringed the campus. The iron gate was open, so the students could leave the academy and spend some time over in the Cypress Mountain shops today, but I looked up at the top of the wall, where two stone sphinxes perched on either side of the gate. Normally, the sphinxes would be watching me with their open, lidless eyes, tracking my movements, just like the rest of the statues on campus always did. But today, the sphinxes didn't seem to be staring at me at all. Instead, their expressions were blank and neutral. They didn't look angry, upset, or worried. They both stared straight ahead at each other, as if they were resigned to whatever was about to happen. My own dread kicked up another notch.

"Come on," I said. "Let's get over to the library. I want to know what's going on."

"Just because Mr. Quinn is here doesn't mean that it's something bad," Carson said in a faint voice. "Right?"

I gave him a look. Carson winced, but he and the others fell in step behind me as I walked through the open gate and onto campus.

My friends and I followed the ash-gray cobblestone walkway all the way up the hill to the main quad that was the heart of Mythos Academy. Five buildings stood on the quad, all made out of dark gray stone, and arranged like the points of a star—math-science, English-history, the gym, the dining hall, and the Library of Antiquities.

We headed for the library. At seven stories, it was the largest building on campus and featured a variety of towers, balconies, and statues—lots and lots of statues. Gargoyles, chimeras, dragons, a Minotaur. Mythological creatures covered the structure from the first-floor balcony all the way to the tops of the towers that jutted up into the sky. But my attention was focused on the two gryphons sitting on either side of the main library steps.

Eagle heads, lion bodies, wings tucked in next to their sides, tails curled close to their front paws. The statues looked the same as ever, but I still stopped to study them a bit more closely.

Like the sphinxes by the main gate, the gryphons' expressions were carefully blank, as though they were playing a game with me and didn't want to give me any indication of what they were really thinking. The gryphons had always seemed so fierce, so lifelike, but now, they just looked tired—tired and slightly sad.

I shivered. Somehow, I found their flat, noncommittal stares even creepier than if they'd been openly glaring at me and obviously thinking about busting out of their stone shells to attack me, like I always imagined they could.

"Gwen?" Logan touched my arm.

"Yeah. I'm coming."

I dropped my gaze from the gryphons, trooped up the steps, and went into the library with my friends.

Despite its dark and foreboding exterior, the inside of the Library of Antiquities had a light, airy, open feel, thanks to the white marble that rolled out in every direction and the enormous dome that arched over the main space. I glanced up. For months, all I'd been able to see whenever I peered at the ceiling were deep, dark shadows. But a few weeks ago, Nike had shown me what lay underneath the blackness—a fresco of me and my friends engaged in a great battle, each of us holding an artifact or two.

This afternoon, a bit of silver glinted through the shadows—the mistletoe and laurel bracelet that I was wearing on my wrist. My fingers crept down to the bracelet, and I started fiddling with the leaves, wondering what I was supposed to do with them. But after a few seconds, I forced myself to let go of the metal. My gaze zoomed over to Nike's statue, which was part of the circular pantheon on the second-floor balcony, one that featured statues of all the gods and goddesses of all the cultures of the world.

A long, toga-like gown wrapped around the goddess's body, while wings rose up and gently curved over her back. A crown of silver laurels perched on top of her head, even as the rest of her hair cascaded down in thick ringlets. Nike looked the same as ever, although her expression was as neutral as the gryphons' had been. Whatever was going on, the goddess wasn't going to give me any clue about it. I sighed. Sometimes, being Nike's Champion was even more frustrating than waiting for the next Reaper attack.

"Come on, Gwen," Daphne said, grabbing my arm and pulling me forward. "Let's get on with this."

She led me down the main aisle, past the shadowy book stacks that filled much of the library. Since it was Saturday, the study tables that sat on either side of the aisle were deserted, along with the coffee cart that perched off to the right. Most of the kids were over in Cypress Mountain having fun, and they wouldn't start panicking about their homework until late Sunday afternoon. This time tomorrow, there wouldn't be a free seat at any of the tables, and the line at the coffee cart would be even longer than the one at Kaldi's today.

But my gaze moved past the empty tables and cart to the end of the aisle. Linus was already there, standing by the checkout counter that lay in the center of the room, along with the glass complex that housed the librarians' offices. I looked through the glass, but I didn't see Nickamedes sitting at his desk.

"This way," Linus said, gesturing with his hand. "Everyone else is already waiting for us."

We followed him around the office complex and into the back half of the library. The lights were turned down low in this section, and I couldn't help but peer into the shadows and drop my hand to Vic's hilt, wondering if any Reapers were hiding in the stacks, watching us from between the rows of books. I didn't see anyone, though. I never did—until it was too late.

I thought that the others might be waiting for us at the study tables on this side of the library, but no one was here. Linus walked past the tables and led us over to a door set into the back wall of the library. He drew an old-fashioned, iron skeleton key out of one of the pockets of his gray robe and opened the door, revealing a flight of narrow stairs that spiraled downward.

"Great," I muttered. "Another creepy basement."

Linus gave me a sharp look over his shoulder before stepping onto the stairs. I sighed, but I had no choice but to follow him, with Daphne and Carson behind me. Logan brought up the rear and shut the door behind us.

Down, down, down we went, until it seemed like we were going to keep walking all the way through to the other side of the world. Linus used that same skeleton key to open a few more doors, as well as saying some magic mumbo-jumbo code words. Eventually, though, we reached the bottom of the stairs, walked down a short hallway, and stepped into another room.

I was expecting something similar to the prison in the bottom of the math-science building, something stark, depressing, and utterly gloomy, but dozens of lights dropped down from the ceiling, casting the entire area in a bright, golden glow. The bottom level was one enormous room that seemed to be as large as the main floor above and almost an exact mirror image of it. And just like up there, stacks stretched out as far as the eye could see, arranged in the same, familiar pattern.

But they weren't filled with books. At least, not all of them. Instead, clear glass cases of varying shapes and sizes covered many of the shelves from floor to ceiling. Through the glass, I could see everything from swords and staffs to fine silk garments to elaborate jeweled headdresses that some ancient kings and queens had no doubt worn.

"What is this place?" I asked.

"This," a familiar voice sounded from somewhere deeper in the stacks, "is *my* reference section."

A faint *tap-tap-tapp*ing sounded, one that made my

heart squeeze tight with guilt. A man slowly hobbled into view, leaning on a cane for support. He wore black pants and a blue sweater vest over a white button-up shirt. The colors set off his ink-black hair and ice-blue eyes, the ones that always reminded me so much of his nephew. Not only was Nickamedes the head librarian, but he was also Logan's uncle.

Nickamedes stopped in front of me. My gaze flicked down to his cane, and that wave of guilt surged through me again. A couple of weeks ago, Nickamedes had accidentally ingested some poison that had been meant for me, and he'd been using that cane ever since. I was the reason he was hurting, I was the reason his legs had been damaged, but he still smiled at me. I don't know that I would have been as forgiving, if our positions had been reversed.

"Really, Gwendolyn," Nickamedes said, a faint teasing tone in his voice. "I would have thought that it was quite obvious."

I dramatically rolled my eyes, playing along with him. "Well, you know me. I never seem to get the obvious."

Nickamedes chuckled, and his face brightened. I was on my best behavior around the librarian these days, trying to do everything I could to make him laugh whenever I could. It wasn't much, but I hoped that it helped him in some small way.

At least, until I figured out how to use the silver laurel leaves to fix his legs. Eir, the Norse goddess of healing and mercy, had given me the leaves and told me that they had an unusual property—the ability to heal or destroy, based on the will and intent of the person using them. I didn't know how many of the leaves it would take to kill Loki, but I was saving at least one of them for Nickamedes. He deserved to be whole again, after everything he'd suffered—all because of me.

"Come along then," he said. "I still have chores to do when our meeting is finished."

Nickamedes led us past the stacks and into the center of the room, where a long conference table stood. The table sat in the same spot that the checkout counter did on the main floor above our heads, adding to my sense of déjà vu.

In addition to Sergei and Inari, two guys my own age were also sitting at the table. One had sandy blond hair, green eyes, and a sly grin, while the other looked like a younger, leaner version of Sergei with brown hair, hazel eyes, and tan skin—Oliver Hector and Alexei Sokolov.

"It's about time you guys got here," Oliver quipped. "Alexei and I were starting to think you'd gotten lost."

Daphne sniffed. "Please. We weren't lost. We were shopping."

"That doesn't make it any better," Oliver retorted. "In fact, I'd say that makes it *worse*."

She glared at him, which only made Oliver's grin widen. He loved teasing everyone.

Daphne slapped her hands on her hips. "Let me tell *you* something, Spartan . . ."

I tuned out their bickering and went to the far end of the table, where a man and woman stood. The man was tall, with a big, solid frame, onyx skin, black hair, and dark eyes. Coach Ajax, who was responsible for teaching all the kids at Mythos how to use weapons. The woman was much shorter, with black hair that was pulled back into a tight bun and green eyes that were warm and kind behind her silver glasses. Professor Aurora Metis, my mentor.

"What's this about?" I asked Metis. "What's wrong?"

She shook her head. "Nothing's wrong, Gwen."

She didn't say the word *yet*, but I got the impression that was what she was thinking. Or perhaps that was my own worry peeking through again.

Metis's gaze flicked past me, and she moved over to Nickamedes, who was having trouble holding on to his cane and pulling out a chair that was wedged up tight against the table at the same time. Metis moved the chair away from the table, and he sank down onto it with a grateful sigh.

"Thank you, Aurora."

"You're welcome."

She was standing behind him, so Nickamedes didn't see her hand hover over his shoulder, as though she wanted to reach out and touch him. A couple of weeks ago, when Nickamedes had been poisoned, I'd flashed on Metis with my psychometry, and realized that she was in love with him. But Nickamedes didn't seem to have any clue about how she felt. I'd been meaning to nose around and ask him if he was dating anyone, but it was such a weird topic that I hadn't quite figured out how to bring it up yet. Especially since Nickamedes had been in love with my mom back when they'd both been students at Mythos.

Maybe that was why Metis hadn't told him how she felt. Maybe the professor was still feeling loyal to Grace Frost, her best friend, even though my mom had been murdered last year by Vivian—

"Since we're all here now, please have a seat, and we'll get started," Linus said.

We all shuffled forward and took a seat at the table. When we were settled, Linus strode to the head of the table and turned to face us. He might not be my favorite person, but I had to admit that he cut an impressive figure with his gray Protectorate robe billowing out around him and a long sword strapped to his thick black leather belt. If there was anyone who could fight Agrona and the other Reapers and win, surely it was Linus Quinn.

"What's up, Dad?" Logan asked. "What couldn't you tell us before?"

"Yeah, or at least upstairs where it's warmer." Daphne shivered and crossed her arms over her chest.

Linus paused, as if he was searching for the right words. He let out a long breath. "There's a shipment of artifacts coming into the Cypress Mountain airport tomorrow," he said. "The items that we recovered from the ski resort that the Reapers were using as their hideout up in New York."

Logan nodded. He'd been with his dad, Sergei, and Inari when they'd found the hideout and battled the Reapers who'd been inside the resort. Logan had told me about the artifacts he'd discovered in a study there, weapons mostly, although there were some more unusual items in the mix.

"We decided to move everything here to the Library of Antiquities for safekeeping," Linus said.

I couldn't help but snort. In my experience, the library was the most dangerous place on campus—not the safest. Not by a long shot.

"The library *is* the safest place for the artifacts right now," Linus said, hearing my derisive snort. "Despite your obvious opinion to the contrary, Miss Frost."

He arched an eyebrow at me, but I shrugged in response. Reapers had been able to waltz into the library and steal artifacts before, and I couldn't imagine what would be different this time around. No doubt, they would try again as soon as they realized that the artifacts were being sent here. I thought of the three guys at the coffeehouse and how they'd bet that the Reapers would ruin the Valentine's Day dance. Maybe I should get in on the action and try to win a few bucks. Because the dance would be the perfect time for the Reapers to break into the library again.

"The shipment will arrive at noon tomorrow," Linus continued. "And the members of the Protectorate will be there to watch over the artifacts from the airport all the way here to campus."

"So that's why you brought so many men with you," Logan said. "To protect the artifacts."

Linus nodded.

"What aren't you telling us?" Metis asked.

"Yes," Nickamedes chimed in, his voice far more sarcastic than hers. "Protecting artifacts is all well and good, but you don't need cars full of guards for that. So what's really going on?"

Linus grimaced, as if he was upset that they'd already realized he wasn't telling them everything, but he nodded. "It seems that the Reapers are particularly interested in one or more of the artifacts. They've already tried to steal the shipment once, when we took it to the New York academy. Three of my men were killed in that attempt."

"And you think the Reapers will try again," Ajax rumbled.

"I do," Linus said.

"And you brought those artifacts here?" Daphne

asked. "Why? You know this is, like, Reaper central, right?"

Linus ignored her and stared at me, and I suddenly realized why he was really shipping the artifacts here—and my part in things.

"You want me to flash on them," I said in a flat voice. "You want me to use my psychometry to see what artifact the Reapers are after and why they want it so badly."

"Yes," Linus said. "That's exactly what I want you to do, Miss Frost."

Nobody spoke, but the others stared at me, then Linus. Once again, I started fiddling with the silver laurels on my bracelet. Sometimes, I thought my entire life revolved around artifacts and all the stupid riddles that came along with them.

Logan shook his head. "No, Dad, no. You can't expect Gwen to use her magic like that. Especially without even asking her in the first place. Who knows what kinds of memories or feelings might be attached to these artifacts? It can't be anything good. Not if the Reapers are after one or more of them."

Frustration filled Linus's face. "I don't like it any more than you do, son. But you didn't see the Reapers. They put everything they had into trying to get these artifacts, and I want to know why. I want to know what's so important that they would risk so many of their own warriors. And Miss Frost is the only one who can help me with that."

Logan opened his mouth to argue with his dad, but I held up my hand, cutting him off.

"It's okay," I said. "I'll do it. I can't see or feel anything worse than some of the stuff that we've been through already, right?"

Logan pinched his lips together. He looked at me, then glared at his father.

"It's okay," I repeated. "Really. I'll be fine. I want to do it. Agrona and Vivian... they've always been one step ahead of us. It sounds like we might finally be able to get one step ahead of them. Right, Mr. Quinn?"

"That's exactly right, Miss Frost," Linus said. "I'm glad you understand."

I did understand, but that didn't mean I liked it. But being a Champion was about making sacrifices. Really, using my magic to flash on an artifact was a pretty small price to pay, considering some of the things I'd seen and done over the last several months. The loved ones I'd lost, the battles I'd been in, the kids my own age I'd had to fight just to survive. No, this wasn't *anything*, in the grand scheme of things. In fact, I was surprised that it wasn't going to be worse.

Or maybe I was fooling myself about that too.

"I would like Miss Frost to look at the artifacts as soon as possible," Linus said. "I was hoping that she might accompany me and my men to the airport tomorrow."

This time, he looked at Metis, as if asking her permission. The professor stared at me.

"It's your decision, Gwen," she said.

"It's okay. I'll go with them. Maybe I'll be able to pick out the artifact on the spot without even touching any of them." I doubted it, but my words seemed to ease some of the worry in her face.

"Then, I'm going too," Logan said.

Linus opened his mouth as though he was going to

argue, but after a moment, he sighed and nodded. "I wouldn't expect anything less from my son." A note of pride rippled through his voice, and he gave Logan a tentative smile.

Logan nodded back at his dad, and some of the tension between them eased.

"There is one more thing," Linus said, picking up a couple of folders at the end of the table and handing one each to me, Metis, and Nickamedes. "I thought that you might like to review the artifacts before the shipment arrives tomorrow. I want to know what the Reapers are targeting as soon as possible."

I opened the folder and flipped through the photos inside. Some weapons, some jewelry, a half-used candle. The artifacts were exactly as Logan had described them to me before. I studied each one of the photos carefully, but they were just glossy sheets of paper, and I didn't get any vibes about the artifacts off them. Not the way I would when I saw the objects in person and then touched them.

"Anything, Miss Frost?" Linus asked.

I shook my head and closed the file. "Nothing that jumps out at me."

"Well, I suppose it was too much to hope, but thank you for looking at the information."

"You're welcome."

"Is that everything?" Nickamedes asked, his voice still as snide as before.

Linus hesitated. "I don't have to tell you that we've reached a critical point in our war with the Reapers. Now that Loki is free, they've become much bolder. It won't be long before they start attacking larger and larger groups. Maybe even one of the academies. Finding this artifact could be our chance to finally turn the tide against them. And you all know how important that is."

He was speaking to everyone, but his eyes were locked with mine, and I felt that same mix of worry and determination roll off him. For the first time, I realized what Linus already knew, what he was trying to tell everyone, even if he hadn't come right out and said the words yet.

Unless we figured out which artifact the Reapers were after and why, we were in danger of losing everything.

Chapter 3

The meeting broke up, and we all went our separate ways.

Logan looked at me, then at his dad, who was talking with Sergei, Inari, Metis, Ajax, and Nickamedes.

"It's okay," I said, seeing the debate on his face whether to go with me or stay here. "Go spend some time with your dad. Daphne and Carson will walk me back to my dorm."

Logan let out a relieved sigh. "Thank you, Gypsy girl. I'll call you later, okay?"

I nodded. We kissed, and then he walked over to his dad and joined in the conversation with the adults. Oliver and Alexei stayed behind as well.

Still holding the folder of artifact photos, I left the basement with Daphne and Carson and climbed back up the spiral staircase to the main floor. The three of us didn't talk as we left the library and stepped outside onto the quad. The sun had gone down while we'd been in the basement, and shadows now cloaked the lush lawns and spread out from the base of the bare, leafless trees like black blood slowly oozing over everything. I shivered, and not because of the bitter cold.

"All right, Gwen," Daphne said as we started walking down the hill toward my dorm. "Spill it. Which one of the artifacts are the Reapers really after?"

I shook my head. "I don't know. I didn't get any big vibes off the photos, and none of the images moved or did anything creepy. I'll have to see the artifacts in person to try to figure it out."

Daphne gave me a suspicious look.

"Really," I insisted again. "I don't know what they're after. At least, not yet."

"But you'll be able to find out with your psychometry, right?" Carson asked. "Once you see and touch the artifacts?"

I shrugged. "I guess I'll have to."

We didn't say anything else, and we reached my dorm, Styx Hall, a few minutes later. I said good-bye to my friends, slid my ID card through the scanner attached to the door, and went inside for the night.

I trudged up the stairs to my room, which was located in a separate turret that had been added on to the side of the building. I unlocked the door and stepped inside.

All of the kids at Mythos had the same sort of dorm furniture, and my room was no exception with its bed, bookcases, TV, mini fridge, and desk. But the small, personal touches were what made it feel like home, like the photos of my mom and Metis that were propped up on my desk, along with a small replica statue of Nike. Posters of Wonder Woman, Karma Girl, and The Killers decorated the walls, while crystal suncatchers shaped like snowflakes hung in the windows.

At the sound of the shutting door, something stirred in a wicker basket in the corner. A moment later, a flash of ash-gray fur exploded out of the basket and leaped across the room, landing on top of my right sneaker. Nyx, the Fenrir wolf pup I was taking care of, sank her teeth into one of my shoelaces and gave it a vicious tug, easily ripping it in two. Her teeth were getting sharper every day.

I laughed, bent down, and rubbed her ears between my fingers. Nyx sighed with pleasure and leaned in to my touch, her tail thumping against my legs.

I finished petting her and straightened up, then crossed the room, unbuckled the leather belt from around my waist, and propped Vic, still in his scabbard, up on my bed. Nyx let out a happy, slightly squeaky yip, then jumped up onto the bed, reared up onto her hind feet, and licked the sword's cheek. Vic's eye snapped open.

"Ugh, fuzzball!" he groused. "What have I told you about licking me when your breath is that bad?"

Nyx let out another happy yip and licked him again. Vic grumbled, but his half of a face curved up into a smile. He would never admit it, but he loved the wolf pup as much as I did.

I plopped down on the bed next to them, sat cross-legged, and opened up the file of photos that Linus had given me.

"I take it you heard everything in the library?" I asked the sword. "About the Reapers desperately wanting to get their hands on this latest mystery artifact?"

"Yep," Vic said.

"What do you think they're after?" I asked, holding the photos up one by one so he could see them all. "From what Logan told me, none of the artifacts seemed particularly powerful."

"You know that doesn't mean anything," Vic said,

his purplish eye locked on to the pictures. "Just look at that bracelet on your wrist. Who would think that those silver laurel leaves could either heal or kill someone? Much less a god?"

He had a point. I wondered if I should have told Linus that I also had an artifact the Reapers would desperately love to get their hands on, should they ever learn of its existence. But that was one of the many secrets I was keeping. I hadn't told my friends much about the bracelet, only that I'd found it in the Eir Ruins, and I hadn't told them I was supposed to kill Loki, either, although Grandma Frost and Professor Metis knew.

"I don't know," Vic said in a thoughtful voice, after I'd finished showing him the photos. "The Reapers could be after anything. Any one of those objects could have more power than the Protectorate realizes. What is your Gypsy gift telling you?"

"Nothing right now. I guess I'll have to wait until I see the artifacts in person tomorrow."

I stuffed the photos back into the folder and put it on my desk. Vic continued chastising Nyx, trying to get her to stop licking him, as I moved around my room, taking a shower, putting on some pajamas, and getting ready for bed. By the time I finished, the wolf pup had wrapped her tail around Vic, and they were both snoring on my bed. I left them alone, not wanting to disturb them.

I grabbed an extra blanket from my closet, curled up in the window seat, pushed back the curtains, and looked outside. Below, partially hidden by the branches of a large maple, Aiko, a Ninja and one of the Protectorate members, stood guard outside my dorm the way she did every night.

My eyes scanned the darkness, but all I saw were

shadows, broken up here and there by a few patches of snow that still clung to the ground from the latest winter storm a couple of days ago. The night was so cold that a killer frost covered everything, from the grass and trees to the cobblestone walkways that wound through them, adding sharp glints of silver to the black landscape. Frost had even crept up onto my window and frozen into delicate clusters of hard, brittle snowflakes around the edges of the glass.

Everything seemed calm, cold, and quiet. Still, I couldn't help but peer out past the frost and stare broodingly into the night, wondering how long it would be before the Reapers struck again.

At noon the next day, Sunday, I found myself standing on the tarmac at the Cypress Mountain airport, shivering in the cold. The sun had already vanished for the day, disappearing into a wall of ominous, dark gray clouds that cloaked the sky like a Protectorate robe spread over the tops of the surrounding mountains. The private Protectorate plane containing the artifacts had arrived fifteen minutes ago, but it was taking the guards *forever* to unload the crates, which was why I was standing around, freezing my ass off.

I tucked my chin down into the dark gray scarf patterned with silver snowflakes that was wrapped around my neck. It didn't help much, though, especially since a winter wind continually gusted across the tarmac, bringing tiny pellets of snow along with it.

An arm wrapped around my shoulders, and I found myself looking up into Oliver's grinning face.

"Relax, Gwen," he said. "Surely, they'll get the plane unloaded in another few minutes."

"You mean before or after I freeze to death?" I groused.

"I don't know what you are complaining about," Alexei chimed in, his Russian accent coloring his words. "It's not even chilly. Not really."

Alexei tilted his face into the wind and smiled, as if he actually enjoyed the cold breeze sweeping over his exposed skin. Oliver and I exchanged a look.

"Hey, now"—Logan stepped up and drew me away from Oliver—"that's my girl you're cozying up to."

Like me, Logan was also bundled up, wearing a black leather jacket and a black fleece toboggan to help ward off the chill of the day.

"It's not *my* fault you left her all by herself," Oliver teased. "You know that's how Gwen gets into trouble."

"I would stick my tongue out at you, but it's too cold," I grumbled.

Oliver laughed. So did Logan, but I didn't mind because he kept his arms wrapped around me, shielding me from the worst of the winter wind.

Linus stood off to the far side of the tarmac, holding a clipboard and talking with Sergei and Inari. More members of the Protectorate, all wearing gray robes over their heavy winter clothes, milled about them, including Aiko. I waved at the pretty petite Ninja, and she waved back at me.

"Well, I'm glad to see that I'm not late after all," a voice called out behind me.

A faint, familiar *jingle-jingle-jingle* rang out across the tarmac. I turned at the sound, a smile spreading across my face at the sight of the older woman walking toward me. A long gray coat covered her black pants and boots, although green and gray scarves peeked out from underneath her collar and trailed down her chest.

The silver coins on the edges of the thin, rippling silk tinkled merrily in the gusty breeze. A purple scarf was wrapped around her head, covering her ears, and holding her iron-gray hair back off her face.

"Grandma!" I said, breaking away from Logan and stepping forward to hug her.

"Hey, pumpkin," Grandma Frost said, enfolding me in her warm, welcoming embrace.

We hugged for several seconds before I drew back.

"What are you doing here?"

"Metis called and told me about the shipment of artifacts," Grandma said, her violet eyes meeting mine. "She asked me to come to the airport to see if I could help you figure out which one the Reapers are after."

That made sense. Like me, Grandma was a Gypsy, part of a family that had been gifted with magic from one of the gods. In our case, our magic came from Nike, the Greek goddess of victory, and Grandma's Gypsy gift was the ability to see the future. Maybe she could simply look at the artifacts and tell which one might be important to the Reapers or the Pantheon in the days ahead. It was worth a shot.

"I'm so glad you're here," I said, hugging her again.

She smoothed down my frizzy brown hair. "Me too, pumpkin. Me too."

Grandma Frost and I broke apart. Footsteps smacked against the pavement, and Linus strode over to us. He held out his hand, pointing at one of the nearby hangars.

"If you'll follow me, Miss Frost, I think we're ready to get started," he said.

I nodded. Grandma Frost squeezed my hand, and we

fell in step behind him, with Logan, Oliver, and Alexei following us.

Linus led us inside the hangar, which was really just a giant metal shell. No planes perched inside the area, no tools covered the concrete floor, and no other kinds of flight equipment could be seen anywhere. There was nothing in the open space at all, except for a table that had been set up along one of the walls.

A table that was covered with artifacts.

Weapons, armor, jewelry, clothing. The long, wide table featured all of the usual items, the objects that had belonged to the gods and goddesses and the warriors and creatures who had served them over the centuries.

As I stepped closer to the table, I realized that most of the Protectorate guards had left the tarmac behind and had followed us inside the hangar—and that they were all staring at me with curious, expectant eyes. No added pressure or anything.

"Any time you're ready, Miss Frost," Linus said. "There's no rush."

Yeah. Right.

"You'll do great," Logan whispered as he squeezed my hand. "I know you will."

I returned his crooked grin with one of my own, then drew in a breath, took off my gray fleece gloves, stuffed them into my coat pockets, and stepped up to the table.

I touched first one thing, then another, systematically going down the table and two rows of artifacts, and spending a few minutes with each item. A large, silver shield that had belonged to Ares, the Greek god of war; a bronze-tipped spear that had once been the property of Sekhmet, an Egyptian war goddess; a set of tiny diamond rings that had been worn by Aphrodite, the Greek goddess of love.

One by one, I picked up each of the items and waited for my psychometry to kick in and reveal all of the artifact's secrets to me. The memories and emotions were exactly what I expected them to be. The shield taking a severe beating as swords screeched across it and arrows *thunk-thunk-thunk*ed against it during the many battles that the shield had been used in over the centuries. Various warriors wielding the spear, stabbing their way through one enemy and one fight after another, shouts and screams rending the air all around them. Still more men and women wearing the diamond rings in hopes of enticing the objects of their affection to love them in return.

But there was nothing surprising among all the flickers and flashes, the cracks and crashes, the images and feelings. Nothing that stood out, and absolutely nothing that told me which specific artifact the Reapers might be interested in and why.

Frustrated, I opened my eyes, pulled the diamond rings off my fingers, and set them back down onto the table.

"Anything?" Sergei asked.

I shook my head. "Nothing out of the ordinary. All of the artifacts have magic, but I'm not sensing anything powerful or unique enough to justify the kind of full-scale Reaper attack that Linus described. They're just weapons and armor and jewelry. They have their uses, sure, but nothing that you couldn't get from other weapons, armor, and jewelry—ones that aren't being guarded by the Protectorate and would be much easier to steal."

I eyed the diamond rings again, wondering if perhaps there was more to them than I'd realized. That's what had happened with the Apate jewels that Agrona had stolen from the Library of Antiquities and had used to control Logan and turn him against me. Back then, I'd thought that the Apate jewels were simply pretty gems and hadn't realized they could be used in a far more sinister way, until it was too late.

So I sighed and reached for the rings again—

Linus stepped up beside me, holding his right arm out to stop me from picking up the rings. "I'm sorry, Miss Frost. But you'll have to look at the rest of the artifacts back at the academy."

"Why? What's going on?"

His face was pinched tight with worry, and he was clutching a phone in his left hand. "I've had a report that some of the guards stationed around the perimeter have seen someone wearing a black Reaper robe and a rubber Loki mask scaling the fence at the opposite end of the airport."

I gestured at the table. I'd only gone about halfway down the two rows, and a dozen more artifacts stretched out before me. "But I'm not finished."

Linus shook his head. "There's no time. If the Reapers are headed this way, then I want you, your friends, and the artifacts out of here and on your way back to the academy, where I know you'll all be safe."

I wanted to point out that the academy wasn't safe, not these days, but I didn't have time to protest before Grandma Frost grabbed my arm and pulled me away from the table. Several Protectorate guards stepped forward and started packing up the artifacts.

"Come on, pumpkin," she said. "Linus is right. You

can look at the artifacts again when we get back to the academy. Let the Protectorate do its job."

"Don't worry, Gwen," Alexei said, coming to stand beside us. "I won't let anything happen to you or your grandma."

"It's not us that I'm worried about right now," I replied. "But Linus is right. We can't let the Reapers get their hands on whatever artifact they're after."

We stood off to one side of the hangar and watched while the members of the Protectorate stowed the artifacts in the back of a large white van.

Ten minutes later, I was sitting in the back of a black SUV, with Logan next to me. Sergei was driving, while Grandma Frost perched in the front passenger seat. Linus and Inari were ahead of us in the van with the artifacts, while Oliver and Alexei actually rode in the back of the vehicle with the crates. Two more black SUVs full of Protectorate guards, including Aiko, idled behind us. Everyone had their weapons out and ready.

"This is bloody ridiculous, if you ask me," Vic muttered, breaking the silence in our SUV. "We should be waiting at the airport for the Reapers. Not running away. It's demeaning, I tell you. Demeaning!"

I had the sword laid out flat across my lap, and I leaned forward so that I could look into his one eye. "Well, it's not up to you, O great slayer of Reapers."

Vic narrowed his eye in an angry glare, but he didn't say anything else.

"All right," Sergei said, pulling his phone away from his ear and laying it down on the console in the center of the SUV. "Linus says we're ready to move out. Here we go."

He cranked the engine and steered away from the hangar entrance, following the van full of artifacts. I looked out the windows, scanning the acres of flat, open land around us, but I didn't see anything but snow, asphalt, and a few trees in the distance. There was no place for the Reapers to hide, and we'd literally see them coming a mile away.

Still, as we drove toward the gate, I couldn't help but think that we were playing right into the Reapers' hands.

Chapter 4

Our convoy rolled toward the edge of the airport. I tensed up as the chain-link fence at the perimeter slid back, expecting Reapers to appear out of thin air on the other side to attack us.

But nothing happened, and Sergei steered the SUV through the opening with no problems.

"Relax, Gypsy girl," Logan said, noticing the worried look on my face. "The Reapers would have to be really crazy or really desperate to attack us with so many members of the Protectorate around."

I gave him a look. "Crazy and desperate is kind of what Vivian and Agrona do, remember?"

He grimaced. He couldn't argue with that.

We rode in silence. For the first few miles, everyone stared intently out the windows, expecting the Reapers to strike at any second. But as the miles and minutes passed, Logan relaxed back against his seat, and Sergei started whistling softly. Grandma Frost remained silent.

I leaned forward, trying to see her face, but Grandma was staring straight ahead through the windshield, and I couldn't get a sense of what she was thinking. Still, I could feel that old, watchful, knowing force stirring in the air around her, the way it always did whenever she was getting a glimpse of the future, but the sensation seemed to vanish as quickly as it had appeared. Or perhaps it had never been there to start with. This wouldn't be the first time that my own worry, coupled with my psychometry magic, had made me see and feel things that weren't real.

Trying to get rid of my nervous energy, I leaned back and started drumming my fingers on Vic's hilt, careful not to poke him in the eye. I kept staring out the windows, but we'd left the open space of the airport behind and were now driving through a patch of woods. Thick stands of trees crowded right up to the edge of the narrow, two-lane road, their bare, brown branches looking as gnarled and knotted as bones swaying back and forth in the steady breeze.

The farther we went, and the closer to the academy we got, the more the others relaxed, and the more I tensed up. Nothing was ever this *easy*, not when it came to the Reapers.

"Don't worry, Gypsy girl," Logan repeated. "A few more miles, and we'll be at the academy."

I nodded, even though my fingers were now curled around Vic's hilt. The sword's eye was still open, although all he could really see was the car ceiling. Still, I knew he'd be ready if the Reapers did attack.

We drove on. The van in front of us slowed and stopped. I tensed again, until I realized that Linus was at a stop sign and getting ready to make a left since this part of the road became a dead end up ahead. A large black truck rolled up at the other stop sign, at a right angle to the van, on the road that we were going to turn onto. Through the windshield, I could see the truck driver waving for Linus to go ahead and make his turn.

Everything seemed normal, but my unease ratcheted up another notch. Something about this whole situation felt slightly off. Worse than that, it reminded me of . . . something . . . something I'd seen before . . . something I couldn't quite put my finger on . . .

My eyes locked on to the stop sign next to the van, and a memory erupted out of the dark of my mind. I flashed back to another intersection and another time—when Vivian had told Preston Ashton to ram their SUV into my mom's car so they could ambush and kill her.

And suddenly, I knew that the Reaper sighting at the airport had been a false alarm—one designed to make us drive to this exact spot.

"Tell Linus to stop! It's a trap—"

Even as I started to yell, I realized it was already too late.

Linus eased the van out into the intersection to make the turn. The idling black truck immediately zoomed forward and slammed into the side of the van, sending it skittering sideways. Sergei cursed and put his foot on the gas, trying to get closer to the van and our friends.

But he didn't realize that there was a second black truck right behind the first one.

It roared up and steered straight at us. I didn't even have time to suck down another breath to scream before the other vehicle smashed into us.

For a moment, the world went completely black.

Then, the SUV stopped rolling, and I snapped back to reality. I shook the fog from my mind and looked at

Logan. He'd gotten the worst of the impact, and his side of the car was smushed in like a tin can someone had stomped under his foot. The left side of his face was bloody from where the window had shattered, and the glass had cut into his skin, while his body was twisted at an awkward angle.

"Logan?" I said. "Logan!"

I thought he wasn't going to answer me, but he let out a weak cough, and his eyes slowly fluttered open.

"Gypsy girl?" Logan rasped, raising his hand to his neck, as though it were aching. It probably was after the jarring impact of the crash. "What happened . . ."

"Reapers," I muttered in a dark voice.

My yells and Logan's voice roused the others, and Sergei let out a low groan from the front seat. So did Grandma Frost. Sergei's face was cut and bloody, just like Logan's, but Grandma didn't seem to have a scratch on her. Neither did I, since we'd both been on the opposite side of the car from the impact.

Since everyone seemed to be more or less okay, I leaned forward and peered through the cracked windshield. Several figures wearing black robes and carrying curved swords had already gotten out of the two trucks and were approaching the artifacts van. That was bad enough, but what made my heart clench in my chest was the fact that more and more Reapers poured out of the woods on the right side of the road, including two very familiar figures.

One of the Reapers was a girl my own age, seventeen, with frizzy auburn hair, pretty features, and eyes that were an amazing golden color. The other Reaper was a tall, slender woman, remarkably beautiful with her blond hair and intense green eyes.

Vivian Holler and Agrona Quinn.

The leaders of the Reapers. Here. My enemies were right here in front of me.

And they weren't alone.

Along with the Reapers, several Black rocs hopped out of the woods, some of the birds even larger than the smashed-up vehicles. Even from here, I could see the crimson sheen that streaked through their glossy black feathers and the sparks of Reaper red that burned in the depths of their shiny black eyes.

Agrona waved her left hand in an obvious command, and several Reapers surged toward the van. Another smaller group split off from the main pack and rushed past my SUV, no doubt to engage the Protectorate guards who were climbing out of the vehicles behind us. Even through the closed doors, I could already hear the sharp *ring-ring-ring* of metal hitting metal.

My eyes narrowed, and rage burned in my heart, searing through the rest of my foggy confusion from the crash. Vivian and Agrona were here, and they'd hurt my friends—*again*.

Well, they weren't going to get away with it, and they especially weren't getting their hands on the artifacts. Not if I had anything to do with it.

"Gypsy girl?" Logan rasped again, his blue eyes glassy and unfocused in his face. "What's going on? What happened?"

"Stay here!" I yelled. "Don't move!"

I unbuckled my seat belt, tightened my grip on Vic, opened the door, and sprang out of the SUV.

It was like stepping into a war zone.

Screams, snarls, shrieks, and shouts ripped through

the air all around me, along with the constant *clash-clash-clang* of swords smashing together and the occasional, high-pitched *caw-caw-caw* from one of the Black rocs. The coppery stench of blood mixed with the smell of burned rubber from where the Reapers had spun their tires, building up enough speed to ram the artifacts van and the SUV that I'd been riding in.

I staggered forward, my head spinning and my body aching, a little more shaken up from the crash than I'd realized, but I shoved the feelings away and concentrated on the van in front of me. Vivian and Agrona were standing off to one side of the road, next to a Black roc, while the other Reapers clustered around the van. Apparently, the back doors of the vehicle were locked, because one of the Reapers drew a crowbar out from the folds of his black robe and went to work trying to pry open one of the doors. The left side of the van had been smushed in, just like with our SUV, but there was no sign of Linus, Inari, Oliver, or Alexei, so I had no idea how badly they might have been injured in the crash.

I risked a quick glance back over my shoulder. Reapers surrounded the other two SUVs that had been at the rear of the convoy and were fighting the members of the Protectorate who had hopped out of those vehicles. Aiko moved through the Reapers, spinning this way and that, like a leaf dancing in the wind. She seemed to be trying to break through the line of Reapers to get to the artifacts van. So did all the other members of the Protectorate, but there were too many Reapers between them and the van, and I knew they wouldn't be able to defeat the other warriors in time.

Up to me, then.

"Reapers," Vic said in a low, bloodthirsty voice. "Finally, *finally*, some Reapers to kill. What are you waiting for, Gwen? Charge! Charge! Charge!"

I knew exactly how he felt. "With pleasure," I muttered back to him.

I tightened my grip on the sword and sprinted forward. Vivian, Agrona, and the other Reapers remained focused on the back of the artifacts van. Apparently, they'd thought that the hard crash had incapacitated everyone in my SUV, so they didn't even glance in my direction.

"Get that door open!" Agrona shouted above the commotion. "Quickly! Before the Protectorate calls for reinforcements!"

The van was about fifty feet away from me, and I'd just stepped past the front of our smashed SUV when I spotted a swirl of black out of the corner of my eye. One of the Reapers had been standing on the other side of the vehicle, watching to make sure that no one got out of it. He raised his sword high, ready to bring it down on top of my head, but I darted forward and slashed Vic across his chest. The Reaper crumpled to the ground.

"That's my girl!" Vic crowed. "Let's fight another one!"

I would have preferred not to, but another Reaper had noticed me battling her friend and came running over as well. But once again, I managed to get the better of the other warrior, and she crumpled to the ground as well, moaning and clutching at the stomach wound I'd given her. But fighting the two warriors had cost me precious seconds, and I wasn't any closer to the van than when I'd started—

SCREECH!

The Reaper with the crowbar finally managed to wrench open one of the van's back doors. He must have been a Viking and used his strength to help him get inside the vehicle. He reached through the gap, unlocked the second door, and threw it open as well. Any second now, the Reapers would get their hands on the wooden crates containing the artifacts, load them onto the rocs, and disappear into the woods with them—

Oliver and Alexei erupted out of the back of the van and jumped down into the group of Reapers closest to the open vehicle doors. Alexei clutched the twin Swords of Ruslan in his hands, swinging the weapons at every single Reaper who came near him. Meanwhile, Oliver punched the Reaper closest to him, plucked the other man's sword out of his hand, flipped it around, and stabbed the other warrior in the chest with his own weapon. Spartans had freaky magic like that, the ability to pick up any weapon—or any object—and automatically know how to kill someone with it.

But despite Oliver's Spartan skill and Alexei's Bogatyr bravery, they were still going to lose.

Reapers surrounded them on three sides, severely outnumbering Oliver and Alexei and pinning them back against the van, and I knew it was only a matter of time before they overwhelmed my friends. Even if I stepped up and joined the battle, it wouldn't be enough to save them. There were just too many Reapers for that. Desperate, I looked around, trying to figure out some way to help Oliver and Alexei and at least give them a fighting chance. But all I saw were the smashed vehicles, Reapers, and the Black rocs they'd brought along with them—

My gaze locked on to the flock of birds. The Reapers had left them at the edge of the road, where the pavement gave way to the woods. The Reapers who had been watching the rocs had joined the fight against Oliver and Alexei, so the creatures stood by patiently, waiting for the warriors to climb onto their backs so they could fly off to parts unknown.

I didn't know all that much about Black rocs, just that they were big, strong, and deadly, like Nemean prowlers, Fenrir wolves, and Eir gryphons. But a crazy idea popped into my mind. Maybe . . . maybe if I could startle the rocs into flying off, it would at least draw some of the Reapers away from Oliver and Alexei.

It was a hasty plan at best, but it was the only chance I had—and my friends too.

So I stepped off the pavement and raced in that direction, hard bits of snow and frozen leaves crunching under my boots, all the while wondering how small, pitiful me was going to scare mythological creatures that could easily eat me with one snap of their sharp beaks.

"What are you doing, Gwen?" Vic shouted. "The fight is over there!"

"You'll see!" I screamed back.

At the sound of my yell, Vivian whirled around in my direction. Her mouth dropped open in surprise, but that Reaper red spark flared to life in her topaz eyes. She shook Agrona's arm and stabbed her finger in my direction. Agrona's mouth flattened into a thin line, and she pushed Vivian forward, clearly ordering the Reaper girl to kill me. Vivian stumbled and almost fell to the ground before she managed to right herself.

But I shut the two of them out of my mind and focused on the rocs in front of me. A couple of the birds had realized that I was running toward them, and their heads turned this way and that, as though they were wondering what I was doing.

Yeah. Me too.

I sucked down a breath and shoved my shoulder into the side of the closest roc. It was like hitting a warm brick wall, and I bounced off the creature's side and staggered back. But I sucked down another breath and surged forward, hitting the same roc again. This time, the creature hopped a few feet to the right and flexed its wing, as though I were a bothersome bug that it was trying to shoo away. I ducked, although the roc's soft feathers brushed across my nose, making me want to sneeze at the strange, oddly ticklish sensation.

Okay, then, it looked like more drastic measures were called for, especially since I could see Vivian racing toward me, her talking sword, Lucretia, clenched in her hand and her black robe streaming out around her like a cloud of death—my death in the making.

So I raised Vic high and charged deeper into the group of rocs.

"Fly!" I screamed. "Fly! Fly! Fly!"

I swung my sword this way and that, not really wanting to hurt the creatures, but trying to incite enough panic in them to make them bolt, either up into the sky or better yet, into the Reapers still swarming around Oliver and Alexei. But all the rocs did was jump around me, as though we were all playing some bizarre game of hopscotch.

So I moved as close as I dared and lashed out with Vic again. This time, I managed to clip one of the creatures' wings with the edge of my sword.

The roc let out an earsplitting shriek and lurched

away from me. It slammed into the roc closest to it, which set off a violent chain reaction. A second later, all the creatures were in motion, in a panic, exactly like I'd wanted. I ducked down in the middle of the flock of birds and put my hands up over my head, trying to shield myself as best I could from the roiling mass of wings and beaks and long, black talons.

With one thought, the rocs stepped onto the pavement and raced across the flat, smooth surface of the road, like airplanes trying to gain enough momentum to take flight. The Reapers who'd been fighting Oliver and Alexei whipped around in surprise at the sound of the rocs' frantic, high-pitched *caw-caw-caw*s. The Reapers were right in the path of the rocs' stampede, and the birds slammed into the warriors, knocking several of them down and giving Oliver and Alexei some much-needed breathing room.

I grinned. That had worked out even better than I'd hoped—

"Gwen!" Vic screamed. "Watch out!"

I ducked down, and a blade whistled through the air where my head had been a second before. Instinctively, I spun around, raised Vic high, and surged to my feet.

CLASH!

I managed to get my sword in position just in time to keep Vivian from cleaving my head in two with her own weapon. We stood there, seesawing back and forth, our two swords *scrape-scrape-scrap*ing against each other and spitting out red and purple sparks in every direction, even as Lucretia and Vic shouted insults at each other.

"Tarnished tadpole!" Lucretia yelled.

"Mouthy matchstick!" Vic yelled back.

I shut the sound of the swords' bickering out of my mind and focused on Vivian, whose pretty face was twisted into a hate-filled grimace, just like mine was.

"You just had to show up, didn't you, Gwen?" Vivian hissed. "You're ruining everything! Again!"

"Ah, come on, now, Viv," I snarled back. "You know it's not a party unless I'm invited."

She screamed and swung her fist at me, trying to use her Valkyrie strength to shatter my jaw, but I side-stepped the blow and raised my sword for another attack.

Clash-clash-clang!
Clash-clash-clang!
Clash-clash-clang!

Vivian and I fought and fought, moving back and forth along the edge of the road, our boots kicking up thick wads of snow and then the hard, frozen dirt underneath.

Out of the corner of my eye, I saw a bit of gray swirling around, and I realized that Linus and Inari had finally gotten out of the front of the van and were helping Oliver and Alexei battle the Reapers. The two men had helped turned the tide in my friends' favor, and it wouldn't be long before the four of them cut down the rest of the Reapers. Behind me, Aiko and the other Protectorate guards were steadily working their way through the Reapers there.

"You should go ahead and surrender now, Viv," I sneered into her face. "And maybe, just maybe, the Protectorate will let you and Agrona live for a few days before they execute you."

"Never!" Vivian hissed back. "I'll die before I give up—"

"Vivian!" Agrona screamed, running toward us. "We're leaving! Now!"

"No, you're not!" another voice chimed in.

I whipped around. Grandma Frost had managed to get out of the SUV. She wobbled on her feet, but she hurried toward Agrona as fast as she could, a sword clutched in her wrinkled hand.

Vivian's golden gaze flicked from me to Grandma Frost and back again, and her eyes narrowed. "This isn't over, Gwen!" she hissed.

Vivian raised her fingers to her lips and let out a loud whistle. A shadow fell over the two of us, and a Black roc dropped down from the sky. I thought I'd scared all of the birds away, but Vivian's must have been better trained than the others, because it landed right beside her, looking completely calm and unconcerned by the battle raging all around it. I charged at her, determined not to let her get away again—

Vivian let out another loud, sharp whistle, and the roc lashed out with one of its wings, knocking me off my feet. I hit the ground hard, and white spots winked on and off in front of my eyes.

Still, I raised my sword, expecting Vivian to try to end me while my defenses were down, but she was too busy climbing onto the roc's back and pulling Agrona up behind her to attack me.

Vivian grabbed the black leather reins attached to the harness on the creature's back and slapped them down hard.

Even as I scrambled to my feet, I knew I was going to be too late to stop her from getting away—*again*.

"Fly!" This time, it was Vivian screaming the word instead of me. "Fly! Fly! Fly!"

The Black roc let out a loud screech, pumped its wings once, and zoomed up into the sky, taking Vivian and Agrona with it.

Chapter 5

All I could do was stand there and watch the Black roc grow smaller and smaller as it flew away. I let out a vicious curse, but that wouldn't bring back Vivian, Agrona, and the roc. Nothing would—

A hand touched my shoulder. I whipped around and raised Vic, thinking that one of the Reapers was getting ready to punch me in the face or ram his sword into my chest. But it was only Grandma Frost standing behind me. I let out a breath, lowered Vic, then reached forward with my free arm and hugged her tight.

Her arms wrapped around me, hugging me back even tighter, and I felt a wave of love and concern wash over me. I drew back.

"Are you okay?" I asked, scanning her face.

She nodded. "Fine. Just a little shaken up from the crash. How about you, pumpkin?"

"I have a few bumps and bruises from the wreck, Reapers, and rocs, but that's all. Let's go check on the others."

By this point, the battle was over, and Aiko was helping the other members of the Protectorate round up the few Reapers who hadn't been killed. I hurried over to Oliver, who was sitting on the back bumper of the artifacts van. Like me, he was covered with cuts, blood, and bruises from the fight. In front of him, Linus and Inari were crouching over the dead Reapers and murmuring softly to each other. They too had taken a few licks during the crash and subsequent battle, but all three of them seemed to be more or less in one piece.

"Are you guys all right?" I called out.

Oliver nodded and waved his hand at me, so I ran over to the smashed SUV, the one that I'd been riding in. By this point, Sergei and Logan had both gotten out of the vehicle and were sitting on the pavement a few feet away. Blood and bruises covered their faces from where the windows had shattered and the flying glass had sliced into their skin, and they both sat stiffly, each with one hand braced on the ground for support, as if it hurt to be fully upright. Alexei was kneeling by Sergei's side, speaking softly to his dad.

I dropped down in front of Logan. "Are you okay?"

He smiled at me, despite the blood on his face. "I'll live, Gypsy girl. Don't worry. It's only a few cuts. Besides, it was worth it to see the look on Vivian and Agrona's faces when you made those rocs run right into the middle of all those Reapers."

"You saw that?"

He nodded. "Through the windshield. My seat belt was stuck, or I would have come and helped you fight Vivian and Agrona."

He started to push himself up and onto his feet, but the motion caused more blood to well up out of the deep, jagged cut on his forehead and dribble down into his eyes. I unzipped my coat and used Vic to cut off the bottom part of my sweater. I held the fabric up to Logan's forehead.

"Stay still," I commanded. "Don't try to move."

His lips quirked up into another smile, but pain glinted in his eyes. "Yes, ma'am."

I stayed by Logan's side, keeping pressure on the wound and trying to get the bleeding to stop. All around me, the members of the Protectorate moved through the Reapers, checking to see which ones were alive and which ones were dead. I glanced at the van, but it looked like all of the boxes containing the artifacts were still intact and inside. The Reapers hadn't managed to get their hands on any of them.

I let out a long, weary breath, although my relief was short-lived. Because I knew that it wouldn't be long before Vivian and Agrona struck again.

At least two dozen dead Reapers lay crumpled on the ground around the vehicles, and another half-dozen were rocking back and forth on the pavement and moaning from the pain of their wounds. I'd never seen so many of the other warriors in one place before, not even when they'd taken people hostage at the Aoide Auditorium during the winter band concert.

The more I looked around at the bloody chaos, the more my heart sank. Linus was right. The Reapers wouldn't stop coming until they got their hands on whatever artifact it was they wanted so badly.

I just wondered if we'd be able to stop them the next time they attacked.

Three hours later, I was in one of the patient rooms in the academy infirmary, leaning against the wall and watching Professor Metis use her healing magic on Logan. She'd already used her power to take care of my minor injuries.

The professor held her hand up over the nasty cut on Logan's forehead, a golden glow emanating from her palm and seeming to sink into his wound. A minute later, his skin knit together, and the deep gash seamlessly healed and disappeared completely. I let out a quiet sigh of relief that Logan hadn't been hurt worse—and that none of my friends had been killed.

"There you go," Metis said, dropping her hand. "Good as new."

"Well, if I'm good as new, then why can't I leave?" Logan groused.

Metis arched her black eyebrows. "Because you and Sergei took the full force of the crash, that's why."

A knock sounded, and Linus opened the door and stepped into the room.

"How is he?" he asked Metis.

"He'll be fine," she answered. "So will everyone else. But I'd like to keep Logan and a few of the others here overnight, as a precaution."

Linus nodded. "That sounds like a good idea."

He went over and gently touched Logan's shoulder. The Spartan reached up and squeezed his dad's hand.

"I'm glad you're okay, son," Linus said, his voice husky with emotion.

"The same goes for you," Logan replied.

Linus nodded, squeezed Logan's hand back, and cleared his throat. Then, he turned toward me. I knew what he was going to say even before he spoke the words.

"The artifacts have been taken to the library basement," Linus said.

I nodded. "Okay, I'll be right there."

Logan sat up in the hospital bed. "I'm coming too."

Linus shook his head. "You should stay here and get some rest. Nothing's going to happen to Miss Frost, son. I promise you that."

"Just like you promised that nothing would go wrong on the trip back from the airport?" Logan countered.

Linus grimaced.

"It's okay," Metis said. "I'm finished up here, so I'll walk Gwen over to the library. Nickamedes will be there too. Linus is right. She'll be safe, Logan. We'll make sure of it."

I put a hand on Logan's arm. "See? Everything will be fine. You should stay here and rest, okay? Besides, I want to go check on my grandma too."

Logan grumbled under his breath, but he leaned back against the pillow and let Metis pull the blanket up over him. That alone told me he was still feeling the jarring impact of the crash.

I kissed his cheek and left him alone with his dad. Metis led me to the next room over, where Grandma Frost was sitting on the edge of the bed, swinging her legs back and forth and making the scarves wrapped around her body merrily *jingle-jingle-jingle* in time to the motion.

"Finally," she said, sliding off the bed and standing up. "I was wondering where you were, pumpkin."

"You should sit back down and rest."

Grandma waved her hand at me. "I feel fine. I was a little rattled by the crash, but Metis checked me out, and she says that I'm okay."

I looked at Metis, who nodded.

"Geraldine didn't even have so much as a cut on her," Metis said. "She was very lucky."

"And now, this very lucky lady is going home," Grandma said, picking up her coat from the chair in the corner and shrugging into it. "I'll feel much better after I take a long, hot bath, have a cup of tea and something sweet to eat, and get some sleep."

"Are you sure?" I asked. "Maybe you should stay here in the infirmary tonight. Just in case."

I didn't add that part of me wanted her to stay. That part of me wanted to pretend I wasn't Nike's Champion, curl up in the hospital bed beside her, and have her stroke my hair and hum a soft lullaby until I drifted off to sleep. The way she had so many nights right after my mom had been murdered.

But I *was* Nike's Champion, which meant that I couldn't do any of those things. Not while there was still work to be done. Because it was up to me to stop the Reapers, and the first step to doing that was figuring out which artifact they wanted and why.

Grandma must have seen the worry and the weariness in my face, because she came over and cupped my cheek with her warm, strong hand. "Don't worry, pumpkin," she said, stroking her thumb over my skin. "I'm fine. Really."

"But what about the Reapers?" I asked. "Vivian and Agrona are still out there. Who knows what they'll do next?"

"Inari is driving Geraldine home, and Aiko and some of the other guards are going to stay there and watch over her tonight," Metis said. "Don't worry, Gwen. The Reapers won't get anywhere near your grandmother."

Well, that made me feel a little better, but not much. Because I hadn't thought that the Reapers would poison Nickamedes in the Library of Antiquities, either. Or attempt to put Loki's soul into Logan's body. Or murder my mom to try to find out where she had hidden the Helheim Dagger. Or any of the other horrible things that they'd done over the past several months. If there was one thing I'd learned during my time at Mythos, it was that the Reapers were predictably unpredictable, and that all of the guards in the world couldn't stop them when they put a plan into motion.

Grandma Frost winked at me. "And I'm going to use this chance to fatten up all those guards. It seems to me like these Protectorate folks could use some homemade cakes and cookies. I'll bake something for you too, pumpkin."

"I'll come get it tomorrow afternoon," I promised.

"I'll see you then."

Grandma Frost drew me into her arms and hugged me tight. I hugged her back, holding on to her for as long as I could, and trying to blink back the tears in my eyes before she or Metis saw them.

Chapter 6

Grandma Frost, Professor Metis, and I stepped out into the front part of the infirmary. As promised, Inari was waiting there to take Grandma home. She gave me one final wave before looping her arm through his and disappearing from sight.

"Come on," Metis said. "We should get over to the library. Linus is probably waiting on us by now."

I nodded and followed the professor out of the room and then out of the building. It was late afternoon now, and the sun had already started to set behind the mountains. The soft lavender twilight was giving way to the shadows as the darkness slowly swallowed up the last bits of purple and gray that streaked the sky. With the short winter days, it seemed like the academy was dark and gloomy more often than not. Or maybe that was just my perpetual worry, since I still wasn't any closer to figuring out how to kill Loki than when I'd started. And I couldn't help but feel like time was running out, something that the Reaper attack today had only reinforced. The final battle was coming—probably much sooner than I realized—and I still didn't know how we could win it.

I still didn't know what I could possibly do to save the people I loved.

Metis and I walked in silence, both of us with our chins tucked down into the scarves wrapped around our necks, our breath still steaming in the cold air despite the layers of cloth. Still, I didn't mind the schlep across campus. It seemed like the first time in ages that Metis and I had been alone, and there was something I had wanted to ask her about for weeks now—Nickamedes.

"We haven't had a chance to talk much lately," I said as we crested the hill and stepped onto the main quad.

Metis sighed. "I know, and I'm sorry about that, Gwen. It's just with everything that's been going on ..."

I waved my hand. "There's no need to apologize or explain. I've had a lot going on too." I hesitated. "And I've learned a lot of things these past few weeks."

"Really? Like what?"

I drew in a breath. "Like the fact that you're in love with Nickamedes."

Metis stopped cold. Seriously, she just—stopped, as though she'd been somehow frozen in place. If not for her breath still steaming in the air, I might have thought her some lifelike statue, like the ones perched on the towers of the English-history building that loomed above our heads.

"I flashed on you the night Nickamedes was poisoned in the library," I said. "I wasn't looking for anything or trying to see anything. My fingers brushed yours, and it just happened. You were so worried about him, and I realized how much you loved him."

Metis nodded, accepting my explanation, although she kept her gaze averted from mine. "I suppose I shouldn't be surprised. Your touch magic is so strong. I should have known that you would figure out how I felt about him sooner or later. Sometimes, I think it's so painfully obvious that I wonder if everyone doesn't already know, especially Nickamedes."

She laughed, but the sound was small and bitter, and she reached up and smoothed back her black hair, even though every strand was already securely tucked away in her usual bun.

"Why don't you tell Nickamedes how you feel?"

Her face darkened. "There are a lot of reasons."

"Is it because of my mom?" I asked. "That's the only reason I can think of why you wouldn't tell him."

A faint smile flickered across Metis's face, softening the tight pinch of her lips. "Sometimes, I forget how perceptive you can be. And not only because of your psychometry."

She started walking again, her steps much quicker than before, as though she could scurry away from the truth and her emotions if only she moved fast enough. I wondered if I'd made a mistake asking her about her feelings for Nickamedes. But before I could catch up to her and apologize, Metis slowed, turned, and then sat down on the library steps, right in between the two gryphons. I hesitated, then plopped down beside her, feeling the bitter chill of the stone even through the thick fabric of my jeans.

Metis ran her fingers back and forth over the dark gray stone of the step that we were sitting on. After about a minute, her hand stilled, although she kept staring at the stone, her green gaze dark and distant with memories.

"You know, your mom and I used to sit out here on the library steps and talk all the time. About everything. Boys, classes, life. I think that's the thing I miss about her the most. The fact that I can't talk to her anymore."

I had to clear my throat to get the words out. "Me too," I whispered.

Metis sighed, drew her hand away from the cold stone, and slowly curled her fingers into a loose fist in her lap. "But you're right. Grace is the reason I never told Nickamedes how I felt about him."

"How long?" I asked. "How long have you loved him?"

A faint smile pulled up her lips again, but her expression was even sadder than if she'd been openly crying. "Sometimes, it seems like forever. I was in the library one day, trying to find a book that I needed to finish a homework assignment. This was long ago, during my very first semester at Mythos. Nickamedes was sitting at one of the study tables near me. Even back then, he was always so serious, always such a stickler for the rules. I think that my muttering about not being able to find the right book annoyed him more than anything else, since he was trying to study. Anyway, he saw that I was in trouble, and he helped me find the book I needed. We became friends. And slowly, I realized that I felt much more than friendship for him."

"So what happened?"

She drew in a breath. "A few weeks later, I introduced him to Grace. He took one look at your mom, and she at him, and the two of them fell head over heels for each other. They were inseparable after that."

I could see it all as clearly as if it was a movie that

was playing right in front of my eyes. Metis secretly crushing on Nickamedes, even though he was totally into my mom. The two of them not realizing that Metis always felt like the odd person out. Her keeping quiet, not wanting to ruin her best friend's happiness with her boyfriend. In that moment, my heart broke for Metis.

"But you never said anything to him?" I asked. "Not even when my mom left him and the academy for good?"

Metis shrugged. "After Grace left, Nickamedes was so angry for such a long time. He threw himself into his job here at the library, and I did the same thing by getting my teaching degree and then working at some of the other academies. Several years later, I came back here to teach. We had kept in touch while I'd been gone, but seeing him again . . . all of my old feelings came rushing back. But there just never seemed to be a good time to tell him how I felt."

She paused. "No, that's not right. There were times that I could have told him. I just . . . didn't. I suppose I didn't want to ruin our friendship, in case he didn't feel the same way. Or couldn't, because of Grace."

I could understand that too. Before we'd gotten together, I'd told Logan how I felt about him, and he'd told me that we couldn't be together and then went off with another girl. That had been painful enough. I couldn't imagine how much harder it would have been for Metis if Nickamedes had rejected her, since they'd been friends for so long. Even if he'd let her down easy, which he would have, she was right. It would have made things awkward between them for a long time, if not forever.

"And then you came to the academy last fall . . ." Metis's voice trailed off.

"And I reminded him of my mom all over again and how much he'd loved her," I finished. "How much you both loved her."

She nodded. "And I felt it would be...disloyal to Grace to say anything to Nickamedes."

We sat there in silence, both thinking about my mom and everything she'd meant to us. Finally, I let out a breath. My mom was gone, but Metis and Nickamedes were still here, and I wanted them to be happy together, if they could. And I knew that's what my mom would have wanted too. In fact, I was willing to bet that nothing would have made her happier than knowing her two best friends were finally together.

"You should tell him how you feel," I said. "Before it's too late."

Metis cocked her head to the side and looked at me. "Why do you say it like that?"

"Because I still don't know how to kill Loki," I said in a flat voice. "I still don't know how to use the silver laurel leaves that Eir gave me. I don't even know which artifact the Reapers were after today, and I doubt that looking at them again will give me the answer. Some Champion I am, huh?"

Metis leaned over and put her hand on top of mine, and I felt a wave of understanding surge through me— along with rock-solid faith.

"I believe in you, Gwen," she said. "You'll figure it out, and I'll be here to help you. Along with Nickamedes, Geraldine, and all your other friends too."

"I haven't told them. I haven't told Logan or Daphne or any of the others about the bracelet or the fact that I'm supposed to kill Loki. I don't know *how* to tell them."

"Why not?"

I looked at her. "Because what if I fail? What if Vivian or Agrona or one of the other Reapers kills me before I figure things out? I don't want them to give up. I don't want them to think that I'm their only hope, even though Nike made it sound like I pretty much was. I . . . I just don't know what to do. About *anything*."

Metis squeezed my hand, and I felt another wave of understanding and faith surge through her and into me. "Being a Champion is never easy, Gwen. But Nike believes in you, and so do I. She wouldn't have made you her Champion if she didn't think you could somehow defeat Loki."

"But all she ever talks about when she appears to me is free will and things happening because they're supposed to and other stupid riddles," I muttered. "I'm sick of it. I'm sick of *all* of it. Sometimes, I just wish that it was over—one way or the other."

"I know," she said. "Your mom said the same thing to me so many times."

"And what did you tell her?"

Metis looked at me, her green gaze somehow sympathetic and stern at the same time. "That you're a Champion. That it's your duty to do the best you can do and to keep going, to keep fighting, as hard as you can for as long as you can. Because that's what Champions *do*."

"Now you sound like Nike," I muttered again.

She shrugged, as if she didn't know what to say to my comparison. Sometimes, I forgot that Metis was a Champion herself, one who served Athena, the Greek goddess of wisdom. So she definitely knew what she was talking about, especially since she'd been fighting Reapers ever since she was my age. Still, despite my own doubts, talking with her made me feel better, the way it always did. Or at least it gave me the strength to keep on going, to keep on fighting, for a little while longer. Just like she said. Just like she always did.

"Well," I said. "You're right about one thing."

"What's that?"

I sighed, then got to my feet. "We might as well go on inside. Duty calls, and all that."

Metis nodded and got to her feet as well. She started to head up the stairs, but I put my hand on her arm, stopping her.

"But promise me you'll tell Nickamedes how you feel," I said. "No matter what happens. My mom would want that. Because you deserve to be happy, and so does he." I grinned. "Even if he always gets way too grumpy when I'm late for work."

Metis laughed, her face a little lighter. She nodded and looped her arm through mine. Together, we went up the steps and headed into the library.

Metis led me through the library, through the door in the wall, and down the stairs to the basement. We moved past the stacks to find Nickamedes and Linus standing at the conference table we'd all gathered around yesterday.

Only now, the table was covered with artifacts.

The shield of Ares, the spear of Sekhmet, the diamond rings of Aphrodite. They were the same artifacts that were in the photos Linus had given me yesterday, the same artifacts I'd seen and touched earlier today at the airport. Weapons, jewelry, armor, garments, and other miscellaneous objects. All just sitting there, glinting dully underneath the lights, and looking perfectly innocent, perfectly *ordinary*, and not at all like the powerful objects they really were.

Linus and Nickamedes stopped their conversation and turned at the sound of our soft footsteps on the marble floor.

Nickamedes glanced at his watch, then arched his black eyebrows at me.

I sighed. "I know, I know. You were expecting me here ten minutes ago."

The librarian sniffed. "More like fifteen, actually. Really, Gwendolyn. This is no time to dawdle. And Aurora, I expected you to hurry her along, at the very least."

"Oh, it's not Metis's fault," I said in a snarky tone. "She couldn't wait to come down here and see *you*, Nickamedes."

His eyebrows drew together, and he looked at Metis in confusion.

"What Gwen means is that I couldn't wait for her to get started," she said in a smooth voice. "The sooner she identifies the artifact, the sooner we can figure out what the Reapers want with it and how to keep it safe from them."

It was a nice save, and I was the only one who noticed the faint blush that stained her bronze cheeks. Still, I wasn't about to let her get off that easy. I nudged Metis with my shoulder, but she shook her head and moved away from me, going to stand next to Nickamedes.

"Tell him," I mouthed. "Tell him now."

She shook her head at me again. Linus looked back and forth between the two of us, obviously wondering what was going on, but he didn't comment on it.

Nickamedes shuffled over to the far end of the table, his cane *tap-tap-tapping* on the floor again. He picked up a thick notebook and an ink pen, then pulled out a chair and sat down.

"What are you doing?" I asked.

He peered up at me, his blue eyes bright with excitement. "Well, since you're going to be using your magic to flash on the artifacts, I thought it would be an efficient use of time and resources to have you describe their properties to me in detail. It will save me a great deal of time researching them later on if you can tell me about them and what they do now."

I eyed him. "That sounds suspiciously like research to me. And I'm not working today, remember? Um, hello, I battled a group of Reapers. I think I've been helpful enough for one day. For several days, actually."

Nickamedes sat up straight in his chair and gave me a stern look that I knew all too well. "A librarian's work is *never* done. You should know that by now, Gwendolyn."

I rolled my eyes, but I knew there was nothing I could do but go along with him and his obsessive need to catalog every single thing in the entire library. And not just because I still felt guilty that he had been poisoned instead of me. Once Nickamedes sank his teeth into something, he wouldn't let go of it.

"Fine," I muttered. "But this totally gets me out of one of my shifts this week."

Nickamedes raised his eyes heavenward, as if asking all the gods and goddesses above for patience to deal with the likes of me. "Oh, very well. But just one."

"Anytime you're ready, Miss Frost," Linus chimed in.

I took off my jacket and scarf, pushed up the sleeves

of my sweater, and got to work. Once again, I went down the two rows on the table, picking up and touching each one of the artifacts in turn. I started with the weapons I'd already examined at the airport, double-checking to see if I might have missed anything, but the vibes I got off them were the same as before. Images of battles, warriors, and blood everywhere. Not the most wonderful memories, but sadly, nothing that I hadn't felt before with my psychometry or experienced in real life, given all the fights I'd been in recently. Vic, on the other hand, would have enjoyed seeing and feeling all of the memories, all of the harsh victories and brutal defeats. The sword would have probably demanded that I get him some popcorn and a giant soda, so he could experience *a right proper show*, as he would put it.

After I finished with an artifact, Nickamedes would ask me about what I'd seen and felt, and I dutifully answered all of his many questions. He scribbled down page after page of notes, his face creased with concentration and his eyes bright with pleasure. Nothing made him happier than research, even if I was the one who was doing all the hard work. But I knew he would put his extensive notes to good use. No doubt some of the information he was recording would be used to make the identification cards that would be placed with the artifacts once they were put on display on the main library floor.

Minutes passed, then turned into an hour. And still, all I did was touch artifacts, get sucked into memories of the past, and then regurgitate everything for Nickamedes.

I'd gone through about half of the artifacts when I stopped and looked over at Linus. "Are you sure that what the Reapers want is on this table? That nothing was left behind at the airport? Or lost somewhere along the way? Because there is nothing here that justifies the sort of massive, full-scale attack they launched this afternoon."

Linus's thoughtful gaze moved from one artifact to another. "This is everything we recovered from the Reaper ski lodge in New York, as well as a few more items that we discovered and confiscated from other hiding places. It has to be here somewhere."

I nodded, sighed again, and reached for the next artifact.

Another hour passed, and I still didn't have any luck. I put down the latest sword I'd flashed on and looked down. Five more objects lay on the table. I sighed, a little louder and deeper this time. The way my luck was going right now, the mystery object would be the very last thing I picked up. Naturally.

So I shuffled forward and grabbed the next artifact, a small, slender, half-used candle made out of white beeswax that had belonged to Sol, the Norse goddess of the sun—

And I immediately knew that I had finally found what the Reapers were after.

For a moment, my vision went absolutely, blazingly, blindingly white, as if I were staring straight into a star. Then, heat blasted over me, so hot, searing, and scorching that I felt like I was holding the sun itself in the palm of my hand. The intense light dimmed down to a single spark—white-hot and beating steadily, almost like a heart. In fact, it seemed as if that single, solitary spark contained all of the candle's magic, condensed down to one bright, glistening point. But it wasn't only heat and light that the candle offered. It was power, it was strength.

It was *life*.

All I could do was stand there, clutching the candle, and let the intense rush of power wash over me again and again, each wave a little hotter and brighter than the one before, and sweeping more and more of me away with it, as though the violet spark at the center of *my* being was melting like the white wax of the candle should have been. It took my breath away. Still, try as I might, I couldn't make myself let go of the candle, I couldn't unwrap my fingers from the smooth wax, and I knew that I was in serious danger of falling so far down into the artifact and the immense power it contained that I might never come back to myself again. I felt like I was drowning in the heat, being burned alive from the inside out . . .

A cool bit of metal pressed into my palm, and I realized that I was clutching the silver laurel and mistletoe bracelet with my free hand. The sharp tip of one of the leaves had pricked my palm, drawing a drop of blood. Somehow, despite the intense heat, light, and power that the candle was giving off, the bracelet remained strangely cool and untouched by the other artifact's magic . . .

But the sharp prick cut through the waves of power and helped me come back to myself. I shuddered out a breath and managed to open my eyes. Sure enough, I was clutching the candle in my right hand, but my left hand had wrapped around the laurel bracelet on my wrist. I kept one hand on the bracelet, letting the feel of the cool metal ground me, as I carefully set the candle back down onto the table. It took me several more seconds before I managed to uncurl my fingers from around the white wax and step back, out of reach of the candle. Because right now, I wanted nothing more than to pick it up again, to feel all of that heat and power and life coursing through me.

"Well, Gwendolyn?" Nickamedes asked. "What did you see?"

"This," I said, pointing at the candle and not daring to touch it again with my bare hands. "This is what the Reapers are after."

Chapter 7

Linus, Metis, and Nickamedes all leaned forward, peering at the candle. It looked the same as before, a slender taper of snow-white wax that had burned halfway down. I shuddered and averted my gaze from it, not even wanting to look at it right now. I'd held a lot of powerful objects since coming to Mythos, but the candle was one of the strongest—and most dangerous.

"Are you sure, Miss Frost?" Linus said. "It doesn't look like much."

"Trust me, looks can be deceiving, especially in this case."

I shivered again, thinking of the immense power that had flowed through me, that steady, white, burning spark of strength. If not for the laurel leaf on my bracelet digging into my palm, I might have drowned in that intense heat, in that sense of absolute, utter, unstoppable power. I might have been lost forever, my mind trapped by the candle's overwhelming sensations, and never been able to find my way back to myself.

I fingered one of the leaves, wondering why the bracelet had remained cool against my skin when every other part of me had felt like I was burning alive.

Maybe because Eir had told me that the silver laurels could be used to destroy as well as to heal? I wondered if whatever magic the leaves contained was enough to overcome the power flowing through the candle. Or at least counteract it in some way. That was the only explanation I could think of.

"Hmm," Nickamedes said, pushing his chair back and getting up from the table.

He shuffled off into another part of the basement, and I could hear his cane *tap-tap-tapp*ing as he moved from one aisle and one shelf to the next. A few minutes later, the librarian reappeared, cradling a thick, slightly dusty book in one hand. He put the book down onto the table, then started flipping through it. The old, worn pages crackled as he slowly turned them, and a faint, musty odor drifted up from the book, one that reminded me of the soft scent that always seemed to cling to the corners of the deepest part of the stacks on the main library floor.

"Where is it . . . where is it . . ." Nickamedes muttered to himself as he flipped through the pages. "Yes . . . yes. Here it is."

He cleared his throat and began to read.

"The Curing Candle of Sol, the Norse goddess of the sun, is thought to be one of the most powerful artifacts in existence, one of the Thirteen Artifacts that helped the Pantheon win the Chaos War centuries ago, since its magic was supposedly used to heal many warriors on the field during the final battle. However, after that battle, it disappeared and was thought to be lost forever. Many reproductions have surfaced over the years, but none have been the genuine article."

Metis stared at the candle. "So how do we know this one isn't a fake as well?"

I thought of the great, burning, terrible power that had filled me the second I had touched the smooth wax. "Trust me. That one is the real deal."

Nickamedes cleared his throat again and continued with his reading.

"What makes the candle unique is that it is filled with the healing power of both the sun and the goddess Sol herself. Whoever holds the candle will reap those benefits—finding strength, health, and vitality. It is thought that the power of the candle is so strong, it can heal any wound, no matter how severe. There are some who believe that the candle can even bring the dead back to life . . ."

Nickamedes's voice trailed off. He read a bit more to himself, then shook his head and looked up from the book. "That's the most important passage. The rest speculates on the history of the artifact, and some of the people who may or may not have used it over the years."

We all stared at the candle again. Not for the first time, I wondered how something so small and innocent-looking could contain such great power. How had the Reapers found it? Where had they uncovered it? Did they even realize what it was before the Pantheon had seized it, along with the other artifacts at the ski lodge up in New York? I didn't know the answers to my questions, and I supposed they didn't really matter. What did was that we had the candle—and that the Reapers wanted it. And now, we all knew exactly what they planned to do with it.

"So the Reapers think the candle will return Loki to

his full strength." I spat out the words. "They failed in trying to put his soul into Logan's body, and they didn't get their hands on the Chloris ambrosia flower to heal him. So now, they're coming after the candle and hoping it will finally do the job."

Silence. No one said anything, but we all knew how bad it would be if the Reapers *ever* got their hands on the candle.

Finally, Linus cleared his throat and turned to Nickamedes. "How soon can you put the candle on display in the library?" he asked. "Out in the middle of the main floor, someplace where everyone can see it."

Nickamedes frowned. "But why would you . . ." Understanding flared in his blue eyes.

He, Metis, and Linus all looked at each other, grim expressions on their faces.

"Are you out of your mind?" I hissed, finishing the librarian's thought. "Why in the world would you want to put the candle on display? Um, hello, there are Reapers *everywhere* at Mythos, despite all the statues and other magic that is supposed to keep them out. You put that candle on view, and you are just asking for it to get stolen . . ."

My gaze zoomed over to the candle, which was still sitting on the table. Then, I looked at Linus, finally understanding what he was really up to. "You want to use the candle as a trap. That's why you want to put it on display. So the Reapers will come after it."

He nodded. "Exactly right, Miss Frost. If what you and Nickamedes say is true, then the Reapers will have no choice but to try to steal the candle from the library. As you've said, they've run out of options trying to heal

Loki from his time spent in Helheim. So they'll come after the candle, and we'll be waiting for them when they do."

I shook my head. "No. No way. It will backfire on you. Things *always* do when the Reapers are involved. Vivian and Agrona will find some way to get their hands on the candle, no matter how many guards you put around it or how clever your trap is."

Linus's face darkened, and anger shimmered in his pale blue eyes. "And Agrona and Vivian are *precisely* the reasons I'm doing this. The two of them are the leaders of the Reapers. If we manage to capture or kill them, then we can stop the second Chaos War before it ever really gets started."

Loki's face loomed up in my mind the way it had so many times over the past few weeks. One side of his face so smooth and perfect with its rippling golden hair, chiseled cheekbone, and piercing blue eye. The other side so ruined and melted with its limp strings of black hair, smushed skin, and burning red orb. All put together, his features were horrible and twisted, the stuff of nightmares. But they weren't nearly as rotten as his soul—and the evil god's burning desire to kill or enslave every single member of the Pantheon, starting with me.

Sure, capturing or even killing Vivian and Agrona would severely hurt the Reapers, but there was no stopping the coming war—not until Loki was dead. And I knew that letting the Reapers so much as *look* at the candle would lead to nothing but trouble.

"But you don't understand—" I started.

Linus made a sharp motion with his hand, cutting me off. He straightened up to his full height, his gray Protectorate robe elegantly hanging off his shoulders as though he were some sort of ancient king, imposing and in command.

"I'm sorry, Miss Frost, but my decision has been made," Linus said. "We're putting the candle on display as soon as possible. The Reapers can try to steal it at their peril."

I argued with Linus some more—okay, okay, until I started to lose my voice—but I didn't change his mind. The Protectorate leader saw this as a way to finally turn the tide against the Reapers, and he wasn't about to pass it up. Part of me understood where he was coming from, but the other part of me thought he was just being stupid. If he was smart, if the Protectorate was smart, then Linus, Nickamedes, and Metis would figure out some way to destroy the candle for good, so that Loki could never, *ever* get his hands on it. Not put it out in the main part of the library for all the Reapers to see— and start plotting a way to steal it and take it to the evil god.

But there was nothing I could do, and an hour later, I found myself leaning against one of the walls of the library's office complex, watching Nickamedes hand a glass case over to Raven, who was one of the more unusual staff members at the academy.

Raven was an old woman with a face full of wrinkles and long white hair that seemed to melt into her floor-length white gown. In contrast, her eyes were as black, bright, and shiny as a Black roc's, while faint, white scars marred her hands and arms, as though she'd been in a fire long ago. Today, she had a black leather belt bristling with hammers, screwdrivers, and other tools slung low around her hips. It matched the black combat boots she always wore. Apparently, putting together artifact cases was another one of her many odd jobs around the academy, like running the coffee cart in the library, sitting in the infirmary, or watching over any Reapers who were being kept in the prison at the bottom of the math-science building.

Raven was stronger than she looked, because she lifted up the heavy glass case with no visible effort and carefully set it on top of Sol's candle. Raven secured the glass to the wooden stand, locking the artifact away. She dusted off her hands, turned, and realized I was watching her. She paused a second, then nodded at me. I nodded back. I'd never heard Raven utter so much as a single word, and a nod was about as friendly as she'd ever been to me. I always meant to ask Nickamedes or Metis if they'd ever actually heard her speak, or if she even could speak, but I'd never gotten around to it.

Still, I stared at Raven as she walked past me. For a moment, her face seemed to flicker like, well, a candle flame, as though she was wearing a mask of wrinkles, and there was a younger, prettier face lurking underneath her old, wizened features. I blinked, and the image was gone, snuffed out like that same candle flame, and Raven was simply Raven again.

Nickamedes moved off to talk to Linus, who was standing in front of the checkout counter, talking to some of the Protectorate guards. But I stayed where I was by the offices, my gaze still locked on the candle. I couldn't believe how innocent, how ordinary, it looked sitting there on its black velvet stand.

Linus had decided to place the candle in one of the most visible sections in the entire library, right in the middle of the main floor, close to the checkout counters. When I'd first come to Mythos, another artifact case had stood in that exact same spot, one that had held the Bowl of Tears. A Reaper named Jasmine Ashton had tried to use that powerful artifact to get revenge on Morgan McDougall for messing around with Jasmine's boyfriend.

Seeing Sol's candle in the exact same spot gave me a creepy sense of déjà vu. Because Jasmine had almost succeeded in using the Bowl of Tears to sacrifice Morgan to Loki and kill me the night of the homecoming dance. And now, here was another powerful artifact, sitting right out in the open, just begging the Reapers to come and steal it.

I glanced around the library, my gaze taking in the other kids hunched over their books at the study tables, browsing through the stacks, and standing around the coffee cart, waiting for Raven to unbuckle her tool belt and get back to fixing their lattes, espressos, and hot chocolates. Everything looked perfectly normal, perfectly ordinary, perfectly *innocent*, but I still couldn't help but wonder if the Amazon texting on her phone a few feet away was telling Vivian that the candle was on view. Or if the Viking leaning against the checkout counter fiddling with a tablet was e-mailing the information to Agrona. Or if one of the members of the Protectorate gathered around Linus was dreaming up a way to kill all of the other guards and take off with the candle.

But the really frustrating thing was that there was nothing I could do about any of those things—not until Vivian, Agrona, and the other Reapers decided to strike.

"Come on, now, Gwen," a low voice said. "Staring at

the candle won't change anything. If you ask me, you're simply attracting more attention to it. And yourself too."

I glanced down at Vic, who was hanging from my belt as usual. The sword stared at the candle, his purple eye bright against the white marble all around us.

"Look around," Vic said, still keeping his voice low so that I was the only one who could hear him. "Everyone's wondering what you're doing."

I glanced around again and realized he was right. All of the other kids had been doing their own thing, but now, more than a few had turned in my direction, wondering what I was doing staring at some boring old artifact. If only they knew that this boring old artifact might mean the difference between whether we all lived, died, or spent what was left of our lives as Loki's slaves.

"Okay, okay," I grumbled. "I'm leaving. But I want to go on record as saying that this is a Bad, Bad Idea."

Vic rolled his eye. "Well, *obviously*. But there's nothing we can do about it tonight, so why don't you quit worrying and go see the Spartan in the infirmary?"

He was right. There was nothing more I could do here, and I did want to check on Logan. So I pushed away from the glass wall, went around the checkout counter, and headed for the doors that led out of the library.

Still, right before I left the main space, I couldn't help but glance over my shoulder one more time. For a moment, it seemed like the candle glowed with a brilliant inner light, making it burn as bright as a star underneath the smooth glass. I blinked, and the light was gone. The candle was simply a candle again.

I shivered, dropped my gaze from the artifact, and left the library.

Chapter 8

Despite my unease, the night passed by in a quiet fashion. Metis gave Logan, Sergei, and everyone else who'd been more seriously injured in the Reaper attack a clean bill of health and let everyone leave the infirmary bright and early the next morning. After weapons training in the gym, Logan and I wound up in the dining hall to eat a quick breakfast before trudging to our morning classes.

Like everything else at Mythos, the dining hall was way more upscale than what you'd find at a regular high school. White linens and fine china covered the tables, instead of plastic trays and sporks, while paintings of mythological feasts decorated the walls, and suits of armor stood guard in the corners. But the dining hall's most interesting feature was the open-air indoor garden that lay in the center of the room, complete with statues perched among the almond, orange, and olive trees planted in the black soil and the curling tendrils of the grapevines that wound around, through, and over everything. Since this was where all of the students chowed down, the statues were mostly of food and harvest gods, like Dionysus and Demeter, instead of the fierce mythological creatures that adorned the outsides of the buildings. But once again this morning, the statues had strangely neutral expressions on their stone faces, instead of cocking their heads to the side and leaning forward, as though they were listening to all of the student gossip, the way they usually did.

"Still worried about the candle?" Logan asked, cutting into my thoughts.

I dragged my gaze away from the statues. Last night, I had filled Logan in on Sol's candle and his dad's plans to leave it on display as bait for the Reapers. "Why do you think that?"

He gestured with his fork at my plate. "Because you've barely touched your peach waffles."

"Are they peach?" I groused. "I couldn't really tell with all of the whipped-cream flowers on top of them."

That was the other way in which the dining hall had little resemblance to a regular cafeteria—the food was far fancier than the usual boxes of cereal and bottles of milk you'd find at breakfast time at any normal school. Instead, the Mythos chefs were standing behind a series of cooking stations along one of the walls, whipping up made-to-order gourmet waffles, omelets, and other delicacies that featured everything from creamy feta cheese to buttery lobster to crispy pancetta. I wasn't particularly hungry this morning, so I'd grabbed the first thing I'd come to on the breakfast line that looked like regular food—peach Belgian waffles. Although the chefs had still managed to add their own froufrou twist to the waffles by decorating the tops of them with mounds of whipped cream swirled into the shape of fancy flowers and curlicued leaves, all dusted with bits of orange, lemon, and lime zest. In fact, there were so many flowers and leaves on the top of the waffles that I almost thought I was eating a frosted birthday cake, minus the candles.

Thinking about birthday cake and candles made me focus on Sol's candle, sitting in the library, waiting for some Reaper to come along and steal it right out from under our noses—

"My dad knows what he's doing," Logan said, interrupting my thoughts again. "He won't let the Reapers get the candle."

"I know he'll do his best," I replied. "And so will all of the other Protectorate guards. But Vivian and Agrona take scheming to a whole new level of evil. They always have a plan within a plan within a plan. You should know that better than anyone."

Logan grimaced, then reached up and rubbed his throat with his hand.

"I'm sorry," I said, regretting my snarky words. "I didn't mean to remind you—"

"That I tried to kill you?" he said. "It's okay, Gwen. Trust me. I don't need you to remind me of that. It's not like it's something I could forget—ever."

Oh no. He only called me *Gwen* when he was being dead serious—or when I'd struck a nerve. Logan's attack was like an invisible live wire sparking in the space between us, one that brought sharp, stinging jolts of pain and misery whenever we got too close to it. That distant, haunted look filled his icy eyes again, the one that had been there on and off ever since Agrona had snapped that gold collar full of Apate jewels around his neck at the Aoide Auditorium. The one that always seemed to come back just when I thought it was finally gone for good. The one that always seemed to come between us no matter how much we tried to pretend that everything was fine.

I let out a breath, leaned over, and gripped his hand. "Look, I'm sorry. I'm just worried right now about *everything*. Vivian, Agrona, the Reapers, the candle, Loki. It's like your dad said. Everything seems to be coming to a turning point. But I don't know what that turning point is or if things will even go the way we want them to."

Logan looked at me, his gaze sharpening. "I know there's a lot going on, but are you sure that nothing else is bothering you? You've been really distracted these last few days. Ever since we came back from Colorado, actually."

I thought of all the things I hadn't told him, all the secrets I'd been keeping from him, all the pressure I felt to find some way to save us all from the unending horror that was Loki.

I let go of his hand, not wanting to accidentally let him feel any of my turbulent emotions since my skin had been touching his. "Nothing's wrong." I tried to smile. "At least, nothing more so than usual."

Perhaps the biggest secret I was keeping was the fact that I hadn't told Logan that I was the one who was supposed to kill Loki. I'd especially kept quiet about that because I knew exactly what he would say. That it was impossible. That no one could do it. That it was a suicide mission. But even worse was my fear that Logan might try to do the job for me, in order to try to protect me. Because that was one fight I knew he wouldn't win, much less survive.

I didn't think I would survive it, either, but I was determined not to take the Spartan or any of my other friends down with me.

"Everything will work out," Logan insisted, still trying to reassure me. "You'll see."

I wished I could have shared in his confidence, but I didn't—I just didn't. I'd already lost too many battles to Vivian and Agrona to think that they wouldn't win this one too. But I knew Logan and his dad were trying to work things out, trying to fix their relationship, so I kept my mouth shut. Arguing with him and undermining his new fragile trust in Linus wouldn't solve anything, and it certainly wouldn't stop the Reapers from striking.

"Yeah, you're probably right," I said, forcing myself to smile at him.

Logan grinned back at me. "Of course, I'm right. I'm *always* right."

I rolled my eyes, leaned over, and lightly punched him in the shoulder. "And now you sound like Vic."

"No, he doesn't," Vic piped up from his spot in the chair I'd propped him up in. "I am *much* more confident than the Spartan is." He sniffed. "And with good reason."

Logan and I both laughed, and the tension between us eased.

We ate our food in silence for the next several minutes. Despite all of the whipped cream, I had to admit that the peach Belgian waffles were surprisingly good. The batter was light and airy, with thick chunks of fresh, ripe peaches sprinkled throughout it, and the peach syrup drizzled over everything added even more sweetness to the dish. I'd also gotten a stack of bacon, which was perfectly crispy, while the hash browns were oozing with sharp cheddar cheese, just the way I liked them. I washed everything down with a glass of fresh-squeezed apple juice, enjoying the cool fruity concoction.

I had finished eating and had pushed my plate away when Logan reached over and grabbed my hand again, threading his fingers through mine. A soft, lighthearted sensation surged through me at the contact, and I sighed, enjoying this rare moment of peaceful happiness.

"So," he said. "Do you think we can talk about the Valentine's Day dance now?"

"What's there to talk about?"

"What time you want me to pick you up, what color dress you're wearing so I can get the right kind of corsage, where you want to go to make out after the dance is over with." Logan gave me a wink. "You know. All the usual stuff."

I laughed. "You must be feeling pretty confident to say something like that."

His grin widened. "Always."

I arched my eyebrow, then leaned forward and crooked my finger at him. Logan leaned in as well, as though we were conspiring about something terribly important.

"Well," I said in a husky voice, staring into his blue, blue eyes. "The answers to your questions are seven o'-clock, silver, and anywhere you want to take me. How do you like that?"

Logan's grin widened. "I like those answers just fine."

He kissed me, his lips just barely brushing mine, although the soft, feathery touch still sent a wave of heat scorching through my veins. With everything that had been going on, we hadn't had a lot of time to focus on us, and I knew Logan was trying to take my mind off things by asking me about the dance, by trying to pretend, at least for a few minutes, that we were a normal couple, eagerly planning our big night out. But instead, he only made me think about how far I'd come from that naïve, clueless girl who'd fallen in love with him at the homecoming dance last year—and how far I still had to go before things were settled.

One way or the other.

Logan drew back, grinned again, and opened his mouth, like he was going to tease me some more, but I didn't give him the chance. I leaned in and kissed him again, wrapping my arms around his neck and desperately trying to ignore the little voice in the back of my mind that whispered that if the Reapers had their way, the dance would never take place.

And I probably would be dead soon, regardless of anything else that happened in the meantime.

Logan and I finished breakfast, and I schlepped to my first class, trailed as usual by Alexei. To my surprise, the rest of the day passed by in a completely normal and utterly boring fashion. Morning classes. Lunch with Daphne, Carson, Oliver, and Alexei in the dining hall. More classes in the afternoon. And then, finally, it was time for me to go visit Grandma Frost, as I'd promised her I would.

When I'd first come to Mythos, I'd snuck off campus to go see my grandma a few times every week before coming back to work my shifts at the Library of Antiquities, even though students weren't supposed to leave campus during the week. But Linus Quinn and the rest of the Powers That Were at the academy had eventually realized they couldn't stop me from going to visit my grandma; nobody batted an eye at my off-campus trips anymore.

But today, instead of riding the public bus down the mountain to the nearby town of Asheville where my grandma lived, I was in the back of another black SUV owned by the Protectorate. Alexei sat beside me in the back seat, while Sergei was driving. Nyx was nestled on the floorboard at my feet, napping, and I had Vic laid out flat across my lap, while I stared out the windows, waiting for Vivian and a group of Reapers to appear at any second and attack us.

"Relax, Gwen," Alexei said. "Nothing's going to happen today."

I looked at him. "Really? Because that's exactly what Linus said to me yesterday, right before the Reapers ambushed the Protectorate convoy. Funny, how you've forgotten about that already, especially since you were in the van that they smashed up."

"I haven't forgotten," Alexei said. "But you're overlooking the obvious."

"Really? What's that?"

He shrugged. "We don't have anything the Reapers want this time."

I wanted to point out that that wasn't true—not by a long shot. The Reapers had already tried to get their hands on Vic, as well as the Swords of Ruslan, which were sticking up out of the black backpack at Alexei's feet. Besides, even without our artifacts, Vivian would have been perfectly happy to kill me, and I felt the exact same way about her. But I kept my mouth shut. I knew Alexei and the rest of my friends were trying to go about their days and lives as though everything was normal, the way they always did, as though we weren't in danger of being attacked and slaughtered at any second. So I decided to stay quiet and let him keep the illusion—even if I knew exactly what a thin, pitiful smokescreen it really was.

"My boy's right," Sergei chimed in, his hazel eyes meeting mine in the rearview mirror. "At the very least, the Reapers will need some time to lick their wounds. Linus and Inari are down in the academy prison right now, questioning the ones we captured yesterday after the attack. After that, the Reapers will be shipped to a more secure facility."

I wished I had their confidence, but I didn't—I just didn't. I didn't see the future like Grandma Frost did, but I couldn't help feeling that time was running out to find a way to kill Loki. The silver laurel bracelet, Sol's candle, all the other artifacts that Logan and the Protectorate had recovered from the ski lodge up in New York. There were too many powerful things floating around out there, and too much of a sense of the centuries-long conflict between the Reapers and the Protectorate finally building to its ultimate conclusion for me to relax. Not now.

Not until Loki was dead—or I was.

Still, I made myself smile at both the father and son, hiding my turbulent thoughts from them as best as I could. "You're probably right."

We rode in silence the rest of the way down the mountain. Grandma Frost lived in a three-story, lavender-painted home near downtown Asheville, among other similar houses that had been cut up into apartments. Sergei pulled up to the curb and parked in front of the house. Aiko was sitting on the porch reading a comic book, her gray Protectorate robe draped around her slender body like a winter cloak to help ward off the chill of the day. Two more Protectorate guards stood down the street at the bus stop, wearing gray leather jackets instead of their usual robes. I supposed they were trying to blend in and look casual, although they weren't succeeding, since they still looked exactly like the tough warriors they were.

Sergei's phone chirped, and he picked it up from the console and stared at the message on the screen. "Linus needs me at the academy. I'm afraid I'm going to have to leave you two here for a little while."

"We can always take the bus back," I said. "You don't need to drive all the way back down here just to pick us up. Even I don't think that the Reapers would be bold enough to highjack a bus full of regular mortals who don't know anything about the mythological world."

Sergei shook his head. "You're probably right, but it's better not to take the chance, Gwen. If I haven't returned by the time you want to leave, tell Aiko or one of the other guards, and they'll drive you and Alexei back to the academy. Okay?"

I wanted to point out that riding the bus would have been far more anonymous than cruising around in an SUV right out of some spy movie, but I kept my thoughts to myself. "Yeah. Okay."

I woke Nyx up from her nap, and we got out of the car, along with Alexei, waved good-bye to Sergei, and trooped up the gray steps to the house. A bronze plaque beside the front door read *Psychic Readings Here*—since Grandma Frost used her Gypsy gift to tell people's fortunes and make a little extra cash. Alexei stayed on the porch to talk to Aiko, but I opened the door and went inside the house.

"Pumpkin?" Grandma called out. "Back here in the kitchen."

I grinned. Thanks to her ability to see the future, Grandma always seemed to know when I was coming over. Nyx let out a happy growl and strained on the end of her leash, ready to run forward, since she loved Grandma as much as I did. I walked through the living room, down the hallway, and into the kitchen, which was my favorite room in the house with its white-tile floor and sky-blue walls.

Grandma Frost was dressed in her usual Gypsy gear—a purple silk shirt, black pants, and black shoes with toes that curled up slightly. Rings studded with various gemstones glinted on her fingers, while a green scarf was knotted loosely around her throat, the silver coin-fringed ends trailing down her chest.

She stood in front of the stove, clutching a couple of gray oven mitts. A timer *tick-tick-tick*ed on one side of the counter, next to a jar shaped like a giant chocolate chip cookie.

I drew in a deep breath, enjoying the scents of butter, sugar, and melted chocolate that filled the air, along with a hint of spicy cinnamon and sweet vanilla swirled together. My stomach rumbled in anticipation.

"What smells so good?"

"Cookies," she replied, her face crinkling into a smile. "Chocolate chip, oatmeal raisin, and sugar cookies. I thought that you and Alexei might like a snack, and I made enough for you to take some back to Daphne too."

Daphne loved Grandma's sweet treats as much as I did, and I always had to fight her off for the last cookie. Logan too. But I didn't mind sharing with them. Too much.

The timer dinged, and Grandma Frost pulled the trays of cookies out of the oven. A blast of heat filled the kitchen, adding to the cozy atmosphere. We sat at the table, eating cookies and drinking glasses of cold milk, while Nyx plopped down on her tummy and gave us sad, mournful looks, wanting us to share our food with her.

Despite everything that was going on, I felt myself slowly relaxing. I hadn't been over to Grandma's much lately, not with all the problems of the past few weeks, and it felt good to sit here and share this quiet time with her.

Even if I knew it wouldn't last—and that Vivian and Agrona were probably plotting some way to steal the candle right now.

The thought soured my good mood. I finished the rest of my chocolate chip cookie, but I had a hard time choking down the sudden, hard lump in my throat that fear and worry left behind.

"What's wrong, pumpkin?" Grandma asked, picking up on my unease.

There was no use trying to hide anything from her, so I drew in a breath and told her everything that had happened since the Reaper attack yesterday, including the fact that Linus had put the candle on view for everyone at the academy to see—Reapers included.

When I finished, I let out another tense breath. "I don't know. I . . . have a bad feeling about things. I think putting the candle on display is a big mistake. I feel like it's just *asking* for trouble. At least, more trouble than we already have with the Reapers."

Grandma reached over and put her hand on top of mine. As always, I felt that wave of warm, familiar, comforting love surge off her and wash over into me.

"It'll be all right, pumpkin," she murmured. "You'll see. Everything will work out okay in the end."

Her violet eyes grew glassy, and I felt that old, knowing, watchful force stir in the air around her. Grandma was having one of her visions, so I kept quiet and held her hand. After a few seconds, the blank look disappeared from her face, and she smiled at me again, although her features seemed dimmer and sadder than before.

"Are you okay?" I asked.

She patted my hand. "I'll be fine, pumpkin. Perfectly fine."

The door at the front of the house creaked open, and Alexei walked into the kitchen. Grandma got to her feet to get him some milk and cookies, so I didn't get a chance to ask her about what she might have seen. She probably wouldn't tell me anyway, since it was hard for her to have crystal-clear visions about friends and family.

Grandma Frost also got out some chicken that she'd cooked special for Nyx. The wolf pup perked up as soon as she took the food out of the refrigerator, and Nyx started dancing around her feet in anticipation.

Grandma laughed. "Patience, little wolf. I'll feed you soon enough."

Nyx plopped down on the tile, threw back her head, and let out a squeaky howl, encouraging Grandma to hurry up already. We all laughed, except Vic, who was well into his latest nap.

Alexei started joking with Grandma, and I let their cheery conversation wash over me. Everything was fine— everything was *great*—and I knew I should be making the most of this happy moment while I could. But as I sat there in Grandma Frost's kitchen, surrounded by my friends, I couldn't help but think that this was the calm before the storm.

Chapter 9

Despite my worries, another hour passed, and before I knew it, it was time for me, Nyx, Alexei, and Vic to head back to the academy, since Nickamedes still expected me to work my usual shift. Truth be told, I wanted to be at the library so I could keep an eye on the candle. Oh, I knew that Linus had guards posted in and around the library, as well as throughout the rest of campus, but I'd feel better if I could see the artifact for myself—and try to stop Vivian and Agrona when they finally tried to steal it.

Grandma Frost packed the extra cookies into a tin, also shaped like a chocolate chip cookie, which I tucked into my gray messenger bag.

"You make sure to give your other friends some of these before Daphne eats them all," she warned me.

"I'll try, but you know how Daphne is," I said, laughing.

She smiled back at me. "That I do. I love you, pumpkin."

"I love you too, Grandma."

I hugged her good-bye, and she did the same thing to Alexei, making a faint blush bloom in his face. She'd just let him go after pinching his cheek when a car horn sounded outside.

"That must be my dad," Alexei said, leaving the kitchen. "I'll go tell him that you'll be out in a minute."

"Yes, pumpkin, you need to scoot if you want to make it back to the library on time," Grandma Frost said. "Besides, I've got dishes to wash."

"All right," I said, sliding Vic back into the scabbard belted around my waist and taking hold of Nyx's leash. "I'll call you if anything happens."

She nodded. "You do that, pumpkin."

Grandma Frost went over to the sink, stopped up the drain, and turned on the hot water, humming a soft tune. I stared at her a moment longer, feeling so grateful that she was in my life and wondering what I would ever do without her, before leaving the kitchen and walking down the hallway. I put my hand on the front doorknob and turned it, ready to step outside and go back to the academy—

Nyx let out a low growl. Surprised, I looked down and realized that the pup was turned back toward the kitchen. She let out another low growl, as though she wanted to tear into something with her baby teeth. A cold finger of unease crawled up my spine.

"What's wrong, girl—"

CRASH!

I jumped at the sharp, sudden bang from the kitchen. A muffled sound followed a second later, along with a soft, but steady *scrape-scrape-scrape*—almost like someone's feet being dragged across the tile floor.

I froze, wondering if I was hearing what I thought I was.

"Mmph!"

A muffled voice sounded from the kitchen, and I knew that Grandma was in danger.

I dropped my messenger bag and Nyx's leash and threw the door open, surprising Alexei and Aiko, who were talking on the porch. They stared at me with wide, startled eyes.

"Reapers!" I screamed, yanking Vic out of his scabbard.

Then, I turned and ran into the back of the house as fast as I could.

"Grandma? Grandma!" I yelled as I raced down the hallway and into the kitchen.

I couldn't hear anything over the rapid drum of my own heart, so I raised Vic high and burst into the kitchen, ready to cut into any Reapers who might have broken into the house.

But no one was there.

My head snapped left and right, but Grandma Frost wasn't in front of the sink, washing dishes like she should have been. Instead, one of the metal sheet trays she'd baked the cookies on rested on the floor. That must have been the cause of the crash I'd heard. It looked like someone had interrupted her, since the water was still running in the full sink, overflowing down the sides and spattering onto the floor. It took me a moment to realize that the back door was cracked open. I tightened my grip on Vic, threw open the door, and took a step forward—

A sword whistled toward my head.

I ducked and brought Vic up into a defensive position. *Clang!*

My sword met the one of the Reaper who'd been

lurking out of sight beside the back door. He raised his weapon for another strike, but I twirled Vic up, around, and down, and stabbed him in the chest with the sword. The Reaper screamed and fell to the ground.

"That's it, Gwen!" Vic shouted, his mouth moving underneath my palm. "On to the next one!"

Next one? What next one?

It took me another few crucial seconds to realize that the warrior wasn't alone. Half a dozen Reapers stood in the backyard, all with their curved swords up, ready to attack me. One of them, a woman, stood on a smooth patch of dirt to one side of the yard, her black boots trampling the purple and gray forget-me-nots that I'd planted there on Nott's grave. Anger surged through me at the sight, but I looked past the Reapers, searching for Grandma Frost.

But she wasn't there.

She wasn't there.

The Reapers grinned, twirled their swords in their hands, and charged at me. I tightened my grip on Vic and stepped up to meet them, even though I didn't know how I would manage to take on all of them at once—

Two figures moved between me and the Reapers— Alexei and Aiko. The two warriors drew their own weapons and rushed forward to meet the charging Reapers. Frantic, I scanned the yard again, searching for any sign of Grandma Frost. Where had the Reapers taken her? What had they done with her? How had they kidnapped her so quickly?

A sharp, high *yip-yip-yip* sounded, and I realized that Nyx had darted outside as well and was standing next to the fence at the edge of the backyard, trying to hurdle it with her short legs. If anyone could find Grandma Frost, it was Nyx. After all, her mom, Nott, had tracked me to the academy from a ski resort miles away. I just had to hope that Nyx had the same nose and instincts that her mom had had.

Nyx howled, and I raced in her direction, rushing past Alexei, Aiko, and the Reapers they were battling.

"Gwen!" Alexei yelled. "Gwen! Wait!"

But I didn't have time to stop and explain what I was doing—and that I was saving my grandma no matter what.

I reached the part of the fence that Nyx was still trying to hurdle. I grabbed the pup, picked her up, and set her down on the other side. Nyx put her nose to the ground. After a few seconds, she went tearing up the hill behind the house. I hopped over the fence and followed her.

"That's it, fuzzball!" Vic shouted out his encouragement to her. "You find Geraldine! Track her down!"

Nyx howled again in answer. I scrambled up the bank after her, not caring that I was tearing through a thicket of briars and other bushes that clutched at my clothes and scratched my hands. All that mattered was getting to Grandma Frost.

I finally crested the hill, but the other side was even steeper, and I had to put a hand down to keep my feet from sliding out from under me. Below, the bottom of the slope gave way to a small, grassy park that I used to play in all the time when I was a kid. Two black SUVs sat at the far side of the park, and I could see Grandma Frost struggling with the three Reapers who were trying to force her into the back of one of the vehicles.

"Grandma!" I screamed. "Grandma!"

Below, in the park, Grandma fought with her captors,

but I knew she wasn't going to be able to break free of them. And they weren't the only Reapers here.

Agrona stood by one of the SUVs, dispassionately watching my grandma's struggles, while Vivian swung her sword from side to side and headed in my direction.

"Gwen! Gwen!" I could hear Alexei yelling again, his voice getting closer and closer. "Wait for me!"

He and Aiko must have taken care of the Reapers in the backyard and were hurrying in my direction. But I didn't have time to wait, not if I wanted to save my grandma.

So I sucked in a breath, raced down the hill as fast as I could, and ran straight at Vivian. Nyx charged along with me, heading toward the SUVs, as though she could save Grandma all by herself. Meanwhile, Vivian smiled, and she raised her sword high so that I could see the half of a woman's face and the burning red eye inlaid into the hilt of her weapon.

"Come on, Vic! You miserable coward!" Lucretia called out in her low, throaty voice. "Come over here, and let me cleave you in two!"

"The only one who's going to get cleaved in two is you, you overconfident bit of scrap metal!" Vic crowed back at her.

Those were all the insults the two swords were able to exchange before I raised my weapon and brought it down, aiming for Vivian's head.

CLASH!

Our blades crashed together, sending out a cascade of red and purple sparks. Red sparks of magic also dripped out of Vivian's fingertips, another sign of her Valkyrie power.

"Give it up, Gwen," Vivian taunted me. "You've already lost this battle."

"Never!" I snarled back at her.

We broke apart and went right back on the attack, each one of us trying to skewer the other. Still, I couldn't help but look past Vivian. By this point, the Reapers had forced Grandma Frost into the back of one of the SUVs and closed the door, hiding her from sight. Nyx was closing in on the vehicles, but the wolf pup wasn't going to get there in time. Agrona gave me a mocking wave with her ruined right hand, then slid into the front passenger's seat.

The vehicle rumbled to life and drove away a second later.

She was gone.

Grandma Frost was *gone*.

"No!" I screamed, feeling like my heart had just been ripped out of my chest.

"Ah, Gwen," Vivian purred. "You don't know how long I've waited to hear you scream like that."

I ignored her taunt and lashed out with Vic. Vivian lurched to one side, and I ran past her, racing after the SUV, even though I knew that I wasn't going to be able to catch it. Nyx was still chasing after it as well, moving as fast as she could on her short, pup-sized legs.

But Vivian wasn't about to let me go that easily. She whipped her sword down and out, and I felt the blade bite into my left shin even as I tripped over it.

I landed facedown, my forehead hitting the ground and momentarily stunning me. But I forced the dizziness away and rolled over onto my back to block the attack I knew was coming—

Vivian put the tip of her sword against my throat and

planted her black boot on my right wrist—the hand that I was using to hold Vic. I couldn't move without her breaking my bones, but I tightened my fingers around the sword's hilt. I wasn't letting go of my weapon. If she wanted Vic, she'd have to pry him out of my cold dead hand.

"Do it," I said through gritted teeth. "Go ahead and kill me."

Vivian stared down at me, that Reaper red spark flickering in her golden eyes. She turned her sword, the point digging into my skin and drawing a bit of blood. Her golden Janus ring glinted on her finger, the ruby chips in the god's two faces, one looking forward into the future, and one looking back into the past, flashing in the sunlight.

"As much as I would enjoy it, I'm afraid that's not the plan," she said. "At least not for today. But there's nothing to stop me from hurting you—"

"Gwen! Gwen!" I heard Alexei shout again.

Vivian glanced over her shoulder. Alexei and Aiko must have been closer than she would have liked, because her mouth turned down into a petulant pout. She whipped around to me again.

"The deal is simple. You either bring us the candle, or your precious grandmother dies," Vivian hissed. "I'll call you with the details later, but the choice is yours, Gwen."

I opened my mouth to say something—I wasn't quite sure what—but Vivian raised Lucretia high and slammed the hilt of the sword into the side of my head.

The world snapped to black.

Chapter 10

Something warm, wet, and sticky touched my cheek, jerking me out of the darkness that I'd been drowning in for what seemed like forever. A small, hopeful *yip* sounded, and a solid weight bounded up onto my chest.

I opened my eyes to find Nyx wagging her tail and staring down at me with her bright, twilight-colored eyes. When she realized that I was awake and looking at her, she let out another happy yip and licked me on the cheek again. I wrinkled my nose. Vic was right. Her breath wasn't the best in the world, but I was so happy to see her that I didn't care. I rubbed her ears between my fingers, and Nyx's tail thumped against my ribs in contentment.

I sat up and realized that I was in the academy infirmary, lying on one of the hospital beds. I still had on the same clothes I had been wearing earlier. They were ripped, torn, dirty, and bloody from where I'd scrambled up the hill and down the other side, but the briar scratches on my hands and arms had disappeared. Other than a slight headache, I felt fine, and I knew Professor Metis or maybe Daphne had used her magic to heal me.

Nyx licked my cheek again, then hopped from the bed over onto a chair where Vic was propped up. She licked his cheek as well, and the sword's eye popped open.

"Ugh, fuzzball!" he groused. "I told you not to wake me up until Gwen was awake too."

Nyx let out another happy yip and hopped back over onto the bed. Vic realized that I was in fact awake and sitting up, and some of the worry eased out of his metal face.

"How do you feel?" he asked.

"I'm okay. What's going on?" I asked. "Where's Grandma Frost?"

Vic gave me a serious look, his purple eye dark and solemn. "I'll let the others tell you."

A hard knot of fear formed in the pit of my stomach. "The Reapers have her, don't they?"

"I'm afraid they do."

I pressed my fist to my mouth, fighting back tears, nausea, and the urge to scream all at the same time. Vivian and Agrona had Grandma Frost at their mercy—something I knew they didn't have a single shred of in their entire bodies.

The door opened, and Metis stuck her head inside. "Oh good," she said. "You're awake."

She stepped into the room, along with Linus and Coach Ajax. Nickamedes shuffled in as well, leaning on his cane. The librarian shut the door behind him, and the adults formed a row in front of the hospital bed.

"What are you doing to find my grandma?" I demanded. "Do you have any idea where the Reapers have taken her?"

Linus shook his head. "Unfortunately not, Miss Frost. Alexei and Aiko told us what they witnessed of the attack, but I'd like to hear your version of events."

I told them about fighting the Reapers, chasing after Grandma, and my confrontation with Vivian—including what she wanted.

"I *told* you that putting the candle on display was a bad idea," I said, staring at Linus with accusing eyes. "Only the Reapers aren't going to be stupid enough to try to steal it from the library like you wanted them to. Oh no. They're going to make us hand it over to them instead."

Linus look at Metis, then Ajax, and finally Nickamedes. Metis and Ajax stared back at him with sad but resigned faces, but anger burned in the librarian's eyes, making them glint like chips of hard blue ice.

"I'm afraid that's not going to happen," Linus said, squaring his shoulders and facing me again.

That ball of fear in my stomach morphed into a lump of cold, hard lead. "What . . . what are you saying?" I whispered, barely able to force out the words.

"We do not negotiate with Reapers," Linus said. "We are not giving the Reapers the candle. We can't afford to. Not after you told us what it does, and how they could use it to return Loki to his full strength."

For a moment, I cocked my head to the side, wondering if I'd heard him right—and really, really hoping that I hadn't.

"You're . . . you're not going to *save* her?" I sputtered in disbelief. "You're not going to give the Reapers the candle?"

Linus straightened up to his full height, his face harsher and sharper than ever before. "No. We are not giving the Reapers the candle. We cannot do anything that will potentially make Loki stronger."

My gaze snapped over to Metis and Ajax. They both looked back at me with tired, weary faces.

"I'm sorry, Gwen," Metis said. "We tried to convince him to change his mind."

"We all did," Ajax chimed in. "You know how much we all care about Geraldine."

Nickamedes didn't say anything, but he looked at the others, his own features pinched tight with disgust.

"But I'm not going to budge," Linus finished. "I can't. Not as the head of the Protectorate."

"Can't? Or don't want to?" I said in a clipped voice.

Linus sighed. "Can't, Miss Frost. Believe me, I take no pleasure in this. No pleasure at all."

"But you . . . you can't just *leave* her with the Reapers," I protested, my hands balling into tight fists. "Vivian and Agrona will kill her—they'll *torture* her—just out of spite."

"I'm sorry, Miss Frost," Linus repeated. "Truly, I am. But there's nothing I can do in regard to the candle. Rest assured that I have every available member of the Protectorate out looking for your grandmother. We are doing everything in our power to find her."

I glared at him. "Just not everything in your power to actually *save* her, right?"

Linus's lips pressed into a hard, thin line, but he didn't argue with me. He couldn't.

I looked at them all in turn. Linus. Metis. Ajax. Nickamedes. They stared back at me, a mixture of pity and resignation on their faces. Well, except for Nickamedes, who looked as angry as I felt. And I realized that they were actually going to do it. They were actually going to stand by and let my grandma die. Anger roared through me at the knowledge, melting that cold ball of lead in the pit of my stomach, and leaving behind a hard, sizzling determination, more intense than any I'd ever felt before.

"Well, if you won't save her, then I *will*," I snarled. "No matter what it takes."

I got to my feet, grabbed Vic, and stormed out of the room.

I knew that there was no use arguing with Linus, so I hurried into the waiting room, with Nyx scrambling to keep up with me. My friends were all there—Daphne, Carson, Oliver, Alexei, Logan. So was Raven, sitting at the reception desk, her black combat boots propped up on top of the smooth wooden surface, reading through one of her celebrity gossip magazines like usual. Raven gave me a curious look, then flipped another page. The faint crackle was the only sound in the room.

I stopped in front of my friends and stared at Logan. The sad, stricken look on his face—on all their faces— told me that he already knew Linus wasn't going to trade the candle for my grandma. I'd thought that Logan going all Reaper and trying to kill me had been bad, but this—this felt like a whole new level of betrayal.

By everyone I cared about.

"Miss Frost, please wait," Linus said, following me into the room.

Metis and Ajax trailed after him, with Nickamedes bringing up the rear.

I whirled around to face him. "Why? So I can stand around and count down the hours until my grandma dies?"

"It's not like that at all, and you know it," Linus said. "As I said before, we will do everything in our power to find your grandmother."

"Before or after the Reapers kill her?"

Linus pressed his lips into a tight, thin line and crossed his arms over his chest.

Daphne came over and tentatively laid a hand on my arm, pink sparks of magic streaking out of her fingertips and landing on my dirty clothes before quickly winking out. "Gwen, why don't you take it easy?"

I shrugged off her hand. "Take it easy?" I let out a harsh, bitter laugh. "I can't take it easy. I can *never* take it easy. Not until Loki is dead."

Daphne frowned. "What do you mean?"

I looked around and realized all of my friends were staring at me with the same wary, curious expression as she. Suddenly, I was so tired—tired of all the lies, all the secrets, all the problems that never seemed to end.

I let out another bitter laugh. "You really don't get it, do you? You don't know what's going on at all. None of you do. Except for her."

I jerked my head at Metis, but she stared back at me, her face neutral.

"What do you mean?" Logan asked, coming to stand beside me. "Gwen, I know you're upset, but what are you talking about?"

"The candle," I said. "I'm talking about the damn *candle*. Yeah, the Reapers want it to heal Loki, but that's not all they're going to get out of it."

Linus frowned. "What else could they possibly do with it? What else could they want it for? Surely, returning Loki to his full strength is their top priority."

"It may be the Reapers' ultimate goal, but it's not

his," I said. "Loki wants to be whole again, sure, for one specific reason—so he can finally murder me."

"And how do you know that?" Logan asked.

"Because," I spat out the words. "I'm the one who's supposed to kill *him*. I'm the one who's supposed to kill Loki."

Chapter 11

Silence. Complete, utter silence.

Linus whirled around to face Metis, his gray robe snapping around his body before falling free again. "Aurora? Is this true? How long have you known about this?"

"Yes, I'm afraid it's true." She lifted her chin. "And I've known ever since the incident at the Garm gate when Loki was freed in the first place. That's when Gwen told me that killing Loki was the ultimate mission Nike had given her, something the Reapers believe she can do as well."

"And why didn't you tell me about this?" Linus demanded.

"Because I knew you'd probably take Gwen away from the academy, her friends, and her grandmother," Metis said. "Knowing you, Linus, you would have kept Gwen under lock and key until you thought it was time for her to finally complete her mission."

An angry flush stained his cheeks, but he didn't deny her accusations.

"I would have done what was best for Miss Frost," Linus said in a stiff voice.

"Yeah," I sniped. "Because letting the Reapers kill my grandma is what's best for me."

He turned to stare at me, but I glared right back at him. Anger didn't even begin to describe what I was feeling. Neither did rage. It was . . . I just felt . . . *fury*. Molten, unending, white-hot fury. Because of all the evil that Loki and the Reapers had done, because of all the hard choices and sacrifices I'd been forced to make, because of all the loved ones I'd lost. And now, my grandma's life was hanging in the balance, and no one seemed to want to save her but me.

"But Metis is right," Linus said, finally breaking the silence. "You need to be protected at all costs, Miss Frost."

He pulled his phone out of his pants pocket. "I'm going to get Sergei and Inari over here right now. We'll get you to a secure location—"

"No," I cut in. "I'm not going anywhere."

"I'm afraid you don't have a choice, Miss Frost," Linus said. "If you can somehow actually kill Loki, then you need far more protection. At the very least, we need to relocate you from the academy to somewhere much more secure."

"Where I can do what? Twiddle my thumbs until the Reapers find me and try to kill me again? I don't think so," I said. "And I do have a choice. I *always* have a choice. It's a little thing called free will. Maybe you should read up on it. I'm sure there are some books about it in the library that Nickamedes could find for you."

That angry flush darkened on Linus's pale cheeks. "You are leaving the academy, Miss Frost. It's not a request. It's an order."

"I don't take orders from you." I raised Vic. "You so

much as lay one finger on me or order any of your Protectorate guards to do the same, and I will fight back with everything I have. Worse than that, I'll use my magic on you. My touch magic. Remember at my trial when I told you that I used it to kill Preston Ashton? Well, I could do the exact same thing to *you*, Mr. Quinn."

Carson gasped at my threat, and my other friends all looked shocked. Logan kept glancing back and forth between me and his dad, not sure what to do. Even Linus looked a bit uncertain, his eyes flicking to my hand, which was wrapped tight around Vic's hilt.

"I'm a Champion, remember?" I snarled. "Nike's Champion, the best of the best. That's what you told Nickamedes once. Believe me when I tell you that you don't want me to prove it to you."

"You're angry right now," Linus said. "I understand that. I know how hard it is to lose the people you love to the Reapers."

His gaze went to Logan, and the raw, naked hurt in Linus's eyes cut through my fury, leaving nothing behind but a hollow, bitter ache in my heart.

"I understand that," I replied, echoing his words. "And I'm so sorry about your wife and daughter. Sorrier than you will ever know. But you have a chance to help me save my grandma. Will you do that? Please? Or are you going to leave her to the Reapers?"

Linus stared at me, and I could see the struggle in his eyes. I knew he was weighing my grandma's life against all of those he was responsible for, every single member of the Pantheon. And I knew what his decision would be, what it *had* to be. If our positions had been reversed, I probably would have done the exact same thing. I'd already lost so much to the Reapers—we all had—and I didn't want to give them the candle, either. I didn't want to make Loki stronger. I didn't want to potentially bring about the destruction of the Protectorate and the Pantheon.

But I couldn't bear the thought of losing my grandma— I just couldn't *bear* it.

"I'm sorry, Miss Frost," Linus said. "But I cannot give the Reapers the candle under any circumstances."

I gave him a stiff nod. "You don't want to trade the candle for my grandma? That's fine. I understand your reasoning. Really, I do. But don't expect me to save you in return."

I turned, pushed past my friends, and stormed out of the infirmary.

I didn't get far. I'd just stepped back outside when Nyx and my friends caught up with me. Daphne, Carson, Oliver, Alexei, Logan.

Daphne was the quickest, and she darted forward and latched on to my arm, stopping me in my tracks with her Valkyrie strength. "Nike told you that you're supposed to kill Loki? Why? Why didn't you tell any of us about that?"

The others gathered around me, forming an unbreakable ring, and I found myself sighing.

"Because I didn't want you to worry," I said. "I figured I was worried enough for all of us."

"How does she expect you to do that?" Oliver asked, his green eyes dark and serious.

I thought of the laurel bracelet hanging off my wrist. "I have no idea."

I figured it wasn't actually a lie, since I didn't know

how to use the bracelet to kill Loki, or if it could really even hurt him in the first place.

"Why didn't you tell us, Gwen?" Carson asked again, peering at me through his black glasses. "Why didn't you let us know what you were dealing with? We would have helped you through it. You should have known that."

The hurt and sorrow in his eyes made the rest of my anger evaporate. "I do know that, and I'm sorry I didn't tell you guys before. With everything that's been going on, there never seemed to be a good time to bring it up."

I winced even as I said the words. Because they were some of the same lame excuses that Grandma Frost, Metis, and Nickamedes had used to keep secrets from me, like my mom being Nike's Champion, or my dad, Tyr Forseti, being a Reaper at one time. I never thought I would do the same thing to my friends, but I had plenty of secrets of my own to hide from them.

Especially now.

Logan stepped forward and put his hand on my arm, just like Daphne had done, but I didn't shake him off. I was suddenly too tired for that.

"I'm sorry about my dad," Logan said, his blue eyes warm and sympathetic. "I couldn't believe it when he said that he wasn't going to trade the candle for your grandma. None of us could when he told us about it in the infirmary. We tried to get him to change his mind— we all did—but he wouldn't."

"And you're okay with it?"

Logan sighed, looking as tired as I felt. "No, I'm not okay with it—not at all. But my dad's right. Even if we handed the candle over to the Reapers, we don't have any guarantee that they wouldn't kill your grandma anyway. Or try to murder you too. Especially if they think you can somehow kill Loki."

"Really?" I asked, my voice dipping to a low, dangerous level. "And what if it was your dad that the Reapers had kidnapped? Or your mom or your sister? What would you do then? Would you stand by and let the Reapers kill them when you knew that you could save them?"

Logan stared at me, a stricken look on his face.

"I didn't think so," I said in a sad voice.

I knew it was wrong, taking my hurt, worry, and fear out on Logan and the rest of my friends, but I was just so *angry*. Not only at the Reapers, but at Linus Quinn and the stupid Protectorate too.

But most of all, I hated Nike for putting me in this situation to begin with. Not for the first time, I wondered why the goddess had chosen me to be her Champion, out of all the people in the world. Why *me*? I'd never asked for the responsibility, and I certainly didn't want it. Not only that, but I wasn't the smartest person around, or the best warrior, or even the bravest. But the goddess had picked me for some mysterious reason, and now I was stuck here, trapped in a tangled web of schemes, prophecies, and riddles that made no sense. Trying to figure out the best thing to do, and knowing I would lose something—or somebody—no matter what decision I made.

I let out a breath. "Look, I'm sorry for everything. I just . . . didn't expect Linus to tell me that he wasn't going to rescue my grandma. I know you're all worried about me, but I'm going to go back to my room. I . . . need to be by myself for a little while, okay?"

I looked at my friends. Daphne with the pink sparks

of magic still hissing out of her fingertips. Carson pushing his black glasses up his nose. Oliver with his arms crossed over his chest. Alexei looking as stoic as ever. And Logan, staring at me like I was some stranger he'd never seen before—one he didn't want to know.

"Okay," Daphne said. "But at least let us go with you back to your dorm."

I nodded, too tired to argue with her. About this, at least.

My friends walked me back to Styx Hall in complete silence. We reached the steps that led up to the front door, then stood there, not sure what to do, not sure what to say to each other now that I'd had my complete and utter meltdown.

Finally, Daphne stepped forward and hugged me, cracking my back with her strength. "I'll call you later, okay?"

Tears stung my eyes, but I blinked them back. "Yeah. Sure. Thanks."

She drew back, then she and Carson turned and walked away, holding hands and whispering to each other.

Oliver came over and slung his arm around my shoulder too. "It'll be okay, Gwen. You'll see."

I nodded, too choked up to speak. Alexei nodded at me and touched my shoulder; then he and Oliver hurried away as well.

That left me standing alone with Logan.

"I'm sorry I yelled at you and your dad," I said. "That I threatened him with my psychometry magic. That was wrong of me. It's just . . . she's all the family I have left. Well, besides Rory."

Logan nodded. "I get it, really, I do. And if I were you, I'd be just as angry at my dad. But he really does know what he's doing. He's managed to keep the Reapers at bay this long. He'll find a way to save your grandma too. You just have to trust him. Okay, Gypsy girl?"

I made myself smile at him, even though I didn't really feel like it. "Yeah, I'm sure you're right."

Logan nodded. He hesitated, then drew me into his arms. He started to kiss me, but I turned my head, and his lips brushed my cheek instead. Logan drew back, a hurt look on his face, but there was nothing I could do to fix it—or this chasm that suddenly separated us once again. Sometimes, I felt like the Spartan and I spent more time apart than we ever did together.

"I'll call you later too, okay?" he said in a low voice.

I nodded and bit my lip, trying to hide how much I was hurting—and how much I would hurt him and the rest of my friends before this was all said and done.

Logan left, and I went into my dorm. I trudged up the steps to my room, with Nyx still following along behind me. I propped Vic up in the bed, and Nyx scrambled up and lay down beside him, as was her custom. I went over and peered out of one of the lace curtains. Linus must have called Aiko, because the Ninja was once again standing guard outside my dorm, but I didn't see any other Protectorate guards. Just kids walking by on the quad, going to their afterschool clubs, activities, and groups, or trudging up the hill to the main quad to get some supper in the dining hall.

"What are you doing?" Vic asked.

"Checking to make sure my friends actually left."

"They're just worried about you," he said. "We all are."

"I know, but I don't want to see them right now. Not when I know what I have to do next."

"What does that mean?" Vic asked.

But I didn't answer him. Instead, I turned away from the window, went over, and sat down at my desk. I looked at the photos of my mom and Metis; then my gaze flicked over to the small replica statue of Nike. I waited, but the goddess didn't open her eyes and acknowledge me. I didn't know if what I was going to do was the right thing or not, but it was the only chance I had to save my grandma.

"Uh-oh," Vic said. "I know that look. What are you thinking, Gwen?"

I swiveled my chair around to him. "I'm thinking that if Linus Quinn won't give me the candle, then I'll just have to steal it myself."

Chapter 12

Vic's eye bulged so far out I thought it might actually pop right off the sword's shocked face.

"What?! You can't be serious!" he said, his voice rising to a near scream.

Nyx whined, as if the high pitch upset her. I winced too. Vic could shriek worse than, well, a teenage girl sometimes.

"You heard Linus," I said. "He's not going to give me the candle to give to the Reapers. They'll kill my grandma if I don't get them the candle. You know they will."

Vic sighed. "Of course I know that. But you need to think about what you're doing. Like it or not, Linus has a point. You can't risk making Loki stronger by giving the Reapers the candle. His injuries and broken body are probably the *only* reason that the Reapers haven't attacked the academy outright yet."

"I know, and I don't like it any more than you do. But I can't leave Grandma Frost to the Reapers. I just *can't.* If my mom were here, she'd try to find some way to save her. I know she would, because that's what Champions do—that's what *I'm* going to do."

"Okay," Vic said. "Let's say that you actually decide to go through with this insanity. Linus will probably put even more guards around the candle now. He's sure to realize that you might try to steal it. So even if you do somehow manage to get your hands on it, how are you going to get out of the library with it?"

"Oh, that's the easy part," I said. "Because you're forgetting one thing."

"What's that?"

I stared at the sword. "The candle isn't the only thing in the library with magic. I've spent more time in that library over the past few months than Linus Quinn and all the other Protectorate guards put together. I know things they don't. More important, I know about *artifacts* they don't."

Vic stared back at me. "You know you're going to have to do this alone, right? Because you can't ask Logan to help you with this. Or any of your other friends. Because if it doesn't work, and they're involved, then it's not only going to be your neck on the line. It's going to be theirs too."

He was right. I couldn't involve any of my friends. Not with this. I'd seen their reactions in the infirmary and then again out on the quad. They felt sorry for me, they really did, and they wanted to help me find a way to save Grandma Frost, but the threat of Loki getting stronger was one they couldn't ignore. Maybe it was wrong of me to ignore it too, but my grandma's life was at stake, and I was going to do whatever it took to save her.

Even if I had to sacrifice my friends' trust—and Logan's love.

"I didn't have any friends when I first came to Mythos, and I did okay," I said, answering Vic's question. "I can make it through this without them."

No matter how much it would hurt all of us.

"Okay," he said again, still trying to discourage me. "Let's say you actually manage to steal the candle from the library, get off campus with it, and take it to Vivian, Agrona, and the Reapers. They're not going to let you and Geraldine go, Gwen. You know that. As soon as he gets his hands on the candle, Loki will order them to kill you both."

I got up, walked over, and plopped down on the window seat, pushing the curtains aside and staring out the window again. "I know. And that's what I have to figure out—how to get us away from the Reapers and steal the candle back at the same time before Loki ever gets the chance to use it."

Vic eyed me. "Well, wake me up when you figure it all out, Gwen. Because there's no getting around it. If you don't have an escape plan, you can't risk taking the candle to the Reapers in the first place. Linus is right about that. You'll doom us all, including yourself."

I wanted to point out that we were all pretty much doomed anyway, since I still had no idea how to actually kill Loki, but I didn't say anything. Vic let out another sigh, then slowly closed his eye. A few minutes later, snores started rumbling out of his mouth. Nyx curled her tail around the sword's blade and settled down for her own nap.

I sat in the window seat and brooded.

As much as I hated to admit it, Vic was right. I couldn't trust the Reapers to keep their promise and let me and Grandma go after I handed over Sol's candle. I might be reckless sometimes, but I wasn't completely stupid. So how could I get Grandma Frost and myself to safety? How could I swipe the candle right out from under the Reapers' noses? Or at least come up with some way to rig it so that Loki couldn't use it, couldn't heal himself with it? I didn't know the answers to my questions, and if I didn't figure them out, then my grandma would die.

So I pulled my knees up to my chest and continued my brooding, staring out into the growing darkness, as if the shadows would suddenly part and give me the answers I so desperately needed.

There wasn't much to see out the window, except Aiko leaning against one of the trees below my windows, standing guard. So I looked past her, idly scanning the rest of the grounds, my brain churning and churning, trying to come up with solutions to all of my many problems.

Besides Aiko, the only other thing of interest was a white marble bird feeder that someone, Raven probably, had set up in the grass close to the dorm. Despite the cold, a few birds flitted around the feeder, grabbing bits of black birdseed out of the holes in the sides. My gaze locked on to one bird who kept returning to the feeder time and time again. Some sort of crow, I thought, although its dark, shiny feathers made it look more like a miniature Black roc than anything else. I sighed. It was so sad that I couldn't even look at a simple bird now without automatically comparing it to its mythological equivalent. Oh yeah. I'd been at Mythos Academy for *way* too long.

Still, the crow circling around and then dive-bombing back to the bird feeder made me think of all the times Vivian had escaped from a battle by hopping onto her

Black roc and soaring up into the sky. She'd done it at the Garm gate, the Crius Coliseum, and even at the Eir Ruins out in Colorado. And she'd pulled the same stunt yesterday after the fight had turned against her and Agrona.

I snorted. If only I had a Black roc, then I could do the exact same thing to help my grandma escape from the Reapers. Problem solved. Of course, the Reapers would never let me get close enough to a roc to actually climb on top of the creature. Even if I could miraculously do that, there was still the small matter of getting the roc to fly me and Grandma away of its own free will—

A bolt of an idea shot through me, and I sat upright in the window seat, jerking to attention so fast that I almost went careening down onto the floor. I didn't have a Black roc, and I would never, ever have a Black roc. But I didn't need one of the birds.

Because I had something *better*.

If I could figure out a way to make it work—and call in some serious favors.

I sat there, my eyes closed, my fingers drumming against my jeans, trying to figure out all the pieces in my mind, all the angles, all the ways my crazy plan might succeed—or fail miserably. And slowly, I puzzled out a way to make it actually *work*. At least, I thought I did. Even the best plan could bite the dust when the Reapers were involved, but it was the only chance I had to save Grandma Frost, and I had to take it.

But first, I had to reach out to someone to make it happen.

I pulled my phone out of my jeans pocket and hit a

number in the speed dial. "Yeah?" a voice answered on the third ring, as snarky and sarcastic as ever.

"It's Gwen."

"Yeah?" came the response, a little more interested— and much more wary.

"The Reapers have my grandma, and I need your help. How soon can you get here with our mutual friends?"

After I finished my call, and set the first part of my plan into motion, I took a shower and got ready for bed. Daphne and Logan called just like they'd said they would, and I talked to both of them. I didn't say a word to either about my plan to steal the candle, though. Vic was right. I couldn't involve them in what I was about to do, no matter how much I would have liked their support and understanding. Besides, I didn't want to wreck things between Logan and his dad by asking the Spartan to help me. They'd just started talking again, and I wasn't going to come between them. Not when I knew how much Logan had missed his dad and yearned for his love, support, and approval all these years.

Oh, I knew Logan, Daphne, and the rest of my friends would be angry when they found out what I'd done, but that was a consequence I was just going to have to live with.

So the next day, I went about my usual routine. Weapons training in the gym, where I apologized to everyone for pitching such a massive fit in the infirmary the day before. Morning classes. Lunch. Afternoon classes. The day passed by in a perfectly normal fashion, right up until it was time for me to work my usual shift at the Library of Antiquities.

Alexei was waiting in the hallway outside my dorm room when I was ready to leave, and he walked me over to the library. He didn't say anything to me, and I didn't speak to him. Other than my apology, I hadn't said a lot to any of my friends today, and they'd given me the space they thought I needed. I did need the space—just not for the reasons they assumed. I couldn't exactly steal the candle if they were all watching me like, well, Black rocs.

Alexei and I entered the library, walked down the main aisle, and went around the checkout counter. Alexei put his black backpack down on the floor, then slid onto a stool that was sitting up against the glass wall of the office complex. I threw my messenger bag down as well, while Nyx hopped up into the basket behind the counter that she stayed in while I was working. I propped Vic up next to Nyx.

"You two be good," I murmured. "I've got a lot to do tonight."

Vic gave me a knowing look, but he didn't say anything. Not in front of Alexei, anyway, although the sword had practically talked my ear off whenever we'd been alone today, trying to get me to change my mind. Still, in the end, Vic might not like it, but he was going along with my plan. Something I was so grateful for— more than the sword probably realized.

I'd barely settled myself at the counter and logged on to one of the computers when sharp footsteps sounded on the marble floor, heading in my direction. I looked past the monitor to find Linus striding down the main aisle, followed by Inari and Aiko.

"Miss Frost, there you are," Linus said, striding up to

the counter and stopping directly on the other side from me. "I'm glad I found you. I wanted to give you an update."

"And what would that be?" I sniped.

He stared at me, his face hardening at my snarky tone. Well, too bad. He was going to be a lot more pissed at me before this was over.

"The Protectorate guards are still out searching for your grandmother," he said.

For a moment, my heart lifted because it sounded like there was an *and* coming. Something like *and we found her alive and well and she's on her way back to the academy right now*. Maybe I wouldn't have to go through with my plan after all...

"And, unfortunately, we haven't been able to find where the Reapers are keeping her," Linus finished.

And just like that, my heart plummeted back down into my stomach and kept right on dropping, like an elevator sliding out of control.

"Of course you haven't." I couldn't keep the bitterness out of my voice. "And you won't."

But I will, I silently vowed. I'd already put my plan into motion, and I was moving on to the second stage of my scheme as soon as Linus left.

"I really am sorry about this, Miss Frost," he said. "And I think you understand that, underneath all the attitude."

"Maybe," I snarked back. "But that doesn't make it any easier on me. And especially not on my grandma, now, does it? If you have things your way, attitude will be the only thing I have left."

My gaze shot past him to the candle, which was sitting in the same case in the same spot as yesterday. None of the students sitting at the study tables or the professors standing in line at the coffee cart paid any attention to the candle, but that didn't mean some of them weren't Reapers, secretly trying to figure out how to get their hands on the artifact, should I not come through for Vivian.

"Well, that, and the great view," I snarked again.

Linus turned to the side to see what I was staring at. When he realized I was looking at the candle, his own eyes narrowed, and a spark of anger shimmered in his gaze. He whirled back around and stepped even closer to the counter, leaning down over it so that his face was level with mine.

"I know you're angry and upset," he said. "But I also know how you think, Miss Frost."

"What does that mean?"

"It means you are what I am kindly going to refer to as a *loose cannon*, the sort of person who thinks the rules do not apply to her, just like your mother was before you," Linus said.

My hands curled into fists on top of the counter. "If you say one more word about my mom, I will knock your teeth out of your mouth, head of the Protectorate or not."

A rustle sounded behind me. I glanced over my shoulder. Alexei had slid off his stool and was standing a few feet off to my right. I wondered whose side he would be on if I really did attack Linus. It saddened me to realize that I wasn't sure it would be mine. On the other side of the counter, Inari and Aiko drifted a little closer to Linus, clearly ready to protect his back.

"Fair enough," Linus said. "But let me be crystal

clear, Miss Frost. Should you make any sort of attempt to interfere with the Protectorate guards watching over the candle, should you be foolish enough to make an attempt to actually *steal* the candle yourself and take it to the Reapers to trade it for your grandmother, then I will throw you in the academy prison quicker than you can blink. And you will stay there until I decide otherwise. Nike's Champion or not."

He stared at me, his gaze cold and hard, and I glared right back at him. I knew he meant every word he said, but I didn't care. I was going to do whatever it took to save Grandma Frost. Truth be told, winding up in the academy prison would probably be a far better fate than what the Reapers had in store for me. But those were the risks I had to take.

"Are we clear, Miss Frost?" Linus's tone had become as angry as mine.

"Oh yeah," I snapped. "I get it. Message received. Loud and clear. Now, can you leave? I've got work to do."

Linus gave me one more angry, suspicious stare before he pivoted on his heel and strode away from the checkout counter. He walked over to the case and stared down at the candle. Then, he glanced over his shoulder and watched me watch him. Linus pivoted on his heel again and stepped over to the coffee cart where Raven was mixing up frappés and espressos for the professors in line. Linus pulled Raven aside and started speaking to her in a low voice, no doubt telling her to keep an eye on me in case I went anywhere near Sol's candle. I rolled my eyes. No doubt that would be another one of her odd jobs now.

"Well, that went well," Vic piped up from his spot below the checkout counter.

Nyx yipped her agreement. I arched my eyebrow at the sword, but I didn't respond to his sarcasm.

A hand dropped lightly onto my shoulder, and I looked up to find Alexei standing beside me.

"He's just trying to help," Alexei said.

I opened my mouth to let loose another snarky retort, but the sympathetic look on his face made me hold back my angry words. Instead, I sighed.

"I know," I said. "I know he's trying to help. That's what makes this even harder. We're all trying to do the right thing, and none of us seems to be on the same side. Logan told me that once, and it's more true now than ever before."

Alexei frowned at my cryptic words, but I didn't clue him in to their real meaning. He'd find out soon enough.

When I stole Sol's candle from the Library of Antiquities.

Chapter 13

For the next hour, I went about all my usual chores, as though everything were fine, as if this was a typical night in the library. Shelving books. Helping other students find reference materials for their homework assignments. Picking up odd sheets of paper, pencil stubs, and other trash that the kids left behind in the stacks.

Finally, I made it down to the last pile of books that needed shelving. I grabbed the metal cart and steered it around the checkout counter, heading back toward the stacks.

Alexei slid off his stool and started to come with me, the way he had every other time I'd ventured away from the counter tonight, but I waved him off.

"There's no need for you to follow me," I said, bitterness creeping into my voice again. "We all know what the Reapers want, and it's not me. Trust me. This is probably the safest I've ever been in the library."

Alexei took a step forward, like he was going to come with me anyway, but he nodded and sat back down on his stool. Good. I didn't want him to see what I was really up to right now. I didn't want anyone to see.

I pushed the cart back into the shadow-filled stacks,

and I really did shelve the books, like I was supposed to. All the while, though, I kept glancing around, my eyes scanning the spaces between the rows of books, to make sure no one was watching me. At first, I thought someone might be following me, since a shadow always seemed to be lurking just out of my line of sight, but a couple of quick zigzags through the shelves took care of that, and anyone who might have wanted to spy on me.

A few times, I passed couples back in the stacks, their bodies pressed up against the shelves, eagerly kissing and doing other things I didn't want to look at too closely. I quickly moved past those aisles. Every once in a while, I would pass a Protectorate guard sitting at a table in some remote corner, as though he or she was a professor who'd come back here to get away from the noise that surrounded the coffee cart and study tables instead of really being on the lookout for any Reapers. A few of the guards gave me respectful nods, but most of them stared at me with narrowed, suspicious eyes. No doubt Linus had told them to watch out for me.

Well, he was right about that, at least.

Finally, I shelved all of the books. I left the cart at the end of one of the aisles, looked around one more time to make sure no one was watching or following me, then moved even deeper into the stacks.

Most of the artifacts were located on the first floor, but I snuck up the stairs to the second level. Nickamedes didn't send me up here all that often, but I'd shelved my share of books on this floor. More important, I'd dusted the artifact cases on this level. And right now, I was looking for one very specific item.

I stopped and looked left and right at the top of the stairs, but no one else seemed to be on this level, although I could hear a soft, faint, tapping sound coming from somewhere, probably drifting up from the main floor. I left the stairs behind and eased over to the balcony, looking down at the students below, but everyone was clustered around the study tables or coffee cart, getting their caffeine buzz on, and no one was paying any attention to me.

Being as quiet as possible, I made my way around the balcony, looking at all of the shelves that lined the walls. They were filled with books, like the stacks below, although the volumes on this level were more obscure titles that rarely got used, except for the occasional overachieving student who really wanted to wow Professor Metis with an unusual research source.

My eyes scanned over each shelf, then the artifact cases that crouched beside them. No, no, no, no . . . I kept walking around the balcony. Had Nickamedes moved the artifact I was looking for? That would be just my luck, especially since I needed this one item in order to get the others I was interested in. My plan wouldn't work at all without this particular artifact, and if I couldn't find it, I didn't know what I would do.

Finally, just when I was about to get seriously worried, I spotted it. I let out a relieved breath and stopped in front of a case that was standing by itself along the wall.

A silver key lay underneath the glass.

It was a small, old-fashioned skeleton key, simple in design, with only two grooves carved into it, although fancy scrollwork had been etched into the metal. Nickamedes had me put the key on display a few weeks ago, since it was the focus of one of Metis's myth-history lectures, and all the second-year students had to do some research on its history, origins, and the magic that it supposedly possessed. I hadn't paid much attention to the key or the assignment, not with everything that had been going on with the Reapers, me, Logan, and everyone else. But thanks to my psychometry, I never forgot anything I saw or heard, and ever since I'd decided to steal Sol's candle, I'd been flipping through my memories, calling up images of every single artifact I'd ever seen inside the library and trying to figure out which ones would help me the most. And when I'd remembered this one, I knew that it was the key—literally—to my entire plan.

I glanced at the small, white identification card that was propped up next to the key, although I already knew what it said.

Janus's Master Key supposedly belonged to the Roman god. In addition to being the god of beginnings and endings, Janus is also associated with doors and gates. It is thought that Janus himself created this key, which will open any door, gate, or lock, no matter how strong or complicated it may be...

Vic had wondered how I was going to steal Sol's candle from the library. Well, this was my answer. Or, at least, the first part of it. With this one key, I could open any artifact case in the entire library, which would give me access to another item I needed. In a strange way, Vivian had given me the idea by wearing her Janus ring at the park. I'd replayed that confrontation with her over and over again in my mind, and when I'd started think-

ing about the artifacts that might help me, I'd thought
of Janus and then his key.

Maybe what I was doing was wrong. Maybe the risk
of making Loki stronger was too great to take. But I'd
do anything to save my grandma—even this—so I
forced myself to push my doubts aside. Nike had always
said that she believed in me, that she had faith in me, in
my instincts, in my decisions, as her Champion. Now, it
was time to have a little faith in myself. I'd been smart
and strong enough to survive everything the Reapers
had thrown at me so far. I'd find a way to get through
this too.

At least, that was what I kept telling myself.

Still, thinking about the goddess made me realize exactly where I was on the second floor. I slowly turned
around.

Nike's statue stood directly across from the artifact
case.

Of course she would be here. She always seemed to
be in all the places I ended up. I wondered what kind of
karma, destiny, or fate that might be. If it was my own
free will drawing me to her time and time again, or
something else entirely.

I walked over and looked up at the goddess's face. I
held my breath, wondering if she might appear to me, if
she might open her eyes and wink, or smile, or give me
some sort of indication that I was doing the right thing.
But she didn't, and her face remained as smooth and remote as ever. I let out my breath. Well, if she wasn't
going to give me any guidance, then I'd have to trust my
instincts. And they were screaming at me to find some
way to save Grandma Frost.

Because I knew I'd never forgive myself if I didn't—no matter what the price might be.

So I turned away from Nike and went back over to the case. I looked around again, but the balcony was as deserted as before, although the murmurs of students talking drifted up from the first floor below, along with that soft, faint, tapping sound again, which seemed to be getting louder. I paused, listening to the sounds, especially the other kids talking, but they seemed to be the usual sorts of conversations and not more excited murmurs like, *Oh, look at the Gypsy girl up on the second floor getting ready to steal an artifact.*

Since the coast was clear, I reached out, put my hand on the case, closed my eyes, and concentrated, trying to see if any spells or protection measures had been placed on the wood or glass. But I didn't sense anything, and the only flash I got was of Nickamedes standing by and watching while I put the key into the case a couple of weeks ago.

I opened my eyes and dropped my hand. Well, it was good there was no magic mumbo jumbo on the case, but there was still a small metal padlock that hooked the glass to the wood—one that I couldn't pop open with my driver's license like I did all of the flimsy door locks in the dorms. I had no lock pick, so I couldn't get past it that way. Maybe I could find out where Raven had put her tool belt, and see if she had a pair of bolt cutters or some sort of metal saw—

"Gwendolyn?" a low, familiar voice called out behind me. "What are you doing up here?"

I bit my lip to keep from shrieking with surprise—and fear. I quickly plastered a bored, nonchalant look on my face and turned around. Nickamedes slowly walked toward me, and I realized that faint tapping sound I'd heard earlier had actually been his cane hitting the floor.

My heart sank. He was the *last* person who I wanted to figure out what I was doing. He'd never forgive me for stealing one of his precious artifacts, not even to save my grandma.

But before I could scurry away from the case, he had reached my side, leaning on his cane and carrying a stack of books in the crook of his other arm.

"Here," I said. "Let me get those for you. They look heavy."

I stepped forward and took the books from him before he could protest, putting myself in between him and the case so he wouldn't realize how interested I was in the key. That was my hope, anyway. Yeah, it was totally lame, but it was the only thing I could do.

"You ready to go back to your office?" I asked in a bright voice, edging away from the case.

"Actually, I was looking for you," Nickamedes said. "I've found out something interesting about your silver laurel leaves."

He reached forward and pulled one of the books out of my hands. Then, Nickamedes stepped past me, put the book down on top of the case, and opened up the thick, heavy volume.

"Come here and look at this," he said. "I think you'll find it extremely interesting."

I wanted to scream, but I kept that blank look fixed on my face and did as he asked. "What is it?"

Nickamedes started flipping through the book. "Remember how we thought you actually had to find a way to grind up the leaves in order to get them to work?"

I nodded. In their attempt to poison me, the Reapers

had used a plant called Serket sap, by drying and then grinding the plant's leaves and roots into a fine white powder. So Nickamedes and I had thought that maybe we had to do the same thing to the laurel leaves. Of course, the only problem was that the leaves on my bracelet were made of solid silver, so they weren't something you could throw on a cutting board and chop up with a knife. In fact, we hadn't figured out any way to use the leaves so far. Otherwise, I would have used as many as it took to heal Nickamedes's bum legs, since I was the reason he'd been injured.

"Well, it looks like we don't have to grind, boil, or do anything like that to the leaves," Nickamedes said. "Here. Take a look at this."

He reached the passage he wanted and stepped aside so that I could read it.

Not much is known about how to use silver laurel leaves to heal or injure. However, one thing is clear. The leaves' metallurgic properties make it impossible for them to be administered in the way one might boil, cut, or grind up a more typical plant, herb, or root. There is one school of thought that suggests getting someone to swallow one of the leaves is enough to activate their power, although that is a risky proposition at best. But another, more interesting idea is that the leaves can actually be used in conjunction with other artifacts to augment or influence their power, or perhaps even intensify a person's own magic . . .

The book went on to give a few examples of how laurel leaves had been used in combination with other artifacts. The Greek goddess Hera had added a leaf onto a jeweled ring that her husband, Zeus, had planned to give to one of his many mortal lovers. Only when Zeus had given his lover the ring, she had dropped dead because of Hera's jealousy and the malicious intent with which the goddess had used the leaf.

But apparently, the most famous example was of the leaves being stitched onto a pair of long, white silk gloves that Sigyn, the Norse goddess of devotion, had once worn, in order to help heal some horrible wounds. She'd gotten the injuries on her hands and arms while being splattered with snake venom when she'd been holding the Bowl of Tears up over her husband, Loki's, head while he'd been imprisoned by the other gods.

"Great," I sniped. "So all I have to do is tie one of the leaves to Loki's finger, and he'll drop dead. No problem. I'm sure he'll let me close enough to do that, not to mention hold still while I slip the laurel onto his finger in the first place."

"There's no need for sarcasm, Gwendolyn," Nickamedes said, picking up the book and shutting it. "Of course, I will research this further, but I thought you would want to know. I thought it might take your mind off . . . things."

I tried not to look at it, but my gaze still flicked down to the key. *That* was what I needed to take my mind off things. Or at least to start working on the rest of my plan to rescue Grandma Frost—

Too late, I realized that Nickamedes had noticed me staring at the key. He frowned, then stepped forward and read the index card inside the case.

"Janus's Master Key," he murmured. "A very unusual artifact with some very unusual magic. Not the sort of thing most warriors would look at for more than a few seconds. They're far more interested in weapons that kill people, rather than simple objects like keys."

I didn't say anything. I didn't know what to say to get him to go away and not think about what I was really doing here.

"But then again, you are not most warriors, are you, Gwendolyn?"

Nickamedes looked straight into my eyes, and I could see the knowledge of my own scheme reflected back in his icy blue gaze.

My breath caught in my throat. He knew *exactly* what I was up to. Of course he would. Nickamedes knew everything that went on in the library, from the kids hooking up in the stacks to the professors who always returned their books late to why I would suddenly be so interested in an artifact that opened locks.

I sighed, fully expecting him to tear into me for even thinking about taking the key out of its case and using it to help me steal the candle. But to my surprise, Nickamedes kept staring at me. Finally, after what seemed like forever, he reached into his pants pocket and drew out a ring of keys.

My breath caught in my throat again because I recognized these keys too—they were the ones to the library doors, as well as the artifact cases. Nickamedes flipped through the ring until he found the right sort of key, then inserted it in the lock on the case, and opened it.

He reached inside and pulled out the Janus key. I expected him to walk away with the artifact, saying that he was going to move it somewhere else for safekeeping. In other words, far, far away from me and my thieving hands. But instead, Nickamedes shut the case and slowly placed the key down on top of the smooth glass.

"You should take that downstairs and make sure it gets a good cleaning," he said. "It needs polishing. Take your time, though. There's no rush—no rush at all."

I couldn't keep my mouth from gaping open. Of all the things that I thought might happen, Nickamedes actually *giving* me the key had never crossed my mind.

"Why do you think that it needs polishing?" I asked in a careful, but curious tone. "It looks fine to me the way it is right now. You know how . . . clumsy I can be with things, especially artifacts. Who knows? I might . . . lose it or something."

"It's a risk I'm willing to take, Gwendolyn," Nickamedes replied in a soft voice. "Even if others are not."

The librarian stared at me again, and I saw the certainty blazing in his eyes, along with his faith—in me.

Once again, my mouth gaped open, but Nickamedes didn't seem to notice my surprise. Instead, he nodded at me, gathered up his books, including the ones I was still holding, then turned and walked away, his cane tapping softly on the marble floor.

After a few seconds, I shook off my shocked daze and carefully picked up the key, waiting for my psychometry to kick in and show me all of the feelings, emotions, and memories that were attached to it. But all I got from the key was a sense of smoothness, as if it would slide into any lock it encountered and easily open it. I hoped that was exactly what it would do.

I tucked the key into the front pocket of my jeans, then went back down to the first floor. I grabbed the empty book cart from where I had left it in the stacks and pushed it back to the checkout counter, still wondering about my encounter with Nickamedes. But for the first time, I actually felt hopeful about my chances of rescuing Grandma Frost.

Alexei was in the same spot as before, sitting on his stool against the glass wall of the office complex, although his tense features relaxed a bit when he saw me—and realized that I didn't appear to have gotten into any trouble while I'd been gone.

If only he knew.

"What took you so long?" he asked.

I shrugged, then parked the cart next to him. "I ran into Nickamedes, and he gave me some more books to shelve. You know, the usual."

It wasn't exactly the truth, but it seemed to satisfy Alexei. He relaxed back against the wall, and I slid onto my own stool and busied myself with more chores.

Another hour passed. All the while, though, I was aware of Janus's key in my pocket, but I didn't dare reach for it while Alexei was with me. He'd ask too many questions about what it was and why I had it.

Eventually, Alexei got up and wandered over to Raven's coffee cart to get a snack. He'd barely been gone a minute when my phone rang. Odd, but not unexpected. In fact, I'd been anxiously waiting for this particular call all day. I looked out over the sea of students still studying at the tables in front of me, but no one paid me any attention. However, I was willing to bet that at least one of the students was a Reaper—and that they'd been waiting for precisely this moment so they could signal their bosses.

The screen said the number was blocked, although I knew exactly who was calling and what she wanted.

"What's up, Viv?" I drawled into the phone.

"How did you know it was me?" Her voice flooded the line. "I'm the one who's telepathic, not you."

"I had a hunch," I retorted. "Besides, it seemed like it was about time for you to call and threaten me some more. You'd said that you'd be in touch yesterday at the park, remember?"

"Well, the next time I see you, they won't be threats," Vivian replied in a syrupy sweet tone. "Because you'll be dead. You and your grandma. Unless you get me what I want—Sol's candle."

"I heard you before at the park." My hand tightened around the phone. "Don't worry. I'm going to deliver. I just need another day, maybe two. That's all."

"Really? You're giving in? Just like that?"

"Just like that," I snapped. "You kidnapping my grandma and holding her hostage doesn't give me a lot of options, now, does it?"

"Well, no," Vivian chirped in a cheerful voice. "But I at least thought you'd hem and haw a little more about it. You know, try to reconcile such a bad, bad deed with your do-gooder conscience and your hero complex and all that."

"My hero complex will be just fine once I kill you," I snapped back. "But I'm not simply handing the candle over to you. I want some assurances first."

"Like what?"

"Like the fact that my grandma is still alive. So why don't you put her on the phone right now before I decide to hang up?"

"You do that, and your grandmother dies," Vivian hissed.

"You kill her, and you die," I hissed back. "And even worse for you, you won't get the candle. I imagine that Loki wouldn't be too happy about his Champion failing to get her hands on the one thing that can finally heal him. But if you want to take that chance, go ahead, Viv. Hurt my grandma. Because it will be the last thing you *ever* do—one way or the other."

Silence. The seconds ticked by and turned into a minute. Worry flooded my body, and I started to wonder if I'd finally pushed Vivian too far.

"Fine," she muttered. "But only because you asked so nicely."

More silence. My fingers gripped the phone even tighter, wondering if Vivian was stalling or bluffing or simply messing with me. If maybe my Grandma Frost was already dead—

"Pumpkin?"

Grandma's voice flooded the line, and I slumped over the counter in relief.

"Grandma? Is that really you?" I whispered.

"It's really me, pumpkin," she said, her voice a little stronger.

"Are you okay?"

"I'm fine. I just want to say that I love you."

"I love you too."

"Good," Grandma Frost said. "Then you need to forget about me. You can't give them what they want, pumpkin. You can't give them the candle. Promise me that you won't—"

"Shut up," I heard Vivian growl.

A sharp *smack* sounded, like someone getting slapped

across the face. A low groan echoed through the phone. I closed my eyes. That was my grandma's voice, her groan. But I couldn't do or say anything to help her—not one *thing*. All I could do was sit there and try to pretend I wasn't hearing the sound of someone I loved being hurt by my enemies—all because of me.

Finally, after what seemed like forever, Vivian came back on the line.

"You have until noon tomorrow," she said. "Bring the candle to the address that I'll text you and come alone—or your grandma dies."

She ended the call before I could say anything else. A moment later, the phone beeped again, and an address appeared on the screen, one that wasn't too far from the academy. I'd search for the directions to it later. Right now, I was too angry to do anything but sit and glare down at the phone, wishing I could crush it with my bare hand—along with Vivian's smug face.

"Who are you talking to?" a voice cut in.

I was so startled I almost dropped the phone. But the worst part was who it was that was asking the question.

I looked up to find Logan standing in front of the counter.

Chapter 14

"Gypsy girl?" Logan asked again. "Who are you talking to?"

I slid the phone back into my jeans pocket. "Nobody. It was one of those stupid spam texts, telling me I'd won some giveaway. You know how it is."

I let out a laugh, but my voice sounded strained and hollow to my own ears. I hoped Logan wouldn't notice. I hated lying to him, but this was the only way to save my grandma. Besides, if it had been his dad, Logan would have done the same thing. At least, that's what I told myself. That's what I had to tell myself to get through this.

He stared at me like he wanted to ask about the phone again, but instead, he jerked his head back at the stacks.

"Can we go somewhere a little more private and talk?" he asked.

"Sure."

I glanced over at the coffee cart, where Alexei was still waiting in line. He saw me with Logan and waved, telling us to go ahead. So I slid off my stool, walked around the counter, and followed Logan back into the stacks.

He moved from one aisle to the next, like a Nemean prowler stalking through the library in search of some sort of prey. Every time I thought he was about to stop, he would keep walking, as if he wasn't quite sure what he was going to say when we faced each other.

Finally, though, he stopped in a remote corner of the stacks, an area that I knew particularly well, since this was the spot where Vic's case had once stood. I glanced up. Nike's statue loomed above us on the second-floor balcony, but the goddess's face was still completely neutral. She wouldn't appear to me until she was good and ready. Of course not. Because that would make things way too easy for me.

"Can we sit?" Logan asked in a soft voice.

I nodded, and he plopped down on one side of the aisle, while I sat on the other, facing him. We stared at each other for several long seconds before Logan finally sighed.

"I've spent all afternoon trying to convince my dad to change his mind about the candle," he said. "But he's not going to."

I nodded. It didn't surprise me, although I was touched that he had tried to help.

"I'm sorry, Gwen," Logan said. "So sorry. How is it that things are always such a mess around here? Even if we're good, it always seems like there's something else that gets in the way of us."

"I know," I replied. "And I hate it too."

"I know you feel like my dad is against you, like he's leaving your grandmother to the Reapers, but he's doing everything in his power to find her," Logan said. "Most of the day, he's been out following down all the leads the other guards have gotten about where the Reapers might have taken her, about where they might be holding her."

I thought about the address Vivian had texted me. I wondered what would happen if I gave the information to Logan. I could picture it all in my mind. No doubt he'd tell his dad, Linus would get a group of Protectorate guards together, and they'd storm into whatever buildings they found at the address. But Vivian was too smart to give me Grandma Frost's location in advance. My grandma wouldn't be there until I'd shown up alone with the candle, and it was too late for me to get any help from my friends or the Protectorate. No, if I gave the address to Logan or Linus, I'd probably get my grandma executed that much faster. I had to do what Vivian wanted me to, or my grandma was dead.

Logan looked at me, waiting for some sort of response.

I sighed. "Look, I appreciate what your dad is trying to do, that he and the other members of the Protectorate are out searching for my grandma. But we both know they're not going to find her in time. If Linus doesn't give the Reapers the candle, they'll kill her. And that will only be the beginning of it."

Logan frowned. "What do you mean?"

"Think about it," I said. "Linus told me, told all of us, that he wouldn't trade the candle for my grandma. But what's to stop the Reapers from trying again? Maybe next time, they'll go after someone closer to him. Someone like . . . you."

I also sent the info about Vivian's order to turn the candle over by noon, along with the address that the Reaper girl had given me.

"Is that who I think it is?" Vic asked.

"Yep," I said. "Our friends are here and ready to rock 'n' roll."

I put the phone away and looked at the sword. Vic stared back at me, his purple eye as serious as I'd ever seen it.

"I still think this is a crazy plan—at best," he said.

"I know. Me too. But crazy is sort of what I do, right?"

He didn't return my halfhearted grin.

I sighed. "Look, if you don't want to go with me tomorrow, I understand. I don't want you falling into Reaper hands any more than you do. So it's okay if you want to stay here."

Vic rolled his eye. "I said it was a crazy plan. That's all. I didn't say anything about not going with you, Gwen. C'mon. At the very least, there will be dozens of Reapers there—Reapers that I can kill. You know I would never pass up a chance to do that."

This time, I rolled my eyes at his bloodthirsty words. Sometimes, I thought the only reason Vic hung around me was so that he could kill Reapers, since I was like a magnet, always attracting them whether I wanted to or not.

"Besides," he continued. "I was your grandmother's sword long before I was yours, Gwen. I want to save Geraldine as much as you do."

I nodded. Sometimes, I forgot that Vic had had all of these other lives before me—that he'd been the weapon for all the women, all the Champions, of the Frost fam-

Logan blinked. "You think the Reapers would kidnap me?"

I shrugged. "Maybe Linus would feel different if you were the one they were threatening to kill instead of my grandma. Maybe then, he wouldn't be so stubborn about things and unwilling to part with the candle." I couldn't keep the anger and the bitterness out of my voice.

Logan didn't say anything, but hurt shimmered in his icy eyes, and his shoulders slumped. He was right. Every time it seemed we were finally on track, something else came up to knock us off course again. And most of the time, it wasn't even anything either one of us had done to the other. But as long as the Reapers were still out there, as long as Loki was free, this was our life—for better or worse.

I just hoped we could survive the worse this time around—especially since I was going to be the one to inflict it on us.

"Look, I know you're sorry about all of this," I said in a low voice. "And I am too. I really don't mean to take my anger out on you. I know it's not your fault. *None* of it is your fault. Not the Reapers kidnapping my grandma, and not your dad refusing to hand the candle over to them, either. It's . . . just our life, and right now, it sucks."

Logan looked at me. "So what can we do to make it better? What can we do to make it right?"

I shrugged. I didn't know the answer to that any more than he did. Logan kept staring at me, his gaze dark and troubled. Yeah, I knew the feeling.

Still, I also knew this might be the last moment we ever had together, given what I was planning on doing tomorrow. So I crawled across the aisle to where Logan was sitting. He wrapped his arm around my shoulder and drew me close. I let out another sigh and rested my head on his shoulder, enjoying the warmth of his body seeping into mine.

"I love you," I said. "No matter what happens, no matter what we do, no matter who or what comes between us, I love you, Spartan. I will *always* love you. I want you to know that."

Logan put his other arm around me and hugged me tight. "I know, Gypsy girl. And I love you too. I always will."

I turned my head, and we kissed. I felt all the love radiating off Logan and flowing into me, along with fear, sorrow, and frustration about everything that was going on. His feelings mirrored my own. After a few seconds, we broke apart, and I rested my head on his shoulder again. Maybe for the last time.

I just wondered how much he would hate me when he realized how I'd lied to him and everything I'd done.

Logan and I stayed back in the stacks until Nickamedes called out in a booming voice that it was time for the library to close. The two of us went back to the checkout counter. I slid Vic into the scabbard on my waist and gently shook Nyx awake. The wolf pup let out a sleepy yawn and licked my hand. I scratched her head, and she sighed in happiness.

Logan walked me back to my dorm. Alexei followed us, then split off to go back to his own room for the night. Logan and I stood outside in the pool of golden light cast by the street lamp closest to the dorm steps.

"I'll talk to my dad again," he said. "We to save your grandma, I promise you that."

I nodded, although I didn't tell him that doubted Linus Quinn ever changed his mind thing once it had been made up.

"Thanks. I appreciate that."

"See you in the morning at weapons training, Logan said.

I nodded. "Yeah. Okay."

We kissed, and the Spartan turned around, stuc hands in the pockets of his black leather jacket, walked away across the grass, which was already ered with that killer frost once again. I watched him then went up the steps, slid my ID card through th reader, and trudged up to my room, with Nyx follow ing me.

I shut the door behind me and locked it. I put Vic on the bed, then sank down beside the sword, letting out a long, tired sigh.

"What's wrong?" the sword sniped, his English accent a little more pronounced than usual. "You don't like lying to your boyfriend?"

"Of course not," I snapped back. "But you know I can't tell him what I'm going to do. He'd try to stop me. Or worse, tell his dad."

Vic didn't respond.

We sat there in silence for a few seconds before my phone beeped. I pulled it out of my jeans pocket and stared at the message on the screen.

We're here. U so owe me for this.

And I'm sure you'll make me pay, I texted back. C U tomorrow.

ily over the years. And that he'd seen a lot of them die too, in the same sort of battle I would be facing tomorrow.

Still, his devotion to my grandma and me too touched me more than anything he'd ever said or done before.

"Thank you," I rasped out through the emotion that clogged my throat.

"For what?"

"For always being there for me when I need you. For being something and someone I can always depend on, no matter what. You've never let me down, and I know you never will. You don't know how much that means to me. Especially right now."

Vic sniffed, as if he was dismissing my words, but I could see the gleam of a tear in his eye before he managed to blink it away.

"Oh, come on now," he said, his voice as gruff as mine was. "There's no need to get all bloody *maudlin* about things. We'll go, we'll kick some Reaper ass, and we'll be home in time for dinner."

I had to smile at his snarky confidence. Vic could always make me feel better about things, no matter how hopeless they looked.

"So when are you going to get the candle?" he asked.

"Tomorrow morning," I said. "That's when I'm going to steal it."

Chapter 15

The next morning, I went about my routines as if everything was normal. As if I wasn't planning to steal perhaps the most important artifact known to the Pantheon. As if I wasn't going to turn said artifact over to the Reapers. As if I wasn't going to make Loki stronger.

As if I might not be dead by noon.

But there was nothing I could do but face things head-on and hope everything worked out like I wanted it to. Still, more than once, I found myself on the verge of hyperventilating, and I had to force myself to breathe in and out, in and out, like my mom had always taught me to do whenever I was nervous, scared, worried, or upset. Those words didn't even *begin* to describe my emotions right now. But the breathing helped, so I kept doing it, over and over again, until I felt like I could actually go through with this.

"Are you okay?" Logan asked me more than once during weapons training. "Do you need to take a break?"

"Nah," I said. "I'm just a little tired today. I didn't get much sleep last night."

It was true. I'd spent most of the night tossing and turning, going over and over everything that could go wrong with my plan, and all of the ways my grandma could die, even though I knew I would need all of my sleep and energy for what was to come today.

"Oh. I'm sorry," he said.

I shrugged, just trying to get through the rest of the training time. I didn't want Logan's sympathy, and I certainly didn't deserve it. Not given what I was planning.

We kept sparring, and, finally, weapons training came to an end. My friends and I left the gym and headed over to the dining hall to get some breakfast. After that, I went back to my dorm room to take a shower and get ready for the day. I dressed carefully, putting on a sturdy pair of boots, my favorite jeans, and the warmest T-shirt and sweater I had, along with my purple plaid jacket. If things went according to plan, then my trip back to the academy would be a short, cold one. I also grabbed a few more items I would need and stuffed them into my pockets as well.

Finally, it was time for my first class of the day. Alexei walked me over to the English-history building.

"I have a meeting with Linus and the other Protectorate guards," he said. "I'll come back when the bell rings to walk you to your next class."

"Sure," I said, my voice far happier than it should have been. "Sounds great."

I'd been wondering how I was going to get away from Alexei long enough to go steal the candle, but he'd given me the perfect opening without even realizing it.

Alexei looked at me, suspicion filling his hazel eyes, but he didn't say anything else. Neither did I. After a moment, he nodded his head, then turned and walked away. I thought about slipping away right then and there, but I headed into the building like I really was going to class after all. I stopped at the first window I came to and peeked out through the glass. Alexei was standing at the opposite end of the quad, staring back in my direction.

I froze, my breath catching in my throat, but he couldn't see me through the glass at this distance. After a moment, he nodded, as if satisfied that I was where I was supposed to be. Then, he hurried on and headed into the gym. That must be where the meeting was.

As soon as I was sure that he wasn't going to double back to check on me, I went against the flow of students streaming inside and stepped out of one of the side doors. Kids were now racing across the quad, trying to get into the buildings, their classes, and their seats before the first bell of the day rang. I put my head down, burying my face in the scarf wrapped around my neck, and scurried along with them, heading straight for the Library of Antiquities. A few kids ran out of the building, having gone into the library during breakfast in a last, desperate attempt to get their homework done for the day. I stepped to one side so they could pass me, then approached the gryphons that sat on either side of the main steps. Yeah, I could have gone in through a side entrance, but that would have made me seem even more suspicious than I already was. Besides, I wanted to see the statues.

Because this might be the last time I *ever* saw them.

Eagle heads, lion bodies, wings, tails. The statues looked the same as always, if a bit fiercer today, with all the bits of snow clinging to them, as though they'd been rolling around in the fine white powder.

"Well, guys, this is it. For better or worse."

Silence.

By this point, all of the other kids had disappeared into the buildings, and I was the only one on the quad. My stomach clenched at the thought of what I was about to do, but I knew there was no going back.

"Wish me luck," I whispered.

The gryphons didn't respond, not really, although it seemed like they dipped their heads to me the slightest bit. That, at least, made me feel a little better about things. Like I could actually pull this off. Like I could steal the candle and use it to rescue Grandma Frost.

Like I might not doom us all in the process.

I nodded back at the gryphons. Then, I sucked in a breath, went up the stairs, and stepped into the library.

Instead of going in through the main double doors, I stayed in the hallway that ran around the building and went over to one of the side entrances. The door was open, and I slipped through to the other side. I could have strolled down the center aisle, but that was a sure way to let everyone know what I was up to. So instead, I slid into the stacks and eased up so that I could peer out into the main part of the library.

Sol's candle stood in the case in the same spot as before. In fact, the glass was so smooth and shiny that it didn't look like anyone had so much as approached the artifact, much less put their grubby hands on the case. Of course, they wouldn't. None of the other kids would have any interest in a half-used candle, unless they were Reapers and knew how important the artifact really was. Even then, they'd wait to see if I'd deliver it to Vivian, before trying to steal it themselves.

No one was sitting at the study tables since all of the students were supposed to be in class right now. Excellent. That would make this easier. I didn't need someone to pull up that stupid phone app that practically everyone had on campus, the one that let them track me all around the academy, and give away my location. That would be a good way to bring Linus and all of the other Protectorate guards down on top of me before I even got close to the candle.

But the library wasn't completely deserted. Aiko was here, along with two other Protectorate guards. Aiko sat at one of the study tables close to the candle, reading through a graphic novel. The two other guards patrolled through the stacks, moving from one section of the library to the next, and looking supremely bored all the while.

I slid back into the shadows and crept through the stacks until I was standing in the section that was closest to Raven's coffee cart. It too was deserted, given the early hour, and the old woman was nowhere to be seen. Good. There was one more artifact I needed in order to put my plan into motion, and I didn't want Raven spotting me and wondering what I was up to.

Being as quiet as possible, I hurried over to the appropriate aisle and walked down it until I came to a case sitting in the middle, one that housed a small silver box with a large, shimmering opal set into the top of it. I glanced at the card that was propped up next to the box, although I already knew what it said, since I'd dusted this particular case more than once during the months I'd been working in the library.

The Dreambox of Morpheus supposedly
belonged to the Greek god of sleep and dreams. It
is thought that Morpheus stored some of his

*dream dust in the box, and that he would blow
the dust into the faces of his enemies in order to
make them go to sleep so he could pass by them
undetected...*

It wasn't enough that I had a key to unlock the case
that housed the candle. I also needed some way to get
past the Protectorate guards in the library, and the box
was my solution. Because if the guards were all asleep,
then they wouldn't see me take the candle—or try to
stop me after the fact—and I had to steal the candle and
get off campus with it before anyone sounded the alarm.

So I drew in a breath, pulled Janus's key out of my
jeans pocket, and slid it into the padlock on the case.
The lock clicked open, as easily as if the key had been
made specifically for it, and the box was in my hand a
second later. My psychometry kicked in, but the only
vibe I got from the box was a sense of supreme and utter
calm, as though I had closed my eyes and was sleeping
peacefully. Hopefully, that's exactly what the Protectorate guards would feel when I used the dream dust inside on them.

And now, it was time to take out those guards.

So I squared my shoulders, gripped the box a little
tighter, and headed in the direction of the first guard.

I moved from one bookcase and one shadow to the
next. For months, I'd grumbled about having to work
my shifts in the Library of Antiquities, especially since I
wasn't getting paid. But now, I was grateful for all the
time I'd spent here. The Protectorate guards might be
bigger, stronger, older, and more experienced warriors
than me, but no one knew the library like I did, except
for Nickamedes. So I was able to slide from one aisle to

the next, all the while drawing closer and closer to the first guard.

He never even saw me coming, and I waited at the end of a bookcase until he stepped past, heading toward the next aisle over. He finally spotted me lurking there out of the corner of his eye. His hand dropped to the hilt of his sword, and he turned to face me.

He frowned when he realized that I was the one standing beside him. "Hey, shouldn't you be in class right now—"

I opened the top of the box, reached inside, drew out a handful of the sand-like granules, and blew them in his direction. A gust of fine black powder swirled through the air, straight into his face, sank into his skin, and disappeared. For a moment, the veins in his forehead turned black, as though he had ink running through them instead of blood. The guard blinked and waved his hand in front of his face.

"Kid, what do you think you're doing—"

His eyes rolled up in the back of his head. That was all the warning I had, but I darted forward, caught his heavy body, and slowly lowered him to the floor. A moment later, peaceful snores started rumbling out of his mouth. Looked like Morpheus's dreambox and dust did exactly what the ID card had claimed.

"Sweet dreams," I murmured and slipped back into the shadowy stacks.

I did the same thing to the second guard. Snuck up beside him, blew the powder into his face, and caught him before he hit the floor.

A minute later, Aiko was the only thing standing between me and the candle. She was engrossed in her graphic novel, and it didn't look like she was getting up anytime soon. I let out a frustrated breath, but I didn't have any other options. I had no way of knowing how long the other two guards would sleep, and I needed to be long gone before they woke up.

"Now what are you going to do?" Vic asked from his position on my belt. He'd kept quiet while I was dealing with the other two guards. "It's not like you can just walk up to Aiko and ask her to give you the candle."

I thought for a moment. "You know what, Vic? I actually think that's an excellent idea."

"Oh, bugger," he muttered. "This is so not going to end well."

"I guess we'll find out."

I lifted my chin and headed toward Aiko. This time, I did step out into the center aisle of the library, as if I'd just gotten there and hadn't been lurking around in the stacks, taking out the other guards. I didn't try to be loud, but I wasn't trying to be quiet, either. Aiko looked up at the sound of my sneakers scuffing across the marble floor. Like the other guards, she frowned when she recognized me. I marched over to the table where she was sitting, as if she was the person I'd come here to see all along.

"Gwen?" she asked in her soft voice. "What are you doing here? Shouldn't you be in class right now?"

"Yeah," I said. "There are a whole lot of other things I should be doing right now instead of this."

She frowned at my words.

"Anyway, tell Linus I'm sorry," I said. "Sort of."

Her dark eyes narrowed. "Sorry for what—"

I brought a handful of the powder up and blew it into her face just like I had with the other two guards. Aiko's eyes widened. She was quicker than the others in that she started to push back from the table, get to her feet, and draw her sword, trying to stop me. But the powder hit her as hard as it had the other guards, and she slumped down over the table. I glanced around, then darted forward, pulled her away from the table, and carefully laid her body on the floor in between two of the study tables. That way, if someone else did come into the library, they might miss seeing her for a few precious seconds—and every one of those was important to me right now.

Once Aiko was sort of out of sight, I hurried over to the case. Sol's candle lay under the glass, looking as harmless and innocent as ever, even though I knew it was anything but. I grabbed Janus's key out of my pocket, slid it into the padlock on the case, and gently turned it.

Click.

And just like that, the case was open, and the candle was mine.

I hesitated, wondering if some sort of magic mumbo jumbo might flare to life, or if an alarm would blare and give me away, but nothing happened, so I lifted the glass and grabbed the candle, careful to use my jacket sleeve, instead of grabbing it with my bare hands. I couldn't afford to get lost in another intense vibe from the artifact right now, so I made sure that none of the white wax touched my bare skin as I slid it into my messenger bag. I suppose I could have put an ordinary candle into its place to buy myself some more time, but Aiko knew what I'd done to her. Once she and the other guards woke up, everyone would realize that I'd stolen the candle.

Either way, there was no going back now.

"Well," Vic said, his voice a little less snide than before. "That was actually easier than I expected it to be."

"Yeah, me too—"

I spoke too soon. Because the second I turned around, I realized there was one person in the library I'd forgotten about.

Nickamedes.

He stood by the door of the office complex, staring straight at me. For a heartbeat, all we did was look at each other. I wondered if he was going to lunge for one of the phones, call Linus, and tell him what I'd done. It was one thing to hand me an artifact for supposed cleaning. It was quite another to let me walk away red-handed from the scene of the crime.

"I saw what you did to Aiko. The Dreambox of Morpheus," Nickamedes murmured. "I wouldn't have thought of that. Clever, Gwendolyn. Very clever."

I shrugged, not sure what else to do.

Nickamedes leaned to one side, and I realized that one of Aiko's legs was sticking out from behind the study tables. "And apparently, very effective as well."

I shrugged again.

Nickamedes kept staring at me. After a moment, he nodded his head, as though he'd made some sort of decision. "Well, I think I'm going to go back into my office now and do some work for, oh, say, the next thirty minutes or so. Unless I am interrupted before then."

Surprise surged through me again that he was actually helping me with this, but I wasn't going to stand around and waste my good fortune. I slowly started backing toward the doors that led out of the library, in case he decided to change his mind. I started to turn around and run when I thought of one more thing I needed to do before I left.

"If I don't come back, you totally need to ask Metis out on a date sometime," I called out. "Because she's crazy about you."

This time, he blinked, and *his* mouth was the one that fell open, as if he were absolutely shocked by my words. Well, it looked like Metis was right, and he really didn't know how she felt about him, how she had always felt about him.

"She never said anything because of your history with my mom," I said. "But my mom would want Metis to be happy. And you too."

A faint smile pulled up his lips, and his blue gaze softened with memories. "You're so much like Grace, do you know that?"

It was the best compliment he could have possibly given me, and I nodded back, blinking away the tears that burned my eyes.

"Be careful, Gwendolyn," Nickamedes said.

I nodded again, then whirled around and ran out of the library as fast as I could.

Chapter 16

I eased back out onto the quad, looking left and right, but the area was as deserted as before, since everyone was still in class. I stepped off the cobblestone path that led to the library and cut across the grass, trying to get off the quad and down the hill as quickly as possible.

Sol's candle might as well have been on fire, along with the rest of my messenger bag. That's what it felt like anyway. Like there was a big neon arrow over my head that kept flashing the word *Thief! Thief! Thief!* in huge red letters. But I had to go through with the rest of my plan.

So I darted from tree to tree, and building to building, working my way down the hill and toward my ultimate destination—the main gate at the edge of campus. Eventually, I made it to the amphitheater and hurried through there, knowing that area would be empty at this time of day, and over to the far side. I stood at the edge of the amphitheater and peered out across the snow-dusted landscape, waiting for all of the guards I saw to move around the sides of the dorms and other outbuildings before I ran forward.

It took me longer than I thought it would, but I made

it all the way down to the gate without any problems. To my surprise, a guard hadn't been posted by the iron bars. Of course not, I thought in a sour mood. Linus *wanted* the Reapers to sneak onto campus to steal the candle. He didn't want to make it any harder for them than necessary to breach the perimeter.

I wondered what he would think when he realized that I'd done the job for them.

No doubt he'd throw me in the academy prison like he'd threatened, and I doubted he would ever let me out again. But, on the bright side, if the Reapers killed me first, then at least I wouldn't have to listen to Linus yell at me or spend the rest of my life in jail. It wasn't really a bright spot, but it was all I had, so I decided to go with it.

Even though I didn't see any guards, I was still careful as I eased up to the gate and peered out through the iron bars. Just because Vivian had sent me an address to go to didn't mean that she and Agrona couldn't have ordered some Reapers to wait outside the academy, jump me, and take the candle away without even giving me the chance to see Grandma Frost again. That would be *exactly* the sort of cruel, sneaky thing they would do.

But no one was lurking on the other side of the gate, and I didn't see anyone milling around across the street over in the shops in Cypress Mountain, either. That was one reason why I'd decided to steal the candle so early in the morning. So that if the Reapers were lying in wait for me in town, I would at least have a better chance of seeing them coming—

A branch cracked behind me.

I yanked Vic out of his scabbard, raised the sword high, and whipped around, ready to attack whoever was sneaking up on me.

But no one was there.

My eyes darted left and right, wondering if the effects of the dreambox dust had worn off sooner than I'd expected and if Aiko had caught up with me after all. With her stealthy Ninja skills, I wouldn't even see the Protectorate guard coming until she had her sword pressed up against my throat—

"Finally," a familiar voice muttered. "I was starting to wonder if you were *ever* going to get here."

I froze. What . . . what was *she* doing here?

A shower of pink sparks erupted, flickering in the air like fireflies, and Daphne stepped out from behind a tree.

It took me several seconds to get over my shock.

"What are you doing here?" I finally hissed, sliding Vic back into his scabbard.

"I'm going with you to rescue your grandma, silly." Daphne rolled her eyes. "Really, Gwen, what does it *look* like I'm doing?"

An onyx quiver was strapped to Daphne's back, one that contained a single golden arrow, while a black onyx bow with thin golden strings hung off her right shoulder. Her usual pink purse dangled off her right arm. It was almost as big as her bow was. Instead of a skirt and tights, she was wearing a black leather catsuit with a hot pink zipper and other pink trim accents underneath a long, matching, black-and-pink trench coat. Black boots covered her feet, and her golden hair was slicked back into a ponytail. She'd even gone the extra step of swiping some black greasepaint under her eyes like a football player. The Valkyrie was definitely geared up for a fight. All put together, she looked like some superhero straight out of one of the comic books I loved to read.

"But . . . but . . . but . . ." I sputtered, trying to think of something to say.

She arched a golden eyebrow. "But what? And please don't give me some lame excuse that you just *happened* to cut class to go over to the library to finish some homework assignment and then you came running down here to the main gate for *no reason at all*. I hate to break it to you, Gwen, but you totally suck at lying. I knew the second you quit fighting with Linus that you were going to try to steal the candle yourself. Going all lone wolf is sort of what you do."

"See?" Vic piped up from his scabbard. "I'm not the only one who can tell when you're up to something, Gwen. Especially not when that something is as bloody insane as this is."

"Shut up, Vic."

I turned my attention back to Daphne. "Yeah, I stole the candle, and yeah, I'm going to trade it for my grandma. But you are *not* coming with me. No way. It's too dangerous."

Daphne snorted. "Please. I've been dealing with Reapers a lot longer than you have, Gwen. I know the risks as well as you do." Her face softened. "Besides, I love your grandma too. She's like the grandma I never had, since both of mine were killed by Reapers, and I'm just as determined as you are to save her. So I'm going with you, and I don't want to hear one more word about it."

"But—"

Pink sparks of magic hissed out of Daphne's fingertips as she planted her hands on her hips. "Not one more *word*, or I will take that stupid candle away from you and go give it to Vivian myself. Understand?"

She narrowed her eyes, telling me that she meant business, and I knew there was no way I could convince her to stay behind.

"Okay, okay," I finally groused. "If you're so determined to do something dangerous, then who am I to stop you? Especially when you dressed for the occasion."

Daphne smoothed down her coat. "You're just lucky I had this tucked away in the back of my closet for a rainy day. And that the coat and the catsuit were both on sale when I bought them."

I couldn't help but laugh. Only Daphne would be proud of her shopping prowess at a time like this.

"Now, come on," she said. "Are we going to go get your grandma back or what?"

"Have I told you lately what a good friend you are?" I asked, my voice dropping to a choked whisper.

Daphne grinned. "Nah, but I know. I'm *fabulous*, darling. Always have been, always will be."

Truer words were never spoken, but I didn't have to tell her that.

She already knew.

Daphne and I slipped through the gate and jogged across the street. I started to head for the bus stop, since that's how I had planned on getting to the address Vivian had sent me, but Daphne shook her head and grabbed my arm.

"The bus? Get real," she said. "Come on. This way."

She tucked her arm through mine and led me down

the street. The shops weren't open yet, and we were the only ones on the sidewalk. I kept glancing around, still waiting for that Reaper ambush, but it seemed as though Vivian really had wanted me to bring her the candle after all, without trying to take it away from me beforehand. No doubt she wanted me to be there in person to witness Loki's ultimate triumph. But, thanks to Nickamedes, I had an idea that just might turn the tables on Vivian and the rest of the Reapers. At least, I hoped it would work. That was all I could do.

Daphne led me over to one of the many car lots where the Mythos students parked their expensive rides, since students weren't allowed to have vehicles on campus.

"What are we doing here? You don't have a car."

Despite her many, many attempts to beg, bully, and badger her parents into getting her one.

"No," Daphne said. "I don't have a car, but that doesn't mean I didn't get some transportation for us."

She walked straight over to a black SUV. The engine was already rumbling, and the driver's window slid down as we approached, revealing another familiar face.

"Oliver?" I asked, surprised again. "You too?"

He grinned. "What can I say? I like to live dangerously, Gypsy, and you certainly help a guy do that."

His snarky words made more tears spring to my eyes, but once again, I shook my head and tried to talk them out of this—both of them.

"No," I croaked. "This is too much. I can't ask you guys to risk yourselves like this. Not only against the Reapers, but against the Protectorate too. Linus will lock you both up if he realizes you helped me."

"Well, he'll have to lock us all up then," Daphne said in a determined voice.

"What do you mean by that? All of you . . . *all* of you didn't figure out what I was up to, did you?"

"*Of course* we all figured it out," she said, waving her hand and causing more pink sparks of magic to shoot out of her fingertips. "You'd have to be completely out of it not to realize you like to do things your own way, Gwen."

I looked at her, then Oliver. "What did you guys do?"

"Well," Daphne said. "Oliver and I are going with you, obviously, to fight the Reapers. That's why we were standing by waiting for you to swipe the candle, so we could hook up with you down here. Carson was watching outside the library, and he texted me to let me know when you were on your way. Alexei and Logan are busy running interference with Linus right now, keeping him busy at that Protectorate meeting in the gym."

One by one, she ticked our friends and what they were doing to help me off on her fingers.

"Logan really, *really* wanted to come," Daphne said. "But he knew his dad would get super-suspicious the second he tried to leave the academy."

"You wouldn't believe how long it took us to convince him to stay behind," Oliver added. "And the things he threatened to do to both of us if we didn't bring you back alive."

"When . . . did you guys decide to do all of this?" I whispered.

Daphne waved her hand again. "Oh, we had a big powwow right after you had your freak-out in the infirmary, and we left you at your dorm. We divided everything up as best we could. Believe me, Carson's gotten the worst of it, trailing you these past few days, wondering when you were finally going to steal the candle."

I thought someone had been following me in the library last night. Poor Carson. I bet he'd panicked when I'd ditched him in the stacks. I closed my eyes. I thought I'd been so clever, pretending everything was fine, but my friends had known what I was up to all along— *Logan* had known what I was up to all along. I wondered if Linus had figured it out as well, but it was too late to turn back now.

"Okay," I said, opening the back door and sliding inside. "If you two are so bound and determined to come with me, let's go."

Daphne got into the front passenger seat, and Oliver drove out of the lot.

"Where are we going?" he asked. "Where do the Reapers want to meet to make the exchange?"

I handed Daphne my phone and the directions I'd looked up online. "Here. They want to meet here."

She scrolled through the information and told Oliver to take the next right. The three of us rode in silence for several minutes. Using the edges of my sleeves, I pulled the candle out of my messenger bag and looked at it. Out here in the bright sunlight, it seemed even more unremarkable than before. Just a plain, white, wax candle, half-melted, with no other marks or distinguishing features on it.

Well, that was something I was about to change.

I pushed back the sleeves of my coat and sweater so that I could see the laurels hanging off the mistletoe bracelet around my wrist. The heart-shaped leaves caught the sunlight and reflected it back, wink-wink-winking at me like sly silver eyes. I'd been thinking about how to use them ever since Nickamedes had pointed out the information he'd found in that book.

From the passage he'd shown me, it sounded like the laurels just had to touch someone in order for their magic to kick in, and I was hoping they would work the same way if the leaves were touching—or even embedded in—an artifact that someone was trying to use.

So I drew in a breath and reached for one of the laurels. I'd never seen a way to take the leaves off the bracelet before, or even get the chain off my wrist, since there wasn't any sort of clasp on it. But to my surprise, the leaf came off quite easily, as though I'd reached up and plucked it from a tree.

I stared at the leaf in the palm of my hand and concentrated, but I got the same cool, calm vibe off it that I always did. The goddess Eir had said the leaves could be used to heal or destroy, depending on the will of the person using them. So I closed my hand around the leaf, so tight that I felt one of the sharp edges cut into my palm and draw a drop of blood.

Kill, I thought. *Kill, kill, kill Loki.*

Then, I opened my palm and stared down. The leaf looked the same as before, and I had no way of knowing if my silent plea had had any effect on it at all. Only one way to find out.

So I took the leaf and pressed it into the candle, still careful not to touch the wax with my bare fingers. To my surprise, it melted into the wax seamlessly, until it looked like it had been a part of the artifact all along. In fact, the leaf had sunk so deeply into the candle that you could barely see the silver outline of it against the white wax. It gave me a little more hope that this might actually work.

"What are you doing?" Daphne asked, twisting around in the seat so she could see me.

"Hopefully, giving Loki exactly what he deserves," I murmured back, plucking another laurel off my bracelet and pressing it into the wax.

I repeated the process over and over again, until the entire surface of the candle was covered with the laurels. I didn't know how many leaves it would take to hurt Loki, much less kill him outright, but I was guessing it was more than just one, given how strong he still was.

I used all of the leaves on the bracelet except for one. I'd made a promise to myself to try to heal Nickamedes with the last one, and that's what I was going to do.

I'd just finished putting the final laurel on the candle when Oliver slowed and stopped the SUV.

"What?" I asked, tensing up. "What's wrong? Why did we stop?"

I looked through the windshield. Oliver had parked the SUV outside the entrance to a fancy subdivision, the sort of place where each house took up three acres and was then surrounded by five more acres of lawn and woods. Even from here, I could see the walls and gates that fronted each house in the neighborhood. Some of them even had small wooden guard shacks sitting by the gates, although the structures were all empty.

"I stopped because I know this place," Oliver said, staring out the window.

"Oh yeah," Daphne chimed in. "Although it looks a little different in the daylight than it did at night."

"You guys have been here before?" I asked. "When?"

They both glanced at each other, then at me.

"Actually, we're not the only ones who have been here before," Oliver said. "You have too."

I frowned. "When? I've never been here before. Trust

me. I would know. Magic memory, remember?" I tapped my finger against the side of my head.

Oliver and Daphne looked at each other again. This time, she answered me.

"You were here before when Vivian kidnapped you," she said. "When she used your blood at the Garm gate to free Loki from Helheim."

"This . . . *this* is where Vivian's house is?" I asked. "The one with that room full of creepy Black roc figurines?"

I hadn't seen the outside of the house, since I'd been unconscious at the time, but I remembered the inside all too well. I'd woken up in an opulent living room, one that was full of paintings, statues, and carvings of the birds, not to mention Vivian's own personal roc, which had been peeking in through the balcony doors at me, as if the creature wanted to rip me to shreds with its sharp beak. A shudder rippled through my body at the thought of going back to that awful room. But if that's where Grandma Frost was, then that's where I had to go.

"Are you sure this is the right address?" I asked, even though I knew it was.

"Yeah," Daphne said, handing my phone back to me. "This is where the directions said to go. This is the right place."

"What do you think will happen once you go in-side?" Oliver asked in a worried voice. "Do you think they'll take the candle away from you immediately? And how are we even supposed to get inside? They're sure to have a ton of guards."

I shook my head. "You won't have to get inside."

He looked at me. "Why do you say that?"

"Because," I said. "They'll take me out to the Garm gate, just like they did before."

"How do you know that?" Daphne asked.

"I just do."

It was true. I did know it, deep down in my bones. Somehow, I could *feel* it. Besides, it had a certain sort of sick symmetry to it. The gate was where Loki had gotten free, and that's where he would want to be healed as well. Perhaps the gate still had some magical properties left, some way that it might add to the power already burning inside Sol's candle. I wondered if it would be enough to counteract the laurel leaves I'd embedded in the wax, but it was too late to back out now.

"You guys stash the car somewhere and hike through the woods and over to the Garm gate," I said. "That's where they'll take me sooner or later. But whatever happens, don't approach the Reapers."

"Why not?" Daphne asked. "How do you think you're going to get away from them?"

I grinned. "Because you guys weren't the only ones who came up with a plan."

I told them whom I'd contacted and what I'd asked that person to do. Oliver and Daphne were silent for several seconds.

"Well, it's not half bad," Daphne said in a grudging tone.

"Not bad?" Oliver said. "It's brilliant, in a completely twisted sort of way."

"Well, I'm glad the two of you think so," I sniped.

We all glared at each other, none of us wanting to give in. Finally, I let out a breath, leaned forward, and took their hands in mine. I reached for my magic, and I tried to show them how much it meant, their coming with me, helping me, standing by me through this. I tried to show them how much their friendship had meant to me over the past several months, how they had given me a sense of peace, happiness, and belonging I'd thought I would never find at Mythos Academy. Their wonder washed over me in return, along with their own feelings of love and friendship. After several moments, I slowly pulled my feelings, memories, and emotions back into myself and drew my hands away from theirs.

"No matter what happens, promise me you guys won't approach the Reapers," I said. "I may be willing to risk myself, but I don't want you guys to get hurt too. More important than that, if things go wrong, someone needs to go back to the academy to tell Linus, Metis, and the others what happened. Logan too."

Oliver and Daphne stared at me, and they both slowly nodded their heads. I gave them both a bright, brittle smile.

"All right then," I said. "Let's go get my grandma back."

Chapter 17

I left my messenger bag in the backseat and slid Sol's candle into my jeans pocket. Then, I got out of the SUV and started walking into the neighborhood. Oliver cranked the engine again, and he and Daphne drove away, leaving me alone. I pulled out my phone and sent out a quick text message, telling the other person I'd contacted my suspicions about the Garm gate. My phone beeped a few seconds later.

Garm gate. Woods. Got it. We'll be there.

And that was all the message said. That was all it really needed to say. I just hoped I was right about Vivian and the Reapers—or else I'd be dead, along with Grandma Frost.

The smooth, wide street was deserted, and everything was oddly quiet. I didn't see any TVs flickering through the windows, no cars pulling down the driveways, no one putting envelopes in a mailbox, nothing to indicate that anyone lived in this neighborhood at all. In fact, several of the homes had FOR SALE signs planted in their front yards. I wondered if that was why the Reapers had chosen this area for their hideout—because it seemed to be so empty. I shivered and walked on.

It took me about half an hour to find the right house, which, of course, was the one at the very back of the subdivision, set off from all the other houses, with a twelve-foot-high stone wall and an iron gate that was eerily similar to the one at the academy. I looked up, but no sphinxes perched on the wall on either side of the gate. That was probably for the best. No doubt the statues would have looked like they wanted to tear me to pieces, since this was a Reaper hideout.

A black security camera was mounted over the gate. It must have been motion-activated, because it swiveled around and focused on me when I approached it. I waited, but the gates didn't open, so I went over and punched a button on the metal intercom that was embedded in the stone wall. A bit of static crackled back to me in response; then the line started humming faintly, as though it were a phone and someone on the other end was waiting for me to speak.

"Open sesame," I joked.

Silence. Apparently, the Reapers weren't in a joking mood. Neither was I, really.

I sighed. "I have the candle."

The gates started swinging open even before I finished speaking. I looked at the long, steep driveway that led up to the house. I had no choice but to walk up it. Not if I wanted to save Grandma Frost.

"Well, here we are," Vic murmured.

I glanced down. The sword hadn't said anything on the ride over here, but now, his purple eye was wide open, and he was staring straight ahead, his metal face set into hard, determined lines.

"Thank you for being here with me for this."

Vic rolled his eye up so that he was looking at me.

"No thanks necessary. It's what I *do*, Gwen. This isn't the first time I've ever gone into a Reaper stronghold."

I nodded. After that, there was nothing left to say, so I lifted my chin, squared my shoulders, and started walking.

The driveway dipped down before arching up a long, steep hill, with the house sitting at the very top. The structure was made out of light gray stone and looked more like a sprawling mansion than something you would find in a subdivision, even one as ritzy as this. I half-expected it to be covered with creepy statues, like the buildings at the academy, but only elegant balconies and tall glass windows fronted the mansion. Of course it wouldn't have any statues on it. The Reapers probably wanted to blend in with the rest of the neighborhood as best they could, not stand out by having some dark, Gothic mansion. At least, that's what I assumed. Maybe that's why all of those paintings, statues, and carvings of the Black rocs had been on the inside of the house, since the Reapers couldn't put them on the outside.

I glanced left and right as I walked up the driveway, but I didn't see any Reapers patrolling the grounds or peering out at me from the trees in the woods that flanked the edges of the enormous yard. They must all be waiting inside for me.

Yippee-skippee.

The thought made my throat tighten with panic, but I swallowed down my fear. Nothing mattered except rescuing Grandma Frost—and hoping that the laurel leaves would kill or at least injure Loki. Or, really, do anything but make him stronger.

It seemed to take forever, but all too soon, I reached the front door of the house. I trudged up the steps and stared at the brass knocker, which was shaped like a snarling gargoyle. I squared my shoulders again, grabbed the knocker, and let it fall back down against the wooden door.

Thump.

I waited, but I didn't hear anyone moving inside the house, and I didn't see anyone pushing the curtains aside to peek out the windows at me. Was anyone even here? Or was this another one of Vivian's games? Or worse, a wild-goose chase—

The door was abruptly jerked open, and I had to bite back my shriek of surprise.

But the person on the other side was all too familiar. Auburn hair, pretty features, golden eyes. She was even dressed like I was, in jeans, boots, and a gray sweater. Her gold Janus ring flashed on her finger, and I stared at the two faces. I wondered what the god would think of me using his key to steal Sol's candle. After a moment, I shook off my thoughts and raised my gaze to the girl standing in front of me.

"Hello, Gwen," Vivian drawled. "So glad you could make it."

The Reaper girl and I stared at each other for several seconds. So did Lucretia and Vic, since both swords were sheathed in their scabbards and belted around our respective waists. The swords didn't say anything, and neither did Vivian or I. The time for talking, threats, and insults was long past.

"This way," Vivian said.

She stepped aside. I swallowed again and entered the mansion. Vivian closed the door and then moved back in front of me.

"I really hope I don't have to remind you not to do anything stupid or your grandma dies," Vivian said in a pleasant voice.

I glared at her.

She let out a pleased laugh. "Oh Gwen. It's going to be so much fun finally watching you die."

She turned and walked away, and I had no choice but to follow her.

Vivian wound her way through the first floor of the mansion, which featured lots of spacious rooms with high, vaulted ceilings. I looked around at all of the opulent furnishings that filled the house. In some ways, it was like being at the Crius Coliseum or some other mythological museum. Jewelry, weapons, armor, and more lined the walls or were displayed under glass cases, while crystal chandeliers hung down from the ceilings, bathing everything in soft white light. I wondered what all of the artifacts did, but, of course, Vivian didn't tell me, and it wasn't like I had time to stop and actually look closely at anything.

I was too busy staring at all of the Reapers.

As we moved deeper into the mansion, I saw more and more Reapers. They lounged on couches and chairs or hunched over tables, their heads close together as they talked softly to each other. They all snapped to attention as Vivian and I passed them, then got to their feet and trailed after us, each one wearing a black robe, although they'd left their rubber Loki masks off today. I supposed they didn't think I'd be able to identify any of them later.

They were probably right about that. If I lived through the next hour, it would be a wonder.

Vivian strode up several sets of steps, then threw open a pair of double doors, leading me into a large, familiar room.

"I thought you might like to see this again," she purred. "For old times' sake."

Dark wooden furniture, antique sofas, crystal vases full of black and bloodred roses. It was the same opulent living room I'd woken up in the night she'd kidnapped me after I'd found the Helheim Dagger. The one with all of the creepy Black roc paintings, statues, and carvings decorating everything from the walls to the tables to the sofa legs. The room looked the same as I remembered, right down to the chair in front of the desk, the spot where I'd woken up and realized that Vivian was Loki's Champion and that she was working with Preston Ashton.

Only this time, another figure was sitting in that same chair, flanked by two Reapers.

"Grandma!" I said, running past Vivian and over to her.

Grandma got up out of the chair, and I threw myself into her arms.

"I'm okay, pumpkin," she whispered into my ear, even as she smoothed down my hair. "I'm okay."

Tears scalded my eyes, but I forced myself to blink them back. Now was not the time to show any sort of weakness, not in front of the Reapers. I drew away from her and gave her a critical once-over. An ugly, purple, fist-shaped bruise marred her right cheek, and more cuts and bruises dotted her hands and arms, probably from where she'd struggled against the Reapers in the park. But overall, she looked okay.

"Touching," Vivian said. "Really. But let's get on with things."

She snapped her fingers at the Reapers who'd entered the room behind us. "Bring them."

The Reapers already had their long, curved swords out, ready to use them, but Grandma and I didn't give them any trouble as they marched us over to the far side of the room, out the balcony doors I remembered, and down a set of stone steps. After that, we left the backyard of the mansion behind and trooped out into the woods beyond.

Daphne was right. It looked different in the day than it had that terrible night when I'd realized how thoroughly Vivian had tricked me. The woods were only woods now, filled with trees and leaves and rocks and snow, and not crawling with creepy, eerie shadows the way they had been back then. Of course, the Reapers and their swords surrounding me and Grandma Frost on all sides weren't really an improvement, but at least I could tell where we were going now—and we were headed straight toward the Garm gate, just as I'd suspected.

Still, as we moved deeper and deeper into the woods, my gaze flicked up to the trees that towered above our heads, but I didn't see any Black rocs roosting in the tops of the sturdier oaks and maples, peering down at me as though I was a worm they wanted to gobble up.

"What happened to all your rocs?" I asked. "You seemed to have a ton of them on the road the other day, but I haven't seen a single one since I've been here. *So* disappointing."

I made my voice sound as innocent as possible, although my question was anything but. I had a very specific reason for asking about the Black rocs, and where they might be lurking, and the answer might determine whether or not Grandma Frost and I made it out of here alive. Still, I made myself look totally bored, as though I didn't really care one way or the other about the answer and was simply mocking the Reapers for kicks.

Vivian shot me a dirty look. "We're still rounding them up, thanks to you."

Which was exactly what I wanted to hear.

I grinned. "Aw, so sorry to make more evil work for you to do, Viv."

Her golden eyes narrowed, and her hand dropped to her sword, as if she'd like to pull Lucretia and attack me right now. Yeah. I knew the feeling.

But Vivian controlled herself, and so did I, and we kept walking.

It didn't take us long to reach our destination. We left the path behind, stepped into a large clearing in the middle of the woods, and there it was.

The Garm gate.

Once, it had been a smooth, circular, unbroken slab of black marble that had been set into the middle of the forest floor. A hand holding a balanced set of scales had been carved into the very center of the stone.

But that was then, and this was now.

The black marble was cracked, jagged, and split two ways from where Loki had used the Helheim Dagger to escape the prison that the other gods had placed him in so long ago. I rubbed my chest, which was suddenly aching, thinking of the scars there, the ones that were shaped like a weird X that slashed over my heart, the same X shape that had ruined the marble before me. The stone couldn't recover from Loki tearing through it any more than I could forget about my scars and how I'd gotten them from Preston and Logan.

My gaze drifted over to a particular patch of stone, one close to the center of the jagged tears. My heart twisted as the memories washed over me. Nott had been killed right *there*, when Vivian had stabbed her in the side. I'd cradled the Fenrir wolf's head in my hands and stared into her eyes as she'd slowly died. It had been one of the worst moments of my life.

And this was shaping up to be another one.

Because a familiar figure was standing in the exact spot where Nott had died. His back was to us, but I would have recognized him anywhere. He slowly turned at the sound of our footsteps echoing across the stone and faced us head-on.

Loki.

Chapter 18

Somehow, I held back a shudder and forced myself to study the evil god.

Loki was wearing a black Reaper robe that rippled around his body like water, as though the material were made out of some especially fine silk, instead of the more mundane cotton the other Reapers wore. He looked the same as I remembered him the last time we were here at the Garm gate, the same as I'd seen him dozens of times in my dreams—my nightmares.

One side of his face was smooth, perfect, and utterly gorgeous, with its aquiline nose, great cheekbone, alabaster skin, and bright blue eye. His long hair was a beautiful gold that flowed down and brushed the top of his right shoulder. But the left side of his face was completely horrible, smashed and twisted together, as though it had been made out of the same wax as Sol's candle—wax that had been melted down into something almost unrecognizable as a man's face. The hair on that side of his head hung in thin, matted, black and crimson strings, while that eye was red—that awful, awful Reaper red.

Loki was almost seven feet tall, but his shoulders

were slumped forward and uneven, and parts of his body stuck out at awkward angles, because he had been forced to stay in one cramped position in Helheim for so long. Perhaps it was my imagination, but he seemed weaker than I remembered him being before, thin and brittle, as if he would shatter if he moved too fast. I wondered if it was because the ritual with Logan hadn't worked, and Loki's soul had been forced back into his own twisted, broken, ruined body.

Agrona was standing by his side, one of her hands resting lightly on his left elbow, almost as if she was ready to support him should he stagger.

This time, I couldn't hide my shudder. Loki might be weakened, but I could still feel the power rolling off him in thick, malevolent waves. I couldn't imagine actually being that close to him, actually *touching* him, but for Agrona, no doubt it was some sort of great honor.

The other Reapers spread out, forming a circle around us, with me, Grandma Frost, Vivian, Agrona, and Loki in the center. I looked past the Reapers into the forest beyond, but if Oliver and Daphne were out there somewhere, they were hidden too well for me to spot them.

"So," Loki began, his voice smooth and seductive. "This time, I'm faced with not one, but two Frost scions."

I reached down and gripped Grandma's hand. Neither one of us said anything. What exactly *did* you say to the . . . the . . . the *thing* that had defined so much of your life? The evil that you'd fought against so hard and for so long? That you had sacrificed so much trying to stop? I didn't know, but Grandma raised her chin in defiance and met his hateful, two-toned gaze with her own steely violet one.

Loki paused, as if he expected Grandma to say something, but then, he shook his head. I could hear each and every one of the vertebra in his neck *crack-crack-crack-*ing, and the sharp motion made him wince and hunch over. It took him a moment to straighten back up.

"Well," he purred again, his gaze zooming over to Vivian. "At least you get another chance to finally correct your failure, your *many* failures to kill her, to kill both of *them*."

Vivian ducked her head, as though she was ashamed.

Agrona plastered a smile on her face. "Yes, my lord. Vivian can finally do that now. How wonderful of you to point that out to all of us—"

He turned to her. "And you weren't any better, with all of *your* pitiful attempts to kill the mother and grandmother. You never revealed your true self to them, and yet you still never managed to kill them, either one of them. Not to mention what a catastrophe the soul ritual with the Spartan boy turned out to be. A ritual that I am still suffering the effects of, thanks to *you*."

Now, Agrona looked as chagrined—and frightened—as Vivian. And the rest of the Reapers didn't look any more certain—or brave. Perhaps Loki had been a harsher, more ruthless master than they'd ever dreamed he would be. It would serve them right if he wanted to kill and enslave all of them too.

Agrona opened her mouth, probably to make some excuse, but Loki held up his right index finger, stopping her.

"The candle. *Now*."

Agrona and Vivian both looked at me, and the Reapers with their swords crept a little closer.

"All right," I said, holding up my hands so they could see that I wasn't trying to pull some sort of trick. "All right. It's in my pocket."

I reached inside my jeans, my fingers curling around the white wax for perhaps the last time. Once again, I felt that bright, burning flash of power, of health, life, and strength, but I forced myself to push the sensation away and focus on what I needed to do.

DIE, I thought with all the desperate anger in my heart, trying to send the silver laurel leaves one final message, one final expression of my own free will and what I wanted them to do. *Kill Loki. Destroy him. Hurt him as badly as he's hurt the people I love.*

For a moment, the candle went as cold as ice against my fingers. But by the time I sucked in another breath, the wax was simply wax again. I didn't know if it was the laurels at work, or my own imagination playing tricks on me, but I'd done everything I could. All I could do now was hope that I'd made the right choices—and that I hadn't just doomed myself, Grandma Frost, and everyone else.

I slowly pulled the candle out of my pocket and held it out where they all could see it.

Vivian wrinkled her nose. "That's it? Really?"

"What did you expect?"

She shrugged. "I don't know. I thought it would at least have some jewels or something on it. Most of the more powerful artifacts do."

"Shut up, you stupid girl!" Agrona snapped.

She stepped forward and snatched the candle out of my hand. "This had better be the real thing, and not some sort of trick on Linus's part."

I straightened up. "It's the real candle. Not a trick. I wouldn't risk my grandma's life on a trick."

Not on *this* trick, anyway.

Agrona took the candle, then turned toward Loki. She walked over to him and bowed low, holding the candle out and up over her head, presenting it to him like some sort of gift. I supposed that's exactly what it was—a chance to restore him to his full health, strength, and power so that he could finally lead the Reapers in their second Chaos War against the Pantheon.

Loki took the candle from Agrona and held it up, examining it from all sides. I couldn't keep myself from holding my breath, wondering if he'd notice the silver leaves embedded in the wax—and realize they weren't part of the original candle.

"At last," he murmured, both of his eyes brightening. "At last, I can return to what I was before . . . and become even *greater* than ever."

His words sent a shiver down my spine, and worry surging through my body, but there was nothing I could do now but hope the leaves did what Eir had told me they could—destroy *him*.

Finally, finally destroy him and all the terror he wanted to unleash on the members of the Pantheon. On my friends. On my family.

Loki clutched the candle tight with both hands. I thought he might need Agrona or Vivian to light it for him, but apparently, that wasn't how it worked. He stood there, his gaze fixed on the wick, his hands wrapped around it and the laurel leaves I'd pressed into the wax.

At first, nothing happened, and I started to wonder if the leaves would keep the candle from working, if one artifact could completely cancel out another like that. If that happened, then Grandma Frost and I were dead. Loki would order the Reapers to kill us where we stood.

But just when I was about to reach for Vic and try to fight my way through the Reapers, a single black spark sputtered to life on the candle's wick. Despite its color, the spark was bright, as bright as a star burning in the middle of the day, so bright and so intense that I almost had to look away from it.

But I forced myself to watch as the spark grew brighter and brighter still, and Loki slowly began to change—to *heal*.

His body grew straighter and even taller than before, and several sharp *crack-crack-crack*s sounded, as if his bones were being wrenched back into the correct places after being out of joint for so long. Loki let out a long, loud, contented sigh, as if it actually felt good to have his body be pulled back into its proper alignment.

But more than his body, it almost seemed as if I could feel his very presence expand—and grow blacker and fouler at the same time.

When I'd touched Logan while he'd been under the influence of the Apate gems, while he'd been connected to Loki, there had been a solid wall of Reaper red in the Spartan's mind, and that's what I felt when I looked at Loki now. Bit by bit, piece by piece, Sol's candle was making him stronger and stronger and restoring all the parts of him that had been chipped away by his centuries trapped in Helheim.

My heart sank. It was working—the candle and all of its powerful magic was actually making Loki stronger, just like everyone had feared.

The evil god let out a loud, wild, crazy cackle, and I realized I'd just made the worst mistake of my life.

Chapter 19

We all held our breath as Loki continued to cackle with glee. Me, Grandma Frost, Vivian, Agrona, the rest of the Reapers. We all watched him get better right before our eyes. I'd seen Metis and Daphne work their healing magic before, but it was nothing compared to this. Fresh waves of hot, pulsing, malevolent power surged off Loki with every breath he took.

And there was nothing I could do to stop it.

"How does it feel knowing that you're going to be single-handedly responsible for the destruction of the pathetic Pantheon?" Vivian hissed in my ear. "What will all of your friends think of you then? What will your Spartan boyfriend think of you when he realizes that you've doomed every single person the two of you care about to a short, painful, miserable life? Not so heroic now, are you, Gwen Frost?"

I ignored her cruel words and focused my attention on the candle and that black spark still burning in Loki's hands.

Come on! I thought, as if I could get the laurel leaves to work just by yelling at them in my mind. *Come on! You're supposed to be* killing *him. Not* healing *him.*

But all I could do was stand there and scream and scream inside my head.

Seconds passed, then a minute, then another one, and another one. But still, the candle kept burning, kept making Loki stronger—

Suddenly, he let out a surprised, almost strangled gasp, and a treacherous bit of hope erupted in my heart, cutting through the utter despair.

My gaze zoomed to the candle. Perhaps it was my imagination, but I thought I could actually see the silver laurel leaves glinting within the wax, burning almost as bright as the black spark flickering on the wick. I blinked, and I realized that the flame had actually changed from one moment to the next.

Because now, the spark was silver—as silver as the laurel leaves.

"Get ready," I whispered to Grandma Frost, gripping her hand even tighter with mine.

I glanced at the Reapers, but they were all fixated on Loki, smiles of wonder and excitement on their faces as they realized that their goal of finally healing him was within reach. No one seemed to notice that the spark had changed color, except for me. Grandma finally noticed too, and she gave me a sharp look. She nodded, and I nodded back at her. She'd be ready when the time came, and so would I.

Now, I just had to hope that the candle would finish what it had started—the way *I* wanted it to.

But Loki seemed to recover from that first, shocked gasp. He straightened back up to his full height, and the spark sputtered from silver back to black. My heart sank again—

A bright, ominous *whoosh* of silver flame erupted

from the candle, boiling a thick cloud of silver smoke straight up into the god's face, completely obscuring his features for a moment, before dissipating as quickly as it had appeared.

"My lord?" Agrona asked in an uncertain voice.

Loki let out a pain-filled snarl, but he tightened his hold on the candle, his fingers digging into the white wax like claws, as if he could get the artifact to work through the sheer force of his own will. Maybe he could. Worry filled the pit of my stomach once more.

But as quickly as Loki had seemed to regain his health and strength, it all melted away like, well, candle wax. His figure grew shorter, thinner, and hunchbacked, and his bones *crack-crack-crack*ed back into the same, extreme, awkward, twisted positions that they'd been in before. In an instant, he went from being on the verge of a full recovery to looking the same as he always did.

But it didn't stop there.

Loki seemed to shrink down and curl in on himself, like a turtle retreating back into the ruined shell of its own body. His eyes, which had been burning so bright, began to dim, and thick chunks of his hair fell out, drifting to the broken stone like macabre bits of black, red, and golden snow.

"My lord?" Agrona asked again, taking a tentative step forward. "Are you . . . ill?"

Loki screamed in response.

Vivan whipped around to me, her golden gaze locking with my violet one, and I felt a sharp, sudden, stabbing pain in my head, as though a pair of fingers were digging into my skull. Vivian peered at me, using her telepathy magic to root around in my mind. I tried to block her attack, but my gaze flicked to the candle, and the image of the silver laurel leaves loomed up in my thoughts before I could shut it out.

She whirled back around to Agrona and Loki. "Drop it! Drop the candle! She's done something to it!"

Agrona reached for the candle, but Loki hunched over it that much more, keeping her from ripping it out of his hands.

"No!" he screamed. "It was working! It has to work! I'll *make* it work!"

The candle erupted into silver flames in his hands. I threw my hand up against the sudden, intense heat and blinding light. So did everyone else in the clearing. It took me a moment, but I managed to force my gaze back to the candle.

This time, I could see each and every one of the silver laurel leaves burning in the white wax, doing exactly what they were supposed to—killing Loki.

He let out another scream, and the flames seem to engulf his entire body, as though he were some sort of candle himself, burning, burning bright. But he still didn't let go of the artifact. I didn't know if it was because he couldn't or if he still thought that he could figure out some way to reverse the magic and get it to heal him again.

I watched as his legs slid out from under him, and he fell to the cracked stone of the Garm gate, still holding on to the candle. Agrona tried to get close enough to rip the artifact out of his hands, but she couldn't get through the silver flames still washing over Loki's body, making him scream and scream and scream.

Vivian drew Lucretia out of the scabbard belted to her waist. "What did you do? What did you *do*?"

I grinned. "How does it feel, Viv? Knowing that

you're single-handedly responsible for injuring Loki so badly?"

Her gaze cut to the god, who was moaning, groaning, and rocking back and forth on the broken stone, even as the flames continued to burn all over his body.

"You'll pay for this!" she hissed at me. "More than you ever *dreamed* of—"

"Now!" I yelled as loud as I could, cutting her off and hoping the others would hear my voice over Loki's screams.

I waited a second, but nothing happened, and the woods remained as still and silent as before, except for Loki's continued screams.

Vivian smirked. "What's wrong? Did you bring some of your friends with you after all, Gwen? Well, it looks like they decided to abandon you. Smartest decision they've ever made, if you ask me."

I drew Vic out of his scabbard. "Maybe. But I don't need them to take care of *you*."

Vivian let out an angry yell, and I did the same. With one thought, we surged toward each other.

Clash-clash-clang!
Clash-clash-clang!
Clash-clash-clang!

Vivian and I fought over the broken stone, each one of us doing our best to kill the other girl where she stood. The Reapers looked back and forth between us and Agrona, not sure whether they should help Vivian kill me or do something to try to aid Loki.

"Help me, you fools!" Agrona said, tearing off her black robe and using the fabric to beat at the flames still devouring Loki's body.

The Reapers left me to Vivian and headed in Agrona's direction, but they forgot about one thing—Grandma Frost.

Grandma stuck her foot out, tripping a Reaper as he rushed past her. He tumbled to the ground, and Grandma snatched up his sword from where it had fallen. She twirled the weapon around, then brought the point down into the Reaper's side, making him scream with pain. Two Reapers whirled around at the sound. They realized that Grandma Frost had a weapon and headed toward her.

I swung my own sword out in a vicious arc, trying to charge past Vivian to help my grandma, but the Reaper girl parried my blow and lashed out with one of her own that had me leaping back to get out of the way of Lucretia's whistling blade.

Grandma twirled the sword in her hand again and stepped up to meet the Reapers, but the one she'd stabbed reached out and grabbed her ankle, throwing her off balance. Horrified, I watched as she tried to pull herself out of the Reaper's grasp and straighten up so she could battle the other two who were charging at her. She wasn't going to get free in time, and both of the Reapers raised their swords, ready to bring the weapons down on top of her head—

A golden arrow zoomed out of the woods and buried itself in the chest of one of the Reapers who'd been targeting Grandma. A second later, another arrow—this one made of regular metal—took out the Reaper on Grandma's other side. Daphne and Oliver had finally gotten into position in the trees, and they were doing their best to help us escape.

But there were still too many Reapers for that.

Even if I could have gotten past Vivian, there were still more than a dozen Reapers in the clearing, although most of them had gone over to help Agrona with Loki. The Reapers had stripped off their black cloaks and were using the fabric to try to smother the silver flames still crackling over his body.

Finally, Agrona reached down and managed to wrench the candle out of Loki's hands. It must have burned her too, because she hissed and tossed it aside. The candle skittered across the broken black marble, landing a few feet away from me and Vivian.

The silver spark and flames had vanished, as though the laurel leaves and all the magic they had contained had been used up, although a bit of silver smoke continued to puff up from the wick. Other than that, the candle was simply a candle once more, and I didn't see any trace of the leaves remaining in the wax.

But there was still about a quarter of the candle left. I didn't know exactly what that meant, but I wasn't about to let the Reapers get their hands on it.

Vivian saw me looking at the candle, and we both lunged for it at the same time. My hand closed around the wax, and I braced myself, waiting for the awful memories of Loki's pain to fill my mind. But all I got from the candle was that feeling of intense heat, and I realized there was still some magic left in it after all— more than enough magic to heal Loki, despite what I'd done to him.

Vivian threw herself on top of me, and we rolled over and over across the stone, with her trying to tear the candle out of my grasp, and me tightening my death grip on the smooth piece of wax. I couldn't let her get her hands on the candle now. Not when I only had one laurel leaf left on my bracelet and no time to press it into the wax.

"Give it up, Gwen!" Vivian hissed. "I'm stronger than you are. Any second, you're going to let go of that candle, and then you'll lose—just like you've lost to me every single time before now."

"Dream on," I hissed back.

Then, I punched her in the face. I was still holding on to Vic's hilt, and I slammed my fist and the sword into her features as hard as I could. I felt her nose crunch under the metal, and blood sprayed through the air, spattering onto both of us.

Vivian shrieked and rolled away from me. I scrambled to my feet, still holding Vic and the candle, which I stuffed into my jacket pocket and zipped up tight so I wouldn't lose it. Grandma Frost raced over to my side. We turned to run into the woods but found our path blocked by a group of Reapers. We whirled around the other way, but there were more of them coming up on that side too.

Grandma and I stood back-to-back near the middle of the Garm gate, watching the Reapers slowly approach us. More golden and wooden arrows zipped out of the woods, and a few of the Reapers split off to go after Daphne and Oliver. I hoped my friends could avoid them and that they wouldn't be foolish enough to try to get close to me and Grandma with so many of our enemies clustered around us. Besides, I still had one trick left, one that I hoped was enough to save us.

"Kill them!" Loki howled, still rocking back and forth on the stone. "Kill them both! Now!"

The Reapers raised their swords and surged toward

us, and I snapped up Vic, ready to fight them for as long as I could—

SCREECH!

A wild, fierce cry boomed through the clearing, making me wince at its volume. But a smile tugged up my lips all the same because I knew exactly what had made the noise.

The high-pitched screech came again, even louder than before, and more than a few of the Reapers paused, looking up toward the treetops, no doubt expecting to see their Black rocs roosting on the sturdier branches. But it wasn't a roc making that noise.

Not even close.

A second later, two male Eir gryphons landed in the middle of the broken stone. One of the gryphons was large, easily as large as the Black rocs the Reapers always used, but the other one was smaller, although he had grown quite a bit since the last time I'd seen him and was now almost as big as his dad. Both gryphons were beautiful, with bronze fur and wings, black beaks and talons, and bright, shimmering eyes that burned like warm, bronze lanterns.

But the gryphons weren't alone.

A pretty girl with black hair and green eyes was perched on top of the baby gryphon. She wore black jeans, a green sweater, and a green leather jacket that gave her a tough-girl vibe. A woman with similar features and clothes rode the adult gryphon. My cousin, Rory Forseti, and her aunt, Rachel Maddox. The other friends I'd called for help, along with the gryphons.

"Hey, Gwen!" Rory grinned at me, shoving her hair back out of her eyes. "How was our grand entrance?"

"Perfect!" I yelled back at her. "Just perfect!"

Grandma Frost ran toward the gryphons, while I covered her, holding off all the Reapers that tried to get past me to attack her. Rachel jumped off the adult gryphon, and the creature leaped into the middle of the fray, swiping his claws into every Reaper that came near him. In a moment, the gryphon had taken out three of the Reapers, and even Vivian and Agrona were looking at him with surprise—and more than a little fear.

I used their distraction to reach into my other jeans pocket and pull out a wad of material that I'd looped over and over itself, making it resemble a small belt. I snapped the material open, and a length of gnarled, knotted, light gray seaweed unspooled in my hand. The net of Ran, the Norse goddess of storms, which had the unusual property of making whatever it was holding much lighter. I'd used it before to ride the gryphons, and I was going to use it now to get us out of here.

"Hurry, Gwen!" Vic urged. "They're regrouping!"

Sure enough, the Reapers were creeping toward the adult gryphon again, but a couple of arrows from Daphne and Oliver in the woods took care of that. Grandma Frost and I raced over to the adult gryphon, and I threw the net over his back, looped it around his neck, and tied the whole thing together. Then, Grandma and I scrambled onto his broad back, both of us hooking our hands through the net so we wouldn't fall off the creature.

"Get us out of here!" I yelled.

The adult gryphon let out another loud screech, pumped his wings once, and shot up into the air. So did the baby gryphon that was carrying Rory; a third gryphon had appeared to fly Rachel away as well. I knew that Daphne and Oliver would find their own way out of the woods and back to Oliver's car and would meet up with us later at the academy. That was the plan we'd worked out before, and my friends should have no problem getting away from the Reapers and back to Oliver's SUV.

Still, as the gryphon flew higher and higher, I leaned over the side of the creature's back and stared down into the clearing below. Agrona was still hovering over Loki and screaming at the other Reapers, most of whom were staring up at the gryphons, their mouths open wide in utter shock.

And then there was Vivian.

For the first time ever, I had the supreme satisfaction of staring down at my nemesis and seeing the rage and frustration on her face as the gryphons carried me, Grandma Frost, Rory, and Rachel to safety.

Chapter 20

I couldn't help but laugh as the gryphons flew higher and higher and faster and faster.

All sorts of emotions surged through me, but the main one was relief—relief that I'd actually been able to pull off my plan and save my grandma and the candle from the Reapers.

But that emotion was quickly tempered by another, darker realization—Loki was injured, but not dead.

And I still had no idea how to kill him.

I'd used up all the laurels but one. Sure, the leaves had hurt him and probably made his body even more twisted and broken than before, but they hadn't killed him.

And I didn't know what would.

But one thing was for certain—this wasn't over. Because I still had Sol's candle, and the Reapers still wanted it. Loki still wanted it. Because there was enough of it left to heal at least one more person, and I couldn't let Loki get his hands on it, or we'd be right back where we'd started.

No, the Reapers would come after the candle again. It was just a matter of when and how many of them there would be.

Still, I was determined to enjoy this rare moment of triumph because I knew exactly how brief it would be. No doubt Linus had figured out by now that I'd taken the candle, and he'd be waiting at the academy, probably ready to clap me in chains and drag me down to the prison as soon as I showed my face there. But I didn't care, because I'd saved my grandma. At least for the moment. What the next few hours would bring, well, I couldn't say, but I'd face the new troubles head-on, just like I had everything else so far.

Vivian's mansion wasn't all that far from the academy, and it didn't take long before the town of Cypress Mountain came into sight, with its cluster of shops and streets.

I leaned down and pointed to the edge of campus and a spot behind the stone wall that ringed the grounds. I could have told the gryphon to land in the middle of the main quad, like he'd done the last time I'd ridden him out in Colorado, but I wanted at least a few minutes with Rory, Rachel, my grandma, and the gryphons before the Protectorate came and dragged me away.

"Put us down there," I yelled above the roar of the wind in my ears. "Please."

The gryphon nodded, and I felt a wave of understanding surge off him and into me. He let out a fierce screech, and the baby followed his father's lead, as well as the third gryphon. The three of them dove toward the ground in unison, hovering in midair like helicopters, whipping up snow and leaves with the fierce beats of their broad bronze wings, before gently touching down. I let go of the net and slid off the gryphon's back, and Grandma Frost did the same.

I turned toward her. "Are you okay?"

She nodded and grabbed my hands. "I'm better now that we're away from that awful place."

"Come on," I said, untying the net from the gryphon, folding it up, and stuffing it back into my jeans pocket. "We don't have a lot of time."

I led her over to the others. Rachel was already on the ground, stroking the head of the gryphon she'd been riding, while Rory gracefully slid off the baby's back and scratched behind his ears. They both turned to face me as I approached, and the gryphons gathered around the four of us.

"How was your trip out here?" I asked.

Rachel and Rory both grinned at each other, then at me.

"The plane ride was fine," Rachel said. "And the gryphons met us exactly where you wanted them to."

"Although it was a little freaky holing up at your grandma's house with gryphons wandering around in the backyard and hiding out in that park on the other side of the hill," Rory chimed in. "I thought for sure that the Protectorate was going to come in and bust us at any second, but they never did."

That was the plan I'd worked out with Rory. I knew I'd need some way to get myself and Grandma away from the Reapers fast, and the gryphons had aided me once before at the Eir Ruins. So I'd asked Rory and Rachel to hike up the mountain, find the cavern where the gryphons made their home, and ask the creatures to come to North Carolina to help me battle the Reapers. And here they were—my plan had worked like the proverbial charm.

I introduced Rachel, Rory, and the gryphons to Grandma Frost, who nodded her head at them all in turn, then moved forward to shake Rachel's hand, and then Rory's.

"Thank you for helping Gwen," she said, still holding on to Rory's hand. "And me too."

She looked at Rory, and her eyes grew glassy for a moment. I knew she was getting a glimpse of the Spartan girl's future, but Grandma didn't say anything about what she'd seen as her eyes cleared and she dropped Rory's hand.

But Rory had noticed that something was going on, and she gave my grandma a suspicious look. Then again, Rory was almost *always* suspicious about *everything*, and with good reason, since her parents had been Reapers and had hidden that truth from her for years.

"Gwen!" A faint voice drifted over to me. "Gwen!"

I whirled around. To my surprise, Carson was running toward me as fast as he could, his boots slapping against the cobblestone path and his arms pumping in time with his long strides. He'd barely come into view when I realized that several other people were running along behind them—and that most of them were wearing gray Protectorate robes.

I sighed. They'd gotten here sooner than I'd thought they would.

I turned to the leader of the gryphons. "You might want to leave now. This isn't going to be pleasant for me. Or you, either, if you stick around."

The gryphon bowed his head. He let out a fierce screech, and he and the other two creatures flapped their wings and soared up into the air. But they didn't go far, perching in the tops of the trees above our heads, watching over us as best they could.

"Gwen! Gwen!" Carson kept shouting at me.

I sighed again and turned to face the music.

"Whatever happens, I'm so grateful to you for rescuing me, pumpkin," Grandma Frost murmured, reaching over and giving my hand a gentle squeeze. "I'm so proud of you."

"Me too," Vic piped up from his spot in his scabbard. "And I'm sure the fuzzball will be as well."

I looked at Grandma. "No matter what happens to me, make sure Nyx is taken care of. Please?"

She squeezed my hand again. "Consider it done."

Carson finally sputtered to a stop in front of us. His brown eyes were wide behind his black glasses, and he bent down and put his hands on his knees as he tried to suck down some much-needed oxygen.

"Daphne . . . and . . . Oliver . . ." he rasped, panting for breath. "Just . . . texted me. They're almost back . . . to the academy."

The last tight knot of worry loosened in my chest. I hadn't been able to text my friends while we'd been flying back, and I was so glad that they were okay, that they'd gotten away from the Reapers who'd gone into the woods after them.

"Good. Tell them thanks for everything they did," I said. "For everything you all did. I couldn't have done it without you, even if I didn't realize it at the time."

Carson managed to grin in between sucking down more giant gulps of air.

I stepped in front of the others, making sure they were behind me. This had been my idea, not theirs, and I was going to be the one to take full responsibility for it—along with the brunt of the punishment.

So I lifted my chin and waited.

Linus Quinn came striding down the path toward me,

his gray Protectorate robe snapping around his legs, as though it was trying to show me exactly how angry he was with me. In fact, I thought I could see a vein throbbing in his temple from here.

Linus finally reached me, and his eyes locked with mine. Oh yeah. I could *definitely* see that vein throbbing in his temple now. His cold blue gaze met mine for a moment before he looked past me at the others. He carefully examined Grandma Frost, Rory, Rachel, and the gryphons in turn before he stared at me again.

But Carson, Linus, and the Protectorate guards weren't the only ones who'd shown up. Logan and Alexei had come down to the gate too, flanked by Sergei and Inari.

I looked at Logan, who stared back at me. His face was carefully neutral, and his eyes devoid of any obvious emotion. I couldn't tell whether he was angry at me for what I'd done or relieved that I was okay. Probably a little bit of both. Okay, okay, probably a lot of both.

Alexei's face was as stoic as ever, and even Sergei and Inari had somber expressions, telling me exactly how much trouble I was in. It seemed I'd gone from one bad situation to the next over the past few days, and no doubt more trouble was on the way. But at least I'd saved my grandma, at least I'd gotten that much right. So I lifted my chin once more and prepared to take my punishment.

"Gwendolyn Cassandra Frost," Linus Quinn boomed in the loudest voice I'd ever heard him use. "You're under arrest."

I flashed back to the first time he'd said those words to me in Kaldi Coffee. His accusations hadn't been true then, but I couldn't deny the charges now.

So I nodded my head. "Okay."

Linus blinked, as if he were shocked that I was going to go along with him so easily. But his surprise quickly vanished, replaced once more by the anger that made his blue eyes burn almost as bright as Loki's red eye did.

"Take her away," he ordered.

Chapter 21

Linus didn't waste any time ordering the Protectorate guards to escort me down to the prison in the bottom of the math-science building, and fifteen minutes later, I found myself in a familiar position—shackled to a stone table in the middle of the room.

My gaze moved from one side of the prison to the other, but there was nothing new to see. Glass cells stacked up three stories high around the circular room, with the interrogation table sitting in the center of the area. I craned my neck back so I could look up at the domed ceiling and the carving that was embedded in the stone directly above my head—a hand holding a set of scales. The scales had started out being perfectly balanced, but as soon as I sat down at the table, they shifted to one side, the way they always seemed to. I wondered if it was my side or the Reapers', but I had no way of knowing. Still, it made me shiver all the same.

But I wasn't alone at the table. Vic lay in his scabbard off to one side, along with all of the artifacts I'd used over the past few hours. Janus's key. Morpheus's dream-box. Ran's net. The only thing that wasn't here was Sol's candle, which I'd handed over to Linus before the guards had led me away. My mistletoe bracelet with its lone remaining laurel leaf was still wrapped around my wrist, only because no one could figure out how to get it off me.

A key screeched in the door, and I straightened up in my seat. After Inari and Sergei had shackled me to the table, they'd both left, leaving me alone with Raven, who was sitting at her usual desk, her black combat boots propped up on the wooden surface as she flipped through another one of her celebrity gossip magazines.

The door opened, and I thought Linus would come striding in and immediately put me on trial for everything I'd done.

To my surprise, Logan walked through the door instead.

I caught a glimpse of Alexei and Coach Ajax out in the hallway before the door slammed shut behind Logan. He looked at me and slowly walked in my direction. He slid into the seat across from me and raised his gaze to mine.

I could feel so many conflicting emotions surging off him. Relief that I was okay, along with all of our friends. Hurt that I hadn't told him what I was doing. Disbelief that I'd lied to him time and time again over the past few days. Worry about what his dad might to do me now for going against the Protectorate.

I felt each and every one of his emotions without even touching him, and, once again, I didn't know how to make things right between us. But I figured I might as well start with an apology.

"I'm sorry," I said. "That I didn't tell you and everyone else what I was up to. I know it was wrong. I know what I did was wrong, but I couldn't think of any other way to save my grandma."

I drew in a breath. "And I couldn't take the risk that you would tell your dad. That's why I didn't let you know what I was planning."

Hurt flashed in Logan's eyes, making them as cold as ice. "Did you really think I would do that, Gwen? That I would rat you out to my dad like that? Especially when I know how much you love your grandmother?"

"You and your dad are just starting to get back on track," I said, not exactly answering his question. "I didn't want to be the one to come in between you. Not like I did the last time he was here. You guys fought so hard for a fresh start. I didn't want to ruin that for either one of you. I didn't want to make you choose between me and your dad. That wouldn't have been fair to you."

Logan gave me a disgusted look. "So you just decided to go off by yourself? You'd think by now that you'd learn your lesson, but you never seem to, do you, Gwen?"

"And what lesson would that be?" My own voice sharpened in response to his cold tone.

He stared at me. "That people care about you, that people love you, that *I* love you, and that I would do anything to help you—anything."

"Even go against your dad?" I asked in a softer voice.

He couldn't quite meet my eyes as he shifted in his chair. He didn't answer me, but then again, perhaps that was answer enough.

I sighed. "Look, what's done is done. I did what I thought I had to in order to save my grandma. And it worked, and she's safe now. I know that doesn't make up for lying to you—for shutting you out. I know you're angry and upset and disappointed with me right now, so all I can say is that I'm sorry I lied to you, and that I hope you can forgive me someday."

He didn't say anything. And cold dread began to build in my own heart that I had lost him for good. But the worst part was that it wasn't because of anything the Reapers had done this time. No, if I lost Logan, it was because of my own decisions, my own actions, my own free will. For the first time, I began to understand why Nike and Metis were always talking about that and how powerful it could truly be.

Finally, Logan sighed, then reached over and took my hand in his. All of his emotions washed over me, even stronger than before—relief, hurt, disbelief, worry—along with more than a little anger.

But most of all, I felt his love for me.

This great, wonderful, amazing, powerful love. It was like a fire burning steadily in his heart. One that had already weathered so many storms. One that would never, ever die. One that I finally realized could survive anything—even this.

I twined my fingers through his and concentrated, sending my own emotions back to him, that warm, soft, fizzy, dizzying rush of feeling that tightened my chest every time he laughed or smiled or teased me. Every time I saw him. Every time I heard his voice. Every time I thought about him.

Every time I realized just how much I loved him.

I'm sorry. I didn't say the words this time, but I thought them, over and over again, trying to tell him that I really meant what I'd said and that I hoped this wouldn't come between us the way so many other things had.

Logan's fingers slowly curled into mine.

I don't know how long we sat at the table, holding hands and staring into each other's eyes, my psychometry letting us say so much to each other without whispering a single word. Perhaps that was the real power of my touch magic.

But eventually, I heard the scrape and turn of the key in the lock again. Logan stared at me, then slowly pulled his hand away from mine. I touched my fingers to my palm, as if that would let me hold on to the warmth of his love.

"Whatever happens, we're in this together from now on, okay, Gypsy girl?" Logan said. "Promise me that."

I looked him square in the eye. "I promise. No more secrets, no more lies, no more crazy plans." I grinned. "At least not without involving you in them."

He grinned back at me, then nodded and got up from the table.

Linus came striding into the prison, his gray Protectorate robe swirling around him. If anything, he seemed even angrier than before. His gaze flicked to Logan standing by my side, and his mouth turned down that much more.

But Linus wasn't the only one who entered the room. Sergei and Inari trailed along behind him, along with Metis and Ajax. Nickamedes appeared a moment later, trying to keep up with the others, even though using his cane slowed him down. To my surprise, Raven got up and gave him her chair, and Nickamedes sat down in it behind her desk.

Linus took the seat across from me at the interrogation table. His blue eyes met mine, giving me an up-close view of the anger still simmering in his gaze, along with something else. I thought it might have been a tiny bit of grudging respect, but whatever the emotion was, the anger quickly swallowed it up.

"Well," he said, leaning back and crossing his arms over his chest. "What do you have to say for yourself, Miss Frost?"

I shrugged. "I don't really think there is anything to say. Do you?"

Yeah, I was being a total smartass, but I couldn't help it. It was better than letting him see how worried I was about what he and the rest of the Protectorate might do to me.

He sighed and rubbed his forehead, as though it was suddenly aching. I grinned a little. Yeah, I figured I had that effect on him.

"Tell me everything that happened," he finally said. "And everything you did. I want to hear it all, from how you stole the candle out of the library to where the Reapers were hiding, to how you, your grandma, and Ms. Maddox and her niece escaped from them."

"You're just asking me?" I sniped. "Really? Aren't you going to get a Maat asp to bite me so that I have to tell the truth?"

That's what Linus had done before, when I'd been on trial for Vivian's crimes. The asp's venom was a sort of truth serum, one that forced you to be honest, or suffer the painful, deadly consequences.

He gave me a chilly look. "Unfortunately, a Maat asp is not readily available at this time or one would already be wrapped around your wrist. But rest assured that I can get one, Miss Frost, should I feel you are not being forthcoming with me."

I didn't feel like being bitten, so I did as he asked and

told him everything that had happened over the past few days. Well, almost everything. I didn't exactly tell him the truth about certain things, a fact that Linus quickly picked up on when he interrupted me halfway through my story.

"What about the artifacts?" he asked, gesturing to the items on the table. "How did you get them out of the library without setting off any alarms?"

"Janus's key was actually in one of the librarians' offices since it was due for a cleaning," I lied in a smooth voice. "So I snatched it when the offices were empty. Once I had the key, it was easy for me to open the case with Morpheus's dreambox in it, and then, the one with Sol's candle after that."

I resisted the urge to glance over at Nickamedes to see what he thought about my story. But this had been my idea—not his—and I was the one who was going to be punished for it. Not him.

Linus gave me a suspicious look, but I kept my gaze steady and level on his. He gestured with his hand, telling me to continue. So I talked some more before he interrupted me again.

"And what about Rachel Maddox and Rory Forseti?" he asked. "Why did you contact them?"

"Because they're my family," I said. "Both of them, blood or not. Besides, Rory hates the Reapers because of her parents. I knew that she'd help me, especially against Vivian and Agrona."

"And the gryphons?" he asked. "Why did you ask Ms. Maddox and her niece to get them to come here? Why did you think that the creatures would cooperate?"

"Because the gryphons had helped me before at the Eir Ruins, and using them was the only way I thought I could get my grandma away from the Reapers before they killed us both," I said. "And it turns out that I was right."

I didn't mention that Daphne and Oliver had been in the woods as well, picking off Reapers with their bows and arrows, and I didn't tell him what Daphne had told me about how all of my friends had been doing what they could to help me on the sly the past few days—including Logan.

Linus rubbed his forehead again, as if my words had only made his previous headache intensify. Yeah, I could totally see that happening. But he gestured at me with his hand again, and I finished my story.

"So you used another artifact, these silver laurel leaves, to counteract the effects of the candle?" Linus asked. "You're absolutely sure that the leaves, combined with the power of the candle, injured Loki, instead of healing him?"

I thought of how the silver flames had washed over the god, making him scream with agony. "I'm sure."

Linus stared at me, as if still debating whether or not I was telling the truth. Then, he reached into his cloak, drew out the candle, and placed it on the table.

Sol's candle looked much smaller and thinner than before, and there was only about a quarter of it left now, just as I'd thought when I'd grabbed it at the Garm gate. I leaned down and peered at the candle, but the white wax was smooth once more, and I didn't see any trace of the silver laurels glimmering in the surface. They must have all burned up when the candle had exploded into flames.

"I must say I'm rather stunned that you actually managed to bring back the artifact, along with your grandmother," Linus said. "At least you did one thing right, Miss Frost."

"I had to bring it back—because the Reapers still want it."

He stilled. So did everyone else in the prison. "What do you mean?" he asked in a sharp voice.

I gestured at the artifact. "Look at it. There's still some candle, some wax, some magic left. From what I saw at the Garm gate, it seems to take about a quarter of the candle to help someone. That's how much is left now, so that means that there's still enough power in it to heal one more person. And the Reapers will want that person to be Loki. They'll try to get the candle again. Trust me on that. It wouldn't surprise me if they tried to kidnap someone else in order to make you give it to them. They might even try to grab *you* so that the other members of the Protectorate will be forced to give it to them."

Linus sat back in his chair, a thoughtful look on his face. "I would never do that, Miss Frost. I would never *allow* that. And neither would any other members of the Protectorate. We all know what's at stake here, even if you don't."

"I think I know *exactly* what's at stake," I snapped.

He looked at me, but he didn't say anything else.

For the third time, a key sounded in the lock, and the door opened. Another man wearing a gray Protectorate robe came hurrying into the prison. He went straight over to Linus, bent down, and started whispering in his ear. I strained to listen, but I couldn't hear exactly what he was saying. Still, I could tell from the low, urgent pitch of his voice that it wasn't anything good. Had the Reapers struck again already? I would have thought that we'd have at least a few hours of peace, but I'd been wrong before.

"How reliable is the source?" Linus asked.

The man bent down next to him and started speaking again. I looked at Metis, but she shrugged at me. So did Ajax and Nickamedes. They didn't know what was going on, either.

"When?" Linus said in a sharp voice. "How long do we have?"

The man whispered a few more words into his ear before straightening back up. He waited, as though expecting Linus to give him some order.

For a moment, the head of the Protectorate looked utterly shocked, then defeated, and then finally resigned, as if something had happened that he had been both dreading and expecting for a long, long time now.

"Go," Linus said. "Prepare the others. Protocol Three. Now."

The man nodded and scurried out of the prison, shutting the door behind him. Inari and Sergei's faces both darkened at the mention of *Protocol Three*. Whatever that was, it sounded serious.

"What's the matter?" I asked. "What's going on?"

Linus's mouth flattened out into a thin line. "It seems that you were right about the Reapers still wanting the candle, Miss Frost. According to our reports, Vivian, Agrona, and a large contingent of Reapers plan to attack the academy before sunset. And Loki will be leading them. Apparently, the Reapers want the candle badly enough to make this their last stand—or ours. Because Loki is still a god, and we are not. Unless you have any other bright ideas about how to kill him?"

His words filled me with dread, worry, and fear, but I

Fifteen minutes later, I walked out of the math-science building.

Linus had already sounded the alarm to evacuate campus, and kids were running in every direction across the quad, yelling to each other, and clutching their bags and weapons. At first, there didn't seem to be any kind of method to the madness, but after a few seconds, I realized that most of the kids were running from the dorms, up the hill, across the quad, and toward the gym.

"Why the gym?" I asked Alexei, who was walking with me and still acting as my guard.

"That's where the buses are gathering that will take the students off campus," he said. "It's standard operating procedure at all of the academies in case of a large-scale Reaper attack."

"Where will everyone go?"

"To a secure location nearby," he said. "From there, some will go on home to their families, if they are close by." He paused. "Depending on what happens here, of course."

I swallowed. He didn't say the words, but I knew what he meant. Depending on whether we won—or just died.

But I pushed my unease aside, although I was aware of some of the kids stopping and staring at me before hurrying on their way. And I could feel the desperation and fear rolling off all of them—along with the faintest bit of hope.

Hope that I really was Nike's Champion. Hope that I could find a way to end this. Hope that I could finally rid everyone at our academy and all the others from the constant threat of Loki and his Reapers.

had to shake my head. Unfortunately, that was the one thing I still hadn't figured out how to do. And as long as Loki was alive, the Reapers would keep fighting and keep trying to topple the Pantheon, one warrior, one battle, one death at a time. Unless someone found a way to stop the evil god.

Unless *I* found a way to stop him—for good.

"So what happens now?" I asked, my voice sounding weak and small to my own ears. "Now you know that the Reapers are coming here? That this is . . . the end, one way or another?"

Linus sighed. "We have long planned for this, and we will immediately begin to evacuate campus, for starters. I don't want any students getting caught in the battle with the Reapers."

"What about the Protectorate? Are you going to stay? Are you going to fight?"

He squared his shoulders. "Of course we're going to stay and fight. This is the battle that we've been waiting for, that we've been planning for, that we've spent all these long years training for. We might not have thought it would have arrived this soon, but we will do our best, Miss Frost. Rest assured of that."

I nodded. Well, if there was going to be a fight, then I wanted to be a part of it—I *needed* to be a part of it. Because, like it or not, I was still the best chance the Pantheon had of stopping Loki and the Reapers once and for all.

"All right then," I said. "Are you going to leave me down here to rot or are you going to let me go and do something useful?"

Linus narrowed his eyes. "Define *useful*."

"You said the Reapers have been going around stealing artifacts, right? And you've been finding stockpiles of them at their hideouts?"

He nodded.

"Then they are sure to be carrying them with them. We need to level the playing field. Loki has enough power on his own without adding artifacts to it."

"What do you suggest?" Linus asked.

I nodded my head at Nickamedes. "Let me go back to the library with Nickamedes. Nobody knows the artifacts there like we do. If we're going to stay and fight, if this could be our last stand, our final battle, then I want to make sure we do everything we can to win it. Don't you?"

Linus stared at me for several long seconds that seemed to stretch on . . . and on . . . and on . . .

Finally, he nodded. He pulled a key out of one of the pockets of his robe, leaned forward, and undid the shackles that chained me to the table.

"You're right," he said. "Despite your other actions, we're going to need every single advantage we have if we hope to defeat Loki and the Reapers."

"Even if that means trusting me?" I asked in a wry voice, rubbing first one wrist, then the other.

The faintest of smiles curved Linus's lips. "Yes," he said. "Even if it means that."

I grinned back at him. In this case, I didn't mind being the lesser of two evils.

Chapter 22

Linus stepped out into the hallway and start out orders, and everyone rushed away to d they'd been assigned.

Logan nodded at me before he hurried ou returned the gesture, knowing I'd catch u later. Right now, we both had work to do.

I stood up and started stuffing all of the the table back into my pockets. I might stil I also belted Vic and his scabbard around my which meant the only thing left on the tal candle.

"Hey," I called out to Linus. "What do do with this?"

I pointed at the white wax. Linus stoppe sation with Ajax, came back into the prisor over to the table. He considered the candle several moments.

"Why don't you hang on to it, Miss Fro said. "As much as I hate to admit it, you' care of it so far."

I nodded and slid the candle into my je

That hope gave me the determination to swallow down my own fear and get on with things.

Alexei and I hurried across the quad and over to the Library of Antiquities. Perhaps it was my imagination, but the library seemed darker and gloomier than ever before, with the statues, balconies, and towers casting out long shadows that stretched all the way to the opposite side of the quad. Or perhaps it was because I knew death, destruction, and chaos were coming our way—and wondering how we could possibly survive.

Still, despite my rush, and everything that needed to be done before the Reapers arrived, I stopped a moment to talk to the gryphon statues on either side of the library steps.

"Today would be a good time for you guys to actually, you know, *move*," I said. "Rip right out of your stone shells and attack any Reaper who dares to set foot on the quad. I'm just saying. It would be really great if you could do that, please. Okay?"

Of course, the gryphons didn't respond, but I still patted first one statue, then the other, before heading into the library. Alexei followed me.

Nickamedes was already inside and standing behind the checkout counter, talking to Metis. Apparently, he'd already enlisted Daphne to help search through the library's electronic catalog of artifacts, because she was sitting in my usual spot behind one of the computers, furiously pounding on the keyboard, pink sparks of magic shooting out of her fingertips with every letter she hit.

She looked up as Alexei and I stepped up to the counter in front of her.

"How's it going?" I asked.

"Slowly," Daphne said, her eyes focusing back on the monitor. "I had no idea there were this many artifacts in the library. I don't know how Nickamedes keeps them all straight."

I nodded and moved around the counter, hurrying toward Metis and Nickamedes. They turned in my direction.

"Professor?" I asked. "How are things? Where is everyone?"

"As well as can be expected, so far," she replied. "Ajax is over at the gym, helping with the evacuation. So are Sergei and Inari. Oliver and Carson are back in the stacks, gathering up some of the artifacts that Daphne has already found. Rory, Rachel, and Geraldine are down at the dorms, getting Nyx and dealing with the gryphons."

One by one, she ticked our friends off on her fingers.

Metis frowned, as though she were reviewing a mental list in her head. "And I think that's everyone."

But it wasn't everyone, because she hadn't said a word about Logan. I opened my mouth to ask her about him, but Metis's phone chirped. She touched my arm, then went back into the stacks to take the call.

Nickamedes watched her go, a longing look on his face, and some sort of deeper emotion flaring in his icy eyes. I couldn't tell exactly what he was feeling, but it almost seemed as if the librarian was seeing Metis for the very first time. I wondered if I was the cause of that, if he was thinking about what I'd told him. If perhaps he was actually giving some thought to the idea of him and Metis as a couple. Provided they made it through the battle, of course.

Provided any of us did.

Nickamedes snapped out of his thoughts, whatever they might have been. A bit of a blush tinted his cheeks when he realized that I'd been watching him watch Metis, and he quickly stepped over to one of the metal carts, which was piled high with daggers, swords, and other weapons, instead of books.

"And Logan?" I asked, still staring at Nickamedes. "Where is he?"

"Right here, Gypsy girl."

I whirled around to see Logan come striding out of the stacks, several weapons bristling in his arms. He laid the weapons down on one of the study tables and started sliding them apart. He also reached into his jeans pocket and drew out the ID cards that had been in the cases with the artifacts and started arranging them side by side with the sword, spear, staff, or other weapon they belonged to.

My gaze roamed over the weapons, most of which I recognized from my time back in the stacks, dusting all of the glass cases. There were some powerful artifacts in the library, things that would make you quicker, stronger, harder to injure, faster to heal. But no doubt the Reapers had the exact same types of artifacts, and in the end, I wondered if it would all just be a draw, at least when it came to the weapons.

Logan finished laying out the ID cards. His hand closed over a long silver sword, which he held up so that I could see it.

"It says that belonged to Thanatos, the Greek god of death," he said. "Pretty cool, huh? What would you think about me using it?"

He twirled the sword around in his hand, getting familiar with the weapon the way he always did. I glanced up at the domed ceiling where the fresco was. Sure enough, I could see a silver sword glimmering through the shadows, the same sword that Logan was holding right now.

I grinned at him. "I think it looks great on you. A perfect weapon for a Spartan warrior."

He grinned back, his face creasing into a wide, happy smile. And suddenly, it felt like everything was right between us again, despite the craziness of the last few hours.

"It is an impressive blade," Vic piped up from his scabbard, which was belted around my waist. "Although not nearly as impressive as I am, obviously."

I rolled my eyes. Logan laughed.

"No, Vic," Logan said. "Nothing could *ever* be as impressive as you are."

If Vic had shoulders, they would have puffed up in pride at Logan's words. "Of course not. But I'm glad that you finally realize my brilliance, Spartan. It's been a long time coming. In fact, I think . . ."

And Vic was off, talking about how he was the ultimate sword of swords, how he was going to rip into all the Reapers that were coming to the academy, and other such nonsense. Logan and I exchanged a look, both of us amused by Vic's antics. He leaned over and squeezed my hand, and I squeezed back.

Together, still listening to Vic rant, we started sorting through the rest of the weapons on the table.

I spent the next hour in the library, working alongside my friends. Nickamedes helped Daphne search through the electronic catalog of artifacts, telling her which items might be the most useful and important. She printed off a long list, which I divided up among me, Logan, Carson, Oliver, and Alexei. The five of us went back into the stacks, retrieved all of the items, and brought them to the study tables in the center of the library.

By the time we were finished, we had enough weapons, armor, garments, and jewelry to outfit a small army.

And we had the warriors to use them.

To my surprise, not all of the kids, professors, and staff members chose to evacuate the academy. Instead, many of them came to the library, determined to fight alongside us. Folks like Kenzie Tanaka, one of Logan's Spartan friends, and his Amazon girlfriend, Talia Pizarro. Morgan McDougall, a former mean-girl Valkyrie who'd helped me out more than once over the past few months. Even Savannah Warren, the Amazon who was Logan's ex-girlfriend, showed up.

I'd put Logan in charge of the weapons, and he quickly sized up every kid and adult and gave them the blade, bow, staff, or spear he thought would best suit them. Then, the other kids clustered around the study tables, familiarizing themselves with the weapons the way I'd seen them do so many times before in gym class.

But this wasn't a class, and no one was going to pull their punches today.

Meanwhile, Raven manned the coffee cart, passing out free drinks and snacks to anyone who wanted something, although most folks just stood there, holding their food, instead of actually chowing down on it. I knew I was far too full of fear, worry, and dread to even think about eating right now.

Instead, I wondered *why.*

I wondered why the other kids and adults would risk themselves in a battle that we had a very real chance of losing, instead of evacuating to safety with the others. I asked the question out loud to Daphne, who was still typing furiously on the computer, searching for more artifacts, but she wasn't the one who answered me.

Instead, Savannah piped up from her spot at a nearby study table.

"You're not the only one who's lost people to the Reapers," Savannah said in a quiet voice, twirling a staff around and around in her hands. "This is our chance to finally confront the Reapers who took away the people we love."

From what Daphne had once told me, most of Savannah's family had been murdered by Reapers. I winced, thinking that I'd taken Logan away from her too, but she came over and laid a hand on my arm, as if she knew exactly what I was thinking.

"It's okay, Gwen," Savannah said, her green eyes serious. "I've moved on. In fact, I'm happier than I've ever been."

She turned and smiled at a Viking I recognized from my English-lit class, one who gave her an adoring look in return. When he realized that we were both watching him, he blushed, ducked his head, and went back to hefting the battle-axe in his hand.

"His name is Doug," she said, answering my silent questions. "Apparently, he'd been into me for a while, and wanted to ask me out, but I was with Logan, so he thought he didn't have a chance. Once I wasn't, well, you know what happened. He's great."

"I'm happy that you're happy," I said. "I really mean it."

Savannah nodded. "I know you do. And I'm happy for you guys too."

She smiled at me, then went back over to her boyfriend. The two of them kissed and started working with their weapons again.

Another hour passed, and we were still grabbing artifacts from every part of the library and passing them out to whoever wanted one.

Finally, though, we stripped the library bare, everyone had all the weapons and artifacts they could wear and carry, and there wasn't anything else left to do but wait. I was sitting at a table with Rory, Rachel, and Grandma Frost. Nyx was back in the office complex with Nickamedes, where she would be safe. My other friends were roaming around the library.

We hadn't said much, but I was glad they were here with me. It made me feel better about things, like we might actually have a chance to win the looming battle after all.

But it wasn't long before I realized that all the kids and even some of the adults were staring at and whispering about me, the way they always did.

"The Gypsy girl will get us through this . . ."

"She won't let the Reapers win . . ."

"Surely, she has to have *some* sort of plan . . ."

That last hushed comment made me grimace. Right now, the only plan I had was to try to kill as many Reapers as I could and not die myself. Other than that, well, I was open to suggestions. But I couldn't tell any of them that. They were already frightened enough. We all were.

"You should go talk to them," Rory said, hearing the same comments and whispers.

I looked at her. "Why? What good would that do? They all know what we're up against. They don't need me to spell it out for them again. Or to remind them how we're probably going to lose. And die."

She shrugged. "Because you're their hero, and that's what heroes do."

I shook my head. "I'm nobody's hero. Trust me on that. I'm just a girl who is always in the wrong place at the wrong time."

"Or maybe it's the right place at the right time," Rachel suggested. "You've come this far, Gwen. I didn't know your mom, and I only met your dad a few times, but I think they'd both be very proud of you, for fighting against the Reapers the way you have."

I shifted in my chair, uncomfortable with her words. I'd never really known my dad, Tyr, so I had no idea what he would or wouldn't think, but I couldn't help but wonder whether or not my mom would be proud of me. She'd been Nike's Champion before me, and she'd done a lot of good, including keeping the Helheim Dagger hidden from the Reapers for years. But she'd also stopped being Nike's Champion, and she'd withdrawn from the mythological world. My mom hadn't wanted me to be a part of it, but I'd been sucked into it anyway.

"Rachel's right," Grandma Frost chimed in. "Grace would be so proud of you, pumpkin. And Rory's right too. You should go talk to your friends. Let them know that you're going to do the best you can for them. It'll help. I know it will."

I looked at her, wondering if she was getting another vision of the future, maybe even of *my* future, but her violet eyes were clear and firmly focused on me. So I nodded, got up, and did what she and Rory had suggested.

I went from one table to the next, talking to all of the kids in turn, and even a few of the adults, asking how they were, joking about how we were all getting out of classes and homework assignments today, and making other small talk. Just trying to lighten the mood and get everyone to take a collective breath before the Reapers arrived. I didn't know that it helped, but at least it took everyone's minds off the coming battle for a few minutes, including mine.

But all too soon, I'd made my rounds, and I found myself standing behind the checkout counter, looking out over the library. In some ways, it seemed like a typical evening. Students sitting at the study tables or clustered around the coffee cart. The soft murmurs of conversations. The constant *squeak-squeak-squeak* of sneakers on the marble floor. The faint, musty smell of the books permeating everything.

But in so many other ways, it was completely different. All of the kids with their weapons, fingering the sharp edges of the blades. Everyone glancing nervously toward the closed doors, as if they expected the Reapers to storm inside at any second. Everyone flinching, jumping, and jerking at every little sound, no matter how small or innocent it was.

There was nothing we could do but wait. So I went over to another table, where Daphne was sitting with Carson. They'd been my very first friends at Mythos, and it felt right, sitting with them here, now, at what could be the end—of everything.

Daphne was plucking the golden strings on her onyx

bow over and over again, listening to the faint, *thwang*y chimes they made, almost as if they were some sort of harp that she was playing. Meanwhile, Carson was studying his own artifact, the Horn of Roland, which looked like a small, handheld tuba. He kept turning it over and over in his hands, peering at the ivory surface, and studying the onyx keys, as though he was using his Celt warrior bard instincts to try to figure out how to get it to work.

I sat down with them, but none of us spoke. There was nothing left to say.

Logan, Oliver, and Alexei had been practicing with their weapons, but they came over to the table too. Logan sat down beside me and threaded his fingers through mine. He put his arm around me, and I leaned my head on his shoulder.

We'd only been sitting like that for about five minutes when Metis stepped out of the office complex and walked over to us, her phone in her hand. Nickamedes appeared in the door of the office complex, cradling Nyx in the crook of his arm. Everyone slowly hushed as Metis approached me.

She stopped and touched my shoulder. "I just got off the phone with Linus. The guards down by the main gate have spotted the Reapers. They're here, and Loki is leading them, along with Agrona and Vivian."

I nodded and got to my feet. Everyone turned to stare at me. I stared out over the faces, so many of them strangers to me, kids and professors and staff members I'd only seen from a distance. One by one, I looked at them, then focused my attention on the people who were so very familiar—my friends, my family, all the people I loved.

Logan. Daphne. Carson. Oliver. Alexei. Metis. Nick-amedes. Grandma Frost. Rory. Rachel. Nyx. Vic.

I wondered if this would be the last time I ever saw them, but I couldn't let myself think about that right now. For a moment, I focused on my breathing—in and out, in and out—letting each inhalation and exhalation ground me and prepare me for what was to come.

"It's time," I finally said.

Chapter 23

Everyone grabbed their weapons and started trickling outside, except for a few folks like Grandma Frost, who were staying here to protect the library from any Reapers who might try to sneak inside. Those armed with bows and arrows, including Rory and Rachel, climbed to the upper levels of the library to head out onto the balconies and serve as archers from those vantage points.

I also stayed behind to talk with Nickamedes. He put Nyx down on a nearby table and leaned on his cane. The battle hadn't even begun yet, but he already looked tired, which told me how much he needed what I was about to give him.

I grabbed what was left of Sol's candle out of my jeans pocket and put it down on the table where Nyx was. She came over and started sniffing it out of curiosity. Then, I reached down, pushed up my sweater sleeve, and plucked the last silver laurel leaf off the mistletoe bracelet around my wrist. I held it out to him.

"What's this?" he asked, staring at the leaf, which glinted underneath the library lights.

"It's for you. I saved the last one for you, so you can

use it to heal your legs. You should hold on to the candle too."

Nickamedes shook his head. "You don't have to do that, Gwendolyn. It's not your fault that I was poisoned, and it's not your fault that my legs haven't fully recovered."

"Yes, it is," I insisted. "And there's a very real chance I won't make it through the battle today. So I want you to have this. Just in case."

Nickamedes stared at me. "You should keep it. You need it more than I do."

"I can't see the future like Grandma Frost, but whatever happens today, this is the end for me. But it doesn't have to be for you. Besides, if we fail, if *I* fail, someone will have to pick up the pieces. Someone will have to go on, will have to keep fighting the Reapers for as long as possible, and I know that someone is you."

He opened his mouth like he wanted to argue with me, but he clamped his lips shut. I held out the leaf again, and he finally, reluctantly, took it.

"All right," he grumbled. "But I'm just holding on to it for you. That's all."

He slipped the leaf into his pants pocket. Nickamedes stared at me, his blue eyes bright. Then, he did something I never imagined he would do in a million years. He stepped forward, reached out, and hugged me tight with one arm.

"If I am ever lucky enough to have a daughter, I hope that she's just like you, Gwendolyn," he whispered.

Emotion clogged my throat, and I nodded and tried to blink back the tears from my eyes. That was one of the nicest things anyone had ever said to me.

"And you've been more of a dad to me than anyone else ever has," I whispered back.

He hugged me even tighter.

Slowly, I drew back, and Nickamedes and I both dropped our eyes, not quite looking at each other.

Nyx let out a soft whine from her position on the table, and I went over and rubbed her ears between my fingers, the way I had a hundred times before. She gave a contented sigh, and I let my emotions flow into her, trying to show her how much I loved her. Her tail thumped against my side in response, and I petted her one final time before forcing myself to step away.

"Keep an eye on Nyx for me, okay?"

"Don't you worry, Gwendolyn," Nickamedes said, straightening up as much as he could. "I'll put her in my office. I will protect her with my life."

I nodded. I knew he would.

There was nothing left for me to do but draw Vic out of his scabbard. He'd been quiet the last few hours, resting up for what was to come. I held the sword up so that we were eyes-to-eye.

"Are you ready for this?" I asked.

His mouth split into a wide grin, and his purplish eye gleamed with anticipation. "I was *made* for this, Gwen. And you too. You'll see. We'll come through this battle just fine. With dead Reapers all around! And Loki cringing at our feet!"

The sword went off on another one of his rants. I let his loud, quick, excited words wash over me, but I kept staring at him, memorizing his features, in case this was the last time that we ever went into battle together.

"Well, then," I said, when he finally wound down. "I guess we should get on with things then."

I saluted Nickamedes and Nyx with Vic, then hurried outside to join the others.

* * *

I left the library and headed down the main steps, stopping at the two gryphon statues. I wasn't the only one. Carson was also there, crouched down beside them, still rubbing his hands over the Horn of Roland. He kept glancing at the horn, then at the statues, as though the two were somehow connected.

Daphne was right beside him, her bow, Sigyn's bow, out and ready. If things went badly, she was to head up to one of the balconies and cover us while we retreated back into the library, something I thought was bound to happen, given that Loki was leading the attack. I didn't know what magic the Protectorate might have, but how was it supposed to stop a god? I didn't know, but I had a bad feeling that I was going to find out.

Logan was waiting for me out on the quad, so I headed in his direction. He was carrying the Sword of Thanatos that he'd shown me before and had thrown a gray Protectorate robe on over his clothes for extra warmth. So had all the other students. I was the only one who wasn't wearing one, but my purple plaid jacket was thick enough. Besides, we'd be fighting soon enough, and then no one's clothes would matter. Nothing would but surviving.

All around the quad, the other kids and adults were getting into defensive positions, with archers stationed on the balconies of the buildings and the other warriors in small groups below so they could watch each other's backs. The Reapers might come in at the edge of campus, but I wouldn't put it past them to have Black rocs fly over to the quad and drop some warriors off so they could attack us from multiple sides at once—

A large shadow zoomed over the quad, and my breath caught in my throat, thinking that the Reapers were already here. My head snapped up, and I realized that the leader of the gryphons had landed on top of one of the library towers. And he wasn't the only one up there. The baby was there too, along with the third gryphon I'd seen before, and several more besides that. They must have been the ones that Rory had said had been staying in the park near my grandma's house.

I waved, and the leader let out a loud *screech*. One by one, all of the gryphons joined in his fierce battle cry. My heart lifted, and I knew that they would fight with us to the end. The Eir gryphons hated the Reapers and how they enslaved gryphons, Black rocs, Nemean wolves, and other creatures.

"Come on," Logan said when the sound of the gryphons' cries had faded away. "My dad's down by the front gate."

I nodded, and we headed toward the far edge of the quad. Once again, I was aware of everyone staring and whispering about me. So I raised my head and tried to look as strong and confident as possible, although my legs trembled, and my knees threatened to buckle with every step I took.

As we walked down the hill to the lower quad, we passed more and more Protectorate guards, each one wearing a gray robe and carrying at least one sword. The guards were going to be the first lines of defense, with the students and adults on the quad serving as backup and the library being our final fallback point.

We found Linus, Sergei, Inari, Alexei, and Oliver standing behind a cluster of maple trees about fifty feet away from the main gate. Like everyone else, they all wore gray robes and were carrying swords. Two swords, in Alexei's case, since he had the twin Swords of Ruslan clutched in his hands.

"What's happening?" I asked.

Linus jerked his head at the gate. "Nothing at the moment, but our sources in Cypress Mountain say they've seen a multitude of SUVs gathering in some of the parking lots and that several Black rocs carrying riders have been spotted overhead."

My head snapped back as I peered up into the sky, but I didn't see any of the creatures flapping their wings and zooming through the air above. Perhaps the gryphons could at least keep the rocs and their riders away from the academy long enough to give us a fighting chance.

"You two should get back up to the main quad," Linus said. "Where it's safer."

I looked at Logan, and we both shook our heads.

"This is our fight too, Dad," Logan said.

"He's right," I said.

I didn't add what we were all thinking—that I was supposed to be the one to kill Loki. To do that, I had to get close to the god, which meant being at the front of the fight.

"Well, at least get out of sight then," Linus said. "For now. Please."

This time, Logan and I did as he asked, sliding behind the stand of maples and out of view of anyone who might be looking through the main gate. Alexei and Oliver moved to join us, the two of them flanking me.

Then, I hunkered down beside my friends and waited for Loki and the Reapers to attack.

Chapter 24

Someone had grabbed a pair of binoculars from somewhere, and we all took turns peering through them and then passing them along to the next person. Finally, it was my turn. I focused the lenses on the gate and the sphinxes that were perched on either side of it.

The sphinxes' features were sharper than I ever remembered them being before, so sharp, so real, so lifelike that I thought I could almost see their hearts beating in their stone chests—

Caw-caw-caw.

Caw-caw-caw.

Caw-caw-caw.

I froze, my hands tightening around the lenses, before slowly lowering them.

There was no mistaking the high, eerie cries of the Black rocs, and a few seconds later, the birds came into view, dozens of them, all with at least two Reapers on their broad backs. One by one, the birds spiraled down from the sky and landed in the middle of the street on the far side of the academy wall.

And they weren't alone.

In the distance, I heard the rumble and screech of vehicles heading our way. A minute later, it looked like all of the cars in Cypress Mountain were parked outside the gate.

The Reapers weren't hiding in the shadows anymore—not today.

"Here they come," Linus said. "Everyone, get ready."

Every single warrior checked his or her sword and other weapons one more time. I tightened my grip on Vic and handed the binoculars over to Inari, who slid them into one of the pockets in his cloak. Then, we all looked toward the gate.

One of the rocs hopped forward, and through the iron bars, I could see the two riders on its back—Vivian and Loki.

They were both wearing black Reaper robes, and Vivian had Lucretia strapped to her waist. Loki wasn't carrying a weapon, but then again, he didn't need one.

Vivian slid off the roc first, then turned to help Loki. Agrona got off another roc and moved to aid her protégé. It took them longer than I thought it would to unbuckle the god from the roc's harness and get him on the ground. It took Loki longer still to shuffle toward the gate.

Loki paused outside the gate and peered in between the bars. Somehow, I could have sworn he was staring straight at me, despite the distance that separated us.

And I realized just how much havoc the silver laurel leaves had wreaked on him.

Before, one side of the god's face had still been beautiful, perfect, normal even.

Not anymore.

It was as though the smushed, burned, melted look of one half of his face had infected the other. Now, all of his features were red, raw, and waxy-looking. All of his blond hair had fallen out, leaving only a few black and crimson strands behind to cling to his scalp, which was as red, mottled, and melted as the rest of his features.

That was bad enough, but it was his eye that caught my attention. The once-blue orb was now as red as his other one, both of them burning, burning bright, as though hot coals were embedded in the sockets instead of eyes. My stomach dropped down and flipped over at the sight.

Loki managed to straighten up to his full height, but his body seemed much thinner and frailer than before, and he wavered slightly on his feet, as if his muscles were constantly being pulled in a dozen different directions at once, and he had a hard time maintaining his balance. A faint *snap-snap-snap* sounded with every move he made, every breath he took, as though his bones were constantly cracking, popping, and trying to settle back to where they were supposed to go.

It was an awful sound, but one that filled me with satisfaction all the same. Because I'd hurt him—badly. And that made me *happy*. Maybe it was wrong, but I wanted him to suffer. I wanted to wound him as much as he and the Reapers had hurt me and the rest of my friends.

But he was still Loki, still a god, still far more powerful than any of us could possibly imagine. And he seemed ready to prove that to everyone—especially me.

Loki took a few more steps toward the gate. He paused, then looked up at the stone sphinxes positioned on top of the wall on either side. Loki stepped forward and put a hand on one of the iron bars.

The sphinxes immediately sprang to life.

One second, the creatures were just statues, just solid stone, still and frozen in place. The next, they'd torn themselves free from the rest of the wall, jumped up onto their feet, and were glaring down at Loki, low growls rumbling out of their throats in a clear warning for him to step back or else.

A shocked gasp escaped my lips. Ever since I'd come to Mythos, I'd heard rumors that there was some sort of protective power attached to the sphinxes, some sort of magic mumbo jumbo that would make them actually come to life if there was ever a major Reaper attack. It looked like those weren't just rumors after all.

But it didn't matter.

Loki waved his hand, as though he were swatting away a bothersome fly. A surge of power rippled off him, so sharp and intense that I could almost see the waves cutting through the air. A second later, that power slammed into the sphinxes, crumbling them to dust.

A second shocked gasp escaped my lips. The statues were gone. Just like that. The first wave of defense had fallen and was now nothing more than stone chips flying off the walls.

Loki reached up and dusted a few bits of the sphinxes that had landed on him off his shoulders. Then, he stepped forward and wrapped both hands around the gate.

And I watched as the metal began to bubble, burn, and melt away.

I didn't know exactly what sort of magic Loki had, but it caused the iron bars to disintegrate like they were made out of paper instead of solid metal. Once that was done, Loki slowly moved out of the way, and the first wave of Reapers surged through the opening, their swords up and ready to attack.

"Here we go," Linus said, signaling the other members of the Protectorate.

They all gave him grim nods, then left their spots in the shadows and behind the trees and ran toward the Reapers. For their part, the Reapers picked up their pace and let out wild, loud cries.

The battle had finally begun.

Logan, Alexei, Oliver, and I held our positions behind the trees and watched the fight unfold in front of us.

Fueled by the ease with which they'd infiltrated campus, the Reapers crashed into the Protectorate guards, almost overwhelming them with that first brutal charge. But Linus managed to regroup the warriors, and they held the Reapers at bay, although the clash and clang of swords ripped through the air.

I watched while Sergei slammed his two swords into first one Reaper, then another, before whirling toward a third enemy, as though the Bogatyr were doing an elegant dance instead of fighting for his life.

"We should be out there helping them," I muttered, my hand tightening around Vic's hilt. "Not hiding here in the shadows."

"You said it, sister," Vic piped up, his mouth moving underneath my palm.

"Linus told us to stay back," Alexei said. "We want to take out as many of them down here as we can. We can't afford to let Reapers overrun us on the main quad. The more of them we kill down here, the safer everyone up there will be."

I nodded. I knew that. Really, I did, but it was still hard to crouch down, wait, and not be in the middle of the fight.

So we watched while the Reapers and the Protectorate guards cut into each other. My eyes flicked from one of the warriors to the next, but I didn't see Vivian or Agrona anywhere in the fray. They must be hanging back and protecting Loki. No doubt he wanted the warriors to clear a path before he expended any more of his energy trying to kill us.

And slowly, it started to happen.

One of the Protectorate guards fell under a Reaper's slashing sword. Then another. Then another. Soon, it was all the guards could do to keep the Reapers from advancing. And then, one of the Reapers broke through the ranks of the Protectorate and started running up the cobblestone path toward the main quad.

Logan, Alexei, Oliver, and I all checked our weapons for the last time. It was up to us to stop the Reapers now.

"Wait," Logan murmured, his eyes locked onto the Reaper racing toward us. "Wait."

In the distance, another Reaper broke through the Protectorate line and started hurrying this way. Then another one. Then another one, until there were half a dozen Reapers headed in our direction.

"Hold your position," Logan murmured again, his icy eyes almost glowing with anticipation of the battle to come. "A few more seconds . . . they're almost here . . . now!"

The four of us leaped out from our hiding spot and attacked the Reapers. Alexei engaged the first two, the twin Swords of Ruslan whipping back and forth from one enemy to the next, just like his dad was doing with his own swords down at the gate. Logan punched one Reaper in the face, making the warrior stagger back, before whirling around and burying his sword in the chest of the next closest Reaper. Oliver engaged the one Logan had punched, ramming his sword into that man's stomach. And that was all that I saw before one of the warriors rushed at me, and I stepped up to battle him.

Clash-clash-clang!
Clash-clash-clang!
Clash-clash-clang!

I parried each one of the Reaper's blows before slamming Vic into the warrior's chest. He collapsed to the ground, but I barely had time to raise my sword again before another Reaper stepped up to take his place.

Back and forth and around and around, my friends and I fought the Reapers. Every time I thought we were finally making some headway, finally turning the tide in our favor, another wave of Reapers would surge toward us. They just kept coming and coming, pouring through the gate and even climbing over the stone wall and dropping down to this side.

And I realized we were going to lose this round.

There were too many of them, and we were too spread out, trying to keep them contained here by the gate. I whipped first one way, then the other, lashing out with Vic over and over again, bringing down Reaper after Reaper after Reaper, but it wasn't enough. Around me, Logan, Alexei, and Oliver were fighting just as furiously, and it was all the four of us could do not to get separated.

Eventually, the Protectorate guards got pushed back to our position, and then we all started giving ground, inch by inch, foot by foot. And still, the Reapers kept

coming. To make matters worse, the Black rocs had finally hopped over the stone wall, and the enormous
birds added to the chaos of the fight, stabbing their
beaks at any members of the Protectorate who got close
to them. One of the guards fell down screaming, clutching at the ugly wound a roc had opened up in his gut.

"To the quad!" Linus finally yelled out, wounding
the Reaper in front of him and backpedaling at the same
time. "Fall back to the quad!"

And so we turned and began our first retreat of the
fight.

Chapter 25

We raced up the hill to the main quad. The Reapers were right behind us, and I could hear their footsteps smashing against the stone paths, and their cruel shouts cutting through the air, chasing after us like a pack of Fenrir wolves nipping at our heels.

"Death to the Pantheon!"

"Take out the Protectorate guards first! Then whoever's left!"

"Kill everyone you can!"

And on and on it went. I gritted my teeth and tried to shut the shouts out of my mind, but I couldn't. I'd been in battles before, but nothing like this.

Nothing so horrible.

Still, I made myself run faster and pump my legs that much harder as I struggled up the hill. Of all the times I'd trudged up that slope, it never seemed as steep as it did right now. Every breath came in a painful rasp, and the cold winter air seemed to burn my lungs worse than ever before.

"Come on, Gwen!" Alexei shouted beside me. "Hurry! They're right behind us!"

I didn't dare look back, but I sucked down another

breath and finally surged up over the top of the hill. The quad stretched out before me, seemingly deserted, but I knew that the other guards, students, and adults were holding their positions, waiting for the Reapers to step into the middle of the area before flanking the warriors on all sides.

I headed for the library steps, where Carson was still crouched down beside the gryphons, his staff in one hand and the Horn of Roland in the other. I spotted Rory and Rachel on one of the second-floor library balconies, with Daphne right beside them. The Valkyrie looked as cool and calm as ever, already taking aim with her onyx bow and golden arrow, waiting for a Reaper to get close enough for her to fire.

I reached the library steps and whirled back around, already raising my sword to give the signal to the archers above.

"Now!" I screamed.

A hail of arrows darkened the air above my head before slowly starting their inevitable, downward arcs. The arrows slammed into the first wave of Reapers that had crested the hill and stormed into the quad, knocking them back. Screams and shouts cut through the air, and the archers sent another volley of arrows at the second wave of warriors. But I could already tell it wouldn't be enough. There were too many Reapers, and we didn't have enough archers to stop them all, even though they were shooting as fast as they could.

Caw-caw-caw.

Caw-caw-caw.

Caw-caw-caw.

And just when I thought things couldn't get any worse, the Black rocs finally got involved in the fight.

They appeared in the sky like thunderous storm clouds, hovering over the quad for several seconds before abruptly dive-bombing, just as I'd feared they would. The Reapers riding them made the rocs target the archers on the towers and balconies, and the creatures raked out with their talons, catching more than one archer across the chest and making them fall from the balconies to their deaths on the ground below.

The sound of cracking bones was horribly loud.

"Take out the rocs!" Logan screamed, waving his hand at the archers above our heads. "Before they kill you all!"

That's what Daphne, Rory, Rachel, and the other archers were trying to do, but there were simply too many rocs and not enough of them. Daphne, in particular, sent arrow after arrow after arrow at the creatures. Every projectile she fired was true, but she couldn't launch the arrows fast enough, even though they were leaving her bow in a golden blur, one after another—

Daphne sent three arrows straight into three different rocs.

I blinked, wondering if I was only imagining things. But she reached back, drew three more arrows out of the quiver strapped to her back, and sent them into three more rocs, all of which plummeted to the ground, taking their riders down with them.

For a moment, Daphne looked as startled as I did. She stared down at her weapon, Sigyn's bow, the one she'd had ever since the Reaper attack at the Crius Coliseum, the one that had kept reappearing in her room no matter how many times she gave the weapon back to Metis. Then, she grinned, gave me a thumbs-up, and reached back for three more arrows.

Nike had once told me that Daphne would know what to do with the bow when the time was right. It looked like Daphne had finally figured out what her artifact did, and she put it to deadly use.

But more and more rocs still swooped over the quad. I heard a loud screech and realized that one of the creatures was heading for me, its talons outstretched as it aimed straight for my throat. I threw my hand up, trying to block the attack, although I knew how useless my hand was against the creature's sharp claws—

A bronze blur moved in front of me, slamming into the roc and driving the bird back. The leader of the gryphons landed on the quad, threw back his head, and let out a loud screech. The rest of the gryphons rose up from where they'd been hiding and launched themselves off the tops of the towers and balconies, clashing with the rocs in midair. Caws and screeches and spits and hisses tore through the quad above my head as the two sets of creatures slashed out at each other with their beaks and talons, and their wings crashed together, sending them all spinning down to the ground.

But with the gryphons involved in the fight, the archers got some much-needed breathing room and focused their arrows back on the Reapers. Wave after wave of warriors flooded the quad, their boots flattening the grass, their bare faces free of masks, their lips curved into evil grins, their black robes swirling out around them like clouds of deadly fog slowly spreading and infecting everything they touched.

Still, as I waited for the Reapers to reach my position, I looked past the ones rushing toward me, searching for Vivian, Agrona, and most important, Loki.

And I finally saw them.

Vivian and Agrona came striding onto the quad in the middle of the waves of Reapers. The two of them flanked Loki, who seemed to float rather than actually walk across the grass. Whatever the laurels had done to him, he wasn't showing any visible effects from it now. If I hadn't seen how completely ruined his face was, I might have thought the laurels hadn't injured him at all.

And then the Reapers reached the library steps, and I was in the thick of things once more.

Clash-clash-clang!
Clash-clash-clang!
Clash-clash-clang!

I cut down every Reaper who came close to me. Logan, Oliver, and Alexei did the same, and I got glimpses of my other friends fighting farther out in the quad. Kenzie stabbing at Reapers with a spear, with Talia slashing her sword across another warrior's chest. Savannah twirling her staff from one hand to the other before smacking the heavy wood into the Reaper in front of her. Then Doug, her Viking boyfriend, stepping in to deliver the killing blow with his battle-axe, protecting her as much as he could. Morgan alternating between sending cross-bow bolts into Reapers, then stabbing them with the dagger she clutched in her other hand.

Linus, Sergei, Inari, and Ajax were also fighting together in the middle of the quad, with Reapers all around them. And I saw Professor Metis heading in their direction, her staff in her hands, whipping it back and forth and clearing a path to Linus and the others.

I blinked again. I'd never really thought too much about what kind of warrior Metis was, but she had to be an Amazon to move that quickly. One second, she was fifty feet away from Linus and the others. The next, she was right beside them, taking some of the pressure off their flank. Soon, the five of them were fighting back-to-back, creating a ring of death in the middle of the Reapers.

But it still wasn't going to be enough to save us.

Because even more Reapers streamed into the quad behind Loki, Vivian, and Agrona, and I could tell we were in danger of being overrun—and then executed.

"We have to push them back!" Logan screamed. "We have to get them away from Dad and the others!"

I knew that as well as he did, but I didn't see how we could make it happen. Linus and the others were near the center of the quad, and we'd have to kill half the Reapers simply to get to them. Not to mention the fact that Vivian and Agrona were just standing by, as if waiting for Loki to do something spectacularly deadly.

I didn't know if the god had that kind of magic, but it wouldn't surprise me. Because it would be just our luck if we managed to take out all of the Reapers only to fall to Loki instead. I wondered if he could wave his hand and reduce us all to dust like he had the stone sphinxes down by the main gate. I shivered at the thought.

A sharp, sudden, clattering sound caught my attention, and I whipped my head to the right to discover that Carson had dropped his staff, and not because he was fighting and a Reaper had knocked it out of his grasp. No, the band geek seemed to have let go of the weapon of his own free will. To my surprise, Carson stepped forward, clutching the Horn of Roland in both hands, as though it were some sort of shield that would protect him from the Reapers and all of their slashing swords.

"Carson?!" I yelled, burying Vic in the chest of another Reaper before shoving the warrior away. "What are you doing?!"

"I'm not really sure," he mumbled. "I feel . . . weird."

He looked at me, and I realized that his eyes had darkened to an absolute black and had the same odd sheen that the bits of onyx on his horn did. The strange, unrelenting color of his eyes seemed to bleed into his glasses, making it look like the lenses were completely black and yet somehow glowing faintly at the same time.

Carson turned away from me and walked farther out into the quad, into the very heart of the battle. I cursed and went after him. I had to protect Carson. He was going to get himself killed, and Daphne would never forgive me if that happened.

"Gwen!" I heard Logan scream behind me. "Watch out!"

I whirled around. Too late, I saw the Reaper who had snuck up on my blind side. I raised my sword, blocking the brutal blow that would have split my skull open, but the Reaper kicked out with his foot, catching me in the leg and making me stumble to the ground. Still on my knees, I lifted Vic, desperately trying to get him into position to counter the deadly blow that was coming my way—

CLASH!

Suddenly, Logan was there, darting in between me and the Reaper, and saving my life the way he had so many times before.

Logan banged his weapon against the Reaper's, taking the blow meant for me, before spinning around and attacking the other warrior. The Sword of Thanatos gleamed a ghostly silver in his hand, the edges seeming to blur, as though the entire weapon were made out of mist. The sword didn't seem to cut into the Reaper so much as it passed right through him, like a cloud of death. That's what it was in Logan's hand.

The Reaper collapsed without a sound, and Logan spun the sword around in his hand. I blinked, and the illusion was gone, the weapon solid metal again.

Logan stretched out a hand and helped me to my feet. "You okay?"

I nodded. "Thanks to you—again."

He grinned. "Anytime."

"Carson!" Daphne shouted from the library balcony.

A golden arrow zipped past us and buried itself in the back of a Reaper who'd been about to bring his sword down on top of Carson's head. But the band geek walked on, completely unconcerned by the bloody chaos raging around him. His steps were slow and measured, and I had a feeling that if I could see his face, his features would be completely slack and blank. The Horn of Roland must have turned him into some sort of zombie, like the Bowl of Tears had once done to Morgan. That's why Carson was walking into the middle of the fight instead of staying with me and my friends. I didn't know what sort of power the artifact had, but it was obvious that it had taken control of Carson.

Logan looked at me and nodded, his blue eyes blazing with the same determination that I felt. I gripped Vic a little tighter and nodded back. Now, the two of us had to make sure that Carson lived long enough to use his artifact.

Together, Logan and I hurried after the band geek, trying to keep close enough to protect him. He was like a calm little bunny hopping into a den of angry, hungry lions. The Reapers realized that Carson didn't have a weapon and that he wasn't fighting back, and they all scrambled to try to take down such an easy target.

"Faster, Gwen, faster!" Vic shouted, his mouth moving underneath my palm. "You can't let the Reapers get in between the two of you or the Celt is dead!"

"Don't you think I know that?" I yelled back at the sword, although I had no idea if he or Logan could hear me over the sounds of the fight.

A Reaper stepped in front of me, but I slashed Vic across his chest, shoved the other warrior out of the way, and hurried after Carson.

Ducking and dodging, sidestepping and leaping, whirling and twirling, Logan and I managed to keep up with the band geek as he moved from the library steps all the way over to the center of the quad.

Carson finally stopped, and I almost slammed into his back. Another Reaper came at us, but before he could attack, Daphne put an arrow into his chest. The Reaper crashed to a stop at our feet. But Carson continued to stand there, staring down at the horn in his hands as if nothing else mattered. I bit my lip. I wanted nothing more than to reach out and shake him, but I didn't want to ruin his concentration . . . or whatever he was doing.

The Celt will know what to do with the horn when the time comes, Nike's voice whispered in my mind. That's what the goddess had said to me when I'd questioned her about why my friends had the artifacts they did.

I cut down another Reaper charging at us. Logan did the same. Whatever it was, I hoped that Carson figured it out soon. Otherwise, the three of us were dead.

Another Reaper fell at my feet, thanks to Daphne and her arrows, and I looked over at the far edge of the quad, where Vivian, Agrona, and Loki were still standing, out of the main part of the fight. Vivian spotted me, then her golden gaze flicked to Carson. She frowned and pointed us out to Agrona. Loki followed Vivian's finger, but instead of staring at me with hate in his eyes as usual, his angry gaze locked onto Carson instead. His eyes bulged in surprise, then his face mottled with red rage.

"Kill him!" Loki screamed at the Reapers. "Don't let him blow that horn—"

But it was too late. Carson slowly brought the Horn of Roland up to his lips, closed his eyes, and started to play.

Chapter 26

One sweet, simple note drifted out of the horn, so soft that I thought I had only imagined it at first. Carson opened his eyes, drew back, and frowned, staring at the horn as if he was confused, as if it hadn't done what he'd thought it would or what he wanted it to.

"Now would be a great time for you to use your music mojo to get us out of this!" I yelled at him, even as I battled a Reaper who was creeping up on his blind side.

"Gwen's right!" Logan shouted, fighting off another Reaper.

Carson was a Celt, sort of like a warrior bard, and he could play practically any instrument he picked up. I hoped he found a way to make the horn do whatever it was supposed to do before the Reapers overwhelmed us—

"Don't worry, guys," he said, his voice soft and almost dreamy-sounding. "I think I've got it now."

Carson nodded, and that strange black gleam in his eyes brightened, as if he'd finally figured out some sort of great secret about the horn.

More and more Reapers started heading in our direction, urged on by Loki's continued screams about killing Carson. I watched in horror as one Reaper broke away from the other warrior he was fighting and raced in our direction. Then another one, then five more, then ten more, until it seemed as if every single Reaper on the quad was running toward us with the sole intention of killing Carson where he stood. Even as Logan and I stepped in front of him, I knew we wouldn't be able to stop the Reapers from swarming over us and taking him out.

"Carson!" I screamed. "Play the horn! Now!"

"Okay," he said in that same soft, dreamy voice. "I can do that."

He brought the horn to his lips. Once again, a single, sweet note sounded, but the Reapers kept coming. Daphne dropped three more of them with her arrows, sending the projectiles into three different targets at once. But more and more Reapers rushed forward to take their places.

"Carson!" I screamed again, slashing Vic back and forth as fast as I could, lashing out at every single warrior I could reach, with Logan doing the same thing beside me. "Carson!"

Just when I thought the Reapers were going to overrun us, Carson drew in another breath and began to play in earnest. Note after note erupted from the horn, each one stronger and sharper than the last. Carson blew and blew on the horn, his fingers pressing into the onyx keys as though it were a regular tuba he was playing instead of a powerful artifact.

At first, the music didn't seem to have any effect. The Reapers kept coming and coming, and Logan and I kept fighting them off, one after another, even though my arms ached from the effort of holding on to Vic and driving the sword's blade into my enemies over and over again. Meanwhile, Daphne kept shooting arrows, and between the three of us, we managed to keep Carson safe.

But then, through the music, I heard another sound.

Crack.

Crack-crack.

Crack.

At first, I thought I was just imagining the sounds through the yells, shouts, and screams of the fight. Then, I heard it again . . . and again . . . and again . . .

Crack.

Crack-crack.

Crack.

Each successive *crack* sounded louder than the one before it, as though someone was firing a cannon over and over again. I instinctively ducked down, and so did everyone else, wondering where the sounds were coming from and what they really were. Out of the corner of my eye, I saw something move.

A statue.

One of the gargoyles perched on the steps of the English-history building slowly began stretching and moving, as though it was waking up after a long, long sleep. In a way, I supposed that's *exactly* what it was doing. I thought I was only imagining the statue moving, that maybe I'd been fighting too hard for too long and had taken one too many blows to the head. But then, the gargoyle on the other side of the steps began to move and stretch as well, and I finally realized what the Horn of Roland did and why it had fallen into Carson's hands.

Because it brought the statues of Mythos Academy to *life*.

Carson kept playing and playing, the sounds of the Horn of Roland rising up to drown out everything else. It was a soft, sweet sound, but yet, somehow fierce and wild and loud and free all at the same time. It was the kind of music that made you want to dance and dance and dance until you laughed with joy and simply collapsed from the fast, sheer thrill of the movement and the music. Slowly, the Protectorate guards and the Reapers stopped fighting, all of us hypnotized by Carson's wonderful playing.

Meanwhile, the statues on all of the buildings began breaking free of their stone foundations, as drawn to the music as everyone else was. The gargoyles, the chimeras and dragons and basilisks, even the Minotaur, leaped down from their lofty perches and started ambling toward Carson, bits of stone cracking off their bodies from where the creatures had been standing in the same positions for so long.

And leading the procession were the two gryphons from the library steps.

They looked even fiercer and more lifelike than I ever could have dreamed, as though their dark gray stone was the thinnest sort of skin that housed their utter wildness. The gryphons came to stand beside Carson, one on either side of him, flanking him just like they always had the library steps. Both of the gryphons turned and bowed their heads to me and Logan. All I could do was bow back and hope that Carson knew what he was doing.

Finally, five minutes after it had started, Carson lowered the horn from his lips. By that point, all of the fighting had stopped on the quad, and everyone was still and silent, mesmerized by the band geek and how he'd brought the statues to life with his music.

Carson stared at the statues all around him, his black eyes gleaming with delight, as though he were the ultimate sort of Pied Piper.

"No!" Loki screamed again, breaking through the spell that Carson had put all of us under with his music. "Stop him—"

Carson brought the Horn of Roland back to his lips and started to play again, the tune harsher and angrier than before, the notes coming faster and faster as though he were building toward something dark, dangerous, and utterly deadly.

But spurred on by Loki, several of the Reapers had started to creep forward again, their eyes flicking back and forth from Carson to the statues even as they raised their swords and eased closer and closer to the band geek.

The statues began to grumble in time to the music, low, angry snarls ripping out of their stone throats. The Reapers paused and looked at each other, uncertain what was going on. Yeah. I think we all felt that way at that moment.

"Kill him!" Loki screamed again. "Now!"

The Reapers looked at each other and charged forward. And still, Carson kept right on playing, his eyes closed, completely unconcerned about the danger coming his way.

"Carson!" I screamed in warning, raising Vic and moving toward the oncoming warriors, with Logan still right next to me, his own weapon in an attack position.

But we didn't have to battle the Reapers.

Because the statues did it for us.

A Reaper neared Carson and raised his sword high, ready to bring it down on top of the band geek's head. One of the library gryphons reached out and casually swiped his massive paw across the Reaper's chest, the sharp, stone talons easily ripping into the warrior's flesh and bones. That Reaper screamed and fell, and the fight began in earnest again.

This time, the statues plowed into the Reapers, clawing, biting, and scratching for all they were worth. One wave of Reapers fell. Then another, then another. Everyone in the Protectorate drew in a collective breath and got back into the fight as well. Logan and I stayed where we were by Carson's side while the two library gryphons protected him—and us too.

Every time a Reaper got within five feet of me, Logan, and Carson, the gryphons would lash out with their paws, talons, and beaks, and either drive the Reaper back or kill the warrior outright. It was one of the most bizarre, wonderful, and frightening things I'd ever seen.

And it slowly turned the tide in our favor.

With the statues fighting by our side, helping us, the Protectorate guards and the rest of my friends were finally able to make a dent in the Reapers' numbers. Warrior after warrior fell on the quad, and this time, the Protectorate forces were the ones who advanced, instead of retreating. The last notes of Carson's song finally faded away, but no one seemed to notice, and everyone kept right on fighting, including the statues.

Suddenly, Alexei and Oliver were by my side, and we all pressed forward, cutting down Reaper after Reaper.

Logan was grinning, and so was I. New energy, new determination, surged through my body. Because, now, I thought we might actually win this battle after all—

An angry snarl sounded, lower and uglier than all the others, and I realized that Loki was striding forward through the Reapers, shoving his own warriors out of his way. He stopped close to the middle of the quad, not that far from where Carson, Logan, Oliver, Alexei, and I were standing. A gargoyle bounded across the grass, heading straight toward him. Loki looked at it with disgust, then gave a sharp, short wave of his hand, sending a burst of power forward.

The gargoyle disintegrated into dust, and my heart sank.

One by one, the stone statues moved to attack Loki, and every time—every single *time*—he waved his hand at them.

One by one, the statues crumbled to dust, breaking into bits and tumbling to a stop at the god's feet. One after another, they all just . . . shattered. I wasn't even aware that I was crying until I felt the cold wetness of my own tears on my cheeks. The statues . . . he was destroying them all.

Every last one.

Somehow, that hurt worse than any other part of the battle so far. For months, I'd been creeped out by the statues, always feeling like they were watching me, and now I knew why—because they'd been protecting me. And now, they were being destroyed for their watchfulness.

"No!" I screamed. "Stop it! Stop killing them!"

I would have surged forward and tried to attack Loki myself, but Logan caught my arm and pulled me back.

"No, Gwen!" Logan yelled. "It's too late! There's nothing you can do! Not against his magic!"

Loki stepped forward and raised both of his hands. This time, a blast of magic swept over the entire quad, rippling through the air like a heat wave, smashing every single statue that it touched, until the only ones that remained were the two gryphons from the library steps. But even they seemed to be weakened, stumbling around from the powerful blast like the rest of us were.

I kept crying, the tears rolling down my cheeks. I'd been able to ignore the horrors of the battle up until now, but everything hit me at once, and I fell to my knees on the quad, trying to find the strength to get back up.

"She's down!"

"Nike's Champion is down!"

"Death to the Protectorate!"

The Reapers pressed their advantage and began engaging the Protectorate guards again, their attacks even fiercer than before. This time, without the statues to help us, the Reapers advanced.

I staggered back up onto my feet and swung Vic in arc after furious arc, but it didn't change the battle at all. Finally, I felt Logan's hand on my arm again, pulling me back. Oliver and Alexei grabbed Carson, who still had a dreamy look on his face. It seemed as if the Horn of Roland was still working its magic on him.

This time, Vivian and Agrona made their way to the front of the Reapers, and I saw Vivian finally start swinging Lucretia and getting into the fight. From the triumphant look on her face, she thought they had already won, and that it was just a matter of getting rid of the guards one at a time before she could come and kill me and the rest of my friends.

And I couldn't help but think that she was right.

"Retreat!" Linus yelled out, his voice booming through the quad, even as he scrambled back over the piles of stone that now littered the grass. "Fall back to the library! Now!"

The Protectorate guards turned and raced toward the library, and my friends dragged me and Carson along with everyone else.

And so we made our second and final retreat up the steps and into the Library of Antiquities.

Chapter 27

Logan and I staggered up the library steps along with everyone else. Linus, Sergei, and Inari were the last ones inside, and Metis and Ajax slammed the doors shut behind them. I didn't know where they'd gotten them from, but Metis, Ajax, and some of the guards raised a couple of thick iron bars and slid them across the doors, locking us inside and the Reapers out.

I stared at the doors, waiting for the Reapers to start trying to break through them, but nothing happened, and everything was eerily silent.

"They need some time to regroup," Metis said, putting a hand on my shoulder. "And so do we. Come on."

I nodded and let her lead me away from the doors, more than a little numb after everything that had happened. Still, I couldn't help but wonder what was taking place outside on the quad, especially to the two stone gryphons. Had Loki raised his hand and turned them to dust like he had all the other statues?

The sadness, worry, and grief just kept on coming as I stepped into the main space of the library—because it had already been turned into a sick bay.

The remaining Protectorate guards slumped over the

tables and chairs or had collapsed onto the floor, and the students and other adults weren't much better. I saw blood everywhere I looked, on every single arm, hand, leg, and face. My gaze locked on to a guy who wasn't that much older than me. He was cradling his arm, which had a nasty gash in it, and it almost seemed as if I could hear each and every drop of his blood plopping against the white marble floor.

I stood there in the middle of the chaos, that numb feeling spreading through my body.

"Quickly!" Nickamedes said, hobbling around and trying to get everyone's attention. "Get the injured and the wounded into the back of the library! This way! This way!"

Grandma Frost was with him. Her eyes met mine, and I could see the relief in her face that I was okay. She clapped her hands together. "Do what Nickamedes says. Now!"

The two of them waved their hands, urging the others to follow them as they hurried into the back section of the library. Everyone who was able put their arms under the shoulders of the wounded and helped them in that direction.

"Gwen?" Alexei said, touching my arm. "Are you okay? Do you need to be healed?"

"Why would you say that?" I murmured.

"Because you look half-dead," Oliver said.

I snapped out of my daze and stared down at my own body, which was covered with dirt, blood, bruises, and shallow cuts. I'd been so caught up in the fight that I hadn't even noticed my injuries before now. None of them was serious, but still, all I wanted to do was curl up into a ball on the floor and cry. But I couldn't do that.

"Gwen?" Alexei asked again.

"I'm fine. What about you guys?"

"I think we're all okay," Logan said, coming to stand beside me. "Just some cuts and bruises, for the most part."

One by one, my gaze swept over my friends. Logan. Alexei. Oliver. Carson. All of them covered with just as much dirt, blood, and sweat as I was. Oliver had a knot on his head the size of a goose egg from where a Reaper had slammed the hilt of his sword into the Spartan's temple. A cut dripped blood on Logan's cheek, while one of Alexei's eyes was starting to blacken from where someone had hit him. But Logan was right. We'd all been lucky to escape with minor injuries—so far.

Carson, miraculously, didn't have a scratch on him, and some of the dreaminess seemed to have leaked out of his gaze, along with the strange magic that had darkened his eyes. Still, he kept a tight grip on the horn, and I wondered if he was thinking about what else he might do with the artifact.

"Are you okay?" I asked.

Carson looked at me, his eyes dim with sadness. "He killed them all. Loki. I made them come to life, I set them free, and now, they're all gone. Just . . . gone."

I thought of how the statues had shattered one by one, then how all of the others had crumbled to dust with a wave of Loki's hand. I put my own hand on his shoulder.

"I know how you feel," I whispered. "I'm sorry."

Carson reached up and pinched the bridge of his nose above his black glasses, as if he was trying to hold back tears. "I know that it's stupid. That people died out on the quad today—good people. But I can't stop thinking about the statues . . ." He glanced down at the horn he was still holding. "If I'd known that they were going to be destroyed, I never would have started playing in the first place. I never would have even picked up the stupid horn that day at the coliseum. I wish I'd never even *seen* it."

"Maybe the statues being destroyed was what was always supposed to happen," I said.

"What do you mean?"

I shrugged. I didn't really know, but it was something Nike had said to me more than once. I'd hoped that Carson would find some comfort in the words, but his face seemed as troubled as before. I didn't know what to say to him. I didn't know what to say to anyone right now.

"Come on," I said. "We should help the others and find Daphne and my grandma."

He nodded, and we headed toward the checkout counter. Logan, Oliver, and Alexei stayed behind with Linus and the guards.

I noticed Morgan McDougall trying to hop around on a bum ankle, so I went over and put my arm under her shoulder. The Valkyrie leaned on me, a few sparks of green magic hissing out of her fingertips.

"You okay?"

"Never better," Morgan quipped. "You know, for being in the middle of the most epic fight *ever*."

I grinned at her black humor and helped her to the back of the library.

Nickamedes was already there, along with Metis, who was healing the most seriously injured. She went from one warrior to the next, the golden glow of her magic bathing the wounded in its soft, warm light. Nickamedes followed her, hobbling around on his cane and helping her as best he could. Metis finished with a particularly nasty wound in a guard's stomach and staggered back from the table, but Nickamedes was there to catch and steady her. Metis looked at him a moment, then hurried on to the next person who was injured. Nickamedes followed her again. Raven was there, too, trailing both of them, carrying rolls of bandages that were the same ghostly white as her dress.

My eyes swept over the study tables, and I finally spotted a splash of pink among all the blood. Daphne had come down from the second-floor library balcony and was holding hands with Savannah, who had an ugly cut over her right eye. A rosy golden glow moved from Daphne's body into Savannah's, and I watched while the gash over the Amazon's eye seamlessly healed.

"You good?" Daphne asked.

Savannah nodded, and Daphne got up and started to move to the next person. But she caught sight of Carson trailing along beside me and Morgan, and stalked over to us.

"What were you doing?" she hissed at him. "What were you thinking, strolling out into the middle of the quad like that? You could have been killed, you idiot!"

Carson gave her a sheepish grin and held up his artifact. "Um, the horn made me do it?"

Daphne grabbed the front of Carson's robe, drew him forward, and pressed her lips to his. A cascade of sparks erupted all around them, bathing them in a soft, princess-pink shimmer.

"Wow," Morgan drawled. "Maybe you guys should get a room."

Daphne wrapped her arms around Carson's neck and kissed him even harder.

I helped Morgan over to one of the empty chairs so she could sit down and take her weight off her ankle. Then, I went over to my grandma, who was holding the hand of a Protectorate guard who'd been laid out flat on one of the study tables.

"Is he going to be all right?" I asked.

"No," she said.

And I realized that the guard was staring at the ceiling, his gaze glassy with death. Grandma sighed, then leaned forward, and gently closed his eyes. She turned to me and opened her arms. I let out a choked sob and stepped forward into her embrace. We stood like that for a long time, rocking back and forth, drawing what strength we could from each other.

"I have to go," I finally whispered. "And see what the plan is now."

She nodded, and we both drew back. Grandma cupped my face in her hands. She leaned forward and pressed a kiss to my bloody forehead before moving over to help Metis and Nickamedes.

I returned to the front of the library. By this point, all of the injured had been taken to the back, and all of the warriors that were more or less in one piece were milling around the study tables.

There weren't many of us left.

Maybe thirty warriors were at the tables, clustered around Linus, Sergei, Inari, and Ajax. Thirty warriors to try to defeat Vivian, Agrona, Loki, and the rest of the Reapers out on the quad. It wasn't enough.

We weren't going to be enough.

My heart sank, but I forced myself to look up at the second floor, where Nike's statue was. The goddess's face was neutral, although her lips were turned down, almost as if she felt the same weary, aching sadness that

I did. And I couldn't help but wonder if Loki would wave his hand and destroy her statue as easily as he had the ones outside. My stomach clenched at the thought, but there was nothing I could do about it.

Because I *still* didn't know how to kill Loki.

But I shook off my worry and hurried over to where Linus was standing with Logan, Oliver, and Alexei. Linus noticed that we were listening to him, and he stared at me a moment before turning to address the rest of the guards.

"We all know what we're up against," he said in a low voice. "We all know that there is no escape. Not for us."

The Protectorate guards nodded their heads in grim agreement. We'd all hoped we would win the battle, but we had prepared for this too—including me.

"I'm afraid all we can do at this point is try to hold them off long enough to get the wounded to safety."

Linus looked at Rory and Rachel, who had come down from the balcony with the other archers and were now standing with the rest of the warriors. I'd lost track of them during the fight outside, and I was glad to see they were both okay.

"You two seem to be the most familiar with the gryphons," he said. "Do you think you can convince them to fly the wounded out of here?"

Rory looked at me, and I nodded at her. She, in turn, nodded at Linus. "We're on it."

Rory and Rachel disappeared into the back of the library to climb up to one of the balconies to talk to the remaining gryphons.

"It will still take the gryphons several trips to evacuate everyone," Inari said.

Linus ran a hand through his hair, leaving streaks of blood behind in his blond locks. "I know. We need to think of a way to buy ourselves some more time. It won't be long before the Reapers try to enter the library, if that's not what they're doing already."

"So how do we stall?" Sergei asked, clutching his hand to his side, blood trickling out from the wound he'd gotten there.

Linus shook his head. "I have no idea."

I thought for a minute, then pulled my phone out of my jeans pocket. To my surprise, the device was still intact, and I quickly scrolled back through my call history until I could pull up Vivian's number. When I was sure I could reach her, I stepped forward.

"I might have an idea that can buy us a little more time."

Linus looked at me. "And what would that be?"

"We give the Reapers exactly what they want. We let them walk right on into the library."

"And why would we do that, Miss Frost?" Linus asked. "We're trying to keep them out of here, in case you haven't noticed."

I stared back at him. "We let them in here so they can finally kill me."

I quickly outlined my plan. Nobody liked it, especially not Logan.

"No," he said, shaking his head. "No way, Gypsy girl."

I looked at him. "You know it's the best option we have at this point. The only option, really. They'll go for it. You know they will. Especially Vivian, since she's failed to kill me so many times in the past. She'll want to prove herself to Loki by finally taking me down."

Logan opened his mouth, but his dad cut him off.

"She's right," Linus said. "The Reapers know they have us trapped and outnumbered. They'll want to savor their victory. I know Agrona. She'll agree to it."

"And Vivian will be practically salivating at the thought of killing me," I added before Logan could protest any more. "And while the two of us are fighting, it will give the Protectorate more time to evacuate the folks in the back of the library. Trust me. It will work. Besides, this is what you've been training me for all these months, right? Surely I didn't get up early all those mornings for nothing."

I gave him a wobbly grin. Logan tried to return the expression, but he couldn't. Yeah. I knew the feeling.

Logan didn't like it, but he realized it was our only option, and he reluctantly agreed. We worked out a few more of the details. When everyone knew what their part was, I hit the button to dial Vivian's number. Of course, it wouldn't matter how clever my plan was if the Reaper girl hadn't bothered to bring her phone with her—

"What on earth could you possibly want?" Vivian's voice filled my ear.

"Hey, Viv. I've decided to make this your lucky day. I'm offering you a trade."

She laughed. "Trade? What sort of trade? You don't have anything we want, Gwen. Especially not when we're going to come in and take it from you anyway."

"Sure I do," I replied. "Because you still want my head on a platter, and you still want to be the one to give it to Loki. Besides, isn't it your *duty* as his mighty Champion to finally kill me?"

"Oh, don't you worry," she said in a smug voice. "I'll be doing that as soon as we get into the library. It shouldn't be too much longer now. I noticed all those shiny new weapons your friends had out on the quad. Well, you weren't the only one who thought to bring some artifacts with you."

In the background, I heard a kind of loud whining sound, almost like a power saw. I wondered what sort of artifact could cut through the library doors and the bars that held them shut, but it didn't really matter. Part of me didn't want to know anyway.

"Sure, you can get into the library eventually," I said. "But who knows how long that will take? And yeah, you'll probably end up killing us all, but who knows what Reaper might get to me before you do? I wouldn't want to rob you of your chance to finally prove that you're worthy to be Loki's Champion."

She didn't say anything for a moment, and I knew I had her. "And what do you want in return?"

"You and me fight in the middle of the library, nobody else, and with just Vic and Lucretia," I said. "No other weapons or artifacts."

"And when I finally kill you?" she asked. "What do you want in return for the promise of your own death?"

"You let everyone else live," I said. "That's the deal."

Silence.

"Let me ask Agrona," Vivian said.

More silence. In the background, I could still hear that saw buzzing, which effectively drowned out any chance I had of overhearing Vivian and Agrona. No matter what they said, I wouldn't believe them. They would never let anyone live, especially not Linus, Sergei, and Inari. Vivian and Agrona knew that they were too important to the Protectorate. Without them, the Pantheon resistance would quickly crumble, and there would be nothing to stop Loki from enslaving the entire world, just as he'd tried to do all those centuries ago.

Still, every second I kept Vivian talking and distracted was another one that the gryphons had to evacuate everyone who was injured. Finally, after about two minutes, just when I was starting to get a headache from the saw's whine, Vivian came back onto the line.

"We accept your deal," she said. "Get ready to die, Gwen."

"You do the same."

"Oh, and don't bother opening the doors for us," Vivian said. "We're almost through them anyway. See you in a few."

She hung up on me. I let out a breath and slid the phone into my pocket. I looked at the others.

"They're going for it," I said. "Let's get into position."

Chapter 28

I stood in the middle of the library and waited for Vivian to come and kill me.

That noise from the saw, or whatever it was, grew louder and louder, until it reverberated through my head like a drill. I grimaced.

I glanced around, searching for my friends. Oliver and Alexei were crouched behind Raven's coffee cart, with Rory peeking out at me from the other side, a dagger clutched in her hand. Sergei, Inari, Coach Ajax, and the other Protectorate guards were hidden in the stacks and behind the marble statues of the gods and goddesses that ringed the second-floor balcony. Daphne was up there too, crouching next to Sigyn's statue, holding the bow that had supposedly once belonged to the goddess. Carson was with her, still clutching the Horn of Roland, although I didn't know what else he might be able to do with the artifact, if anything.

Linus stood beside me, as the head of the Protectorate, with Logan on my other side. Metis was still in the back, healing as many of the wounded as she could while Rachel, Nickamedes, Raven, and Grandma Frost helped them climb to the upper floors so that the gryphons could fly them away to safety.

"Are you sure you can do this, Miss Frost?" Linus asked in the kindest voice he'd ever used with me. "You need to draw the fight out as long as possible. It won't be easy, given what a skilled warrior Vivian is."

I shrugged. "I don't really have a choice, now, do I?"

"No, I suppose not," he murmured.

The whining of the saw grew even louder, making me wince again. But as quickly as the noise had started, it faded away altogether. Silence. Then—

Bang.

Bang. Bang.

BANG!

A great crash sounded, and I knew the Reapers had breached the outer library doors. I drew in a breath and held up Vic.

"Are you ready for this?"

The sword fixed his purplish eye on me. "I'm ready, and you are too, Gwen. Trust me. Nike believes in you, and so do I."

My gaze drifted up to the goddess's statue on the second floor. Her face was as neutral as before, although her eyes seemed to be fixed on mine. I wondered what she thought of the battle so far, the choices I'd made, and the fact that it was all going to end here in the library. Although I supposed that was rather fitting, since this was the place where it had all started, the night I'd grabbed Vic out of his artifact case.

I hope you're proud of me, I thought, still staring at the goddess. *I've done the best I could to save everyone.*

The goddess tipped her head at me, but that was her only response.

The doors flew open, and Vivian and Agrona came striding into the main part of the library. Loki stepped inside after them, flanked by Reapers on all sides. My heart sank as I realized exactly how many Reapers were left. They still outnumbered us three-to-one, if not more.

"So," Agrona purred, stopping a few feet away and looking at Linus. "It's finally come down to this. Your final, ultimate defeat, and here you are, hiding behind a teenage girl, no less. I'm rather disappointed in you, Linus. I would have thought that you would have managed to hold out for at least a little while longer."

Linus straightened up to his full height. His eyes were full of hate as he stared back at his former wife. "Well, not all of us have a god on our side," he snapped back. "Or plot and scheme for years to put his soul into an innocent boy's body."

I frowned. Everyone knew that Agrona had tried to put Loki's soul into Logan's body. That was old news. Still, something about Linus's words resonated in my mind in a strange way. Something about Loki wanting a new body, a *mortal* body . . .

Agrona arched a blond eyebrow. "Still angry about that, dear husband? Tsk. Tsk. You're setting a bad example for your innocent boy there, holding such a grudge."

Logan stepped forward, his hand tightening around his sword. "He's not the only one. One of the happiest moments in my life is going to be the one when I finally kill you for everything you've done to my family."

"Unfortunately, that's not the deal we made," Agrona said. "Vivian and Gwen will do the fighting. And then we'll see what happens to the rest of you."

She smirked at her former stepson. Logan took another step forward, but Linus grabbed his arm and shook his head.

"Let it play out," Linus said in a soft voice that only we could hear. "Remember, every second counts."

Logan didn't like it, but he reluctantly nodded his head and stepped back.

"Well, then," Agrona said. "I say we let the battle begin. My lord?"

She turned to Loki, who nodded his head at her. Then, the god's gaze flicked over to Vivian.

"Do not fail me this time," he said in his silky, but deadly voice. "Or you will not like the consequences."

Vivian trembled the faintest bit. "Of course not, my lord."

She bowed to him, then turned and strode toward me, stopping in the middle of the library floor. I stepped up so that I was standing about five feet away from her. We'd cleared all of the chairs and study tables out of the way, so there was only open space around me and Vivian.

"No interference from anyone," Linus called out in a grim voice. "Those were the terms we agreed upon."

"Don't worry." Vivian smirked. "I won't need any help with her. Not this time."

"Well, well, well, aren't we feeling confident today, Viv?" I mocked her. "But you're going to lose, just like you always have before."

"We'll see about that," she hissed.

She held her weapon up by the blade, and I did the same with Vic so that the two swords could see each other. Lucretia's red eye snapped open.

"So, we meet again, Vic," the other sword purred. "For the last time."

"Of course, it will be for the last time," Vic snapped back. "Because I'm finally going to cleave you in two, you simpering sword!"

"The only one who simpers around here is you, you overconfident hunk of metal!" Lucretia cried back.

I would have stood there and let the two swords trade insults all day long, as it gave Metis, Nickamedes, and the others more time to heal and evacuate the wounded, but Vivian lowered her sword and tightened her hand around the hilt once more.

I did the same, and the fight was on.

Vivian raised her sword high overhead and charged at me, trying to use her Valkyrie strength to end me with that first, hard, sharp, powerful blow. Her sword crashed against mine, sending red and purple sparks everywhere. It took all of my strength to hold on to Vic and not crumple under her attack, but I managed it.

"Die, Gypsy!" Vivian hissed.

"You first!" I hissed back at her.

We broke apart and continued our battle. Back and forth, we fought in the middle of the library, hacking and slashing our weapons at each other over and over again, each one of us trying to kill the other.

I whirled around after parrying Vivian's latest attack and glanced at the clock mounted on the wall of the glass office complex. Only three minutes had passed since we'd started fighting. Funny, but it felt like forever. Or maybe that was because I'd been battling Vivian ever since she'd tricked me into finding the Helheim Dagger for her. Either way, I needed to keep going, even though I was already utterly exhausted from the battle out on the quad.

So the next time Vivian gave me the slightest opening,

I pretended to trip over my own feet instead of slashing my sword across her arm like I should have, like I really wanted to.

The Reaper girl blinked in surprise before her eyes abruptly narrowed. She frowned. "What are you doing? Why aren't you attacking me with everything you have?"

"Because I don't need to," I mocked, not wanting her to realize that I was trying to draw the fight out for as long as possible. "Face it, Viv. You're not half the warrior that I am. I can kill you anytime I want to. I just want to humiliate you first in front of all your Reaper friends—and especially Loki."

I raised my sword and charged at her.

Clash-clash-clang!
Clash-clash-clang!
Clash-clash-clang!

Once more, we fought, and once more, we broke apart and started circling each other. My eyes flicked to the clock on the office complex wall again, but only two more minutes had passed—

"You . . . you . . . you're stalling!" Vivian snarled. "Why? What are you up to, Gwen?"

A golden light blazed in her eyes, and a sharp, sudden pain exploded in my head, as though she had stabbed a knife deep into my brain. I screamed, but the pain intensified. Vivian stepped forward and slammed her fist into my face, adding to the agony. I rocked back, but I didn't go down, so she punched me again. This time, the pain was so intense that I felt my legs sliding out from under me and my ass hitting the marble floor.

"Get up, Gwen!" Vic screamed. "Get up! Now!"

But I couldn't. All I was aware of were those damn invisible fingers digging through my brain again and again, prying into every part of my mind, peering into every single corner, and rifling through all of my secrets. Still, I tried to push back. Tried to imagine my own hands forming fists and pounding at the disgusting, crawling fingers like they were worms that I was squishing, but nothing seemed to work, and the pain continued, seeming to get stronger and stronger with every breath I took.

Above me, I heard Vivian laugh. "Give it up, Gwen. You're no match for my telepathy magic. Why, if I'd known that it was this easy to take you down with it, I would have used it right off the bat. But let's have a little fun before I kill you. Humiliate *you* the same way that you wanted to humiliate me. What do you say? I've been wanting to do this for a long, long time. Let me show you exactly what the Reapers have planned for your precious friends and the rest of your pathetic Protectorate."

Still reeling from the agony in my head, I huddled on the floor as Vivian showed me image after gruesome image. The first thing that popped into my mind was her driving Lucretia through my chest, the sight so vivid that I thought she'd really done it for a moment. Then, she did the same thing to each one of my friends in turn. Oliver. Alexei. Daphne. Carson. And finally, Logan.

I started to scream again, but those images vanished, replaced by one of Metis, Nickamedes, and Ajax all wearing chains, on their knees and bowing their heads as Vivian lorded it over them.

Then, that sight disappeared, and I saw Vivian raising her sword over my grandma's head and killing her just like she had murdered my mom.

One after another, the images flooded my mind, and

there was nothing I could do to stop them. But the more images Vivian showed me, the more she let me see how much she wanted to hurt my friends, the angrier I got. I grabbed hold of that anger and held it tight, using it like a shield to block out the uglier images and all of the horrible hallucinations the Reaper girl kept forcing into my mind. And slowly, bit by bit, I came back to myself, pulling my mind up out of the dark abyss of pain and terror and nightmares. Because they weren't real, and I wasn't about to let them come true—not now, not *ever*.

Finally, Vivian stopped her mental assault long enough to sneer down at me. "Well, Gwen? How does the future look to you?"

I stared up at her. "Not nearly as bleak as yours does."

I lashed out and stabbed Vic deep into her calf. Vivian screamed in surprise and fell to the floor beside me. I pushed the last of the pain away and threw myself on top of the Reaper girl, slamming my fist into her face over and over again as hard as I could. Sometime during the fight, Vic fell from my hand and skittered across the floor, and I slapped Lucretia away from Vivian before she could use the sword against me. Vivian snarled in anger and surprise, and we rolled around and around in the middle of the library floor, punching, hitting, and clawing at each other as fiercely as we could.

I was furious, as furious as I'd ever been, but I was still no match for her Valkyrie strength. Vivian pinned me to the ground, her hands locked around my wrists.

"I was going to slice you open with Lucretia," she said. "But now I think I'll just choke you to death instead. That will be so much more *fun*."

Before I could stop her, she reached up, wrapped her hands around my throat, and started squeezing.

I laughed in her face, although it came out as more of a rasping wheeze.

Vivian frowned. "What are you doing? Why are you laughing?"

"Because you forgot one thing, Viv," I snarled. "You're not the only one here with magic. I have it too, remember? And not just any magic—*touch magic.*"

Too late, Vivian realized that her skin was touching mine. Her eyes widened, and she started to pull her hands away from my throat, but I didn't let her. Instead, I wrapped my hands around hers and reached for my magic.

My psychometry kicked in, and I flashed on the Reaper girl, seeing the bright red spark that burned at the very center of her being. I thought about closing my hands around that spark and slowly crushing it until it was snuffed out completely. But I couldn't forget about all of the awful images she'd shown me, and I wanted to give Vivian a taste of her own medicine.

"You want to see something truly terrible?" I growled. "You like watching other people suffer? Well, let me show you what *real* suffering looks like."

I tightened my grip on Vivian's hands. And then I showed her exactly how much she and the other Reapers had hurt me over the last few months. Every battle we'd had, all the pain I'd felt, all the agony of realizing that she was the one who'd murdered my mom and watching her kill Nott right before my eyes. I showed her all that and more.

So much *more.*

Vivian started screaming with pain—my pain—but I didn't stop. I didn't have any mercy. Not today. Not for her. Not after everything she'd done to me. Not after everyone she'd taken away from me. My mom, Nott, and even Logan and Grandma Frost for a while.

Oh yes, I showed her my pain and all the other pain I'd experienced over the years. All the bloody memories from the artifacts I'd touched. All the cruel, petty emotions I'd felt rolling off people. All the bad things that I'd realized they'd done when I flashed on them with my magic. And then, I showed her one of the most horrible memories I had—that of a girl being abused by her stepdad.

Vivian's screams grew louder and louder, and that red spark flickered inside her, but I kept up with my relentless assault, slamming the images into her brain one after another the same way she had done to me.

And finally, I felt something inside her mind just... *crumble*, the same way that the statues out on the quad had crumbled under the brunt of Loki's foul magic. Her hands fell away from my throat, and this time, I let her go. Vivian scrambled away from me, wrapped her arms around her knees, and started rocking back and forth on the floor. I hurried over to grab Vic and raised up the sword, thinking this might be another one of her tricks, but Vivian didn't even try to reach for Lucretia. She didn't even so much as glance in my direction.

"Make it stop," she whispered in a small, broken voice. "It hurts so much. Please, please, *please* make it stop."

I tightened my grip on Vic, still suspicious, but Vivian put her hands up to her head and kept rocking back and forth on the floor, her golden eyes fixed on something far away that only she could see—all of the horrible memories I'd shown her.

And I realized that the fight was over, and Vivian was

no longer a threat. I let out a breath. Somehow, I knew that the Reaper girl would never be a threat to me ever again.

"Gwen?" Logan asked, coming up to stand beside me. "Aren't you going to . . ." He made a slashing gesture with his own sword.

"No," I said. "Because we don't execute people who are down and out. That's the Reapers' thing. Not ours. That's what they do. Not us."

I stepped away from Vivian, but I didn't move away from the center of the library. Because I knew who my next target was going to be—Loki.

Agrona raced over, picked up Lucretia, and bent down next to her protégé. She started to touch Vivian, but the Reaper girl flinched and pulled away from her, mumbling more nonsense words to herself.

"What did you do to her?" Agrona whispered, watching Vivian rock back and forth on the cold marble.

"She wanted to play in my head," I said in a harsh voice. "So I showed her *exactly* what was in there."

Agrona gave me a sharp look. "You showed her your memories?"

I smiled. "Just the bad ones. Believe me, I have plenty of those, thanks to you guys."

Fear flickered in her green eyes before she could hide it. "You must have overloaded her brain. You've . . . you've *destroyed* her mind."

I looked down at Vivian and shrugged. "Probably. But it was the same thing she wanted to do to me, and no less than what she deserved after everything she's done."

Maybe it would have been kinder if I'd killed her

after all, but I didn't say that. I could tell that was what Agrona was thinking—and my friends too. But I wasn't in a merciful mood, not now, when the real test was still to come.

"Enough of this nonsense!" Loki hissed. "Attack! Attack! Attack! And this time, don't stop until you've killed every last one of them!"

I'd known that was what he was going to say, and I didn't hesitate. Even as my friends leaped out from behind the stacks to engage the Reapers, I pushed past Agrona and ran straight at the god. I raised Vic high, brought the sword up, around, and down, and slammed the blade into Loki's chest—right where his heart would be, if he even had one.

Triumph filled me. I'd done it. I'd beaten Vivian, and now, I'd killed Loki too.

The god looked down at the sword buried in his chest. Then, he raised his head and looked me in the eyes.

He laughed.

He just . . . laughed and laughed, right in my face.

"Oh, you stupid, stupid girl," he sneered, his foul breath kissing my cheeks like a rotten gust of wind. "Did you really think you could kill me with a mere sword?"

"Hey!" Vic snapped. "I'm not just any mere *sword*, pal!"

I yanked the sword free and stepped back, but I wasn't ready to give up. Not yet.

I stabbed Loki again and again, slicing Vic every which way I could across his chest, his neck, even his arms and legs. All the while, he kept right on laughing at me, amused by my frantic struggles. No blood poured out of his wounds, and it seemed like I was slicing my sword through air instead of into someone's body.

All around me, I could hear the shouts and screams of the fight, but I didn't dare turn to look at how the rest of my friends were faring against the Reapers. For a moment, Logan and Agrona stepped into my line of sight. Agrona slashed at him again and again with Lucretia, but Logan easily blocked all of her blows, then whipped his sword up and buried the point in her heart. Grim satisfaction filled Logan's face as Agrona dropped to the floor—dead. Loki laughed again, and I pushed away all thoughts of Logan. I yanked Vic out of Loki's chest and stood there, panting and trying to get my breath back after my last frenzied attack. The god tilted his head to the side, his neck *crack-crack-crack*ing as he studied me, his two red eyes burning into my violet ones.

"You know, what you did to that girl was quite impressive," Loki purred. "Perhaps Agrona made a mistake trying to get me a Spartan body. Perhaps what I've really needed all along was *your* body, Gypsy."

He stretched out a hand toward me. The thought of him infecting my body, my mind, my soul, the same way he had Logan's was so horrifying that I almost leaped back.

Almost.

Self-sacrifice is a very powerful thing, especially if you do it of your own free will. Once again, Nike's voice whispered in my mind. And it didn't stop there.

You have free will, Gwendolyn, just like every creature, mortal, and god does. Remember that because it's the most important thing I'll ever tell you.

Never forget that because it's the very thing Loki and

his Reapers are trying to take away from you—your right to choose your own fate.

One after another, I remembered bits and pieces of all my conversations with Nike, all the times she'd come to me, all the cryptic things and riddles she'd said. And suddenly, I knew what I had to do. Maybe I'd known it somewhere in the back of my mind all along and just hadn't wanted to face it until now.

I couldn't kill Loki. He was a god, simple as that. Immortal. Eternal. Forever.

But I *wasn't*.

I wasn't a god, and my body wasn't immortal, eternal, forever, or anything even close to that.

No, it was—I was—decidedly mortal.

And utterly killable.

So when Loki stretched out his hand toward me, I let his fingers close around my throat, even as I stared up into his burning red eyes. I saw so many things there. Hate, rage, disgust, but most of all, I saw triumph—triumph that he'd finally succeeded in finding a way to defeat Nike once and for all. Not by killing me, but by corrupting me with himself.

What he didn't realize was that the same triumph was reflected back in my own eyes.

So I tightened my grip on Vic, closed my eyes, and let the evil god's soul infect my own.

Chapter 29

It was—Loki was—horrible.

Absolutely, completely, utterly *horrible.*

His soul slammed into my body like a bolt of lightning, frying me from the inside out. I could hear him laughing in my head, and my vision immediately went Reaper red. The only thing that wasn't that awful color was Vic's lone, purplish eye. Everything else just looked . . . *bloody.*

All the while, I was dimly aware that I was screaming—screaming and screaming as Loki infected every single part of me. I thought I'd known what Logan had gone through when it had happened to him, but seeing his memories hadn't prepared me for the intense, unending pain and the sheer, utter agony. But I concentrated on the cold, hard feel of Vic in my hand, and I let Loki do his worst to me.

"Yes," I heard the god murmur in my mind, or perhaps I was the one who was saying the words out loud. I couldn't quite tell. "Oh yes. This Gypsy girl's body will do *quite* nicely."

I screamed again as he dived even deeper inside me, burrowing down farther and farther, drilling into every single part of my mind, my body, my heart and soul, until I could almost see the bright purple spark at the center of my being start to take on an ugly red tint. I was aware of Loki's hand falling away from my throat, and his body dropping to the floor, since it was nothing but an empty shell, now that he was inside *me*.

"Gwen! Gwen!" I thought I heard Logan screaming my name, but his voice sounded dim and distant, as though both of us were underwater.

Eventually, the pain died down to a more manageable level, although I could still feel Loki moving around in my body, rifling through my insides like they were index cards, and murmuring to himself, or perhaps both of us, as he took stock of me.

"Yes, yes, young and strong," he purred. "Oh, the things I'll be able to do in your body, Gypsy. Nike will rue the day she ever *dared* to stand against me. It will be such a pleasure using you against her."

I let him rant. It was all I could do to keep breathing—in and out, in and out—and not lose myself completely in the foul god's rotten core. Even so, I could feel it eating away at me like acid. Slowly, I managed to turn around and realized that the fight had stopped and everyone—Reaper and Protectorate alike—was staring at me with wide eyes and gaping mouths.

"Gypsy girl?" Logan whispered in a horrified voice, slowly creeping toward me.

I could see a burning reflection in his blue gaze, and I realized that my eyes must be red—as Reaper red as his had been that day at the auditorium when Agrona had tried to put Loki's soul into his body.

I tried to smile at Logan, tried to let him know that everything was going to be okay, this was all part of my plan, that it had to be this way, but it hurt too much, so I quickly gave up. Besides, I knew what I had to do now, and time was running out. Another minute, and Loki would have complete control of me. There would be no coming back from any of it.

Not for me—not for anyone.

Of course, I didn't plan on coming back anyway, but if I was going to die, then I was determined to take Loki with me.

Everything felt odd and clumsy and large and heavy, as if my hands suddenly weren't big enough for my body. But then again, it wasn't really my body anymore—it was *his*.

So it took a lot of concentration and a couple of tries to bring up Vic and turn the sword around. I cut my right palm on his sharp blade, but it was a small, dull ache compared to the rest of the pain burning through my body.

I raised Vic up. His eye was still the same purple as before, and I focused on that soft twilight shade, letting it center me for what I had to do next.

"I'll miss you, Vic," I whispered, although it wasn't my voice coming out of my mouth anymore. "I love you."

A single tear streaked down Vic's hilt. "I love you too, Gwen."

I pointed the sword's tip inward at my chest. In front of me, I saw Logan's eyes bulge as he figured out what I was going to do. He ran toward me, trying to stop me, but he was going to be too late.

But he wasn't the only one who finally realized what I was planning. Loki stopped his soft murmuring, and his burning red eyes popped up into my mind, blotting out everything else, and peering at me as if I was doing a most curious and worrisome thing.

"What—what are you doing?" Loki's voice flooded my mind again, rising to a sharp screech on the very last word. "You—you can't do this. Stop! I command you! Stop!"

I let out a long, loud, crazy laugh that echoed from one side of the library to the other and rose all the way up to the domed ceiling before it abruptly bounced back down again. I positioned Vic so that his tip rested against my heart. His point pricked my skin, drawing a bit of blood, and I focused on that small flash of pain. Suddenly, I could feel claws scraping down my insides and seizing onto the tendons and muscles in my arms, tearing, ripping, and trying to get me to drop the sword. But I tightened my grip and held on.

"You will stop this madness at once!" Loki hissed again. "I demand that you stop right now!"

I laughed again.

"That's where you're wrong," I said. "That's where you've *always* been wrong. This whole *time*. All these centuries. You can't stop me. You can't stop me from doing one single *thing*, especially not this."

"And why is that?" he hissed.

I smiled, even though he couldn't see me. "Free will."

Then, I rammed Vic's point into my heart as hard as I could.

There was a bright, blinding flash of pain.

Then . . . nothing.

Chapter 30

I sucked in a breath and sat bolt upright.

At least, that's what I thought I did. One second, I was slamming Vic into my chest and feeling all the pain of the mortal wound I'd given myself and the warm blood that slicked down my hands. The next, I was standing in the middle of the Library of Antiquities, still holding Vic.

I looked down, but I wasn't bleeding anymore. In fact, I was perfectly clean, and my clothes showed none of the wear and tear from the battles out on the quad. I brought my hand up to my chest, and I realized that I could feel a third mark slashing over the other two scars already over my heart. The wound throbbed, but the pain felt dull and far away.

"Here we go again," I muttered.

"Yes," a soft voice called out. "Here we go again."

My head snapped up, and I realized that I wasn't alone.

A lone figure stood in front of me. Her long white gown seemed as crisp and fresh as new snow and draped around her strong, slender figure in perfect fashion. White wings rose up over her back, forming a heart shape above her head, and her hair was curled into bronze ringlets that fell past her shoulders. But it was her eyes that I could lose myself in. Beautiful, beautiful eyes that were a mix of purple and gray and lavender and silver that blended together to form one amazing twilight shade.

Even though I was dead, or mostly dead, or whatever I was, I still recognized her. Nike, the Greek goddess of victory.

She smiled, stepped forward, and clasped my hands in hers, and I felt a wave of cold power blast off her and flow into me.

"Hello, Gwendolyn," Nike said.

I focused on the goddess, trying to make sense of things. "So I'm dead this time, right? Dead-dead. For real? Forever?"

She gave me a mysterious smile. "That remains to be seen. But you have done exactly what I asked of you, and I couldn't be more pleased."

I raised my eyebrows. "So you wanted me to stab myself in the chest with Vic all along? You know, you could have just told me that. It would have saved me a lot of heartache."

The three wounds on my chest throbbed. I winced. My words were true in more ways than one.

"Yes, I suppose it would have," Nike murmured. "But things had to happen this way, Gwendolyn. You had to get to this place and time of your own free will, and so did *he*."

Nike dropped her hands from mine and stepped to one side. I blinked and blinked.

Because Loki was here.

He was on his knees in the middle of the library floor. But he didn't look like the ruined, rotten figure that I knew. No, he looked as he must have centuries ago, before Helheim, before the Bowl of Tears, before everything.

Because he looked *beautiful*.

Golden hair, alabaster skin, piercing blue eyes. All of that had been restored to him, and both sides of his face were as smooth as any of the statues that lined the second-floor balcony. A long white robe rippled around his body, instead of the black one I'd always seen him wear before. The bright, pure color only made him seem that much more perfect.

He was perhaps the most beautiful thing I'd ever seen, even lovelier than Nike herself. But the longer I looked at him, the less his features dazzled me and the more that I saw the cruel cunning in the sly shimmer of his eyes.

Loki glared at me, his mouth turned down into a sullen pout, before his hate-filled gaze moved over to the goddess. His eyes blazed with rage, but they remained the same blue as before and didn't turn that awful Reaper red I'd seen so many times in my nightmares.

"What is he doing here?" I asked Nike.

"He's here because you killed him," she replied. "Just as you were meant to do all along with your magic."

"My magic?" I frowned. "But I thought I was supposed to use the silver laurel leaves that Eir gave me to kill Loki. Not my magic."

Nike shook her head. "The leaves and the candle severely weakened Loki, enough for you to allow your psychometry, your touch magic, as you call it, to pull his soul into your own body—a mortal body that you then sacrificed for the good of all your friends."

"Self-sacrifice is a very powerful thing, especially if

you do it of your own free will," I murmured, thinking about the words Nike had once said to me.

The goddess beamed at me. "And you made the ultimate sacrifice when you gave your life to stop Loki. You have proven yourself worthy of being my Champion, of being the Champion of all Champions."

"You and your damn trickery." Loki spat out the words, still glaring at Nike. "I should have known it was too easy, thinking I could take over your Champion's body and finally complete my victory. Well, I won't stand for it. Take me back. Put me back into my own body. I demand it. *Now*."

"You're simply upset that I beat you at your own game," Nike said, her voice as cold and harsh as I'd ever heard it. "You gave up your immortal body of your own free will, Loki. There is no going back to that body or the mortal realm for you—*ever*."

"Do you mean . . . is he . . . dead?" I whispered. "Like me?"

Nike shook her head. "Not exactly."

"But you told me I had to *kill* him. That's what you and the Reapers have been saying all along. That I was going to kill Loki. Why go through all of this if that's not what I actually did?"

"In a way, you did kill him," Nike said. "You killed his body, and without it, he can never return to the mortal realm."

"But how will his being . . . here . . . wherever here really is . . . help?" I asked, throwing my hands out wide in frustration. "Can't he just escape again and go back to the mortal world? And then we'll have to go through this all over again."

Nike shook her head again. "No, Gwendolyn. He

can't escape. Not this time. He cannot leave this realm, not as long as he is wearing *that*."

She pointed at Loki, and I noticed a thin silver bracelet gleaming around his right wrist—one that was very familiar. I glanced down at my own wrist, but the mistletoe bracelet that the laurel leaves had been attached to was gone. He was wearing it, and he kept glaring at it and grimacing, as though the mere sight of it pained him greatly, along with the feel of the silver actually touching his skin.

"The bracelet was transferred to Loki since you were wearing it when you killed him," Nike said, answering my silent questions. "Mistletoe has very powerful properties. It's what Loki used to trick another god into killing Balder, the Norse god of light, so long ago. And it is what will keep him here where he belongs, along with other things."

"What other things?" I asked.

"Blood," another voice called out. "My blood."

Suddenly, Raven was there, striding down the main aisle toward me, Nike, and Loki.

"What is she doing here?" I whispered to Nike.

"You'll see."

Raven stopped, her white hair and gown swirling around her in a way I'd never seen them do before. Her black eyes locked with mine.

"You always wondered what I was hiding with my wrinkles, Gwendolyn," she said, her voice light, sweet, and pure. "Well, let me show you."

Raven held her hands out wide, her palms up, as though she were somehow drawing the air in around her. And I watched while her hair slowly blackened, her wrinkles melted away, and her skin smoothed out and tightened up, as if she were growing younger instead of older. The only thing that remained the same about her were the old, faded scars that marred her hands and arms. In a moment, she went from a mysterious old crone to a gorgeous goddess. And suddenly, so many things about her made sense to me, including her real identity.

"Sigyn," I whispered. "You're Sigyn, the Norse goddess of devotion. Loki's wife."

Another thought occurred to me, and my gaze flicked up to the second floor, where her statue was. "That's why your statue in the library seemed so hollow and empty that one time I touched it when I was searching for the Helheim Dagger. Because you were in the mortal realm all along instead of being... here."

Wherever *here* really was.

Sigyn smiled. "Yes, Gwendolyn. That is exactly right. I have spent centuries in the mortal realm, watching over the members of the Pantheon, the Protectorate, and the academy students."

"But why?"

Sorrow filled her black eyes. "Because Loki tricked me into helping him escape all those centuries ago. Because I believed he was truly sorry for orchestrating Balder's murder. Because I thought he had really changed and wanted to be a better person, instead of trying to bend us all to his will. If I hadn't been so foolish, none of this would have happened. So much pain and suffering could have been avoided. So much... loss."

She stared down at her former husband, who was still on his knees in the middle of the marble floor. "So I decided to devote myself to setting things right, to making up for my mistake as best I could. And I finally have, with your help."

She stepped toward me and held out her hand. I realized that she wanted Vic, and I handed the sword over to her. Sigyn stared at the blade a moment, then sliced her palm open on it before handing Vic back to me.

She walked over to Loki and stared down at him again.

"I'm sorry that it had to come to this," Sigyn said in a soft voice. "But you gave me no choice."

Loki glared at her, but he didn't say anything.

Sigyn sighed, so much sadness in that one soft sound, as if she felt all of the evil Loki had done more intensely than anyone else. In a way, I supposed she did. Then, she clenched her hand into a tight fist until blood dripped out from between her fingers.

Plop . . . plop . . . plop . . .

One by one, the drops of her blood hit the mistletoe bracelet still wrapped around Loki's wrist. He hissed and struggled with all his might, but some invisible force held him in place. Strangely enough, it felt like that same old, watchful, knowing force I had sensed around Grandma Frost so many times when she was having one of her visions of the future. Somehow, I knew that it was Nike's victory magic at work.

Finally, Sigyn stepped back.

"There," she said in a tired voice. "It's done. The mistletoe is bound on him, and he is bound here—forever."

"And now," Nike murmured. "For the final step."

She waved her hand. I blinked, and Loki was gone, and the floor was empty again. I whirled around and around, but Nike placed a hand on my shoulder and pointed up to the second-floor balcony. For as long as I'd been at Mythos, there had been a lone, empty spot there in the circular pantheon of the gods—an open space where Loki's statue would have been.

But now, the god himself stood in that spot.

Nike, Sigyn, and I looked up at him, and I realized that we weren't the only ones in the library anymore. All of the statues had turned their heads in his direction, and they weren't statues anymore, but real, live people.

Real gods and goddesses.

My breath caught in my throat, even as I tried to look everywhere at once at all of the figures I'd read about in my myth-history books, since they'd all come to life right before my eyes. Bastet, the Egyptian cat goddess, with her sleek, feline body. Athena, the Greek goddess, with her wise, solemn features. Coyote, the Native American trickster deity, with his wide, mischievous grin. And hundreds of others from all the cultures of the world.

All gathered here to watch this—Loki's final defeat and punishment.

"We have all agreed as to what his fate is," Sigyn said. "He has brought this upon himself."

One by one, all of the gods and goddesses nodded their heads in agreement, giving their approval for what was to come.

"Eir," Nike said. "If you will be so kind, please."

On the balcony above, a goddess stepped forward. Black hair, green eyes, pale skin. I recognized her from my trip to Colorado—Eir, the Norse goddess of healing and mercy. The one who had given me the silver laurel leaves and the mistletoe bracelet.

Eir stepped forward and held out her hands. A force rippled off her, shot through the air, and slammed into Loki on the far side of the balcony.

The evil god let out a scream, and I realized that the mistletoe bracelet around his wrist was glowing with an intense silver light.

And then it started to spread.

I watched as the mistletoe sprouted, and more and more vines slowly began to curl out of the bracelet, reach up, and wrap around his body. Loki screamed and screamed, but there was nothing he could do to stop the slow, steady onslaught. The vines quickly crept up his arms, trapping his hands against his sides before climbing up his chest and neck. He tried to keep his face up out of the greenery, but the vines wrapped around his head, pulling it down, before swallowing him whole. After a while, even his screams faded away to nothingness.

That silver light flared a final time, pulsing brighter and more intensely than ever before, and I had to close my eyes against the burning brightness.

When the light faded away, and I finally opened my eyes again, I realized that another statue had been added to the pantheon—Loki.

His head was down, and his eyes narrowed, as though he were glaring at the mistletoe bracelet on his wrist, the source of all the vines that had wrapped themselves around him. But he was solid stone, even while the other gods and goddesses still showed their true forms. I let out a long, tired breath.

And just like that, it was done, and Loki was locked away—forever.

Chapter 31

"So it is done," Nike finally said in a loud, booming voice, echoing my own thoughts. "Forever."

One by one, the other gods and goddesses nodded their heads at her before stepping back and slowly melting into their stone forms once more. In an instant, only Nike, Sigyn, Vic, and I were left in the library.

"What's going on?" I said, staring up at the pantheon. "What's happening? Why are they leaving?"

"The Twilight of the Gods is upon us, Ragnarok, some mortals call it. Either way, the gods are withdrawing from the mortal world," Nike said, glancing at Sigyn. "With a few notable exceptions, of course."

A faint grin pulled up Sigyn's lips. "Some of us still have work to do."

Nike returned her grin. "And warriors to mold. Spartans in particular."

Sigyn's smile widened. "Something like that."

"But why?" I asked, totally not understanding their cryptic talk.

"Because we have caused too much damage here over too many years," Nike said. "Too much pain, too much sorrow, and too much death. We will not risk that happening again. We will not risk another god trying to rise up and enslave everyone as Loki attempted to. It was a mutual decision."

I knew that what she was saying made sense, but I couldn't help but feel a pang of loss and longing all the same. Because the gods' withdrawing from the world meant that Nike would leave too. She'd been such a big part of my life these last few months. I didn't always agree with the goddess, and I'd long since grown tired of her games and riddles, but I also didn't want to lose her the way I had my mom and Nott.

I swallowed. "Will I . . . ever see you again?"

She gave me that familiar, slightly mysterious smile, the one that was so old, knowing, wise, and yet so infuriating all at the same time. "Perhaps. But never fear. I will always be here, watching over you."

"And don't forget about me," Vic piped up, breaking his long silence. "I'll always be with you, Gwen. For as long as you will have me."

"So . . . what do I do now?" I asked. "What happens next?"

"Whatever you want to happen, Gwendolyn," Nike said. "Although Loki is gone, there will still be battles for you to wage as my Champion. And for others as well. Your friends, your . . . family."

Something about the way she said *family* made me think of Rory, but before I could ask her exactly what she meant, she smiled at me again.

"Either way," Nike said. "Your part in this fight is finally finished."

I shook my head, still not understanding.

"Perhaps this will help set your mind at ease."

Nike nodded, and Sigyn stepped forward, a book in her hand. Sigyn opened the cover and held the book out to me. Slowly, the pages began to turn, and I realized the images there held the story of my life, the pictures moving the same way the drawings in my myth-history book always did.

Me growing up. My first day at Mythos. Me sitting in classes, the dining hall, and even the library. All the battles I'd endured right up until the moment I'd stabbed myself in the chest with Vic. After that, the pages were mostly blank, although every once in a while, I caught glimpses of my friends. Daphne. Carson. Oliver. Alexei.

And then there was Logan.

His face was one of the constants, and somehow I knew we would get through this and everything else that came our way, good and bad. Oh, there would be fights through the years. Breakups and makeups. But through it all, we would always love each other. We would always find our way back to each other.

And some day, in the future, there would be a little girl with black hair, violet eyes, and a teasing grin that was exactly like her father's. She would laugh and play and run through the Library of Antiquities while I worked as the head librarian. Late at night, the two of us would lie on a blanket on the marble floor and stare up at the amazing fresco on the ceiling, and I would tell her stories about our battle against Loki. And one day, I would hand Vic over to her, and she would continue on with the Frost family tradition of serving Nike and being her Champion.

The last page of the book fluttered by, and I realized

that it was blank. But before I could ask what it all meant, Sigyn closed the book and stepped back.

She nodded at me. "Until we meet again, Gwendolyn."

Sigyn strolled over to where Raven's, or rather her, coffee cart was, stepped around it, and melted into the shadows.

But Nike stayed where she was in front of me. The goddess took my hand in hers, and I felt the cold waves of power flow from her, into me, and back again.

"So Loki's trapped, and I'm still here," I said. "How am I going to get back this time?"

"You saved yourself, Gwendolyn," she said. "When you gave what was left of Sol's candle to the Spartan librarian. He's using it at this very moment to heal you, along with the last laurel leaf."

I shook my head. "I told him to save the leaf for himself. Not me."

"Nickamedes is making his own sacrifice—for you," Nike said. "Don't dishonor him by not accepting it."

I nodded. I looked down, and I realized that there was a silver glow right where the stab wound was in my heart. I concentrated, and I could feel the power of Sol's candle surging through me and repairing all the damage that had been done to my body, both from my own actions and from Loki ripping into my mind, heart, and soul.

"And now, I must leave you, Gwendolyn," Nike said. "This is good-bye—for now. Know that I am so very proud of you, and so very honored to call you my Champion. Now and forever."

Then, the goddess leaned forward and kissed me on the cheek, making even more of her cold power flow through me. Tears streaked down my face, freezing on my cheeks like tiny snowflakes.

Nike bowed her head. The silver laurels on her brow glinted; then her wings slowly curved forward and closed in on her body. That bright silver light flared again.

And then she was gone.

And so was I.

Chapter 32

Once again, I woke up with a gasp and sat bolt upright. I sucked down breath after breath, trying to figure out what was going on and where I was. Slowly, everything came rushing back to me.

I looked up to find my friends clustered around me. Logan. Daphne. Carson. Oliver. Alexei. Linus, Metis, Ajax, and Grandma Frost loomed over them, while Nyx was sitting on the floor beside me. So was Nickamedes, a small bit of white, melted wax clutched in his hand. They all looked at me with wide, frightened eyes.

I stared past them up at the fresco on the ceiling. It was completely free of shadows now, and I could see all the images of the battle that we'd just been through. Me, Logan, and everyone else fighting the Reapers, from the first attack at the main gate to the final confrontation here in the library. The fresco featured all that and more, and somehow, I knew it would never be covered with shadows again.

Next, I looked down at my right palm. Now, instead of two scars, I had three. But the really weird thing was that they formed a sort of snowflake design—one that was exactly like the necklace Logan had given me, the one I was wearing right now. And I knew that if I pushed my shirt aside, I'd see the exact same three marks in the exact same pattern on my chest, right over my heart. I grimaced, but I didn't really mind. Because the marks would always remind me of the battles I'd survived—and how victorious I'd been in the end.

"Gwen?" Logan asked, his voice hoarse, as though he'd been screaming and screaming for a long time. "Is that really you?"

"Yeah," I said. "It's me. I'm . . . okay. I think."

My gaze flicked up to the second-floor pantheon to the empty spot, but it wasn't empty anymore—a statue of Loki stood there, wrapped in thick, marble strands of mistletoe.

The others followed my gaze. One by one, their mouths dropped open, and they all let out sharp gasps of surprise.

"Is that . . ."

"That looks like . . ."

"Could it be . . ."

"Loki," I said. "He's gone now, and he won't ever be able to hurt us again."

"What happened?" Linus asked.

I shook my head. "I'm not quite sure. Nike came to me. She said that when Loki . . . infected me, he gave up his own immortal body, and I forced him back into the gods' realm by stabbing myself. She said that he would never be able to come back to the mortal realm ever again. So . . . I think we're finally safe from him. I think we're finally *free* from him. Forever."

"Are you sure?" Metis asked.

I looked at the statue again, half-expecting it to glare at me the way all the other ones did, but Loki remained still, frozen, and locked in place, and I didn't sense any vibes rippling off the stone—not a single one.

"Yeah," I said. "I'm sure."

For a moment, there was silence. Carson peered up at the statue of Loki, then around at everyone else.

"So," he said. "I guess this means that we . . . won?"

More silence. Then, slowly, grins spread over my friends' faces. Everyone started laughing and cheering and clapping each other on the back until the entire library was filled with the happy sounds. Logan held out his hand, helping me up and onto my feet. He wrapped his arms around me, holding me tight, and I leaned into him, enjoying the moment.

It was over.

The second Chaos War was over. And we'd won. For good.

Forever.

But our happy respite was short-lived. Because we had been through the battle to end all battles, and we had all paid a high cost. Many Reapers were dead, and Logan had managed to kill Agrona for all her crimes against him and his dad. But most of the Protectorate guards were dead as well.

Including Sergei.

Warm, happy, boisterous Sergei had fallen in the library to a Reaper's sword. Alexei crouched over his father's body, holding his cold, dead hand and crying and mumbling. Oliver stood by his side, his hand on his boyfriend's shoulder. My own heart ached in response to the waves of grief rolling off Alexei.

And Sergei wasn't the only friend we'd lost. The bodies of many of the gryphons littered the quad outside the library, right next to those of the Black rocs they'd been fighting. Still more wounded and dead—mortal and creature alike—could be found in and around the library, on the quad, and all the way across campus and down to the main gate.

The next few days passed by in a blur, filled with an odd mix of tears and smiles. I went from one place to the next, trying to help wherever I could. Carrying bodies down to the morgue in the bottom of the math-science building until they could be properly identified and buried. Cleaning blood off the floor in the library. Returning all of the artifacts we'd used to their cases and original locations in the library. Rounding up the artifacts the Reapers had used, including Lucretia, and putting them in the library basement until they could be examined and catalogued. I got up early, worked all day, and then dropped into bed at night utterly exhausted. And still, there was more to do the next day.

And I wasn't the only one who was busy. Not all of the Reapers had been killed, and the wounded were rounded up and taken down to the academy prison.

Including Vivian.

Agrona appeared to have been right when she'd said that I'd destroyed the Reaper girl's mind, because we found her hiding back in the stacks, curled up into a ball, rocking back and forth just like she had before. All the while, she kept murmuring nonsense. Well, to the others, it was nonsense about hairbrushes, gloves, and Reaper red walls. To me, it made perfect sense because I knew all about the horrible memories she was seeing over and over again in her mind. Either way, she wasn't a threat now, and she was taken to the prison, along with the other wounded warriors.

A few of the Reapers had escaped from the library, and Linus, Inari, Aiko, and what was left of the Protectorate were hot on their trail, but I wasn't too worried. With Loki gone, the Reapers would need some time to regroup—if they ever could. I didn't know what the Reapers would do next, and right now, I didn't care. As Nike had said, my part in the battle was done, and now, it was time to rest and try to recover from all the wounds and scars I'd gotten along the way.

Three days later, I stood in the parking lot behind the gym and watched a group of Protectorate guards load Sergei's coffin into the back of a waiting limousine to be taken to the Cypress Mountain airport. Alexei was taking his father home to Russia to bury him, and Oliver was going with him. Logan had also come to see them off.

"I'm sorry," I said. "I wish we could have saved him. I wish we could have saved *everyone*."

Alexei nodded. He hadn't spoken much since the battle, and I knew he was hurting. We were all hurting, despite the fact that we'd won.

"He died serving the Protectorate and helping his friends," Alexei said. "He always told me there was no greater calling, no greater honor, than that."

His face was as stoic as ever, but I could see the pain glimmering in his hazel eyes and the sad slump of his shoulders. So much pain. And I couldn't help but think that if I'd been smarter or stronger, I might have figured things out sooner and spared us at least some of the grief we were feeling. But it had been a fight to the death, and now, we were paying the price—the loss of those we loved.

"I'll be back soon," Alexei said, finally turning to look at me.

"We both will," Oliver chimed in. "Count on it."

I nodded. I was too emotional to speak, so I settled for hugging them both as tight as I could. Logan did the same.

Alexei laid a hand on his father's coffin before closing the back door of the limo. He got into the back passenger's seat, along with Oliver.

Logan wrapped his arms around me, and together, we watched our friends leave the academy.

We said a lot of good-byes that day, not only to Alexei, Oliver, and Sergei, but to Rory, Rachel, and the gryphons too. I met them down by the main gate in the spot where the gryphons had brought us when we'd escaped from the Reapers. A car was waiting on the other side of the gate to take Rory and Rachel to the airport.

"Well, Princess," Rory said. "I guess this is good-bye again. I'll say this. Things are never boring with you around."

I grinned. "They aren't boring with you around, either. What are you going to do now?"

She shrugged. "I guess I'll go back to the Colorado academy and see how things are shaking down out there."

News of the battle had spread to the other academies around the world. I didn't know much about what was happening at the other schools, but I imagined that everyone felt a collective sense of relief. I certainly did.

"And what about the other kids? And how they were treating you before because your parents were Reapers?"

She shrugged again. "We'll see if this changes anything, but I doubt it."

I doubted it too, since folks had long, long memories when it came to Reapers, but I hoped for the best for her. And I couldn't help but think back to Sigyn and Nike's conversation and wonder what plans, if any, they might have for Rory. But that was for her to discover, not me.

So I hugged her and Rachel good-bye, then turned to the gryphons. Most of them had already left, but the leader and his baby had stayed behind.

"Thank you for coming," I said, laying my hand on his wing and using my psychometry to show him how grateful I was for that and all they'd done for me and my friends. "For fighting with us. For everything."

The gryphon let out a much lower, softer, sadder screech, and I felt his pain about the gryphons he'd lost. He nudged me, and I reached up and scratched his head before doing the same thing to the baby.

Then, the adult gryphon pumped his wings once, and he and his baby rose up into the sky to start the long, wearying journey home, their wings, heads, and hearts drooping from everything that had happened.

I knew how they felt. It would take a while for all of us to fully recover—if we ever truly could.

Chapter 33

"This is pointless," I muttered. "Pointless. *Point. Less.* Valentine's Day was weeks ago. So why are we having a stupid dance tonight?"

Daphne eyed me. "Because this is the first week the academy has been open since the battle, and everyone feels like celebrating. Or if they don't, then they at least are willing to fake it for the rest of us. So suck it up, Gwen."

Three weeks had passed since the final fight in the library. Despite everything that had happened, the Powers That Were had decided to reopen the academy, even though the mess from the last battle with the Reapers was still being cleaned up.

Part of the reopening meant going through with the big Valentine's Day dance that had been planned, which meant I was in my dorm room, wearing the dress Daphne had made me buy weeks ago for the event.

I stared at myself in the mirror, smoothing down the long, silvery silk skirt. With its cap sleeves and beaded waist, the dress was similar to one that I'd worn to the homecoming dance back in the fall, although this one was much more elegant. In fact, it sort of reminded me of the gown that Nike always wore. Daphne had helped me take the whole goddess illusion a step further, by taming my frizzy hair and curling it into sleek ringlets, which brushed the tops of my shoulders. Silver shadow and liner rimmed my eyes, while pale purple lipstick completed the look.

"Besides," Daphne said. "You look fabulous tonight, and so do I."

She bumped me out of the way and peered and preened at her own reflection in the mirror. Naturally, Daphne's dress was pink, with a full skirt studded with tiny white crystals that made her look like a fairy-tale princess come to life. Pink shadow brought out her beautiful black eyes, while darker pink gloss was slicked across her lips.

"Daphne's right," a soft voice chimed in. "You both look beautiful tonight."

I looked over at Grandma Frost, who was sitting in my desk chair, cradling Nyx in her lap. The wolf pup barked her agreement.

"Yes, you do," Vic chimed in from his spot propped up on my bed. "And even warriors need a break from battle every now and then."

I rolled my eyes. "Thanks, Vic."

Nyx bounded out of Grandma's lap, hopped up onto the bed, and started licking Vic's cheek. The sword grumbled, but there was a smile on his face.

Daphne finally quit staring at herself and turned to face me, planting her hands on her hips and causing pink sparks of magic to crackle in the air around her. "Now, are you going to come along quietly, or am I going to have to strong-arm you like usual?"

I laughed and held my hands up in mock surrender.

"Don't worry. You're right. Tonight is a time to celebrate. I'll come along peacefully."

Grandma cleared her throat and got to her feet. Daphne stared at her, then me.

"I'll wait for you downstairs," Daphne said.

I nodded, and she left my room.

Grandma Frost stepped forward. "Actually, pumpkin, there's something I'd like to give you. I've been meaning to do it for a while now, but tonight seems like the perfect time."

She reached up, unwrapped a long scarf from around her neck, and held it out to me. "I thought you might like to have this. It belonged to your mom. She used to wear it whenever she would go out dancing."

The silk scarf was a beautiful swirl of gray and violet, like petals mixed together, with a few bright silver coins hanging off the edges. I carefully took the cool fabric from Grandma, the motion causing the coins to jingle out a soft tune.

My psychometry kicked in, and my mom's face appeared. I let the memories sweep me away.

Images of my mom laughing, talking, and dancing filled my mind. There was music and soft lights and glittering decorations. Metis was in some of the memories, whispering and giggling with my mom. Nickamedes too. But there was one image that was sharper, stronger, and more vibrant than all the others. I let myself fall deeper into that memory.

My mom stood on a balcony, the moonlight painting her brown hair a soft silver. She was dancing in the arms of a man with sandy blond hair and blue eyes. My dad, Tyr. They moved slowly to the music. Other people were on the balcony as well, but they were little more than shadows, and the two of them were completely focused on each other.

"You know what?" my mom asked.

"What?" my dad answered, a faint teasing note in his voice, as though this were a game they'd played many times before.

"Violet eyes are smiling eyes," Mom whispered the familiar words before kissing him.

The memory faded away, but the soft echo of music remained in my ears, along with their happiness in my heart.

I sighed and opened my eyes, stroking my hand over the fabric. "This is one of the best presents anyone could ever give me. Thank you so much."

Grandma gently squeezed my hand, her love surging into me and mixing with the memories of my mom and dad. "I'm glad you think so, pumpkin."

I hugged her tight and wrapped the scarf around my shoulders, feeling the memories soak into my skin.

Grandma Frost stayed behind to talk with Vic and Nyx. I left my room and went downstairs, where Daphne was waiting with Logan and Carson. Both guys wore classic black tuxedoes and looked exceptionally handsome. They were both clutching corsages, silver for me and pink for Daphne, which they quickly slid onto our wrists.

"You know, we could skip the dance," Logan murmured, stepping closer to me, his eyes that wonderful, wonderful blue. "And go straight to the after-party. The one where it's just you and me. Alone."

I stood on my tiptoes as though I were going to kiss him and tapped him on the nose instead. "And you should know that we at least have to put in an appearance at the dance. Besides, I didn't put this dress and makeup on for nothing. So come on."

Logan groaned, but he let me lead him outside.

The four of us walked up the hill and fell into the stream of students flowing into the dining hall, since that's where the dance was going to be held. We stepped inside and stopped, all of us bowled over by the sight in front of us.

The dining hall had been utterly transformed. All of the chairs and tables had been removed, creating one enormous open space. White, pink, and red lights had been strung up in the indoor garden in the middle of the room, wrapping around all of the trees and even the statues there, and casting the entire area in warm, soft light. Silver, pink, and red hearts dangled down from the ceiling, the glitter on them throwing out small sprays of light in every direction. Giant hearts had even been taped up onto the walls, covering many of the mythological paintings there. It was even more impressive than the memories of the dances that my mom had attended here.

But more than the decorations, there was such a sense of peace, calm, and relief in the room. At first, I wondered why, but then I realized that everyone was smiling, from the students on the dance floor to the adult chaperones chatting by the punch bowl to the statues in the garden. I even spotted the three guys from the coffee shop, the ones who had been betting that the dance would be ruined. They were laughing and talking, like everyone else. I didn't know what had happened to their bet, and I didn't care. All that mattered was having a good time tonight.

"Come on," Daphne said, grinning at us. "Time to party."

She led Carson out onto the dance floor, and the two of them were soon rocking to the music.

Logan took my hand. "What do you say, Gypsy girl?" he asked in a teasing voice. "Want to dance?"

I started to answer him when I noticed two people standing off to one side of the dining hall—Metis and Nickamedes. Metis looked lovely in a dark green gown, and she'd even worn her black hair down for a change, softening her features. Meanwhile, Nickamedes looked almost as handsome as Logan did in his tux. Nickamedes seemed to be trying to get Metis to go out onto the dance floor with him, but she kept shaking her head in refusal.

Nickamedes's mouth pinched with frustration. Metis said something to him and started to turn and walk away, but he grabbed her hand, pulled her toward him, and kissed her soundly. She stiffened in his arms at first, clearly shocked by his bold action, but then, she slowly melted into his embrace. By the time he drew back, they were both blushing and flustered. This time, when Nickamedes tugged on Metis's hand, she let him lead her out onto the dance floor.

Logan frowned, seeing exactly what I was looking at. "Metis and Nickamedes? What's that all about?"

I laughed and grabbed his hand. "Well, I thought it would be obvious, but come and dance with me, and I'll tell you all about it."

He stopped, pulling me back toward him. "I've got a better idea. Why don't we sneak off and go have that makeout session we talked about back at the dining hall?"

I wrapped my arms around his neck and pulled his head down toward mine. "Why not start now?" I whispered.

Logan grinned. A moment later, his lips met mine, and I forgot about everything else, including the dance.

I didn't think it was possible, but things slowly went back to normal at Mythos Academy. Actually, they weren't quite normal.

They were *better* than that.

With the threat of Loki gone, and the remaining Reapers in hiding, everyone was far more cheerful and relaxed than I'd ever seen them before. Professors, staff members, students. Everyone just seemed . . . happy. Laughing, talking, joking, out on the quad, in the dining hall, even in the classrooms. Of course, there was a lot of sorrow, sadness, and grief mixed in, especially for those who had lost friends and loved ones, but things were far more hopeful than they'd been in years. As for me, well, I felt like the weight of the world had been lifted off my shoulders, literally. For the first time in a long time, I felt . . . *free.*

And I loved it.

But that didn't mean I didn't have responsibilities. I was still a student, after all, which meant classes and more classes and tons of homework assignments from all the days we'd missed while the academy had been closed for repairs. I was busier with school than ever before, but I made time for the things I enjoyed most, the things that were truly important to me. Weapons training in the morning with my friends, lunch with Logan in the dining hall, afternoon visits to Grandma Frost's house. I even worked my regular shifts in the Library of Antiquities, helping Nickamedes clean up, since the library had taken the brunt of the Reapers' attacks.

Speaking of the library, I was late for my shift, as usual, but instead of hurrying inside the building, I stood at the bottom of the steps, staring at the two gryphons. They were the only statues left on any of the buildings on the quad, since Loki had destroyed all the others. I thought he had obliterated them too, but they'd been in their usual spots when we'd come outside after the battle, perched by the library steps as if they'd never even moved in the first place.

Whatever magic Carson had used to bring them to life had sustained them through the battle, and the gryphons loomed as large and fierce-looking as ever before. Sure, they were a little rough around the edges now, with scars embedded in their stone bodies from the wear and tear of the fight. But they were still here, still watching over me, and still protecting us all. Walking by the gryphons every single day was one of the things that had helped me cope with all the nightmares from the battle. I think that seeing them helped a lot of other folks deal with things too.

Metis said that all of the statues on all of the other buildings would be replaced, a project that Raven was overseeing, which didn't surprise me in the least, given what I now knew about her real identity. I wondered if the new gargoyles, dragons, chimeras, and more would all have that same wary watchfulness as before.

I hoped so.

I patted first one gryphon's head, then the other, whispering my thanks to them before entering the library.

*   *   *

An hour later, I was supposed to be looking something up on the computer for Nickamedes, but really, I was watching him whisper into Metis's ear. Something perhaps a bit steamy, judging from the sly look she gave him in return. She leaned up and kissed his cheek before waving at me and leaving the library. The two of them were officially a couple now, and I couldn't have been happier for them.

Nickamedes shuffled over to the checkout counter. He was still using his cane to get around, but he wasn't leaning on it as heavily, and he said that some of the aches and pains in his legs had finally started to ease. I was hoping he'd make a full recovery after all.

"So," I said, swiveling around on my stool and raising my eyebrows at him. "I take it that things with Metis are going well?"

A blush bloomed in Nickamedes's cheeks, although he still managed to give me an utterly withering look. "Things are going just fine, not that it is any of *your* business, Gwendolyn."

"Of course not," I sniped. "I'm just the reason the two of you got together in the first place. It's not like I'm going to be responsible for your lifelong happiness or future kids or anything."

He gave me a sour look that melted into a smile before he disappeared back into his office.

"You should cut the librarian some slack," Vic piped up from his spot behind the checkout counter. "Love can be a tricky thing, after all. Don't you agree, fuzzball?"

Nyx was curled up in her basket, but she lifted her head up and barked out her agreement.

I laughed and went back to work.

My friends came and went as the evening wore on and turned into night. Daphne. Carson. Kenzie. Talia. Morgan. Savannah and her boyfriend, Doug. And Alexei and Oliver came by too, since they'd gotten back from Russia a few days before. Some of the sadness had left Alexei's eyes, although I knew it would take time for him to fully recover.

Finally, Logan came to the library, and I forgot about everything else. Despite everything that had happened with the candle, the Spartan and I had forgiven each other, and we were in a good place now—and stronger than we'd ever been before.

Logan hung out around the checkout counter while I went about my usual chores. Finally, though, I got caught up enough to take a break, and he flashed me a sexy, wicked grin.

"You know," he drawled. "With all the time we've spent together the past few weeks, there's one thing we haven't done."

"Oh really? What's that?"

He jerked his head at the stacks and waggled his eyebrows. "We haven't been back there in forever. Maybe it's time we see what all the fuss is about for ourselves, huh?"

I leaned closer to him. "That sounds like a plan to me, Spartan."

Logan laughed, and I headed around the counter. Together, and still laughing, we scurried toward the stacks. We'd almost reached them when the inevitable happened, and I heard the door in the glass office complex squeak open.

"Gwendolyn!" Nickamedes called out. "Where are

you going? These books aren't going to shelve themselves!"

I looked back over my shoulder at the checkout
counter. The librarian waved me over before disappearing back into his office. I turned back to Logan and
grabbed his hand.

"Come on," I said. "This way."

"What about the books?" he asked. "And Nickamedes?"

"He can wait," I said. "Just like I waited for you—
and for all of this."

Logan frowned, not quite understanding my meaning. So I tightened my grip on his hand and reached for
my psychometry, letting him see all the memories that
were attached to my mom's scarf, the one Grandma
Frost had given to me the night of the dance, the one
that was carefully tucked away in my messenger bag.
Then I reached for all the images and feelings—good
and bad—from the snowflake necklace around my
neck, the one he had bought me for Christmas.

I showed everything to Logan. All the battles we'd
fought, all the enemies we'd faced down, all the heartache we'd endured. But most of all, I showed him my
love for him and all my hopes for our future—together.

Logan sighed in understanding, and I let go of the
memories and emotions.

"That's what I've been waiting for," I whispered, staring into his blue, blue eyes.

"Me too," he whispered back.

I'd been thinking about that book of my life Sigyn
had shown me, and I'd finally figured out why some of
the pages had been blank. Now, I was ready to fill them

in with new memories—*my* memories of all the experiences I'd have with Logan and the rest of my friends over the years ahead.

"So come on, Spartan," I teased. "Let's go. Unless you changed your mind about wanting to be alone with me."

Logan smiled at me, that slow, sexy smile I loved so much, the one that always made that warm, fizzy, dizzying feeling explode in my heart. "I would never do that, Gypsy girl. Not with you."

"Good."

So I grinned, pulled Logan back into the shadowy stacks, and pressed my lips to his, ready to start the next chapter of my life at Mythos Academy.

The one that I would write myself.

Dear Readers,

Well, we have come to the end of Gwen's adventures at Mythos Academy. I hope you have all enjoyed reading about Gwen as much as I have enjoyed writing about her.

This is really the first time that I have ended a series, and it is a bittersweet feeling.

On one hand, I hate to leave Gwen, Logan, Daphne, Carson, and everyone else behind at the academy. I've enjoyed spending time with all of the characters, getting to know them, and putting them through all the many challenges that they have faced together.

I'm going to miss so many things about writing the series. Visiting Grandma Frost's kitchen. Listening to Professor Metis's myth-history lectures. Hearing Vic talk about how awesome he is. Watching Nyx grow up. Walking by the gryphons and all the other statues on campus. Attending gym classes with Coach Ajax. Working for Nickamedes in the Library of Antiquities.

However, I'm also happy that I got to bring Gwen's story to what I hope is a satisfying conclusion for fans of the series.

Please know that I have appreciated and enjoyed all of the nice comments and e-mails that I have received about the characters and the books. Entertaining folks is one of the reasons that I write, and knowing that folks are reading and enjoying my books is always humbling. So thank you, readers, for taking this trip with me, Gwen, and all of the other characters.

I have been asked if I will ever write more in my Mythos Academy series. I'll never say never. Perhaps someday in the future, I will dream up a new set of adventures for Gwen, Logan, Daphne, Rory, or another character at Mythos Academy.

But, for now, Gwen's story is finished. I see a bright future, good things, and great times ahead for Gwen and her friends, and I hope that you do too. The characters and the world of Mythos Academy will always live on in my heart.

Happy reading!

Jennifer Estep

BEYOND
THE
STORY

Mythos Academy Warriors
and Their Magic

The students at Mythos Academy are the descendants of ancient warriors, and they are at the academy to learn how to fight and use weapons, along with whatever magic or other skills that they might have. Here's a little more about the warrior whiz kids, as Gwen calls them:

Amazons and Valkyries: Most of the girls at Mythos are either Amazons or Valkyries. Amazons are gifted with supernatural quickness. In gym class during mock fights, they look like blurs more than anything else. Valkyries are incredibly strong. Also, bright, colorful sparks of magic can often be seen shooting out of Valkyries' fingertips.

Romans and Vikings: Most of the guys at Mythos Academy are either Romans or Vikings. Romans are superquick, just like Amazons, while Vikings are superstrong, just like Valkyries.

Siblings: Brothers and sisters born to the same parents will have similar abilities and magic, but they're sometimes classified as different types of warriors. For example, if the girls in a family are Amazons, then the boys will be Romans. If the girls in a family are Valkyries, then the boys will be Vikings. However, in other families, brothers and sisters are considered to be the same kind of warriors, like those born to Spartan, Samurai, or Ninja parents. The boys and girls are both called Spartans, Samurais, or Ninjas.

More Magic: As if being superstrong or superquick wasn't good enough, the students at Mythos Academy also have other types of magic. They can do everything from heal injuries to control the weather to form fireballs with their bare hands. Many of the students have enhanced senses as well. The powers vary from student to student, but as a general rule, everyone is dangerous and deadly in their own special way.

Spartans: Spartans are among the rarest of the warrior whiz kids, and there are only a few at Mythos Academy. But Spartans are the most dangerous and deadliest of all the warriors because they have the ability to pick up any weapon—or any *thing*—and automatically know how to use and even kill someone with it. Even Reapers of Chaos are afraid to battle Spartans in a fair fight. But then again, Reapers rarely fight fair. . . .

Gypsies: Gypsies are just as rare as Spartans. Gypsies are those who have been gifted with magic by the gods. But not all Gypsies are good. Some are just as evil as the gods they serve. Gwen is a Gypsy who is gifted with psychometry magic, or the ability to know, see, and feel an object's history just by touching it. Gwen's magic comes from Nike, the Greek goddess of victory.

Bogatyrs: Bogatyrs are Russian warriors. They are exceptionally fast, and most of them use two weapons at once, one in either hand. Bogatyrs train themselves to always keep moving, to always keep fighting, which gives them great endurance. The longer a fight goes, the more likely they are to win, because they will still be going strong as their enemies slowly weaken.

**Want to know more about Mythos Academy?
Read on and take a tour of the campus.**

The heart of Mythos Academy is made up of five buildings that are clustered together like the loose points of a star on the main, upper quad. They are the Library of Antiquities, the gym, the dining hall, the English-history building, and the math-science building.

The Library of Antiquities: The library is the largest building on campus. In addition to books, the library also houses artifacts—weapons, jewelry, clothes, armor, and more—that were once used by ancient warriors, gods, goddesses, and mythological creatures. Some of the artifacts have a lot of power, and the Reapers of Chaos would love to get their hands on this stuff to use it for Bad, Bad Things.

The Gym: The gym is the second largest building at Mythos. In addition to a pool, basketball court, and training areas, the gym also features racks of weapons, including swords, staffs, and more, that the students use during mock fights. At Mythos, gym class is really weapons training, and students are graded on how well they can fight.

The Dining Hall: The dining hall is the third largest building at Mythos. With its white linens, fancy china, and open-air indoor garden, the dining hall looks more like a five-star restaurant than a student cafeteria. The dining hall is famous for all the fancy, froufrou foods that it serves on a daily basis, like liver, veal, and escargot. Yucko, as Gwen would say.

The English-History Building: Students attend English, myth-history, geography, art, and other classes in this building. Professor Metis's office is also in this building.

The Math-Science Building: Students attend math, science, and other classes in this building. But there are more than just classrooms here. This building also features a morgue and a prison deep underground. Creepy, huh?

The Student Dorms: The student dorms are located down the hill from the main quad, along with several other smaller outbuildings. Guys and girls live in separate dorms, although that doesn't keep them from hooking up on a regular basis.

The Statues: Statues of mythological creatures—like gryphons and gargoyles—can be found on all the academy buildings, although the library has the most statues. When she first came to the academy, Gwen thought that the statues are all super creepy. Now, she likes the fact that they are around, especially the two gryphon statues by the library steps, the ones that always seem to be watching over her. . . .

Who's Who at Mythos Academy— The Students

Gwen (Gwendolyn) Frost: Gwen is a Gypsy girl with the gift of psychometry magic, or the ability to know an object's history just by touching it. Gwen's a little dark and twisted in that she likes her magic and the fact that it lets her know other people's secrets—no matter how hard they try to hide them. She also has a major sweet tooth, loves to read comic books, and wears jeans, T-shirts, hoodies, and sneakers almost everywhere she goes.

Daphne Cruz: Daphne is a Valkyrie and a renowned archer. She also has some wicked computer skills and loves designer clothes and purses. Daphne is rather obsessed with the color pink. She wears it more often than not, and her entire dorm room is done in various shades of pink.

Logan Quinn: This seriously cute and seriously deadly Spartan is the best fighter at Mythos Academy, and he wins almost every fight he is in, whether they are mock fights in the gym with other students or real battles with Reapers. Logan is determined to protect Gwen and his friends, especially since Reapers killed his mom and older sister when he was younger.

Carson Callahan: Carson is the head of the Mythos Academy Marching Band. He's a Celt and rumored to have come from a long line of warrior bards. He's quiet, shy, and one of the nicest guys you'll ever meet, but Carson can be as tough as nails when he needs to be.

Oliver Hector: Oliver is a Spartan who is friends with Logan and Kenzie and helps with Gwen's weapons training. Oliver is one of Gwen's friends, too.

Kenzie Tanaka: Kenzie is a Spartan who is friends with Logan and Oliver. He also helps with Gwen's weapons training and is dating Talia.

Savannah Warren: Savannah is an Amazon who used to date Logan. She is friends with Talia and Morgan.

Talia Pizarro: Talia is an Amazon and one of Savannah's friends. Talia has gym class with Gwen, and the two of them often spar during the mock fights. Talia is dating Kenzie.

Helena Paxton: Helena is an Amazon who seems to be positioning herself as the new mean girl-queen of the academy, or at least of Gwen's second-year class.

Morgan McDougall: Morgan is a Valkyrie. She used to be one of the most popular girls at the academy—before her best friend, Jasmine Ashton, tried to sacrifice her to Loki one night in the Library of Antiquities. These days, Morgan is friends with Savannah and Talia, and she has also helped Gwen fight Reapers.

Jasmine Ashton: Jasmine was a Valkyrie and the most popular girl in the second-year class at Mythos Academy—until she tried to sacrifice Morgan to Loki. Gwen battled Jasmine in the Library of Antiquities and managed to keep her from sacrificing Morgan, although Logan was the one who actually killed Jasmine. But before she died, Jasmine told Gwen that her whole family are Reapers—and that there are many Reapers at Mythos Academy. . . .

Preston Ashton: Preston is Jasmine's older brother, who blamed Gwen for his sister's death. Preston tried to kill Gwen during the Winter Carnival weekend at the Powder ski resort, although Gwen, Logan, and Vic eventually got the best of the Reaper.

Vivian Holler: Vivian is a Valkyrie and a second-year student. She is also Loki's Champion and was responsible for the death of Gwen's mom. Vivian wants to kill Gwen more than anything else, and Gwen feels the same way about her.

Alexei Sokolov: Alexei is a third-year Russian student who most recently attended the London branch of Mythos Academy. He's a Bogatyr warrior who is training to become a member of the Protectorate, and he is Gwen's bodyguard.

Rory Forseti: Rory is a first-year student at the Colorado branch of Mythos Academy. She's a Spartan and Gwen's cousin, since her dad and Gwen's dad were brothers. Rory's parents were Reapers, although they never told her about that. However, everyone at the Colorado academy now knows about her parents, and Rory has a lot of pain and guilt about all of the terrible things that her parents did as Reapers.

Who's Who at Mythos Academy and Beyond—
The Adults

Coach Ajax: Ajax is the head of the athletic department at the academy and is responsible for training all the kids at Mythos and turning them into fighters. Logan Quinn and his Spartan friends are among Ajax's prize students.

Geraldine (Grandma) Frost: Geraldine is Gwen's grandma and a Gypsy with the power to see the future. Grandma Frost makes her living as a fortune-teller in a town not too far away from Cypress Mountain. A couple of times a week, Gwen sneaks off the Mythos Academy campus to see her grandma and enjoy the sweet treats that Grandma Frost is always baking.

Grace Frost: Grace was Gwen's mom and a Gypsy who had the power to know if people were telling the truth or not just by listening to their words. At first, Gwen thought that her mom had been killed in a car accident by a drunk driver. But thanks to Preston Ashton, Gwen knows that Grace was actually murdered by Vivian, Loki's Champion. Gwen is determined to find the Reaper girl and get her revenge—no matter what.

Nickamedes: Nickamedes is the head librarian at the Library of Antiquities, who loves overseeing all the books and the artifacts in the library. Nickamedes is also Logan's uncle, and Gwen has learned that Nickamedes once dated her mom, Grace, when the two of them were students at the academy.

Professor Aurora Metis: Metis is a myth-history professor who teaches students all about the Reapers of Chaos, Loki, and the ancient Chaos War. She was also best friends with Gwen's mom, Grace, back when the two of them went to Mythos. Metis is the Champion of Athena, the Greek goddess of wisdom, and she's become Gwen's mentor at the academy.

Raven: Raven is the old woman who mans the coffee cart in the Library of Antiquities. Gwen has also seen her in the academy prison, which seems to be another one of Raven's many odd jobs around campus. There's definitely more to Raven than meets the eye. . . .

The Powers That Were: A board made up of various members of the Pantheon, including Linus Quinn, who oversee all aspects of Mythos Academy, from approving the dining hall menus to disciplining students.

Vic: Vic is the talking sword that Nike gave to Gwen to use as her personal weapon. Instead of a regular hilt, a man's face is inlaid into Vic's hilt, complete with one twilight-colored eye. Gwen doesn't know too much about Vic, except that he's really, really bloodthirsty and wants to kill Reapers more than anything else.

Lucretia: Lucretia is the talking sword that Vivian Holler uses as her personal weapon. Instead of a regular hilt, a woman's face is inlaid into Lucretia's hilt, complete with one burning red eye. Lucretia and Vic always shout insults at each other whenever they meet.

Linus Quinn: Linus is Logan's dad and the head of the Protectorate. He is also a Spartan and has always pushed

Logan to be the best warrior he can be. For many years, Linus and Logan's relationship was strained, due in part to the murder of Logan's mom and sister, but Linus and Logan are slowly working through their issues and growing closer together.

Agrona Quinn: Agrona was Logan's stepmom and a member of the Protectorate before she was revealed to be the leader of the Reapers. Now, she is one of the most-wanted Reapers, and Linus and the other members of the Protectorate are constantly searching for her. Agrona is also an Amazon.

Sergei Sokolov: Sergei is Alexei's dad and a member of the Protectorate. He is also a Bogatyr.

Inari Sato: Inari is member of the Protectorate. He is also a Ninja.

Rachel Maddox: Rachel is a chef who works in the dining hall at the Colorado branch of Mythos Academy. She's a Spartan and Rory's aunt, since she and Rory's mom were sisters. Like Rory, Rachel has a lot of conflicting feelings about the fact that her sister was a Reaper.

Covington: Covington was the head librarian at the Library of Antiquities at the Colorado branch of Mythos Academy before he was revealed to be working with the Reapers. Now, he is in a Protectorate prison.

Who's Who at Mythos Academy—
The Gods, Monsters, and More

Artifacts: Artifacts are weapons, jewelry, clothing, armor, and more that were worn or used by various warriors, gods, goddesses, and mythological creatures over the years. There are Thirteen Artifacts that are rumored to be the most powerful, although people disagree about which artifacts they are and how they were used during the Chaos War. The members of the Pantheon try to protect the various artifacts from the Reapers, although they are not always successful. Many of the artifacts are housed in the Library of Antiquities.

Black rocs: These creatures look like ravens—only much, much bigger. They have shiny black feathers shot through with glossy streaks of red, long, sharp, curved talons, and black eyes with a red spark burning deep down inside them. Rocs are capable of picking up people and carrying them off—before they rip them to shreds.

Champions: Every god and goddess has a Champion, someone that they choose to work on their behalf in the mortal realm. Champions have various powers and weapons and can be good or bad, depending on the god they serve. Gwen is Nike's Champion, just like her mom and grandma were before her.

The Chaos War: Long ago, Loki and his followers tried to enslave everyone and everything, and the whole world was plunged into the Chaos War. It was a dark, bloody time that almost resulted in the end of the world. The Reapers want to return Loki to his full strength, so the god can lead them in another Chaos War. You can see why that would be a Bad, Bad Thing.

Fenrir wolves: These creatures look like wolves—only much, much bigger. They have ash-gray fur, razor-sharp talons, and burning red eyes. Reapers use them to watch, hunt, and kill members of the Pantheon. Think of Fenrir wolves as puppy-dog assassins.

Loki: Loki is the Norse god of chaos. Once upon a time, Loki caused the death of another god and was imprisoned for it. But Loki eventually escaped from his prison and started recruiting other gods, goddesses, warriors, and creatures to join forces with him. He called his followers the Reapers of Chaos, and they tried to take over the world. However, Loki and his followers were eventually defeated, and Loki was imprisoned for a second time. Using Gwen's blood and the Helheim Dagger, Vivian freed Loki from his prison, although he was severely injured from his time in the Helheim realm. Now, Loki wants to be fully healed so he can plunge the world into a second Chaos War. He's the ultimate bad guy.

Mythos Academy: The academy is located in Cypress Mountain, North Carolina, which is a ritzy suburb high in the mountains above the city of Asheville. The academy is a boarding school/college for warrior whiz kids—the descendants of ancient warriors, like Spartans, Valkyries, Amazons, and more. The kids at Mythos range in age from first-year students (age sixteen) to sixth-year students (age twenty-one). The kids go to Mythos to learn how to use whatever magic and skills they possess to fight against Loki and his Reapers. There are other branches of the academy located throughout the world.

Nemean prowlers: These creatures look like panthers— only much, much bigger. They have black fur tinged with red, razor-sharp claws, and burning red eyes. Reapers use them to watch, hunt, and kill members of the Pantheon. Think of Nemean prowlers as kitty-cat assassins.

Nike: Nike is the Greek goddess of victory. The goddess was the one who defeated Loki in one-on-one combat during the final battle of the Chaos War. Ever since then, Nike and her Champions have fought the Reapers of Chaos. She's the ultimate good guy.

Nyx and Nott: Nyx is the Fenrir wolf pup that Gwen is taking care of. Nyx's mom, Nott, was killed by Vivian at the Garm gate the night that Loki was freed. Nott is buried in Grandma Frost's backyard.

The Pantheon: The Pantheon is made up of gods, goddesses, humans, and creatures who have banded together to fight Loki and his Reapers of Chaos. The members of the Pantheon are the good guys.

Reapers of Chaos: A Reaper is any god, goddess, human, or creature who serves Loki. The scary thing is that Reapers can be anyone at Mythos Academy and beyond—parents, teachers, even fellow students. Reapers are the bad guys.

Sigyn: Sigyn is the Norse goddess of devotion. She is also Loki's wife. The first time Loki was imprisoned, he was chained up underneath a giant snake that dripped venom onto his once-handsome face. Sigyn spent many years holding an artifact called the Bowl of Tears up over Loki's head to catch as much of the venom as possible. But when the bowl was full, Sigyn would have to empty it, which let venom drop freely onto Loki's face, causing him great pain. Eventually, Loki tricked Sigyn into releasing him, and before long, the evil god plunged the world into the long, bloody Chaos War. No one knows what happened to Sigyn after that. . . .

Maat asp: A Maat asp is a small snake with shimmering blue and black scales. It is named after Maat, the Egyptian goddess of truth. The Protectorate uses the asp to question Reapers, since the snake can tell whether or not people are telling the truth. The asp's venom can be poisonous—even deadly—to those who lie.

The Protectorate: The Protectorate is basically the police force of the mythological world. Among other duties, members of the Protectorate track down Reapers, put them on trial for their crimes, and make sure that the Reapers end up in prison where they belong.